THE RUN AROUND

BERNADETTE FRANKLIN

The Run Around
by Bernadette Franklin

Arranging a wedding for her brother and a five-time thoroughbride tests Hope's skills and patience. She'd believed the vows would be the most dangerous part of the ceremony, but a baseball to the head during the photography session proves her wrong and lands her in the sights of her brother's best friend, Fredrick.

He wants her to plan his wedding.

She wants to be his bride.

Diving into the treacherous world of wedding planning, Hope keeps her word and arranges the vows for the one man she believes she could love. He doesn't know how much she cherishes him and his friendship.

What she doesn't know lands her in the heart of a royal mess.

Cover design by Ali of The Book Brander (thebookbrander.com)

Caity,

I'm blaming you and those purple pens you sent me for this one. I regret nothing.

P.S.: I ran out of purple pens.

ONE

I made an excellent scapegoat.

A SENSIBLE WOMAN would've been delighted to be her future sister-in-law's maid of honor, as it implied cordial relationships or some sort of bullshit like that. I knew better.

I made an excellent scapegoat.

As the wedding party's weakest link, everyone expected me to trip on my dress, maybe break an ankle along with my neck, or spill the entire wine fountain onto the floor. My brother claimed he loved me, but I believed he'd been the one to spread the rumor I was the world's clumsiest woman.

When I secured my revenge, it would be sweet.

But first, I needed to survive my brother's wedding without being responsible for a single hiccup. Playing to my brother's misconceptions, I'd spent months tripping over nothing on purpose so I could transform myself into the image of traditional beauty and grace.

I'd even lost twenty pounds so my dress would fit.

The wedding would be a disaster, but I would emerge from the chaos smelling like roses, red wine, and garlic bread. Honestly, I doubted the wedding would make it to the reception.

Some weddings had bridezillas. We had a thoroughbride, and if she got it into her head to run, I wished my brother the best of luck catching her before she fled from the church. My proposal to have the wedding on a yacht, where my brother's thoroughbride couldn't escape, hadn't earned me points with anyone.

The bride hated the ocean.

My brother was smart enough to catch onto my implication.

It wasn't my fault Amy wasn't exactly the most reliable woman in the world when it came to marriage. Once was a fluke. Twice was a trend. Five incidents of running from the wedding was evidence the thoroughbride would strike again, and my dear old brother would be saddled with the fifty thousand dollar bill, as he refused to believe Amy would run out on him.

Oh, no. Amy would never run out on *him*.

My brother was an idiot, but I loved him too much to let his wedding fail. My brother deserved to be left at the altar as snubbed groom number six, but I wouldn't back out. I'd play my part, I'd even try to keep her from running or ruining the wedding, and I'd take as many pictures as possible to immortalize the chaos.

Thanks to Amy's awful taste in gowns, I had ample space in my cleavage to hide my phone.

At four in the morning of the big day, I called in every favor owed to me so I could not quite match the bride in the beauty department. In exchange for doing his taxes for two years, Wolfgang transformed my dull, light brown hair into a curled work of art and handled my makeup. Clarice did my nails and toes for dibs on any interesting photos, and she'd even pay for them if she liked them.

My brother would never forgive me for selling photographs of his wedding to a newspaper. If he hadn't wanted me taking pictures, he wouldn't have talked shit about me behind my back.

"This is crazy," Clarice muttered, fiddling with my toes while Wolfgang waged war against my unruly hair. "What did Matthew do for you to pull out all the stops? Wearing those baggy sweaters to hide your waist size was pure brilliance. I heard the thoroughbride bitching about how you'll burst out of your very expensive dress."

"It's a good thing my dress fits me perfectly, isn't it?"

"I worry for the donut supply the instant the reception is over."

Wolfgang snickered. "Do you think there'll be a reception?"

I shrugged. "We'll find out in twelve hours. Did you talk to Ben?"

"If the photographer doesn't show, you're covered," he confirmed. "You're good on the caterer, too. My source confirmed they started their work on the cake an hour ago, and they're doing two just in case. If nothing goes wrong, you'll be paying for the second cake in volunteer work."

I expected the caterer, a business operated by Wolfgang's aunt, would be the most reliable element of the wedding. "The open bar?"

"Aunt Emma has sworn on our family's honor everything will be perfect."

"If this goes off without a hitch, I'll double owe you both. The dresses are confirmed, Clarice?"

"They're in my SUV and ready to roll. I have a list of brides and maids who could use them if they survive through the day."

I had doubts about that. "The flowers?"

"Ten-minute arrival window if needed, and if they're not needed, they'll be sent to the local hospitals and nursing homes to cheer up the patients. Your brother is on his own for the rings. There needs to be limits to your paranoia, Hope."

"You're joking, right? Last week, Matthew warned me if I screwed anything up, my shame would be witnessed by royalty. I told him he was delusional. What sort of self-respecting member of royalty would be friends with *my* brother? He needs to worry about himself. He's the one who wants to marry a thoroughbride."

We laughed. There was little else we could do in the face of impending disaster.

AT EXACTLY EIGHT in the morning, I presented myself for bride-herding duty. Amy opened her door and gaped at me, her expression so stunned I had no doubt she'd expected me to flake from the very beginning. "Rise and shine, Amy. It's your big day."

Take six.

"Hope? You're already dressed."

Not only was I dressed, I wore makeup and had nice hair, which wouldn't survive the day if everything went as I expected. I forced a smile. "Of course. I need to give you my complete attention today so everything's perfect." I kept smiling until my face hurt. The effort to keep from clenching my teeth left me tired and ready to go back to bed. "Did you sleep well?"

"I spilled wine on the dress last night. Mat was over, and we were drinking."

While my brother liked to drink, had she actually spilled wine on her dress while he was present, he would've called me in a complete panic. I questioned my decision to make certain my brother got the wedding he wanted.

I also swore I wouldn't judge until I had a

chance to ask him if he had actually gone over and been a participant in the death of a dress worth more than I was. With my smile fixed in place, I retrieved my phone from my purse and texted Clarice about the first disaster of the day. "Where's your stylist?"

"He quit last night when I told him I'd need him an hour earlier."

There went one deposit, and I'd be lucky if I got any of that money back. Wolfgang might forgive me one day. Maybe. If I groveled sufficiently and became his slave for the rest of my life. The second text of the day went to him. Then again, if I survived the day, I'd consider it a win and sell myself into slavery without regret.

Wolfgang's world seemed so much better than mine.

I drew in a steadying breath. "Any other problems?"

"I think the photographer quit, too."

Any sensible photographer likely would when faced with Amy at her worst. I really couldn't see what my brother saw in the woman, but I couldn't make his important life decisions for him.

Clarice would forgive me. Wolfgang might forgive me. Ben never would. Poor Ben. I texted Ben with a warning we'd upgraded from a thoroughbride to a bridezilla, and if I could somehow procure his skills for the day, my brother's soul would be his to do with as he pleased.

My brother's soul, in the grand scheme, was worth a lot more than mine.

As my bride-induced paranoia knew no bounds, I texted my father, an older man who'd stepped in when my parents had died years ago. The request to bring his parents' rings would be the icing on the wedding cake for him, even if my brother and his goon of a bride didn't manage to screw up their rings.

My father would consider forgiveness in exchange for a son-in-law. He'd be a long time waiting for that disaster to happen, but if he hadn't figured that out on his own, he hadn't been paying attention for the past ten years of my life.

It occurred to me we might have worse problems on our hands than a runaway bride out to ruin the wedding. I texted my mother just to make certain my brother showed up for his big day.

Our parents would be rolling in their graves over my brother's poor choice of bride. The first chance I got, I'd visit their tombstones and tell them all about the woman who'd turned Matthew's life upside down.

Amy stared at me, and I kept on smiling. Careful to keep my tone pleasant, I asked, "What is the situation with the florist?"

"They're the only thing not ruined."

Not only would I walk through the valley of the shadow of death, I'd have tea with the devil to negotiate my takeover of hell before the day was through. Several pings on my phone drew my attention to the screen, with Clarice, Wolfgang, and Ben promising to come to my rescue. My father, in his text, informed me he would bring the rings and recruit Mom to herd Matthew and ensure he showed up without incident.

I wondered if I should warn Dad Matthew might be hungover. On second thought, I wouldn't.

Matthew could handle the Wrath of Mom if she smelled lingering alcohol on his breath.

"The replacement stylist should be here soon. I have a seamstress friend capable of performing miracles, and I'm sure I can handle the rest. If you have any concerns, let me know."

"I might be pregnant."

With how often my brother shacked up with his thoroughbride, I wasn't surprised. "Have you told Matthew yet?"

"No."

"Well, you won't be partaking of the wine fountain. You can surprise him as a wedding gift. Congratulations. Also, that's not a concern. Matthew loves children." I'd consider it the one thing that might go right in the day.

"It's probably not his. He uses condoms religiously."

I'd seen brides with cold feet before, but none quite like Amy. I had no idea on what planet she thought she was fooling anyone; the woman didn't have time for a tryst, and she'd spent every waking moment trying to piss me off or banging my brother.

But if she wanted to play games, I'd play. "Fortunately for you, Matthew loves children."

Her mouth dropped open, and I snapped a photo of her to immortalize the moment I'd rendered the bridezilla speechless. In the time it took her to recover, Wolfgang arrived, his expression the ultimate mask of excitement. "Is this jewel the bride?"

Wolfgang needed to have his head examined as soon as the wedding was over. "She sure is. Work your magic, Wolfgang. I've a dress and bridesmaids to wrangle."

No matter what, the only disaster at my brother's wedding would be Amy.

AMY CONCOCTED a thousand excuses to put the brakes on the wedding, testing my limits, pushing my buttons, and ultimately forcing my hand an hour before showtime. We shared a room with Amy's three poor bridesmaids, who would have to witness the moment I transformed into a dragon and breathed fire.

Amy's friends had already lost their will to live, their dead eyes watching while they waited for the worst.

They had no idea how determined I could be—or how ruthless.

I'd enjoy teaching them why underestimating me was a bad idea.

I smiled, and if Amy had any sense in her head, she would've recognized it as a warning she was about to have her ass handed to her. "Amy, my brother spent fifty-one thousand dollars on this wedding to make you happy. Go ahead. Try to run. I'll haul your ass to the altar myself. If you want to divorce him tomorrow, fine. That's your problem. I don't care if you break Matthew's heart tomorrow. But today? You're getting married. *You* wanted this fancy wedding, and if you want to be a bitch, you'll do so at the altar. Maybe you have the integrity of a newt, but if you're going to spit in my brother's face, you will do so where all five hundred guests, including your father's top investors, can witness how unreliable and petty you really are. So. Are you walking with your father down the aisle? The other option is a literal ball and chain. I'm sure the ladies wouldn't mind helping me lug it to the altar."

Amy's mouth dropped open, and her eyes widened to the point she ran risk of them popping out of her head. Her friends gasped.

The pretty blonde, a woman I believed had more money than sense, smirked, and her expression led me to believe I'd misjudged Kate. At least, I thought her name was Kate. She'd wisely dodged most of the preparations.

"It weighs eighty pounds and cost me a small fortune."

"You wouldn't dare," Amy whispered, and I savored the doubt in her tone.

"I dare. Go on. Try me. I'm in shorter heels, a better dress, and I've already requested backup. And if *that* isn't enough to convince you, I've made a list of every expense leading up to your special day. I have your father's cell phone number and his personal email address. Nice man, your father. It wouldn't take me long to expose everything."

Amy paled, and only her obsessive-compulsive suntanning disorder kept her from matching her dress. "You wouldn't."

"I worked too damned hard on this wedding to watch you ruin it by refusing to go to the altar like some spoiled brat who is just realizing life is work. If you want to chicken out during the vows, go for it. But you're walking to that damned altar, and you'll do so at the stately, dignified pace we practiced for hours yesterday. The entire way to the altar. We clear?"

The thoroughbride-turned-bridezilla gulped. "We're clear."

I turned to Kate. "If she looks like she's going to run, trip her and sit on her long enough for me to fetch the ball and chain."

"You got it," the woman replied. When she smiled, I recognized the expression as one of satisfaction.

"Caterina! You're siding with her?"

"Damn straight I'm siding with her. She's right. Also, sure, you might be pregnant, but we all know you're too much of a chickenshit to cheat on Mat. The condom probably broke, and you puked up your birth control because you have the common sense of a rock. Don't screw this up being stupid. Frankly, it's a miracle you got another chance at this. Just do your part. You'll thank us later."

I appreciated Kate's optimism, but I doubted Amy would ever forgive me for ruining her plans to skip out on her extravagant wedding. Oh, well. I didn't care what she thought. I wasn't the one marrying her.

I just wanted my brother to be happy, and I'd do a lot more than chain a runaway bride to give him what his heart wanted.

AMY MADE one final attempt to abandon ship, and I caught her halfway out the window. A single clearing of my throat froze my brother's future wife in place, one knee braced against the windowsill.

"If you're trying to snitch an extra rose for your bouquet, I've got one here," I announced in my sweetest voice. My phone warned me we had five minutes until showtime. "Your father's waiting outside, and he looks about ready to cry that you're finally getting married. Smile, Amy. It's your big day."

Either aware I'd shackle her to a literal iron ball or she was unable to follow through with disappointing her father yet again, Amy slid back into the room. "Why are you doing this?"

"I love my brother almost as much as he loves you. And since I do love my brother almost as much as he loves you, I won't tell him you tried to run. I'm telling myself at least one of you will have a great day. Maybe after the vows are exchanged, your cold feet will warm up. Also, if you try to run at the altar, I will chase you. You're not giving my brother the run around today. Just be grateful I hired extra staff to cover your cancellations. You'll have your perfect day, and if it makes you happy, you can gloat over how much it cost me to cover your ass."

"You paid for the replacements?"

According to her tone, she couldn't believe it was at all possible I could afford to do such a thing. My brother was the one with the money and connections, not me.

Or so she thought.

My job would never move me too far up in the world, but people trusted me with their money, and that went a long way in the business world.

"With my sweat, blood, and tears. You can thank me later."

Judging from her glare, she wouldn't be thanking me anytime soon. I refused to care. Satisfied I wouldn't have to tell my brother the love of his life had run, I pointed at the door. "It's showtime. Pretend this is the happiest day of your life. It would be embarrassing if your face ended up plastered on the front page of some tabloid. They love calling out runaway brides who sucker their grooms out of tens of thousands of dollars on a wedding. And I really don't think your daddy will be keeping you in his will if you humiliate him in front of his investors today. Hate me all you want, but I am helping you."

"The tabloids? What tabloids?"

"You're a registered thoroughbride marrying a man with some money and influence, Amy. Of course the tabloids are interested in your wedding. The only way you win is if you see this through."

I really hoped she was half as great a person as my brother believed. If not, I'd have to figure out some way to convince him to forgive me.

"I hate you," Amy whispered.

"I'm sure you do. I'm a bitch on a good day. Don't make this a bad one." I glared at her and snapped my fingers, once again pointing at the door. "Time for you to be happily married. Emphasis on the happily. Double emphasis on the married. Now, march!"

TWO

I held my breath through the officiation.

I TOOK my place as the bridesmaid of honor, kept a smile plastered on my face, and wished I could go home and sleep. When I'd suggested shorter vows, I'd pissed off my brother and triggered Amy's indignant wrath. I'd convinced them to cut down the twenty-minute monstrosity to five nerve-racking minutes. Time dragged while I worried my brother's thoroughbride would bolt for the door.

She stayed, and I held my breath through the officiation. Only after they both signed the paperwork did I relax.

Well, as much as I could. One thoroughbride down, one reception to go. If I pretended we weren't booked for three hours of photographs before the reception, could I skip? I'd done my part. For better or worse, my brother was a married man.

I hoped he didn't regret his choice—and that Amy wouldn't wage a war to turn my brother against me. I figured that was part of being an in-law. I gave it twenty-four hours before I became enemy number one.

If I focused on the good things, I'd get through the day. Mom and Dad were happy, beaming that their son had gotten hitched and had wrangled a thoroughbride without her running off. To them, it didn't matter we were adopted; they'd done their jobs as parents and seen their boy safely married off. The bride's parents seemed to be likewise thrilled.

Mom would wait a few weeks before starting her campaign to marry me off. Dad would start dropping hints immediately if not sooner, as I'd seen the gleam in his eyes when he'd watched Amy's father walk her down the aisle.

Maybe I needed to run away before I got caught up in the wedding nonsense.

Per our plan, the happily married couple left the church with the rest of the wedding party in tow. Three limousines waited to cart us to the botanical gardens thirty minutes away.

Amy stuck close to my brother, who did his best to start a conversation with his new wife. In the time it took us to divide into the three limousines, he'd coaxed a single smile out of her.

It was better than I expected, all things considered.

I really could be a bitch sometimes.

Before I could pick a limousine, Kate linked arms with me and dragged me to the last limo in the line. "That was brilliant. No one outside of the bridesmaids has any idea that was almost a disaster."

Well, someone was happy with me. I'd take what I could get. I retrieved my phone from its hiding place in my cleavage and checked the time. If I had gotten one of the larger models, I wouldn't have been able to pull the stunt off. All hail simple, small phones with decent cameras built in. "We have eight more hours of potential disasters ahead of us left. Let's not get overly optimistic here. The only reason the photography shoot might work out is because I handled the arrangements for the limos and the gardens. And yes, I booked a second photographer knowing Amy would somehow screw up the first one."

"Why aren't you a wedding planner?" Kate shoved me into the limo and scooted onto the leather seat beside me, and the other bridesmaids converged to ensure I couldn't escape. "You've worked miracles today. How did you even pull this off? Emily, Sarah, and I? We can't figure it out."

I laughed. The truth hurt, and I'd be spending the next six months of my life ruing and lamenting the choices I'd made to make my brother happy. "I'm a tax accountant, Kate. So far, I'm doing two years' worth of corporate taxes for several small businesses.

Basically, I bribed people, offered to do their personal *and* corporate taxes, and spent the entirety of my vacation fund making certain this wedding happened."

"On top of the fifty grand your brother paid?" Kate's eyes widened.

"Fourteen grand of that went to the church and reception hall. Thanks to Amy's poor life decisions, the rest of the funds went bye-bye."

"That's horrible. You won't get any of that back?"

"I wasn't planning on getting the money back. I don't have time to chase after every cancelled contractor. At most, I could get the payments for the actual work back, but the deposits are gone. And thanks to Amy's poor life choices, the deposits were way too high for the work anyway. Please don't tell Mat. He has no idea Amy lost the deposits and most of the wedding funds with her cold feet. But it's done now, and she signed the marriage certificate—and no one protested their vows. As far as I'm concerned, it was worth every penny."

Kate looked me over before exchanging long looks with her friends. "Are you a queen bitch or an angel, Hope? I can't tell."

"Closer to bitch, but thank you. As long as Mat's happy, that's all I care about."

"Except your brother invested over fifty grand to lose all but fourteen."

I arched a brow and stared at Amy's

friend. "And he would've paid twice as much to make her happy. I'm not going to ruin that for him. Just don't trust her with your event planning. She'll bleed you dry."

IN HER EFFORT TO drive me insane, Amy had insisted on inviting everyone to the botanical gardens for the photography shoot. Getting tickets for everyone had involved a special RSVP on the wedding invitations and hours upon hours of printing and distribution. To add insult to injury, Amy had demanded beautiful, gold-framed tickets.

The stupid envelopes alone had cost my brother a fortune.

The limos arrived first, with a parade of other cars tailing us. Expecting Amy to screw up the admittance to the garden, I bolted from the vehicle to intercept the newlyweds. "Have your tickets?" I chirped, ready to dig into my little clutch for one of the spare tickets if needed.

Under no circumstances would my brother learn I wanted to run away and hide thanks to his new wife.

Mat held up the two gold-gilded envelopes that contained their tickets. "All good, Hope. Even if I screwed it up, I do have my wallet with me. Despite my inability to plan a wedding, I have mastered ticket stalls. And you thought my love of going to the movies would never amount to anything."

One day, my brother would yank my last chain, and I'd go truly crazy. I did have to admit his love of going to the movies had made him the perfect gopher for ticket acquisitions—usually. Unless a wedding and botanical garden visits were involved.

"Try not to get lost. You'll make the photographer cry—and after Ben's done with you, I'll take a turn."

"As I value my life, I promise I won't give Ben any reason to kill me. On my honor. I still don't know how you managed to pull all this off, but thank you."

"You can thank Amy. She helped." I smiled at my masterful disguising of my sarcasm. Amy's embarrassed flush helped curb my desire to make additional snide commentary. "But seriously. Congrats to you both."

My brother beamed and kissed the top of my head, once again reminding me I faced a lifetime of being short. "Try not to cry too much when you can't beg me to kill spiders for you anymore, little sister."

Considering I'd last asked him to kill a spider for me about five years ago, I'd probably manage. If the damned thing hadn't been on the toilet seat in his bathroom, I would've been fine without help. "Well, now you only need to worry about Amy. Also, that was a long time ago."

"It was," he conceded, checking his watch. "Mind doing me a favor?"

While tapped out in the favor department, I resisted my initial urge to strangle my brother in front of the wedding guests. "What do you need?"

"My friend's dog ate his ticket. Can you get him inside? I really don't want Ben to kill me."

There was always one. Always. "Sure. I'll meet him here. Send him my picture so he knows who to look for."

"Thanks, Hope. You're the best." My brother snapped a picture with his phone before escorting Amy into the gardens. The rest of the wedding party followed with the arriving guests hot on their heels. If his friend took longer than twenty minutes, Ben would kill me for interrupting his schedule. Then again, a quick death might be a mercy, an escape from the photo shoot, and a way out of attending the reception.

One way or another, I expected the reception to finish me off, assuming I made it out of the gardens alive. I wouldn't put it past Amy to find some poisonous flower and off me with it. If I cared a little less about my brother's perfect day, I would've considered changing my plans and consuming the entire wine fountain rather than have my picture taken. Given thirty minutes, I could do some serious damage to the wine supply. Liver failure would ruin my day, but my brother would leave with Amy long before I sought out the bottom of the barrel.

"You Hope?" a deep, smooth voice asked with enough of a rumble to curl my toes in my foot-torture devices otherwise known as shoes.

I turned to behold a vision of male perfection, too tall for my good, with warm brown eyes and chestnut hair tinged with red. Add in a smooth jawline, a mouth well accustomed to smiling, and dimples, and I'd need at least a few weeks to recover. "I'm Hope."

"Sorry for the fuss. My dog pulled the invitation off the counter right before my flight." He reached into his jacket and revealed a chewed envelope. "She doesn't like when I leave home."

I'd do a lot more than chew on an envelope to keep him at home if he were mine. "I'm afraid I require pictures of your dog to verify your claim."

His smile widened into a grin, and he retrieved his phone. "You just want to see pictures of my dog."

"And if she's cute, I'll be forced to scold you for accusing her of wrongdoing."

"Let me guess. You think all dogs are cute."

"Was it obvious?" I made a show of tapping my forehead. "Did I finally get it tattooed to my face?"

"Mat hadn't told me about your sense of humor." My brother's friend held out his phone. "This is Annabel Lee."

A big, white, gray, and fluffy dog grinned for the camera. "Well, in good news for you, that kind of dog won't get cold even when near the sea. What is she?"

"For all her paperwork claims she's a purebred, I think she might be a mutt. From the looks of her, she must be part Alaskan Malamute, part pony. Mat neglected to tell me you're a poetry fan."

Annabel Lee didn't look like a Malamute to me, but I couldn't tell what breed she actually was. "I'm more of an abandoned English literature major who ditched to major in accounting instead after translating the original Canterbury Tales. Quoth the Hope, 'Nevermore!' I thought it was wise to quit before I murdered my professor. I see red whenever someone asks me to quote from the Raven. But Annabel Lee is a favorite."

"My mother loved the poem, so I named my dog Annabel Lee."

"I'm sorry."

"Don't be. My mother stopped loving it when eight-year-old me recited it approximately ten thousand times. I live to vex my mother, and she loves my dog despite her name."

There had to be something horribly wrong with my brother's friend, but what? Did he snore? Steal the blankets? Hover sexily at inappropriate times? "Mat didn't tell me your name."

"That's like him. I'm Fredrick, but please

call me Rick." He shuffled his phone to his left hand and offered to shake with me.

Instead of the expected shake, I got a light kiss to the back of my hand.

All right. How had my brother become friends with a gentleman? "I'm Hope, and I don't have any nicknames because the last person who tried to give me one called me Ho, and my brother punched him. I was in high school at the time, and it was a teacher."

"Believe it or not, I heard about that incident from Mat. He got the teacher fired but spent the night in holding. No charges were ultimately filed though, right?"

"No charges," I confirmed. "He recorded the teacher pestering me with his phone and threatened to bring up sexual harassment charges against the school. Honestly, I was about to punch the teacher, too."

Rick released my hand and grinned. "No worries about anything like that from me, Hope. Does my incredibly sweet but mischievous dog earn me a pass for the damaged ticket?"

Laughing, I nodded and gestured to the ticket booth. "I'll get you sorted. I have open tickets, but we need to give them your residency info. You don't mind?"

"Of course not. Honestly, I was just going to buy my own replacement ticket, but Mat got pissy. It seems insulting your hard work is simply not allowed. To be fair, we were betting Amy would run, even him—and he's been working out to make sure he could catch her if she took off. That woman loves running him in circles. How on Earth did you convince her not to run? Everyone's saying you're a miracle worker."

Ew. I didn't want anyone's attention on me as a result of my brother's wedding actually succeeding. I masked my dismay with a roll of my eyes. "If you really must know, I used a ball and chain."

"A ball and chain? Do tell."

A five-minute chat with the poor woman at the ticketing booth sorted the problem of Rick's ticket, who had ventured from Japan to attend the wedding. As Fredrick had as much Asian blood as his dog, I assumed he was one of Mat's overly rich businessmen friends with more money than sense.

Did being an overly rich businessman count as something severely wrong with him? After a fierce but brief debate with myself, I decided I needed to gather additional information before issuing a verdict.

"So, about that ball and chain," he said after we entered the gardens. "I really must know."

"It weighs about eighty pounds, it cost me a small fortune, and it would have looked terrible with her dress. I informed her I would recruit the rest of the bridesmaids to haul it to the altar if she tried to run. She obviously believed me."

"Would you sell me that ball and chain, please? I'll pay good money for it."

"As I have no use for a solid iron ball and chain that was painted white and equipped with the best lock money could buy for below two hundred, consider it yours. Happy belated birthday—assuming it's not your birthday today."

He stumbled a few steps and gaped at me. I took advantage of the opportunity to make my escape, cutting through the first topiary maze to catch up with the rest of the wedding party. Mat would just love having to deliver an eighty pound ball and chain to his friend, a gift from his little sister.

Not.

For the first time that day, I truly laughed.

THE POND in the heart of the gardens made the ideal place for wedding photographs. As I had expected trouble from the very beginning, I'd learned every shortcut through the place to reach the first stop of our picture tour.

Despite waiting for Rick and dealing with his ticket, I beat the rest of the wedding party to the pond. Ben chuckled and waited for me to catch my breath.

"And you laughed at me for spending so much time over the weekends jogging in the gardens."

"I'm impressed but also concerned. Your brother texted me that you might be late. Make yourself as pretty as an ugly duckling can. I'll do your solo shots now. Else, the harpy might try to cut you out of the photographs completely."

"That would annoy my brother, but I can't say I don't deserve being cut out at this point. Am I mussed or sweaty?"

"Surprisingly, no."

"Take pictures." I even smiled for him, as bridesmaids were supposed to look happy for the bride at her wedding. I doubted I'd be able to look anything other than flustered and annoyed once Amy showed up. I'd try, but I'd never been good at dealing with people who created unnecessary trouble for me.

Who had time for that crap?

Ben shook his head and sighed. "You could try posing."

"No one told me I had to pose for this wedding." I posed my middle finger in the upright position. To enhance my no fucks left to give image, I stuck out my tongue.

Ben, being Ben, dutifully photographed my immaturity. "How classy, Hope."

I leaned against the trunk of the nearest tree and showed him both of my middle fingers. "Is this better?"

"Attempt to look demur for once in your life. I'll take pleasantly puzzled if you can't handle the demur look."

"How about the total badass look?"

"No. You're not a badass. You're usually tired and easily annoyed but hide it well. Badasses kick butt, take names, and go home a crowned queen. You go home more like a battered servant."

Damn. Ben didn't pull his punches. "This game sucks."

"I can work with a pretty pout and dewy eyes."

"Gross. I'm not a broodmare up for auction."

"For today, you really are. Just remind yourself it'll make your brother happy. If you can't handle a dewy pout without help, remember you can't smack the bride."

"That's so stupid. Why not? After what she did this morning, she deserves it." I targeted Ben with my most disappointed frown. "You're enjoying my pain too much."

"If you're good, I'll take you out for milkshakes tomorrow night."

After frantically dieting to fit into a dress that Amy had deliberately purchased two sizes too small, I'd cut someone for a milkshake. A milkshake might turn the train wreck of my life around—and help me fit back into my real wardrobe, which was of a healthy size rather than designed for a skeleton barely wrapped in flesh.

Ben snapped a few photos. "Damn, woman. You don't have to actually cry."

"It's been that long since I've had a milkshake. That's worth crying over."

"I can tell. Give me a smile. Think about how you're going to sucker me into paying for your extra large milkshake. I'll even hold your hair if you make yourself sick after so long of trying to eat less than a bird. As an added bonus, you'll get two cherries on top; I'll let you steal mine. You know those damned cherries go straight to my hips."

A laugh escaped before I could stop it. "Why are all the good men gay?"

"You just attract the good gay men because you're too damned sweet, treat us like we're human beings, and don't mind when we go shopping with you. Who else is going to tolerate my taste in clothes and offer helpful advice on what looks best? You don't even beg me to go full gay mode on annoying men to make them go away."

"I don't need you to make annoying men go away. I just act like myself."

According to Ben's expression, I was full of crap. "Cut yourself some slack, Hope. One day, you'll find a man who knows your worth. The rest are just shitty sex fixes, and your battery-operated boyfriend does a better job."

"Remind me of that the next time I'm stood up on a date."

"You got it, babe. Strike some poses for me and show me that smile of yours. In ten minutes, your day goes straight back to hell."

AS PREDICTED, Amy's arrival dumped my skinny ass straight into the bowels of hell. Since my detour dealing with Rick hadn't unseated my throne of perfectionism, she decided she needed someone to photograph every square inch of the gardens to immortalize her wedding day.

I bit my tongue so I wouldn't remind her she hadn't wanted a wedding in the first place.

Unfortunately for Amy, I'd anticipated something of the sort, so I'd begged Ben to come extra prepared. I'd hear his complaints for months over his offended sensibilities, but he'd brought five spare, cheap cameras along just in case. I could find a few extra volunteers to help me take thousands of photographs Amy wouldn't bother looking at.

Amy began her evil work at the pond, but a few kids, a baseball bat, and their ball ensured her victory. I hadn't even registered the crack of them hitting their ball before it'd bounced off my thick skull. I lost a few minutes thanks to their aim, and when I finally rejoined the rest of the world, I discovered I'd spent some time in the pond along with Ben's camera.

He might kill me for trashing even one of his cheap cameras.

Water dripped into my eyes, but when I lifted my hand to wipe my face, someone stopped me. My eyes refused to focus properly, although I identified the person as a man. Men wore suits, women wore dresses. That had been the dress code for Amy's wedding, and the person interfering with my attempts to get the water out of my eyes was definitely wearing a suit.

"You were supposed to photograph the pond, not dive in," Amy complained. "You're a mess. You have weeds in your hair."

I couldn't even tell if Amy was actually upset I'd interrupted her photography shoot. I thought her tone implied glee, but I decided I wouldn't care. I'd threatened her with a ball and chain, so it was fair enough for her to view the incident as karma biting me in the rump. "It's a rule. Someone at a wedding always ends up in the pond. No one told me I'd score a headache, though. I could live without that part."

My brother sighed, and I realized he was the jerk who kept stopping me from wiping my face. Then, since one sigh wasn't good enough, he did it again. "You're not supposed to catch baseballs with your head."

Fine. He wasn't wrong, but did he have to say it? I came bundled with various forms of revenge, and I figured I'd delve into my love of amusing movies to exact my revenge. "'Tis but a scratch."

"Your clock's been cleaned!" He shook his head, confirming he was, indeed, the helpful entity who refused to let me get the water out of my eyes.

When my brother figured out I was yanking his chain, he might kill me. "No, it hasn't. I'm talking to you. If my clock had been truly cleaned, I would not be speaking to you right now."

"You weren't speaking to me thirty seconds ago."

"My clock has not been cleaned."

"If your clock hasn't been cleaned, why is there blood in your hair?"

My brother made it hard to keep from laughing. In my current state, laughing would be bad. Laughing would make my head hurt. "I've had worse," I lied.

"Have you, now?" My eyes focused on him enough to witness the narrowing of his eyes. He inspected the side of my head where I'd been smacked with a baseball. "I can't remember any other time you almost lost your head to a baseball."

Finally, my moment had come. "It's just a flesh wound."

Behind me, Ben snickered.

"You're a force of unrelenting evil," my brother complained.

"Go back to taking pretty pictures with your bride and be happy I got my solo photos done early. I'll be fine." After my head stopped trying to split in half. "I'm just going to sit here for a few minutes and catch my breath."

"You almost drowned because you lost

consciousness due to a baseball to the head. That is not fine."

Damn. I was afraid to ask if CPR had been involved. If it had been, I'd never live it down. I'd heard horror stories about CPR, and my chest didn't feel like someone had beaten me with a baseball bat, so I would assume I'd escaped from that horror. I could think of only one way to distract my brother. I turned to Ben and asked, "Did you get any pictures of that? It'd be tragic if you hadn't caught any pictures of me taking a baseball to the head."

My friend sighed and shook his head. "Maybe. I'll check tonight."

"I demand copies if they exist. Mat, please go back to taking pretty pictures. I'll be fine."

My ploy failed, and my brother glared at me. "I fail to see how my sister, who was hit in the head hard enough she fainted and almost drowned, can possibly be fine."

I checked the gardens for our adoptive parents and spotted them nearby, their arms crossed and glaring at me with matched expressions of disapproval. Unlike my brother, they wouldn't say anything—yet. They'd wait for a moment of weakness and attempt to kill me with kindness.

And they'd arrange it so I wouldn't be able to escape. If they felt I was about to have a breakdown because my big brother had finally grown up, they might bring a puppy or kitten with them and make me care for it.

I'd never had a puppy or kitten before.

Or, worse. They'd finally listen to my childhood dream of owning a horse and make one appear to keep me broke, busy, and close to home.

I'd even like it.

"I'm fine!" I hollered in their general direction.

Neither seemed to believe me.

I wrinkled my nose. "I'm just that amazing. That's how I'm fine. I'm just *that* amazing. Go take your pictures. I'll just sit here and wait for the busybody paramedics you probably insisted on calling to arrive. After they leave, I'll get changed and prepare for the reception." I pointed at my brother. "Are we clear?"

"You're a pain in my ass. You're really going to attend the reception after taking a baseball to the head?"

Duh. Stupid brother. "Today is your wedding day. I wouldn't miss it for the world. A damned baseball isn't stopping this woman, so get used to the idea."

My brother looked like he wanted to be sick. "Hope."

I wanted to tell him he was only going to get married once, but I knew better than to tempt fate, especially when Amy was the second half of their partnership. "Please go do the things handsome grooms do on their wedding day. I'll be fine. Really. It'll take a lot more than a baseball bat to make me miss any part of your wedding."

Except that bit where I'd fallen into a pond and almost drowned. I didn't count that. It wasn't my fault a bunch of kids thought it was a good idea to play baseball in a botanical gardens.

Ben and my brother both heaved sighs but trudged off to do as told.

THREE

Some risks were worth taking.

TO KEEP to the day's frantic schedule, I dealt with the paramedics in record time. They couldn't force me to go to the hospital, I politely turned down their repeated invitations, and I promised I would take myself to a doctor if I suffered from any of the symptoms they rattled off. I promptly forgot the list.

There was no way in hell I was leaving my brother's wedding, and I didn't even care if there was some blood in my hair. The bleeding had stopped, my vision had cleared, and while I had a headache worth writing home about, it was nothing I couldn't handle despite clenching my teeth to get through it. If I left my brother's wedding, it would transform into a nightmare. Leaving Amy in charge of the reception would end the reception. The disaster would be talked about for years. Somehow, she would make it even worse than me taking a baseball to the head.

Luckily for me, the blow had been a graze,

it hadn't hit anything important, and I figured the only reason I bled was thanks to one of the dumbass clips taming my hair.

I wanted to keep the wedding disasters to the things I hadn't planned for. A baseball to the head counted, but it wouldn't kill me.

I hoped.

Some risks were worth taking, and I'd have to remind my brother later I loved him that much.

A call to Wolfgang would fix my ruined dress and makeup problem, but I hesitated. Telling him what had happened would result in well-earned mockery. I retrieved my phone from its cleavage prison to discover it still had some life left in it. Dialing his number worsened my headache.

The rest of the day would suck, but I would make it through somehow.

"What went wrong?" Wolfgang answered.

"I took a stray baseball to the head. I need your makeup skills and my reception dress. Help a woman out? Please? I'm not above begging at this point."

"A baseball? To the head? How did that happen? Are you all right? If you were hit with a baseball—"

"Don't you even dare suggest I go to the hospital."

Wolfgang sighed. "What happened?"

"Fate, karma, the universe, or whatever you want to call it, wishes I would die already. I fell into the pond. I bet I'll make the front page. Who knows? Maybe someone caught the whole thing on video. I might go viral."

The groan on the other end of line promised Wolfgang was at the end of his rope, too. "Your brother must be freaking out."

"Ben's keeping him busy taking pretty pictures to immortalize the day I almost drowned in the botanical gardens pond."

"Where were you hit?"

"It was a graze off the side of my head. My hair should hide any bumps. The bleeding stopped."

"Are you dizzy, have a headache, or feel ill?"

I suspected once I tried to get up and walk around, I would be dizzy. I wasn't a fan of my own head right now, and I could be honest about otherwise being all right. Unfortunately, if I lied, he would know it. He always knew. "Maybe."

"I'll be there in twenty. I'll bring the dress and your makeup, but you're going to the hospital before the reception. If you go to the reception."

"I am not."

"You are, because I am taking you there."

"If you take me there, I'll miss the reception," I hissed.

"My mother can handle the reception organization if we're not done in time. She'll have fun."

She would, too. The woman could probably organize a rally given ten minutes and a bullhorn. "I'm not going to the hospital."

Someone reached over my shoulder and stole my phone, and I recognized Rick's chuckle. "I've no idea whom I'm speaking to, but I'll contain the lady until her ride to the hospital. I've been recruited to make certain she goes. Yes, by Mat. Twenty minutes, you say? Excellent. I'll see you then. I'll bring her to the gate."

My damned traitor of a brother. "Hey. That's my phone. I was using that."

"Now I'm using it to make certain you go to the hospital. The groom's wishes trump yours in this case, princess."

A god-level adversary had crossed my path, and unless I did something about it, I would lose to him and his wicked ways and theft of my phone. "I will get revenge on you both if you make me go to the hospital." Ignoring my brother would earn me a scolding later, but Rick would be the true challenge of the pair; I bet he'd ignore my fussing without any effort at all on his part. "I will begin with stealing your puppy's love."

Rick laughed. "She loves everyone, but I will always be her favorite. I wish you the best of luck with that. Ah, pardon me, Wolfgang. Hope's putting up a fight. Is she, perhaps, allergic to hospitals?"

"Yes, I am. Can I have my phone back now? I need to schedule in a meeting with your puppy to steal her love and become her favorite. You'll be reduced to begging for scraps of affection."

My newfound rival ignored me. "I'll bring the lady to the gate and come with you. Also, Ben wanted me to tell you that Hope could really use a milkshake, and she needs all of the cherries, so we'll have to sacrifice ours."

I was surrounded by traitors. "Ben, too?"

My brother strolled to me, bent over, and dared to look down his nose at me. "You're going to the hospital."

"But it's your wedding day, Mat!"

"And you took a baseball to the head. You're going. Thank you for containing her, Rick. She's slippery, so she will try to give you the run around if you let her. I'd recommend a leash, but I didn't think I needed to bring one today."

My brother did not play fair. Before I could protest, Rick said, "Glad to help. I'll bring her to the reception hall if we're done in time."

"Take your time. I'd rather the hospital be thorough rather than have her try to rush through her examination stubbornly trying to attend the reception. I meant it, Rick. She's slippery. Good luck. You'll need it," my brother announced before turning to leave.

"I'm not dying, damn it."

Mat snorted. "We'll let the hospital decide that. Thanks again, Rick."

Rick snapped my brother a salute, and the

motion reminded me of a professional soldier standing at attention. "Glad to help. Try to enjoy the rest of your day, and I'll text you with updates on how she's doing."

"I didn't even bleed much," I complained. "And the paramedic already checked to see if I'd cracked my skull. And despite being unconscious in the pond, I didn't drown. You're being unreasonable."

"The only reason you didn't drown is because I fished you out of the pond. At least I caught something this time. I usually don't. I love to fish, but I'm terrible at it. This'll go a lot faster if you don't fight it. Anyway, head injuries can be nasty. Be grateful I told Mat you'd be unhappy if he skipped his reception to drag you to the hospital himself."

"But you'll miss the reception."

"Going to the hospital with you is more interesting than attending a reception, even your brother's. I hate watching a bunch of rich prudes get drunk before trying to pretend they're not drunk. I deal with that too often during the week. I hate receptions, and I have to go if you skip your hospital trip. That would be a tragedy. Save me. I'm a defenseless gentleman about to be taken hostage at a reception."

My brows shot up at that. "Do I look like a hero to you?"

"No, but you look like a heroine—possibly a princess in disguise. I'll have to do a closer examination to determine the truth about your secret identity of heroine or princess."

Why did I always attract strange men? Worse, they were either gay, married, or happily in a relationship with someone else. The truth would likely send Rick running. "I'm an accountant."

"A third option has become apparent. You might be a fierce warrior queen. My mistake. Any woman clipped with a baseball and taking a tumble into a pond only to get up ready to rumble must be a fierce warrior queen. Anyway, Mat'll feel terrible if something happened because you went to the reception instead of the hospital. I'll keep you company and show you pictures of my insanely cute dog."

"She is really cute," I conceded.

"Puppy pictures," he whispered in my ear.

Damn it. I'd been had. I couldn't lose the chance to see Annabel Lee's puppy pictures. "I'm doing this under protest."

"Ben gave me the address of your favorite ice cream parlor."

I scowled at the gang of traitors determined to force me to go to the hospital. "He still owes me a milkshake even if you get me one tonight."

"I'll make sure he knows that."

After the day I'd had, some whining was warranted, and I didn't enjoy the thought of having to walk to the gate. "I'm wet, I'm cold, and my shoes squish when I walk."

Rick chuckled, and his gaze dipped to my feet, which I stuck out from under the hem of my ruined dress. "Take the shoes off. I'll carry them, but I can't help you with your wet dress problem. I would if I could, but I neglected to bring clothes suitable for a lady with me today. I'll take care not to be guilty of such an oversight again."

After the reception, I needed to tell my brother he needed to have more friends like Rick. He would have fewer life problems, if only he had better taste in friends.

THE HOSPITAL WANTED to keep me overnight for observation and testing. Baseballs and heads weren't supposed to collide, and according to the doctor, I'd gotten lucky to emerge somewhat unscathed. The entire medical team took a turn with me, scolding me for my refusal to go to the hospital via ambulance.

Wolfgang, who'd accompanied me through the entire wait and triage process, joined forces with Rick and the doctor. To add insult to injury, I was denied my milkshake. I would've accepted even a bad milkshake, but no.

Bad women who didn't go to the hospital right away didn't get a milkshake at all.

While he claimed he was doing it to make me feel better, Wolfgang left to attend the reception in my stead. I knew better. The bastard wanted to escape from my wrath over being denied my hard-earned milkshake.

Rick stayed, and because he wanted to get in on the action, he taunted me with his phone's charger—and his working phone.

After arrangements for me to go to the hospital had been made, mine had died a terrible death, giving the last vestiges of its miserable little life to ensure my captivity. I retrieved the dead device from the table and pressed the power button hoping for a miracle. Nothing happened.

"Mine's dead. This is all Mat's fault. He just had to marry the thoroughbride."

"I'm really impressed she didn't give him the run around today."

"I threatened the ball and chain, and I caught her trying to escape out the window once. The reception's going to be a nightmare, especially without me keeping an eye on things. If I don't show up, it will be guaranteed to be a disaster."

"You're likely right. That said, it's going to be all right. A disaster of a reception is better than not having a reception. Mat can handle his new wife. He is the one who wanted to marry her, after all. I'm sure there's a reason for that. It probably involves blind love and good sex, but there you have it. I wouldn't have married her, personally. I'm still sane."

I laughed at Rick's implication he was not

a fan of my brother's new bride. "Yet you're skipping the reception."

"Well, yeah. Mat bullied me into attending both. While I rather no one be hit with a baseball, I'm eternally grateful for an excuse to skip the reception."

"I don't like receptions, but I never expected to meet someone who dislikes them more than I do. Also, Mat is going to find creative ways to make you pay for skipping his reception. He's lowering your guard pretending to be grateful you accompanied me to the hospital. He might wait years before seeking his revenge, but revenge is coming. Don't say I didn't warn you." It seemed fair to make certain Rick understood he had signed up for my brother at his worst.

"I think I'll be fine. Anyway, I am keeping an eye on you. That's a get out of jail free card, as I know Mat values you more than any reception, even his own. Now, we have more important matters to attend to. As I'm the only one here with a working phone, you should be nice to me. I can be talked into sharing inane news and discussing the circumstances leading up to these unique events. I've found some gems, and I'm willing to share them with you."

I had no idea how Rick wanted me to be nice to him, but it sounded scandalous, and it'd been long enough since I'd had a boyfriend that I was shamefully hopeful being nice involved removing my clothes—

and his. "Inane news? What are you talking about?"

"It usually involves Florida Man."

"Ah. The mystical Florida Man. He's surprisingly durable—most of the time." I giggled, as I often clicked any headline featuring the mystical Florida Man. Without fail, my day seemed a lot better because I'd never done anything nearly as stupid as Florida Man.

"That's one way to put it. I read a lot of news, and Florida Man is a welcomed distraction. Following the news is part of my job."

"Your job sounds tedious and possibly quite awful. I'm sorry your job forces you to watch the news. The news is so depressing lately." I grimaced at how judgmental I sounded. "I'm sorry. That was rude."

"It wasn't rude at all. I like your honesty. And yes, my job can be tedious and awful at times. Let's play a game. Winner takes all."

I got as comfortable as I could on the hospital bed. "Your loss if you bet that."

"What do you mean? We haven't even picked wagers yet."

"I have a packed work schedule for the next two years, and I think I went bankrupt buying the dress I wore into the pond. The only thing I have worth wagering over is the ball and chain, and I already agreed to give it to you."

Rick chuckled. "I'm sure I can think of something you can do for me."

What was adding a little more work to my schedule? I could sleep when I was dead. "Household budget? I'm aces at those, and they're a pain in the ass."

"As my accountant cries whenever I ask her for help with my budget, you're on. Should you win, I'll send you on an all-expenses paid vacation for two weeks, and I'll be responsible for hiring and paying a good temporary to cover your work."

It'd been so long since I'd taken a vacation I couldn't remember what they were like. "What are the rules, and how do we play? How do we keep score?"

"We'll take turns reading crazy headlines and guessing what the article is about. A point for each correct guess. No points lost for incorrect guesses, as we'd both be in the hole if we did that."

"But you read these all the time. You probably know all the stories."

"I'd avoid headlines with Florida Man in them if I were you. Whoever has the highest number of points by the time you're discharged wins."

"You're on. You can go first. Read me a headline."

Rick grinned and tapped at his phone's screen. "Security Camera Catches Prowling Suspect Licking Doorbell for 3 Hours."

I clapped my hands over my mouth so I wouldn't laugh. A cackle burst out of me, which didn't help my headache at all. I snorted in my effort to contain my mirth. A giggle slipped out, and I dissolved into helpless laughter. "Well, some poor bastard wasn't home when that happened. That's just *weird.*"

"I'm giving you a point for directly quoting the article. 'That's just weird' is the general consensus on this one."

I struggled to control my giggling enough to talk. "But why lick a doorbell? That poor homeowner. How long did it take to sanitize that disaster?"

"According to the article, an entire weekend."

"Was the doorbell licker high?"

"No idea. He wasn't caught."

I cleared my throat and drew in deep breaths until the urge to cackle subsided. "That's a pretty good headline. I can understand the allure. If I had an awful job like yours, I'd be looking for those headlines, too."

Rick grinned and handed me his phone. "I haven't read any of the articles on this list, so pick one and go to town."

I scrolled through my selection until I found one about a rambunctious tree rat. "Wanton Squirrel Scarfs Egg Roll as Twitter Drools."

"The internet was obviously bored and hungry. I'm going to guess it happened in San

Francisco, as their Chinatown is the largest in the United States."

"Half point for bored and hungry internet, but it happened in New York."

"I should've guessed that," he groused. "New York squirrels are plentiful and bold. Is the article mostly a vid?"

I nodded and returned his phone. "The squirrel's true crime was forgetting the sauce."

"Now that's just a pity. You can't have egg rolls without the sauce." Like me, Rick took his time scrolling through the list. "Here's a good one. BABY BUNNY CAUSES BOMB SCARE IN AUSTRALIA."

I could think of at least a hundred ways a baby bunny trapped in a bag could unleash utter mayhem in an airport. "He was left in a bag, and he wiggled around inside, thus inspiring fear of a bomb?"

"I'm giving you a point for that. They named him Boeing."

I'd never known a baby bunny named Boeing could sound so wretchedly adorable. "That's just too damned cute, Rick."

"It really is. No one knows why the bunny was abandoned, but the article states Boeing now has a happy home." Rick gave me his phone, shaking his head while smiling.

Rick's motivations for reading the headlines clicked, and it was something I'd do if stuck between a rock and a hard place. "You read these as feel-good stories, don't you?"

"Mostly. The rest of the news is depressing. Sometimes, I read about Florida Man to remind myself there's no way I could ever do something that infernally stupid."

I understood. In keeping with the wildlife theme, I hunted until I found a bird headline to go with the bunny and the squirrel. "RHINESTONE VEST-WEARING PIGEON REUNITED WITH FAMILY."

"Why would anyone put a pigeon in a vest? Why was it wearing rhinestones? It seems to have flown off, but it's wearing clothes. Can I have half a point?"

"You can. So, what's your guess?"

"1920s party, and someone brought their pet pigeon, but it flew away."

I laughed, as reality was far stranger than Rick's guess. "The vest is a diaper so the bird can fly in their home without leaving poop everywhere."

"Take away my half a point. I'm not worthy."

Still laughing, I replied, "I never would have guessed a pigeon wearing a diaper."

"I'm still stuck on someone having a pet pigeon. Add in the vest, and that's a spectacular article."

"It really is. It gets better. The owner replaced some of the pigeon's bling with Swarovski crystals."

"That bird is obviously loved and spoiled." Rick snickered and shook his head. "The world is a strange place."

That it was.

THE HOSPITAL grudgingly released me in the morning, and as to plan, my brother and his menace of a bride left on their honeymoon. I foresaw disaster, but as I'd done since learning he wanted to marry a thorough-bride, I kept my opinions mostly to myself.

My game with Rick ended in a draw, which I found a lot funnier than he did.

"The scoring of this game is obviously flawed," he announced while wheeling me towards freedom. "I should have won."

"You would have, if you hadn't forfeited half a point to the bling-encrusted pigeon," I reminded him.

"For one brief moment, victory had been mine."

"Very brief. All of twenty seconds."

"How is your head feeling?"

"It'll feel a lot better when I have my milkshake. Then I'm going to go home, review all the wedding receipts, and figure out how much that damned wedding ultimately cost, how much she lost him in cancelled bookings, and how long it'll take me to pay everyone back for standing in. I'd appreciate if you didn't tell my brother about that. He'll get pissy."

By pissy, I meant he'd blow his top. Both of us blowing our tops at the same time wouldn't work well. I was about three hours from my first midlife crisis, and damnit, if anyone pushed me, I'd be sorely tempted to bail town, disappear, and show up on Christmas and Thanksgiving because if I didn't, I'd disappoint our parents.

I could cope with two days each year dealing with my brother's bitch of a bride.

I needed to get over my grudge sooner than later for the sake of my sanity.

"Your brother doesn't care about money when he should," Rick conceded.

"Where have you been all his life? Why aren't you a woman? You could have married my brother instead. That way, he'd have a sensible wife instead of a walking, greedy disaster."

"I'd make a terrible woman."

He'd probably be a gorgeous woman so far out of my brother's league it hurt to think about it. Hell, Rick was so far out of my league it hurt to think about it. He was so far out of my league I considered asking him to invoice me for wasting his time. "Think about it this way: man or woman, your dog will still love you."

"I'm not sold on the whole being a woman thing. I love women."

"Women who love other women are called lesbians. I'm friends with a few. They're cool chicks. They'd love she-you."

"Can I stay he-me, please?"

"Got a lady you like?"

"I do."

Bummer. "Lucky lady."

"She has no idea how lucky she is. I've no idea how to approach her. I'm strapped for time," he admitted. "Hey. Would you consider planning a wedding for hire? As a professional planner? You did a spectacular job with your brother's wedding. I'd pay handsomely."

Ugh. More weddings. I considered asking to be executed to be put out of my misery, but Rick had stayed the night with me in the hospital despite having come overseas to attend my brother's wedding. "For a friend?"

"Family member. Mat's met her. She's a lot nicer than Amy, but if given a chance, she'd probably run for the border. Neither bride nor groom like each other too much, but they love their families. I'm hoping that'll change. It's a political wedding. Our families fight a lot, and being in-laws would help—or so everyone believes. She came up with the idea. I figure if you can handle someone like Amy, you can handle this wedding."

"Where would the wedding take place?"

"I'm going to recommend somewhere in the United States, possibly here. It's neutral ground."

"You didn't even see the reception, Rick. You have no idea if that was a train wreck or not. It was probably a train wreck."

"I saw pictures."

Rick gave me a headache. Technically, he worsened my headache. "I'll give you my number, and I'll think about it. But, if I do this, it will be because you're my brother's friend. I don't need to be part of the wedding party, right?"

"The wedding party will be large. Even if you somehow landed in it, no one would notice you."

I frowned. "Just how large would the wedding party be?"

"My mother's wedding party had fifty-two maids."

Now I'd heard of everything. "But why? Why so many maids? That's insane, Rick."

The thought of arranging for fifty-two bridesmaid dresses almost made me throw up.

"One woman for each family close to ours is how it typically goes. You'd be put into the party because your brother is a close friend of mine, which gives you the familial tie."

"Your family has a lot of friends. I'm both impressed and horrified."

"That we do. We're used to it, though. It's not that bad. Well, it's that bad, but we're taught from birth to pretend it's not that bad. Most of them are barely acquaintances, but it's been a family tradition for as long as anyone can remember, so we stick with it. You game?"

"A professional would be wiser, I just feel I need to warn you of this."

"But a professional wouldn't be as good for my family as you. Mat's wedding was perfect. That's what I want for my family: that sort of perfect."

"Do I want to know what sort of surprises will be in store for me should I tentatively accept?"

Rick chuckled. "Why do you think there'll be surprises?"

"I'm breathing."

"That you are. All right. My family is a little crazy, a lot egotistical, and we have a history of surprise double or triple weddings happening on the fly and attached to the original ceremony. When so many young, single people with more money than sense get together to plan a wedding, stuff happens."

"When most people say stuff happens, they mean people sleep together and an unexpected baby comes into the picture. Unexpected marriages aren't the first thing people think about."

"Well, my family is traditional by nature, and they prefer when the marriage happens before the babies. Newly conceived babies are the reason for approximately half of our unexpected marriages, while the rest of the unexpected marriages happen because people meet, fall in love, and lose all common sense. I plan on being a little more meticulous than that when I marry."

"How is one 'a little more meticulous than that' when discussing marriage?"

"I will have dedicated at least six months

to the pros and cons of offering a proposal, I will enter the relationship fully committed, and I will come to the table armed with condoms, promises of any testing she desires, and I'll even get snipped should she not want children. My mother might die of a heart attack when she finds that out, so please don't tell my mother. I love her dearly and don't want her to die."

"Traditionally, we call that an overshare."

"It's relevant information for the wedding planner. You'll find a lot of men in my family have similar thoughts, so you may have to address condom provisions, medical testing, and so on as part of your work."

"Okay. That's fair. That's also insane. I should have demanded Mat have Amy tested before agreeing to marry *or* sleep with her. That would've been smart."

"Traditional doesn't mean sane. I'm going to have to pay you bonuses to deal with the insanity, honestly. You'll be grateful we do unexpected marriages. It saves us from having to plan that many extra ceremonies."

I blinked, spent a minute thinking that through, and nodded at the wisdom of merging weddings. "That's actually pretty brilliant. The odds of this happening?"

"I'm hoping high."

Ah. It clicked. Rick wanted *his* marriage to be the unexpected marriage added to the list, and he wanted me to plan the perfect wedding for him, one which involved his mystery lady, who had no idea he was after forever.

It was crazy, it was oddly romantic, and any woman with half a grain of sense in her head wanted to be her—or at least loved by someone willing to take a crazy gamble on forever.

My brother had no idea how lucky he was to have someone like Rick as a friend. Despite myself, I laughed. "If she gives you the run around for this stunt, you only have yourself to blame."

"As long as she says yes, it'll be worth it."

FOUR

I have a milkshake in my hand, so I'm surviving.

RICK BOUGHT me a milkshake as promised, took me out to replace my phone, drove me to my apartment, and returned to Japan where he belonged. The phone would bother me for a long time; he'd insisted on paying for the entire bill himself, and he had tricked me into showing him my dream phone, something I never would have bought for myself but had lusted after with every fiber of my being.

The pictures it took rivaled dedicated cameras costing thousands of dollars, and I loved taking pictures. It would give me an excuse to do all the little things I'd missed out on because I'd never liked how the images turned out on my cheap phones. My first trip, as soon as I had a moment to breathe, would be to go back to the botanical gardens and explore at my whim rather than Amy's.

He'd even gotten me a phone with a lot of

space so I could take as many pictures as I wanted.

After my brother returned from his honeymoon, I needed to tell him he should've married Rick instead of Amy. Gay men rocked, and I'd always have room for more gay men in my life.

Alas, Rick had been clear that a woman held his attention, and she was likely an old family friend. I didn't understand why he wanted *me* to handle something so precious. I recognized I'd worked a miracle with my brother's wedding, as he made it through the day hitched to a chronic thoroughbride.

In some ways, I regretted my hard work. Would they stay married? I had no idea. No matter how much I worried for Mat, he was a big boy, and he could handle his relationship woes with Amy on his own.

My replacement phone rang, and it annoyed me I had squandered the chance to change my number. I might. Later. Depending on who called me and why. I'd also make a date with my service provider to add Caller ID. "Hope speaking."

"Hey. How are you feeling?" my brother asked.

"I've had better days, but I have a milkshake in my hand, so I'm surviving. Aren't you supposed to be honeymooning rather than calling me?"

"I am honeymooning. Amy's taking a nap, as she's not feeling well."

"I've heard there's a good reason for that." My brother might forgive me later for taking the wind out of his sails—or spoiling the surprise. I'd wait for a hundred or so years, though.

"She told *you* about the broken condom?"

Damn. What the hell had Amy been saying about me for my brother to take that tone with me? I went from headachy to bitchy in half a second flat. I also owed Caterina if I ever saw her again. I resisted the urge to clack my teeth and tear into my brother for being rude. "Call it bridesmaid intuition. Morning sickness?"

"Probably. We're fairly sure she's pregnant at this point."

I wondered if Mat knew about the existence of pregnancy tests and how they were used. I'd ask that question later. Maybe. Or not. In fact, I'd let my brother solve his own damned problems for a change. He wouldn't consider a baby a problem. He'd be throwing a party until the baby was born. "Congratulations, Mat."

"It's not really how we intended to become parents, but I think it'll work out."

In Mat language, he contained his excitement by a thread, and when that thread snapped, he would go on a joy-induced rampage. For his sake, and the sake of his baby, I hoped they made everything work. "I'm a bad sister."

"Why would you say that? You did an

amazing job on the wedding. Everything went flawlessly, even when you couldn't make it to the reception."

As I wasn't about to confess I'd been thinking terrible thoughts about him, I went with the less hurtful of my general bad sister issues. "I seriously think you should've married Rick instead of Amy yesterday."

"Fredrick? That Rick?"

"There was only one Fredrick on the guest list, so yes, that Rick."

"Like him, do you?"

Under no circumstances would I give my brother ammunition against me. "Me? I don't like anyone. I'm a bitchy accountant with a sarcasm problem and surrounded by gay friends."

Mat laughed. "Clarice isn't gay."

"She's married. Close enough."

"That's not how marriage works, Hope."

"Gay and married both equal unavailable."

"While accurate, I know full well you're not in the closet and have an unfortunately healthy interest in men."

Damn. My brother was on a roll. "Are you going to make me plan a baby shower next?"

"No. Amy can plan her own shower." Something about my brother's tone of voice warned me not everything post wedding was sunshine and roses.

"Are you sure you're okay?"

"I'm fine. Did you fight with Amy by any chance?"

Ah. There it was. The moment I'd dreaded. I gave it five minutes before I fully ruined my relationship with my brother and ensured his wife would never speak to me ever again. One of those problems bothered me a lot more than the other. "I wouldn't call it a fight. I would say I issued some ultimatums on what would happen if she attempted to leave my brother at the altar. She was not happy."

"She claims she's upset you had a ball and chain prepared."

"Oh. That reminds me. Rick wants the ball and chain. I'm going to drop it off at your apartment later, assuming I can roll the damned thing up the steps." After all the working out I'd done to fit into the damned dress, I could carry the damned ball and chain over my head if I really wanted.

"It's real?"

"All eighty pounds of it. It's painted white. I had it custom made to hide under her dress if she really tried a stunt. As you can tell, I didn't need the ball and chain, so it was worth every penny I spent on it out of my own pocket."

Mat groaned. "Did you have to?"

"Yes, I did. It got her to the altar."

"She's not that bad."

Like hell she wasn't. "I caught her trying to climb out the window right before the vows. Yes, I did block her from leaving, yes, I did threaten to use the ball and chain on her to make sure she got to the altar, and no, I refuse to be sorry I did that because you love her."

"We'll talk about this later." Mat hung up.

No, we wouldn't. I was done with being stepped on. The first thing I would do was take my headache-ridden ass to the cell store, get a new phone and number, and start doing what I should have done years ago: find a better job somewhere else. With my resumé, my certifications in several states, and my experience despite my age, I could land interviews with good companies anywhere in the United States within a week. If my luck held, I could be on the move before my idiot brother and his pest of a wife returned from their honeymoon.

He wanted a fresh start with Amy. I'd give it to him, and he'd just have to deal with me not being in the picture.

And, because I could be the queen bitch over all other bitches, I'd leave him a meticulous record of everything he'd spent, how much his new wife had lost him, and how much I'd personally paid to make sure he could be happily married.

He could deal with his wife, his financial investment woes, and the rest of his issues on his own.

I'd leave the paperwork under the ball and chain in a corner along with a note to ship it to Rick at his leisure. The fallout would be spectacular, but I wouldn't be around to witness it.

I had a life to live, and damn it, I meant to enjoy it for a change rather than living to make everyone else happy.

I NEEDED to either curb my impulsive tendencies when angry or take the time to fully evaluate the consequences of changing jobs and moving without warning. A smart woman would've slept on it. A smart woman with a concussion would've waited for the concussion to heal.

Instead, I got a cheap new phone as planned, gave the fancy one a new number, and began taking the first steps towards reclaiming my life.

I returned to my apartment, spent a few hours finishing the accounting work on my brother's wedding, made copies in triplicate, and prepared to move forward with my plan to find better waters. Mat's dismissal, after so many grueling hours of dealing with his bridezilla, became the straw that pissed the camel off. My back wouldn't break. No, thanks to Amy's bitchiness and her insistence her bridesmaids wear the same size dress, I'd lost the inches but gained the muscles. Hell, by the time I finished with my day, my back would probably be the only thing in good shape.

After I checked that my numbers made sense and added up as expected, I gathered a copy for Mat, dumped them in my piece of shit car, and headed over to the wedding venue to retrieve my ball and chain.

The church's minister, a kind man with a heart of gold, had promised I could use his office to store the ball and chain. He'd even agreed to the stunt, as he viewed Amy's tendency to run as a symptom of PTSD rather than a serious case of asshole. I'd come to the conclusion my brother had married a serious case of asshole, but it wasn't my problem.

I wasn't the one sleeping with her, doing her accounting, or cleaning up her messes, not anymore.

It was not my fault my brother had fallen in love with a thoroughbride. It was my fault for going to extremes, especially in my reaction to him hanging up on me, but I refused to apologize for toeing the line of my breaking point. When he apologized for snapping at me and hanging up, I'd reconsider a few things.

Except my brazen decision to find better waters. I was doing that for me.

Our parents would forgive me eventually.

I recognized part of my problem, which went a long way towards cooling my flared temper: headaches transformed me into an epic asshole on a good day, and it wasn't a good day.

I arrived at the church, cursed myself for

forgetting Sunday meant services, and broke my four-year record of dodging religious ceremonies. Sitting in the back pew and pretending to listen counted. The singing portions of the sermon murdered my poor head, and I regretted my decision to wait inside the church rather than prowl in the parking lot waiting for Pastor Haulette to finish his god's good work. I survived without making a scene, but it took over an hour for the worshippers to clear out so I could approach the pastor to retrieve my odd property.

"I heard about the baseball, Hope," he said in way of greeting. "I prayed for you last night."

"Thank you," I replied, as my parents—both living and dead—would've turned me over their knees and spanked me if I didn't remain polite to the nice holy man. "It's doing better today, but I've still got quite the headache. I was wondering if I could retrieve the items I left in your office?"

"Of course. I was very impressed with your work yesterday. I had a lot of inquiries about if you would be willing to plan future weddings."

Once again, Rick had come to my rescue. "I've already agreed to help someone plan his wedding, and I can't do more than one at a time, unfortunately. But I'm really grateful people liked the wedding."

"It was classy, tasteful, and respectful. You

obeyed every rule of the church, as did all of the guests. Your crews did a marvelous job of cleaning up, although some admitted they came at the last minute because of the incident with a baseball."

"Taking a baseball to the head was not one of the things I'd planned for going wrong," I admitted. "But next time, I'm definitely going to plan accordingly."

He chuckled and led me to his office, a modest wood-paneled room with an elegant antique desk, two armchairs, and bookshelves filled with religious texts as the only furnishings. The ball and chain waited for me in the corner, and I cracked my knuckles, ready to prove to the world I meant business. The chain and its padded cuff made an excellent handhold.

Pastor Haulette went to his desk and picked something up. At first, I thought he meant for me to drag the ball and chain on a piece of wood to protect the floors from the iron, but then I realized it had wheels.

Wheels would make everything easier. I put my new muscles to good use, set the ball in place, and gave the chain a firm pull.

The ball rolled in my direction.

"Well, that makes this a lot easier. Thank you so much. I'll return this later today."

"Keep it. We have a bunch extra for the kids, and that one's old. I'm not sure it'll survive the trip to your car, truth be told. And if it does, I'll confess they're rather fun to play with when no one is looking."

I could use some fun, and my apartment complex had a nice concrete hallway I could roll down if I abandoned my dignity. "Thank you, sir."

"Feel better. Do you need any help getting that into your car?"

"I don't, but I appreciate the offer. I worked out a lot getting ready for the wedding."

"Do take care of yourself. Concussions aren't to be trifled with. If you do need any help, please ask one of the deacons. There's usually one or two outside around this time."

I bet; right after the sermon, social hour had begun, except I worried it would take several hours before everyone left. And, according to the church's big sign out front, they had another service later in the day.

Before I could be guilted into attending another service, I exchanged pleasantries with the pastor and made my escape. Pride demanded I get the ball and chain into my car without help. Bemused church goers watched me, and I got it shunted into my back seat on the first try. To make certain I didn't get an iron ball to the spine, I buckled the damned thing in and closed the manacle around the seat belt as an extra insurance policy.

I would not be beaten by a damned metal ball.

Armed with my papers and my weapon of

choice, I invited myself over to my brother's apartment, hauled it up the short flight of steps, and let myself in with the key he'd given me and had forgotten to take back during the festivities. I'd mail the key to him to demonstrate I could be a spiteful bitch when provoked.

It took me less than five minutes to do my dirty work, and I kept my wheeled toy so he'd have to figure out how to move the ball on his own—and he'd have to, if he wanted to know the contents of the manila envelope I'd left beneath it.

It served the jerk right for hanging up on me.

With my mission completed, I locked the door behind me and began the next phase of my day: the resumé update.

I would start with Wolfgang, as I'd been doing his taxes from the instant I'd been able to legally handle them for others. As my current company allowed me to do accounting work on my personal hours, I'd be able to build a robust resumé with some work.

"How are you feeling?" Wolfgang answered.

"Like I need a new job. Can I list your business as part of my resumé?"

"Of course. Use my business contact info for a reference. Finally got tired of your old boss making you fix your coworkers' messes?"

Huh. Wolfgang needed an extra special

present for Christmas. "Yes," I lied. "I most certainly am tired of fixing messes. Part of my job is to fix messes, but I would rather fix messes because math and taxes are hard rather than because my coworkers aren't paying attention."

"Should you be making such an important decision with a concussion?"

I laughed at that. "The concussion helped. Otherwise, I'd stay miserable at a shit job getting paid half of what I'm worth. I'd like to aim for three-quarters of what I'm worth if possible, but I'll take anything over half of my current value, really."

"That's sensible. Go ahead and use me as a reference. Which part of town will you be job hunting in?"

New York City, several hours north, would be my first search spot. If New York didn't pan out, I'd take a look at the west coast. It would be an adventure. A very stressful adventure filled with blitz trips.

Then again, maybe it wouldn't be so bad. I would begin with my boss, inform him I'd be leaving unless he got me a transfer and a raise, and go from there. For all I liked to pretend I had no money, I had enough to last me a while.

And even if I didn't, my parents would be game to play ball while I searched for better waters. They might even play along with my plan to dodge Mat for the rest of eternity.

I grunted at my own damned silence. "I

haven't decided yet. It depends on what I find. I've only just made the decision to update my resumé and start trolling for new work. I'm going to give my boss a chance to give me a raise and relocate me to one of the other offices, too."

"That's not a bad idea. Outside of your office having an unfortunate number of idiots on staff, the company is decent."

"I wonder what it says about us that we view a company just being decent as a good thing."

"You make a fair point. But they pay your wages on time, and they let you work for others as long as there's no general conflict of interest."

"And since I'm not auditing the kind of businesses my company has any interest in, it's no big deal."

"They like the stench of money."

"That they do." I rolled my shoulders and grimaced at the various snaps, pops, and creaks. "I'd like to maintain that clause wherever I work next, but a lot of corporations don't allow it. That'll make the job hunt difficult. I can probably get an exemption for the folks I already do accounting for, but I'd have to make a list for them to ensure there's no conflict of interest."

"You'll be fine. You always land on your feet, and you always find that little loophole that lets you get away with just about anything. If you have any issues, give me a call. If you're tired of big corporate, there's a lot of smaller businesses who'd love to hire someone like you."

While true, I'd take a hard kick to my income, which was half-decent for my age and experience. It helped I'd added on as many certifications and extra schooling as I could get—it also helped I'd entered the workforce free of debt thanks to working myself to near death and having a little help from my birth parents, who'd left us enough to get our educations.

My adoptive parents had worked hard to keep us free from debt, too.

"I'll figure something out. Also, my brother is an ass, and I'm going to teach him a lesson. Play along."

"How do you want me to play along?"

"I want you to pretend I don't exist."

"What on Earth has gotten into you?"

"He hung up on me, and you know what you told me once upon a time after a bad day."

"I regret telling you to stop getting mad and start getting even," Wolfgang muttered.

"It'll be fun. All you have to tell my brother if he calls you asking about me is that you don't know anything about what's going on, and since you hate lying, I'm not going to tell you what's going on."

"I don't hate lying, I just hate lying without a good reason. If Mat has gotten you that mad, I'll tell him I don't know what's going on for you. It's his own damned fault, anyway. He should've known better than to poke you with a stick, although I'd appreciate if you didn't take advantage of this situation to use your name in a pun."

I pouted, as there were so many good choices of inappropriate puns for the situation. "That's just not fair, Wolfgang."

"Save them and use them on your brother the next time you speak to him. It'll drive him wild."

"No, Wolfgang. There's no Hope for my brother."

"Damn it, you!"

I laughed. "Thanks for the assist, Wolfgang. I'll call you after I've made a better game plan."

"I look forward to it." He hung up, and I smiled.

Amy wasn't the only one who could give my brother the run around, and Wolfgang wasn't the only one looking forward to it.

FIVE

I enjoyed catching the cheaters.

SOME PEOPLE LIKED to call Washington D.C. a swamp. As a general rule, I agreed with them. In a place where sketchy politics ruled, accountants could make or break most situations. The good ones ferreted out illegal dealings, the kind of transactions that brought the FBI knocking at a business's door. Scattered across the United States were firms with one purpose: to check if a company could pass an IRS—or worse, an FBI—audit.

From the instant I'd stepped into college until graduation, I'd made it my goal to be an auditing accountant, the type of person who could learn any secret from an account ledger.

Had I known the reality of the life of an auditing accountant, I would've run the other way and done something a little easier, a little saner, and a lot less stressful.

In good news, thanks to my inability to leave well enough alone, I'd acquired the appropriate licenses and certifications to work in Maryland, New York, Delaware, New Jersey, and Virginia, along with the prized ability to be hired by the worst Washington had to offer.

They liked when their accountants understood the nuances of nearby states. The wise ones lived on solid ground, doing their best to forget Washington might flood out on them at any given point in time. The flash flooding had done a good job of reminding people Washington could go for a swim at nature's leisure.

I'd been one of the lucky ones; my apartment had dodged being a flood victim by a mere half a block.

As I'd had my fill of floods and swamps populated with politicians, I needed to extend my search to one of the places I was licensed to work without having to pass a test.

New York City made the most sense, would offer the best chance of moving up in the world, and would make it difficult for my brother to track me down. The hustle and bustle of the city would annoy me, as I preferred the green places Washington boasted. But I'd grown tired of fast food joints with bulletproof glass, the awareness I lived at the epicenter of politics in the United States, and the special brand of snobbery the politically inclined brought to the table.

New York City had its fair share of snobbery, but it also possessed a certain charm Washington lacked.

I headed home, got onto my laptop, and began my search. With my skills, licensing, and general certifications, I'd qualify for most accounting positions, although I avoided the managerial hellholes destined to test my patience and not my math skills. If I'd wanted to manage people doing the math, I would've gone in for a standard business degree and joined the ranks of know-it-all snoots out to take over the world.

I liked the math.

The numbers never lied, and if I poked at them enough, they could tell me an entire company's story, including who had ethics, who cheated who, and if someone tried to skim funds to line their pockets.

I enjoyed catching the cheaters.

If I were a little more tolerant of politicians, corrupt government, and the game of making money, I would've applied for a job with the IRS. Alas, I would rather drink shots of rusty nails, broken glass, and battery acid. I supposed the IRS's reputation had something to do with it.

The tax code also contributed. When the documents could break a table when printed, it needed a major overhaul—and a lot fewer loopholes. I'd spent an entire year of my life learning about the loopholes, how to best use them for my clients, and why they existed.

The why of it had taken me all of ten minutes to figure out.

Greed corrupted the heart of the American economy, and it was my job to make sure everyone kept their fair share of their money —and find extra ways to keep the government from taking their hard-earned wealth.

The IRS then went out of its way to find loopholes to get around the loopholes, resulting in an intricate dance with the rich and powerful. The real losers were people like Wolfgang, who worked hard for their money. With the game rigged against him and most Americans, only the lucky managed to claw their way up from the bottom.

I tried my best to give them a chance to be lucky.

Hell, I wanted to be lucky, too.

Turnover happened in New York with alarming frequency, and a plethora of new jobs waited for my application. I spent an hour updating my resumé before I sorted the jobs by the ones I thought would pay the bills and have enough left over to enjoy life for a change. Before I could chicken out and resign myself to the same old same old, I hit submit on the first three.

The first three mattered most; they convinced me I really wanted to bail town at the earliest opportunity.

Having a midlife crisis in my late twenties sucked, but I figured I'd have a chance to have a better midlife crisis in my thirties. Then, I might be able to afford to splurge on a nice new car. I checked my savings account, narrowing my eyes at the number.

Apparently, not having a student loan and paying into my savings account as though I had one had worked some miracles in my bank account. While I wouldn't be splurging on a new fancy car, I could certainly go to the dealership, trade in my piece of shit, and leave the lot with something used but nice. Nice would be a requirement in New York.

Money mattered, and driving a rust bucket would be a black mark against me.

Fortunately for me, politicians churned through cars, resulting in a surplus of good used vehicles with minimal miles, proper rustproofing, and all the bells and whistles. With the three important resumés out the door, I could spare the extra hours to take my car to a dealership and get a new vehicle. It would eat up the afternoon, assuming one was open.

The internet knew everything, and while some dealerships closed early on Sundays, I found a few open.

A new car, a new job, and a new life. I liked it.

Giggling, I grabbed my keys and purse. Conquering the world would take a lot of work, but I could do something for me for a change. I expected my choice to bite me in the ass, but I'd make do somehow.

Despite everything, I always did.

THE USED CAR dealership offered a range of vehicles from rusted antiques to barely used, and while my bank account wouldn't appreciate it, I targeted somewhat sporty vehicles less than two years old with no accident reports. I cared less about the miles than I did about the general conditions of the vehicles, which did a good job of limiting my choices to a handful of possibilities. I gave a hard pass to the cars from brands with a history of being found on the roadside in need of repair, which left me with a choice of three.

The soft-top convertible tempted me, but I'd freeze to death in the winter, so it left my list.

The two-door would crank my insurance bill, which left me with a boring gray mid-range Mercedes with most of the bells and whistles. I liked its mileage, although I wondered why anyone would spend so much money on a vehicle only to drive it fifteen thousand miles.

The dealership liked the mileage, too, along with the car's general good condition and its perks.

After an hour of arguing with the salesman and putting in some serious thought about heading to a different dealership, I got the vehicle for three grand more than I wanted to pay, which was six grand lower than they wanted me to pay. My credit, pristine since the day I'd reached adulthood, would let me walk off the lot with it for a decent monthly payment, but they'd get more interest out of me than I liked.

I took the loan on one condition: the car would no longer be gray when I finished with it, and they would not penalize me in any fashion.

Then I notified my insurance company my new car would be silver and accented with blue glitter.

Keys in hand, I went to the nearest body shop that handled custom paint jobs. The owner, five minutes from leaving for the day, sighed when I entered. "How can I help you?"

"Can you paint a car silver with blue glitter?"

I expected he got a lot of odd requests, but the instant the word 'glitter' left my mouth, he stared at me as though I had lost my mind.

"Blue glitter?"

"I want my car to turn heads when I drive down the street. I also want it easy to spot in a parking lot. It's also less tempting to steal a car that has to be repainted to hide."

"I have worked with glitter before. Let me check if I have any blue in stock." He went into the back of his shop and left me alone to admire the photographs of far fancier cars than mine decorating the walls. Within five minutes, he returned. "I do have blue. I have pink, red, orange, and green as well. What kind of car?"

I pointed outside. "It's a Mercedes. If I pay for a rush job, think you can do the work in a hurry?"

"I can, but it'll take a few days."

"Got a loaner?"

"I got a loaner if you can deal with a piece of shit."

I laughed. "I just traded in my piece of shit. As long as it is street legal and parts don't fall off while I'm driving, I don't care what condition the car is in."

"Just for that, I'm going to loan you the slightly nicer piece of shit. I'll need to see your proof of insurance and license."

As I'd just dealt with the insurance issue at the dealership, I pulled the documents out of my purse and handed them over along with my license. "If you do the protective coats, I don't care if it takes an extra day or two, and if you happen to also do rust proofing, if you could make certain my baby is extra protected, I'd be grateful and show my gratitude in the form of appropriate and immediate payment."

"I charge half up front for supplies and the rest upon delivery."

I took out my credit card, which needed to get some exercise anyway. "Do you have things like those luxury steering wheel wraps?"

"Give me a budget of five hundred, and I

can add some bling to your interior so it matches your exterior."

I would own a glittery masterpiece, and I'd never been so excited in my life. Was a midlife crisis supposed to be so fun? "I am also really sorry for keeping you late."

"When a polite young lady comes into the shop with a good job I can do and a budget, I'm always willing to play ball. Business has been light lately, so your timing couldn't be more perfect for a rush job. I'll even get started tonight so it's ready as soon as possible."

"I hope you're charging me a rush fee for that."

"It won't be much. I appreciate a challenge, and figuring out how to make your car sparkle elegantly will be a good challenge. Your color combination is a good choice, though. The silver should work well with the blue. I only have one question for you."

"What is it?"

"Do you want a standard silver or a metallic silver?"

"I'm not sure I understand the difference."

The shop owner reached behind the counter and pulled out paint samples. He set a silver square in front of me, the color I expected on a car in a lot. "This is standard silver." Then he set another square down, which looked remarkably like molten silver but a lot shinier. "This is the metallic shade; it's a little darker but has a lot better luster and turns heads. The glitter will make it look like there's gemstones encrusted all over the vehicle."

"I don't care what it costs, but I want that," I replied, pointing at the metallic sample. I set my credit card on the counter and shoved it towards him. "Please. I'm not above begging."

He laughed and took my credit card to his register. He set a price list in front of me and explained the charges, adding them to his machine as he did so. Seven thousand dollars later, and I'd have a very sparkly car with some interior surprises. All in all, I viewed it as a most excellent start to my midlife crisis.

Once I wasn't so pissed at my idiot brother, I'd have to thank him. I needed a brand new me, one that wasn't tied to my brother at the hip and involved him nosing about in my daily life anyway.

He had a life to live, and so did I.

It was up to me to make my new life a good one, and it began with putting me first for a change.

AS EXPECTED from my job hunt, the first two days brought in zero results, but I dedicated every free moment to casting a wide net over the entirety of New York City. I also began the tedious search for a new apartment. After paying Washington prices for rent, the cost of living in New York didn't put me off as much as I thought it would, although I'd have to hope I landed one of the better jobs if I wanted to be able to have a decent living. I held some hope.

Accounting work could pay off in the right place and the right time.

To expand my options, I delved into the banking world, something I'd generally avoided due to the insane regulations and its cutthroat nature.

The morning my Mercedes was scheduled to be finished, my new cell rang, and the display informed me someone called me from a New York number.

I viewed the call as a good sign; the last time I'd hunted for a new job, the employers opted for email until they wanted me to show up in a hurry. I answered, "Hope Kensingvale speaking."

"Good morning, Miss Kensingvale. My name is Garret, and I'm calling on behalf of Cercson Investment Group. You submitted a resumé with us several days ago. We have an interview opening on Friday afternoon at two. Are you available?"

"Please give me a moment to check my calendar," I replied, knowing full well I had absolutely nothing scheduled at the time of the interview and would enjoy taking my new car on a long drive if it was ready and opportunity allowed. I headed to my desk and tapped at my laptop to offer the illusion of handling the task. "Yes, I'm available. Can you tell me more about the position, please?"

"It's an unusual one, but you have the skills and certifications we need. While we're typically an investment firm, one of our offices does, from time to time, do accounting audits of businesses to help them better use their finances. We work with their accounting department to determine how they can improve their general operations. Honestly, we're a poorly named business, as we're not really in the business of investments. We're in the business of making businesses work better, and we offer a full range of services for businesses wishing outside assistance. After a legal firm was charged for embezzlement of funds following the assault of an employee, many legal firms in our area have opted to have external audits of their accounting teams done. We've been hired by one such firm, but their operations are much larger than we anticipated, and I don't feel our current staff is capable of handling the job without bringing in another auditing accountant. The position will require a lot of hours at first, as they want the job done in a timely fashion."

"How unusual." I considered Garret's explanation and wondered why so many firms would request auditing at the same time after one firm ran into trouble. "May I ask a question, sir?"

"Of course, Miss Kensingvale."

"While it's not unheard of for a company to do a test audit and bring in a third party to handle the work, especially if they think they may be running afoul of a new IRS rule, why would so many legal firms request outside auditing at the same time? Legal firms typically hire competent accountants and are very careful about IRS regulations."

Garret chuckled, and his amusement implied I'd passed some sort of test. Some employers viewed the initial phone call with a potential employee as the first interview, and my behavior could make or break me with him and his firm. Most disliked the practice, but I thought it wise.

People often behaved differently outside of interviews, and an employer could tell a lot about a person from how they acted outside of work and interviews. Skills played a major part of being hired, but other factors mattered, especially when a firm cared about its reputation. Due to many companies caring about their reputation, mine included, I avoided social media like I'd contract the plague if I delved too deep into its turbulent depths. I avoided a lot of things, the news included, although I'd discovered a new love for Florida Man headlines and other zany news articles.

I waited, aware that employers valued a person with patience, especially when money issues could take a frustrating turn with a single report.

"You're correct. Because the embezzlement involved upper management and someone in accounting, a lot of the local firms want an outside look at their operations. It's very unusual. And with the FBI sniffing around one firm, there is a cause for concern that their attention will turn to others—especially others who have had any business associations with the firm. Unfortunately, the firm handled corporate law matters. There have been falsified invoices for several businesses the firm worked with."

"Well, that's stupid. If the IRS audited either company, the ruse would be discovered."

"We have come to the conclusion that those behind the embezzlement are not what we would call intelligent individuals. But, there's a real risk of other legal firms being investigated by the IRS as a result of this case. Personally, I don't view the risk as all that substantial, but because there are so many businesses with crossover with other firms, it's a possibility. Most legal firms have had dealings with employees or directly with the company that the embezzling firm used."

The reason for concern clicked, and I didn't blame the legal firms for taking a few extra steps to make certain they were in the clear. "The FBI will do an audit on all companies the legal firm worked with, and as such, it's a possibility they will audit the companies who worked with any company audited; it gives them legal grounds to secure the warrant for the audit, which means they could access rival legal firms. Everyone wants to clean up their operations just in case the FBI decides to check just how far the rabbit hole goes."

I loved puzzles, and I especially loved mysteries involving money. For most legal firms, I expected the accounting would be so clean it squeaked when I rubbed it. But sometimes, an audit revealed interesting things, things I would get to investigate and make sense of for my bosses, who would handle the situation as they saw fit.

"Precisely. With so many businesses potentially earmarked for investigation, everyone is making certain their accounting is in order. These businesses are lucky. The trial ensured they had advance warning."

"Trial?"

"One of the firm's employees was assaulted by a partner, and she sued for damages. She won."

"Good for her. I hope she took the firm for everything it was worth."

"She didn't do badly; they called in a good prosecutor from Buffalo, and he definitely did her justice and gave the defense quite the run. The defense played fair ball but not hard ball."

"The attorney tossed the defense?"

"There wasn't a lot he could work with. Only an idiot assaults an employee, tries to frame her, and then attempts to assault a second employee in front of the police. The defense tried to drag it out, but the partner lost rather miserably. He went down with a fight, but he only ended up burying himself deeper. I'm of the opinion the jury caught onto his guilt from the moment they met the woman, who required a great deal of surgery to repair her face. The settlement included a fund for reconstructive surgery and cosmetic repairs, too. Actually, the case has been making the rounds here, not because of what he did, but what she did after the case closed."

I appreciated that Garret treated me like a human, but I questioned why he told me so much that had little bearing on my employment. Well, it mattered none to me; I would rather work for someone who could hold a conversation rather than someone who viewed me as a nameless statistic. "What did she do?"

"She built a relationship with an attorney, and she spent the money to give them a fresh start on a life together. She decided to wear her scars with pride. That takes one hell of a brave woman, especially in our society."

"That's amazing."

"It really is. There is a reason I'm telling you this, of course."

"What reason, sir?"

"Garret, please. I hear enough sirs from everyone daily."

"Okay, Garret. What do I have to do with this woman?"

"She works at one of the firms that we're auditing, and one of our other departments is working on the audit for the firm that her husband works at. The auditing will require you to work with another department, as the firm you'd be auditing had a case involving her husband. If there are links between her current employer, his current employer, and the originating firm, we need to make certain all relationships are disclosed. It could create an unfortunate ripple."

"The IRS could investigate them all because of their romantic connections?"

"The IRS would love to use any loophole possible to get a chance to do an investigative audit on most legal firms. If you find anything linking them to the originating firm, we need to be notified immediately. In fact, we're essentially asking you to pretend you're an IRS auditor who will be seeking to expand an embezzlement case to extend to multiple firms. It's unusual, but that's what they've requested. They want to drill their accountants on handling an IRS audit; apparently, they've kept their accounting so clean neither firm has been officially audited before."

My brows shot up at that. "The IRS loves to audit companies."

"We're aware. So, both companies are freaking out. But they didn't trigger any red flags with the IRS, so they were never selected for auditing."

"Their accountants could just be that good." I grimaced at the doubt in my voice. "I'm not sure I'm qualified to pretend I'm an IRS auditor about to rampage through the entire company's accounting. I'm willing to learn on the job and take supplementary courses if needed, but I'm not sure what the job requirements for an IRS auditor are, and I've never worked for the IRS."

"I've looked over your resumé; you're qualified, and you have licensing in several states, so that benefits us. There is crossover at the firm you'll be auditing with Delaware, New Jersey, and Maryland."

That explained a lot. The accounting would require special work for handling employees in multiple states, and one accountant who was familiar with the rules of all states involved would make the audit a little easier rather than needing to coordinate extra bodies with the right qualifications. "Will we be required to audit employee taxes for this?"

"Employees were offered a chance to have their taxes audited at the same time. Within the firm you will be working on, seven employees accepted."

"Let me guess: this woman was one of the ones who accepted?"

"Yes, she is. She is, understandably, flustered about the settlement and the tax consequences. While she thinks she submitted the taxes correctly, she believes she'll be audited if the IRS were to start poking around her new employer."

I understood that, although there were some protections in place for her unless any evidence she was involved directly with embezzlement came to light. "I can verify her taxes and help her file a correction if it's required. That is absolutely no problem. I've worked with personal and small business accounting in addition to corporate accounting. I'll have to review her specific situation, but unless there are circumstances I'm unaware of, it should be simple enough to handle."

"That is exactly what we would need from you. What would be your time frame for being hired?"

"I am under an at-will contract with my current employer, but I was planning on giving two weeks of notice despite my at-will status. I am planning to hand in my resignation tomorrow morning. In the past, my employer has preferred to immediately terminate resigning employees."

"While that is beneficial for my company, may I inquire why you are handing in your resignation without having secured future employment?"

I was planning on enjoying some time off, and while they may opt to immediately terminate my resignation, I would still be paid out my benefits as part of my contract. "In case of immediate termination, I'm paid out for the two weeks I would have worked as part of my resignation. Between that, my vacation benefits, and personal savings, I'll be quite comfortable even with an extended job search."

"Then I'm looking forward to meeting you on Friday, and should the interview go as I expect, we would be ready for you to begin work on Monday. As I'm aware you do not live in New York, we would be prepared to help you with your move as part of your employment package, but you would be in corporate housing for a few weeks until we have sufficient time to plan for a mover, if one is not readily available."

That checked off a few of my boxes for my requirements for a new employer. "That sounds wonderful, Garret. Can you please email me any information and directions I'll need for the interview?"

"I'll do that for you as soon as I get off the phone. I appreciate your flexibility on this matter."

While a risk, I figured I could make an offer. "Considering the situation and the extensive work required, if you ultimately need me in for an interview earlier, I can probably manage. I expect they'll execute the immediate termination clause in my contract."

"Should they, please let me know. We do have earlier openings for an interview, and I would not say no to being able to start this sooner than later. Frankly spoken, I expect this to be a mess."

I did, too, but unlike him, I liked messes when I anticipated them. Messes earned me better pay, offered me negotiating grounds, and got me out of Washington that much faster.

If working for Garret didn't work out, my resumé floated through New York's murky waters. No matter where it went, there'd be sharks, but even shark-infested waters beat staying in Washington. My brother might not like me no longer being available for his plans, but he had a life as a father in front of him, and I needed to do something for me for a change.

And I would.

It took five minutes of exchanging pleasantries with Garret to get off the phone, and I smiled when I disconnected the call.

For a little while, life would be all about me, and I looked forward to every mistake I made along the way.

Someone else could be Lady Perfection for a while. Maybe I'd even be the star of one of Rick's prized headlines for doing something so crazy yet marvelous everyone wanted to know about it.

In reality, I'd be just one of many women who'd lost her last fuck, and I was all right with that. A little freedom would do me a lot of good. I'd just stay away from Florida until I bothered to take control of my life, as some headlines were too extreme for even me.

SIX

No longer would I be a scapegoat.

AS EXPECTED, when I called in to work to talk with my boss, he opted for immediate termination. Then, in a move that surprised me, he spent several hours doing his best to convince me to stay. When he learned the truth, that I wanted to head to New York for new waters, he tried to secure a transfer for me. His efforts impressed me, although I expected the answer he received. The New York office didn't need yet another accountant, and I didn't have the auditing experience they wanted despite my lengthy history with the company.

He honored my hiring contract's clauses upon resignation, authorized for all my pay to be sent to my bank account on Friday, and wished me well. As he'd spent the hours trying to convince me to stay, he'd drawn up the paperwork for my termination to be effective first thing in the morning.

One day didn't matter to many, but I appreciated the gesture.

With the clock ticking and potential employment on the horizon, I'd have to make arrangements if Garret did want me in for an interview sooner than later. I contacted him, informed him my boss had opted for immediate termination, and waited.

His reply came back within ten minutes, asking if I could be interviewed on Thursday late afternoon with a potential start on Friday, and he requested that I call him at my leisure.

Thursday would work. I'd pick up my new used car on Wednesday, after a short delay due to the paint taking its time to dry, and I would drive up in time to check into my hotel and arrive at his office in time for the interview on Thursday. The few days would make it easy to arrange for my apartment to be packed and put into storage until a moving company could haul it to New York.

Life would change, but change would help me more than anything else.

I had a lot to do and a little time to do it. It reminded me of planning my brother's wedding, although things might have gone smoother if not for Amy. Thinking of the pair fueled my need to get the hell out of town.

Things would be different. I would make certain of it.

No longer would I be a scapegoat or a creature of convenience meant to make the lives of those around me easier. For once in my adult life, I'd be the burden, and I'd refuse to accept any shame for doing something for me. I wouldn't. I lifted my chin, wrote a list of things I needed to do before Thursday, and got to work.

Change began with me.

I started with my vital records, packing up the important papers I'd need to make a transition happen. Once I had everything I needed in hand, I booked a week at a long-stay hotel in Manhattan to serve as my base of operations. The weekly rate would murder me, but I expected the monthly rent wouldn't be a walk in the park, either. I wrote it off as a necessity, triple-checked how long I would need to get from the hotel to where I'd interview, and thanked my lucky stars I could walk between my temporary residence and my potential new workplace.

I rented a truck, braced for chaos, and called Ben.

"How's the concussion?" he answered.

I really needed to start exclusively using my new phone and number. Actually, I'd keep my old phone number for a while and downgrade my plan. "It's fine. The headache isn't too bad. I need to ask for a favor."

"What can I do for you?"

"I'm moving, and I need to put some stuff into storage. I won't be able to get a moving company right away, so I need to get my apartment cleared out."

"When?"

I loved that Ben could work with the crazy and unexpected without question. If more people were like Ben, I believed the world would be a much better place. "As soon as possible. I have a job interview on Thursday. Also, I am invoking the friendship clause in which my activities are not discussed with my cretin of a brother."

"Uh oh. I sense a familial dispute in progress. All right. I have time. How much are we moving?"

"Everything. If it doesn't fit into my car, it doesn't go with me. I'm driving out early Thursday morning."

"Driving where?"

"Somewhere not here."

"I don't know what your brother did this time, but I'm concerned, Hope."

"My new car is silver with blue glitter. You can be as concerned as you want. It's also a used Mercedes. It was in my budget, and I got a decent deal on it. It's currently at the shop getting its new clothes."

"Did you just say silver with blue glitter?"

"I did. And it's that really metallic silver, not the pale gray most people call silver."

"You bought a Mercedes, and you had it painted. Custom painted."

"Go big or go home, and I decided I'm tired of going home, so I'm doing things I like rather than things other people think I'd like. And I won't be including the 'if you please' most expect from me. I have lost my last fuck, Ben. No, I killed it."

"I'll recruit some help. What day would you like to do the move?"

"Ideally, we'd do everything on Wednesday afternoon. Maybe after three. It depends on when my car is finished."

"I'll talk to Wolfgang. I bet he knows some folks who could use the exercise."

I grinned at that. Gay men came in all shapes and sizes, and Wolfgang liked his men big, muscular, and capable of lifting hundreds of pounds over their heads. "I bet he does."

"And how is your work wardrobe?"

"However much I'd like a makeover, that's not in the cards right now."

"It's in the cards. I know your sizes, and I'll pick up what you need. You can pay me back later. I'll return what doesn't fit or work, and we'll make a day of it. With your dinky apartment, we can get everything moved in a few hours. Are we getting budget boxes?"

"I need boxes, and I need them now, and that's not going to be budget friendly. I'll deal with it. I won't like spending the money, but it's a necessity. At least I shouldn't need a moving truck if the job hunt goes well; I'm only interviewing with places that'll help handle the relocation."

"Good for you. I'll see you tomorrow at three, then."

"Let yourself in and get to work if I'm not

back from the body shop, okay? I'll bring milkshakes. Just tell me how many."

"Oh, no. I'm bringing the milkshakes, and there will be plenty of cherries to go on top. It sounds like you need it, and I'd feel guilty if a milkshake spilled in your new car."

"It's used."

"It's new to you, so it's new. I'll see you tomorrow."

WEDNESDAY MORNING, the paint shop called to inform me the work was done and I could pick up my baby. I headed over right away, eager to ditch the loaner and go home in style.

My car waited for me outside, and the shop's owner had decided to go intense on the amount of glitter decorating the front before fading it out along the car's body until the rear was a metallic silver dusted with trace amounts of glitter. She sparkled in the sunlight, and I loved everything about her.

I wanted to hug her hood, but I figured I'd get my filthy fingerprints all over her shiny paint job if I did.

"She's perfect."

"She's definitely going to turn heads. Look inside."

As promised, he'd done a lot of work on the accents in the car, and anything that could be covered in glitter was. I dug out my credit card and waved it. "Take my money, please. This is even better than I thought it would be."

All in all, I thought my midlife crisis was starting off well, and after taking the time to exchange pleasantries with the shop's owner and pay my bill, I headed to my landlord's office to notify him I wouldn't be staying. With the housing market as it was, I expected he'd love getting rid of me so he could bring in someone willing to pay more.

I'd gotten a good deal initially, and the lease, signed through the previous owner of the building, had barred anyone from raising my rent beyond a certain percentage each year. The new landlord, a decent enough fellow, had agreed to keep the terms of my lease, as I paid my rent on time, never caused him any trouble, and usually did my own damned repairs unless I couldn't handle it on my own.

As hoped for, he cut me out of my lease early, and he gave me to the end of the month to vacate.

When I returned home, Wolfgang and Ben waited for me, far ahead of my proposed three in the afternoon, and they had a throng of helpers armed with milkshakes with them. Ben offered me a milkshake, and it had two cherries on top.

Happiness was a milkshake and a new, glittery car, and I questioned why I hadn't snapped prior.

I'd missed out on a lot of good things staying sane.

"Why are you driving a Mercedes covered in glitter?"

"I regret nothing," I announced, plucking off the first of my cherries and popping it into my mouth, yanking off the stem and flicking it into the nearest bush. I chomped until I located the pit, which joined the stem in the bushes. "I have a barren field of fucks, Ben. I've decided the first thing I would do was buy a nice car, paint her how I like, and do the things I want to do for a change."

"And that involves moving where?"

"If I don't tell you where I'm moving, my brother can't get to you. If my brother can't get to you, he can't get to me, and my first act as an independent adult woman is to put that jackass in his place."

"I have no idea what Mat did, but he's very sorry."

"Oh, he will be. I've wasted how long being his scapegoat?"

"I sense some resentment from my favorite accountant. Seriously. What did Mat do that tripped your trigger?"

"He's mad at me because I didn't let his bitch of a bride run from the altar. She, of course, is upset I took special lengths to make sure she married my brother. That plus I paid how much for his damned wedding?"

"I can send him the bill for my share of the work," Wolfgang announced. "And I can make the invoice clear you paid for everything in labor."

"I spent how much time and effort making sure they married? I'd rather not turn their marriage into an early divorce, especially not when Amy's pregnant. But then again, I left all the paperwork in his apartment for him to find, under the ball and chain, so I'm probably signing him up for a divorce anyway. It's their problem, not mine. So, do what you want, Ben."

Ben sighed. "You just can't win, can you?"

"I'm winning right now. I'm doing what I want, for me. Mat is just going to have to deal with it and live happily with his wife. He's a damned grown adult, so he can take care of his own problems."

"I see he's finally gotten on your last nerve."

"As I said, he got pissed over me making sure he got married, and Amy's being a bitch about it, too. I'm not getting involved. I left him copies of all the invoices, and well, he's an adult. He can deal with it. Frankly, I don't care what you do, but I'm not going to be the one who bursts his bubble about how she lost all of the deposits and payments. The wedding happened, and the wedding happened with only a minor hitch or two."

"A baseball to the head is hardly a minor hitch, Hope."

"It barely grazed me, and it only rattled my brain in my skull a little. Actually, outside of the headache for the first night, I walked away the winner there. I didn't have to deal with the damned reception."

"Mat missed you at the reception."

"And then got pissed because there was a reception. Nope, Ben. You're not going to guilt me into backing out of this. I've already quit, I have a job interview on Thursday, and I mean to ace it. It'll be good work for me, and it'll be work I enjoy. I'll still be able to manage your taxes, too, just as I promised, so you don't even need to bring Mat into it. I don't want him to get a divorce because I'm pissed at his drama queen of a wife. He loves her, and that's that."

"He loves you, too."

"He can love me from a distance."

"Just how distant are we talking about here?"

"My barren field of fucks has lost its map. Somewhere."

"You're really going to leave me waiting to find out, aren't you? Or worse, you're going to make us put in effort to figure out where you went."

"Mat can figure it out if he really wants."

"Harsh. All right. I expect you to keep contact and email me at least once a week, especially if you're going to be changing numbers."

"As a matter of fact, yes. I will be changing numbers. I'll be out of the area. I'll keep my old number for a while for emergencies, but it'll be a cheap plan unless my carrier offers no roaming."

"Considering how small Washington really is, that is of no surprise to me. Just how far out of the area are you going?"

"Far enough."

"You're really going to play hard ball on this, aren't you?"

"I already played ball with my head. That actually worked out okay. It knocked sense back into me."

It had also given me time to get to know Rick and his love of Florida Man and other ridiculous headlines. In my new life, I would join him in seeking out the absurd, and I would remember my weird night with my brother's friend. Had I met the new me before Mat's wedding, I might've tried to take things too far.

He was handsome, single, and fun.

I was single, and I wanted to be fun. It wasn't up to me to decide if I fell into the attractive category, but I hoped for somewhat interesting bordering on pretty.

"Or out of you. From where I stand, it looks like your common sense took a lethal blow."

"I disagree. Just because I'm doing something for me doesn't mean I lack common sense. It just means I'm not living my life to someone else's terms or standards. I did too much for Mat. He's married, he can handle his own matters moving forward."

"But do you have to move to do it?"

"Yes. We're talking about Mat here. He'd show up at my apartment until he got what he wanted, which would be, in this case, making his wife happy. Probably. Frankly, I question his taste in women, but she either played him really well or she's a totally different person around him. Right now, I'm in a bad mood about it, so I'm assuming she's played him and is pissed off she's not getting out of that relationship without a divorce hearing."

"While I'm not really fond of the woman, their relationship seems genuine enough."

"Except she went out of her way to sabotage the damned wedding," I muttered.

"You don't have any proof of that."

I stared at Ben. "Really? *Every* provider had an issue for the entire wedding. I had to essentially toss together a wedding on the fly. The only thing that *wasn't* screwed was the church, and I bet that's only because I dealt with the arrangements for the church on Mat's behalf rather than hers."

"While that is suspicious, you don't have any proof."

"One thing going wrong is life. Everything going wrong is intentional. Everything went wrong, Ben. *Everything*. If it had only been one thing, maybe. But not everything. Anyway, she's not my problem, and I'm not going to stick around under my brother's thumb when he's pissed at me for making sure he had a wedding. Maybe that makes me a bit of a bitch, but I'm done being the workhorse."

"What about your parents?"

"What about them? They like when I'm independent and self-reliant. I'm being independent and self-reliant. I'll visit them at the appropriate intervals."

"I just hope you know what you're doing."

"I do, but thank you for your concern. This time, I'm doing something just for me, and well, people are just going to have to deal with it. If Mat wanted me dancing to his tune, he wouldn't have taken me and my hard work for granted—and he wouldn't have taken that tone with me. Not after how hard I worked making sure *his* wedding worked out for the best."

"I'm sorry. I don't know what he said to you that pissed you off so much, but I'm sorry."

"He dismissed me. That's all."

Ben grimaced. "Okay. I can see how you'd get upset over that. But moving and getting a new car?"

"If I'm going to have a midlife crisis, I will have one in style, Ben. Now, let's get this show on the road, shall we?"

IT TOOK until midnight to empty my apartment out and finish cleaning. I thanked everyone with dinner, focusing on everything

I needed to do before Thursday morning. I'd be leaving town with a few new outfits courtesy of Ben and Wolfgang, along with a new hairstyle.

I barely recognized myself in the mirror.

Wednesday night, I slept at a hotel in town. Thursday, I packed my new car with the basic necessities and hauled ass to New York in the wee hours of the morning. My new residence, an extended stay place I would spend too much on until I found an apartment, was a hop, skip, and a jump away from where I'd interview, which made it worth the staggering weekly rate.

Either way, I'd have to find a new apartment—or drive a hefty distance to a cheaper area to find somewhere to live in until I secured work. I would make my new situation work out, and if I had anything to say about it, I wouldn't be unemployed for long.

Thirty minutes before my interview time, I walked to the building, checking out the block before showing up a reasonable fifteen minutes early. The receptionist in the lobby directed me to the third floor, and the man seated behind the tall desk told me to take a seat.

Every business had a different method of hiring someone, and sometimes, an interview began the moment an applicant entered the building. Doing nothing would drive me into fidgeting, something that might ruin my chances of being employed. As I had no idea how long I'd have to wait, I retrieved my e-reader from my purse and settled in to read. I liked that no one could readily determine my books of choice, although I'd used what I was reading as talking points in the past.

If anyone asked, my choice of *The Art of War* might raise a few brows. Sun Tzu's insights, still applicable even in modern times, investigated the nature of humanity in a way I could understand—if I tilted my head to the side. I'd have to put some serious thought into how to apply some of his teachings to my life.

I focused on the section dedicated to the laying of plans, and how I might take control of my life through careful strategy rather than haphazard impulse. I made a foray or two into the chapter about evaluating strengths and weaknesses, as I figured I'd have to focus on my strengths while eliminating my weaknesses if I wanted to get ahead rather than just getting by.

"Miss Kensingvale?"

I recognized Garret's voice, and I pressed the power button on my e-reader, slid it into my purse, and rose from my seat. "I'm Miss Kensingvale."

A man who only appeared a little older than me looked me over before holding out his hand. "Garret. Pleased to meet you in person. If you'll come this way, we'll start the interview. I apologize for being late. Things have been busy."

"Quite all right. I assumed things would be busy due to your circumstances."

"That's a mild way to put it. Rather than the standard question and answer session, I have a test for you. You'll have an hour to go through the papers, and we'll determine if you're appropriate for the job by how well you perform. We'll review the documentation at the end of your test, and we'll discuss your performance. After, we'll notify you of our decision. I expect this will take three hours in total unless there are delays preparing employment documentation."

Well, while the next three hours would be stressful, it beat waiting to find out if I'd be hired. "That seems reasonable."

"It won't seem quite so reasonable once you see the test." Garret led me into a conference room, which was covered with piles of papers.

I'd endured similar audits before, and it would take a lot more than an hour to audit the documents. That was the entire point, however. How I handled the stress of dealing with a mass audit would give Garret a good idea of how I worked under pressure.

I set my purse down and rubbed my hands together. "Anything I should know before I start, sir?"

"Garret, please. These are fictional files founded on an actual audit. We received the company's permission to model our test audit for interviews under the condition we change all names to generic descriptors. When we were hired, the CEO suspected embezzlement and wanted professionals to go over the numbers to find any discrepancies."

"Understood. May I begin?"

"Begin," he ordered.

It would take hours to fully evaluate the number of files, so I dove in and went to work, reviewing every page—or group of pages—to begin making sense of what I had. It didn't take long for me to determine the company did a lot of advertising, although I couldn't tell the nature of the business from the placeholder names. I organized the invoices by who the company was hiring. One company, dubbed Placeholder D, earned the lion's share of money from the company, and payments ranged from several hundred to hundreds of thousands of dollars. While tempted to whistle over the spend, I sorted the invoices into their appropriate piles by date before tackling the smaller stack of employee financials and information sheets.

Once I had all employees isolated into stacks, I went through the invoices again and separated them by date and company to each employee.

Employee A primarily handled Placeholder D's invoices, although Employee C handled all invoices worth more than ten thousand dollars.

Employee C had careful notations on

every invoice, explaining all expenses thoroughly.

Employee A treated their invoices with Placeholder D as things to be paid without question, leaving few clues on what advertising work the company had received.

Making use of a stack of sticky notes and a pen, I flagged all invoices with unknown expenses for further review, marking the oddities as something to fully audit with internal records, and made decent progress on organizing when Garret cleared his throat, which I assumed meant I'd run out of time.

I found it amusing my auditing test lacked any actual accounting or demonstration of real auditing skills.

If they were testing for my general eye and ability to notice anything amiss, I stood a good chance of passing. I set my pen down, took the sticky note I'd been working on, and stuck it to the invoice I'd been reviewing. "May I make a comment, sir?"

"Of course."

"In a real situation, I would've been using a spreadsheet or accounting software to create entries for the invoices while referencing the accountant's files—and I would've been taking notes on a tablet with stylus."

Garret chuckled. "You'll have access to such things during real work. We've already spoken to your previous employer about your applicable job skills."

Crap. While I'd included my former boss

as a reference, I always hoped new employers wouldn't take the time and effort to interview those I'd worked for. But, rather than assuming the worst, I'd hope for the best. "Then this is a logic test to see if I have the skills needed to organize from the ground up on a new project." I regarded my work with a frown. "Which implies you want a ground-up approach to these audits, expecting something to be found and needing every element of the company's operations evaluated to check for errors or potential embezzlement."

"Or even shoddy recording."

Shoddy recording of funds and funds mismanagement happened in many companies. I'd dealt with it at every workplace I'd ever done accounting for. No matter how hard the accountants tried, *someone* found a way to mess things up, even if it was forgetting to file an invoice correctly after payment, resulting in chaos when accounting had record of a payment without having a copy of the invoice they'd paid. "Has anyone told you those are dirty words, Garret?"

"I was asked specifically to use those dirty words in that order to see your reaction. We've learned we can tell a lot about a potential employee by how they react to the hazards of their specific profession."

Well, I appreciated the man's sense of humor, which boded well for my future—if I got the job. "I bet the accounting at the company those files came from really didn't like Employee A after audit."

"As a matter of fact, you would be correct. When we were building the test, our accountants said some rather unpleasant things about Employee A. We've also learned Employee A is unfortunately common."

"Every company has at least one. Or three. Or ten." I grimaced. "Usually closer to ten."

"It's an accounting hazard. So. My question for you is this. Can you handle working with people like Employee A every day for the foreseeable future? That's what we'll probably be dealing with as we dig through this auditing mess."

"That depends. Will the firms cooperate when we request more information on ambiguous invoices?"

"That remains to be seen."

"It's a part of the job, but truth be told? It's a part I dislike. Can I deal with it? Yes. It's necessary, especially if the firm wants to survive an IRS audit without losing their shirts to fines and penalties."

"Thank you, Miss Kensingvale. If you'll follow me, I'll show you to the reception. I don't expect this evaluation will take too long before we can get back to business."

Back in the reception, I considered returning to *The Art of War,* but I decided on lighter reading.

If Florida Man couldn't distract me, nothing could.

The news sites didn't disappoint, and I emailed myself links to the best articles, expecting Rick had already seen them. Fortunately, thanks to planning my brother's wedding, I had Rick's phone number and his email address.

I could be brave and bold, and I could be friends with my brother's friend. I didn't need Mat's permission or blessing.

I dug through my contacts for Rick's email address, and I picked my favorite of the headlines.

Florida Man, upset over the circumstances of his birth, had assaulted his father with a pizza. Compared to the other candidates, he came across as mostly harmless, hilariously funny, and out of his right mind without really hurting anyone. Well, beyond a few of my brain cells, which died terrible deaths trying to comprehend why someone would beat his father for being involved with his birth.

Something about sending the email put me at ease, and I spent the rest of the wait smiling while browsing the internet in search of an even better article.

"Miss Kensingvale?" Garret asked.

According to my phone, I'd spent almost an hour and a half reading news articles, likely grinning like an idiot. I stowed my phone in my purse, rose, and kept on smiling. "Hope, please."

"Come this way. I apologize it took longer

than anticipated."

"It's no problem at all." I fell into step with him, and we returned to the conference room.

We were alone, and I remembered he'd claimed to discuss my odd interview with others. At his invitation, I took a seat.

"We spoke to some of your other contacts," he announced, sitting across the table from me.

I saw writing on the wall, but I had no idea what it said. "Well, this is either about to go really good or really badly."

Humor wouldn't lose me the interview if I'd already lost it in the first and strange part of the process. I'd be disappointed, but New York firms big and small needed accountants, and I'd get hired by someone eventually.

My plan would still work.

"Well, one of your references told me, without preamble, I'd be a bloody idiot if I didn't hire you, and that he resented losing you to me. I asked if he was one of the clients you worked for after hours, and when he confirmed that, I did reassure him you could continue your work with him. He then informed me that I might do. As what, I'm not sure."

Of my friends, Wolfgang would have pulled a stunt like that. I wasn't sure if I wanted to thank him, smack him, or find some other way to get some payback. "That would be Wolfgang. He's one of two candidates who would resent something like that, but he's also vocal with a protective streak."

Garret chuckled. "You would be correct. We appreciate your strong relationship with your clients, and your previous employer informed me he'd taken steps trying to keep you. His sentiments were similar. That's, honestly, why we skipped the traditional first part of our interview and went straight to the logic test."

Ah. I'd have to thank Wolfgang and the others I'd used as references.

"Is it bad form for me to admit I actually like this style of interview better?"

"Not at all. We prefer seeing a potential employee in action. Your logical and methodical approach to seeing the file for the first time is required for this sort of auditing work. Your education is what we're looking for, you have the appropriate licenses in New York, and your ability to prepare for relocation on short notice is exactly what we need. When can you be ready for a full move?"

"My apartment is packed and in storage already. I moved out on Wednesday, as I planned on moving to New York City anyway. I'm currently staying in a hotel down the street, but I will be looking for an apartment soon."

"We'll expense your hotel as part of your hiring bonus." Garret reached down, retrieved a briefcase, and opened it, pulling out a folder filled with papers. "Here is our hiring proposal."

Well, so much for the second discussion and portion of the interview. I took the folder, opened it, and began to read.

From everything I'd read, survival in Manhattan required at least fifty thousand a year, and that was only if I found an apartment with a roommate. Living on my own would require over a hundred thousand. Cercson Investment Group wanted to pay me just shy of one-ninety, and I'd be salaried with overtime pay should my hours exceed forty a week. My brows rose at that, as most firms used salaries to bleed employees dry. Everything else about the company seemed standard with the exception of parking; a reserved spot would be made available for my use in the building's garage at no extra fee to me. The thirty thousand dollar hiring bonus, paid out in cash and calculated to be after taxes, would make my life a lot easier while settling in the city. Three weeks of paid vacation and ten sick days transformed the offer into my personal slice of heaven.

Who knew hard work could actually pay off?

To sweeten the pie, I would have access to a financial manager to handle investments, and the company matched retirement investments handled through them.

I would have to thank my brother at some point for pissing me off enough to bail town and find better waters. All things considered, I saw no need to do much negotiation, although I had one thing on my adult wishlist I'd add. "Would the company be willing to help me find an apartment that would allow a dog?"

"We're a dog-friendly employer. Assuming your dog is trained, you are welcome to bring the animal to work on days you're not required to leave for meetings. Some of our contacts welcome dogs as well, but that's case-by-case."

I foresaw a dog in my future, one as cute, fluffy, and lovable as Rick's. "I don't have a dog yet, as one wasn't an option in my previous apartment."

Garret smiled. "We're used to accommodating pet owners moving into the area, so this is no issue."

I flipped through the pages to locate where I needed to sign over my soul for a chance at a good, challenging job that paid me closer to what I deserved. I swiped the nearest pen, gave it a click, and signed. "As I have successfully negotiated for the ability to have a dog, I'm quite pleased about this proposal."

My new boss—or, who I assumed would be my new boss—chuckled. "Considering I managed to finagle a range for your old salary out of your former employer, I thought you'd enjoy our proposal. It's a tough job, but we try to make sure the pay justifies the headaches."

"So far, the headaches seem comparable," I admitted.

"That's what I gathered after listening to your previous job description. Frankly, your tolerance for an intense work schedule was what bumped you to the front of our list. In our line of work, flexibility is needed. We never know who is going to walk through our door with a proposal, and sometimes, those proposals take us all over the world."

That caught my attention. "It does?"

"Yes. There are many companies who wish to move into New York City and need to know the legal and financial ramifications of such a choice. I've found sending our negotiators with an accountant makes the process go much smoother. People like you are the financial heart of an investment group. You see all the numbers other departments sometimes miss—and you know how the money flows. So, we'd be foolish to exclude accountants from such ventures. I do wish we'd been better named for what we actually do. Auditing challenges are only a small part of our firm's operations, albeit a critical one. I think you'll find your job challenging but rewarding, especially as we issue corporate cards for travel so you don't have to worry about filing as many expense reports. Accounting likes when we have nice, neat, easily tracked credit cards assigned to employees for tracking expenses. We do require expense sheets be turned in that match the expenses on the card, but it's much easier on the accounting at the end of the year this way."

I wanted to cry from joy. "You concentrate the expenses to credit cards?"

Garret's smile widened to a grin. "I do love the moment an accountant realizes we've significantly simplified certain elements of their work. We do. We consolidate many expenses to be easily tracked. Every corporate card is linked to only one employee, and we have an accountant who checks all credit expenses every week to make certain there is nothing fraudulent. We allow traveling employees up to thirty days to turn in expense sheets, but we do confirm what expenditures are going through on a weekly basis. We try to avoid issues."

I slid over the signed papers and matched his grin. "I think I'm going to like it here, Garret."

"As do I. Welcome aboard, Hope."

SEVEN

You should get a nicer model and buy yours new.

SIGNING the hiring proposal started a frenzy of activity, and after two more hours, three meetings with various members of HR, and all the other little things required to hire me in the state of New York, I secured full-time employment. I handed over the key to my storage box, which would be emptied and transferred to my new apartment in New York.

On Monday evening, I had a date with one of their real estate agents, who'd help me find a place within my budget.

Once finished with the necessities to be employed, I hiked to my hotel, grabbed a quick bite to eat on the way, and flopped in front of my laptop, checking my email to see what disasters waited for me.

I ignored the email from my brother, wrinkling my nose at the [NO SUBJECT] gracing his entry. I'd long-since turned pre-viewing off so I could scan more emails with ease. He likely wanted to know where I was and why I'd changed my number and otherwise refused to speak to him.

He'd probably figure it out in a week or two with some prompting from our mutual friends. Holding a grudge didn't make me a good person, but I had lines, and my brother needed a stern reminder he couldn't walk all over me just because we shared blood. I'd planned his wedding out of my love for him.

That love didn't mean I needed to tolerate him stepping on me.

The reply from Rick caught my attention, and I clicked it to discover he'd left his phone number and a request to call him.

As I liked Rick a hell of a lot more than I liked my brother at the current moment, I fell for his bait, picked up my new cell phone, and dutifully dialed, already grimacing over my cell bill for calling overseas.

Then again, thanks to a huge raise and chasing an impulse to do what I wanted in my life rather than what my family wanted for me, I could afford it.

"Fredrick speaking," Rick answered, and I recognized the tone as one a businessman used when he hadn't bothered to check his Caller ID.

"It's Hope," I replied, already worrying I'd made a mistake calling him. The last thing I needed was another reason to like the man who'd made it clear he'd be marrying someone within the next year or two. Being friends with him would hurt, but I'd do my best to make the most of it. I'd even do my best to be friends with the woman who'd won him. She had to be something special to earn the affections of someone like Fredrick. "I got your email. You have successfully corrupted me into reading absurd news articles. I hope you're happy with yourself."

He laughed, and I smiled at the sound. "I'm quite pleased with myself, thank you. Your brother is pitching a fit, and judging from what I've learned, you're doing something sneaky, sly, and concerning for all parties excepting yourself. Also, I have received a picture of your new car. It's spectacular—and I mean that in a good way. I never knew a Mercedes could become something so fun. I'm almost tempted to get a matching one, but I'd go with black and silver glitter."

Yep, the upcoming months of my life would be bitter and sweet. Maybe he had a single brother who wasn't in line to marry someone else. His sense of humor and kindness had to be genetic, right? "You should totally do that. But you should get a nicer model and buy yours new. I'm fairly sure you can afford it. Mine's used, but she runs well, and she likes her new paint job. The interior even has glitter accents. I'd say I'd refer you to the paint shop, but he's in America and you are not."

"At least for the moment. It seems work

may be moving your way at some point in the near future. Can I ask what's going on?"

"It's nothing all that important. Mat said something I'm going to make him regret, and I just secured myself a huge pay raise *with* overtime on a salary. Actually, I'm doing great. Don't tell him this, and please don't tell him you've spoken to me, but this has been the best thing I've done for myself in forever." Mat wouldn't agree with me, but Mat needed to learn my life was my problem rather than his—and that I needed to do things for me.

"As long as you're happy, I'm all right with this. Your friends are worried, as you wouldn't tell them where you went." Rick paused, and then he sighed. "They're hoping I will talk sense into you, but it seems you've already talked sense into yourself. All that said, your friends really are worried about you, and they aren't sure why you won't talk to them about this."

"Well, they're all blabbermouths and would snitch to my brother at the first sign of pressure."

Rick chuckled. "I expect you're right about that, as they did just that with me when I pressed about your situation. Your friends called me."

"They called you?" They must have talked to Mat, Mat must have decided Rick was the best chance of getting through to me and had involved the poor man in my midlife crisis. Then, because Rick was a far better man than

Mat realized, Rick had joined my team—or would play at being on my team.

I'd find out soon enough; if Mat contacted me, I'd know who had given him my new number.

"You like me a lot more than you like your brother right now, I'm a trustworthy party, apparently, and they think I can talk sense into you. I think you've talked sense into yourself, and I gave my immediate approval of your choice of vehicle. It suits you. I then told them sometimes it takes a baseball to the head to knock sense back into people. I hope you don't take offense to this, but you struck me as the type to put everyone over yourself. This is just you doing something for *you* for a change, and you don't expect much in the way of support, so you're doing it on your own."

Yep. Friendship with Fredrick would hurt as much as it helped, and I'd forever envy the woman lucky enough to win him. It might take a few years, but I'd keep reminding myself if one man like Fredrick existed, there were others, too. Billions of people meant *surely* there was a hot, single guy with good manners and a better personality out there for me. I could live without him being hot, as long as he had the good manners and a better personality. "Hot damn, someone who finally gets me."

"Been there, done that. My move to the United States is partly bullshit induced as well. Not your bullshit, as nothing you've done yet has been even close to being bullshit. There are some others, however, who have dragged me right to the end of my rope."

"Sounds like we're birds of a feather right now."

"That we are. Would you be willing to give me a general idea of your location? Just the state will do. I would find it rather amusing and enjoyable trying to locate you through a series of clues you can leave for me. It'll be a scavenger hunt. Put me through the run around. I need a challenge."

"Well, I am supposed to be planning a wedding for you."

"I'd still like your help with that. The wedding date is still up in the air, but I showed my family the work you'd done on Mat's wedding, and I even told them about the ball and chain. My mother wasn't all that happy about it at first, but then I reminded her that the bride was quite prone to running at the altar, and you managed to make the wedding happen, which is a miracle as far as I'm concerned. Actually, I was concerned there wouldn't be a wedding at all after Mat told me who he was marrying. She has a reputation."

Yeah, I'd figured that one out on my own. "Well, she's his problem now—and so is their baby."

"Baby?"

"Baby. It's a very young human that is

born approximately nine months after the start of a pregnant woman's menstrual cycle, which is typically two weeks before conception. They cry, drink milk, and make a mess of diapers. After a period of twelve years, they grow into teenagers determined to drive their parents insane. It seems there was an incident with a broken condom." I shuddered at the thought of my brother having sex with anyone, especially Amy. "And that's how far I want to go down that particular rabbit hole."

"Me, too. However much I enjoy sex with a willing partner, Amy is not what I consider attractive. At all."

"Strangely enough, I don't consider her to be very attractive, either."

"Then we are agreed. Mat can deal with his wife, and we will do our best to avoid thinking about his wife."

I smiled. "It's nice having an ally in this."

"We won't tell anyone what we think about her. So, if you're willing, I have a few questions for you."

"Only if you'll answer my questions," I countered.

"Deal. Are you game to play a scavenger hunt with me? My goal will be to find you, and you have to leave me a clue at least once a week."

"That's a lengthy period between clues." I considered why he might want so long between clues and came up with no reasonable explanation. "Why?"

"I'm in this pursuit for the long haul, and at first, I'll have to get settled, so that frequency should work to begin with. After I'm settled in the appropriate state, I can beg for additional clues to find you faster. I figure we can coordinate wedding planning through email and phone discussions should I fail to find you promptly."

"That sounds good. But no tracing my calls. That would be cheating. You also can't hack into any computers to get my location. You have to find me from my clues or the gentle questioning of those who know my location. No interrogations or anything unscrupulous that might lose me my new job."

Rick clucked his tongue. "I suppose I can agree to those terms. Do you have any other restrictions for me?"

"When you find me, you can't tell my brother. You must also introduce me to your dog. I will even give you permission to grab me specifically for the purpose of meeting your dog. I want to be friends with your dog. I might get a dog, because my employer allows dogs in the office, and I've never had a dog before."

"Can I convince you to hold off on the adoption of a dog until you meet my dog?"

"That depends. Can I steal your dog? She's really that cute, Rick. I might have to steal her and take her home with me."

"Can we negotiate this after I find you?"

I considered. "Maybe. It depends."

"On?"

"How long it takes for you to bring your dog to me, how often I'll be allowed to visit your dog, and how often I'll be able to visit your dog after you're married." Reminding myself he was destined to marry someone else sucked.

Never before had I held much interest in any man. Worse, my job for the next few months—or however long it was for the wedding to be planned—involved marrying a perfect-for-me man to someone else. In some other life, I must have been a terrible person.

Only a terrible person deserved my awful luck.

Rick laughed. "I should be landing in the United States within the next week or two, as I am in progress of finalizing the paperwork required to import my dog. As it would be cruel to withhold my dog from you, I would allow for open visitation outside of work hours, and should I need to take a business trip, I pay well for a trustworthy person to babysit my girl when I can't take her with me. As for the issue of marriage, that depends on a lot of factors."

Of course. If we tried to list all of the factors, we might be done sometime tomorrow, and I'd be even more aware of how I intended on torturing myself for the next few months of my life. "As the answers to my first two questions are acceptable, I'm willing to ignore the third question completely for now. However, I'm not going to throw our game just because I want to meet your dog."

Instead of worrying about Rick, I could have a really good relationship with his beautiful Annabel Lee. She would be easy to love, and I'd happily throw away my dignity in order to babysit her when Rick and his wife went away on their honeymoon.

With my luck, they'd take the dog, and I'd just have to face reality alone.

"That would be boring, and it wouldn't do if I bored you. Which state should I make arrangements for, Hope?"

My name and his lips were a dangerous and potent combination. I may have disliked my brother's choice of wife, but I'd hate myself every minute I worked to make certain Rick had the best wedding day possible. Creating perfect memories for him and his wife-to-be would be my pride. It would be painful, although I'd try to look on the bright side.

Men like Fredrick existed in the world, and I could find another, and the next one might be the one for me. I could handle my crush on him like a sane adult.

He wouldn't realize I admired him, would like a chance for him to be in my life, and work to make sure the rest of his life started with the perfect wedding.

I would need to spend a lot of time repeating that to myself to make sure I didn't screw up.

"New York," I finally replied, aware I'd left

him waiting in silence for an embarrassingly long time. "Unfortunately for you, New York State has a population of over nineteen million with five major cities with populations of over a hundred thousand. I could be in any one of them. I could also be in a smaller city."

"And as you're still on a Washington area code, so if you keep that phone number, I won't be able to tell."

I'd have to thank him for that reminder. "Obviously, I will not be able to change my phone number until you've located me." That wouldn't cost me a lot; I'd learned my plan came with unlimited roaming, so I could stay in New York without worrying about changing my number. "I will also refuse to speak to Mat until you have found me. He can go suck eggs, and you can tell him that for all I care."

"Your brother is not going to take that well, I just thought you should know."

"Well, he should have been a little less of an asshole and a little more grateful for the hell I went through putting his wedding together. I went from a healthy weight to a twig with ribs to fit in the damned dress in the size Amy demanded."

"I am going to insist that you are a healthy weight in time for my wedding, and I will hire a reasonable nutritionist to help make certain you're in good health if needed. And I'll have words with your brother about that. If you don't mind me asking, how much weight did you have to lose?"

"Twenty pounds or so. To be fair, I probably did need to lose five of those pounds. I like milkshakes a little too much."

"Five pounds isn't exactly a lot in either direction. Hell, I'm usually ten pounds over, but I've been told I'm a muscle-bound freak."

"I'm not qualified to say if you're muscular, but you don't seem like a freak to me. If anything, you seem rather normal. I mean, how bad can you be? You have a cute dog, and she obviously loves you so much she ate your wedding invitation so you wouldn't leave her behind. You also have a sense of humor. I never knew how entertaining funny news headlines could be until I took a baseball to the head."

"I'm concerned you might go out of your way to be hit with more baseballs to discover other joys in life."

"Can I pass on that? I didn't want to get hit the first time. I'm just pointing out that the baseball incident had a damned good silver lining. Neither one of us had to go to that reception. I love my brother, but by the time they got through the actual ceremony, I was already done with the entire wedding."

"I'm still amazed there was a reception. That is not a slight against your brother, but his wife is a piece of work."

"I'm glad I'm not the only one who realizes that."

"Well, your brother did make mention he'd allowed himself to be swayed by her without consulting with you on the matter."

"He didn't appreciate my blunt opinion when I spoke to him on the phone, that's for certain."

"His mistake, not yours. There is one more delicate matter I was asked to bring up to you, if I happened to be able to speak cordially with you."

"If it's about our parents, I'll show up for the next major holiday."

"I will not count that as an easy way to get a hold of you unless I become desperate."

"And if you become desperate enough to crash the family dinner, you can acknowledge your defeat at my hands in front of my family. Spare yourself the humiliation. Plus, Amy will be there."

"They'd give Mat your number, wouldn't they?"

"Yes, they would."

"I will provide a phone specifically for you to contact your parents, and you can keep it turned off except when you call them and check your voice mail. That can be my penance for becoming involved with this situation. I'll send you money online to cover the cost of your phone and the line. Would that be fair?"

"I can get a cheap prepaid phone to call my parents. That's not an issue."

"Then you can use the money for that, but

I'm not going to force you to pay for something like that, especially not when I'm a part of why you're avoiding certain people."

"Hardly. You didn't force Mat to act like an asshole. You also didn't force him to marry Amy. You also didn't suggest he ask me to plan the wedding. Well, I hope you didn't. You'll have a lot of penance to pay if you're the one who gave him that idea."

"I invited your brother to attend an event with me, which was where he met Amy."

Well, then. I took a few moments to decide how that changed my perspective of the man. Ultimately, it changed nothing. "You're the reason I spent how long of my life planning my brother's wedding?"

"I deserve to pay some form of penance. Would it help if I told you that I hadn't intended for them to meet?"

"That helps a little, but I feel you have failed to appropriately warn my brother what he was getting into—and you may have failed to warn him about scorned women. You better tell me a good headline. I think I need to hear one after this, Rick."

"Can it be a particularly crude headline?"

In my recent days of pursuing amusing headlines, I'd found a few crude ones, but I wondered how his definition of crude and mine differed. "Sure."

"Florida Man Vapes Semen."

My mouth dropped open, and I spluttered for a few moments before asking, "But *why*?"

"That headline has been haunting me for years. I can't even imagine why. Worse, the article was unclear about where, exactly, he acquired the semen."

I closed my mouth, lifted my hand, and scratched at my scalp. "I think I need another headline, but one not as likely to scar me for life."

"This one was later revealed to be a hoax, but did you hear about the time Florida Man killed his imaginary friend and turned himself in to the police? The mug shot that went with that headline was spectacular."

"But it sounds so real," I protested. "That's a hoax?"

"Fooled me, too. I mean, it's totally something Florida Man would do. This one isn't a hoax, though. FLORIDA MAN BREAKS INTO JAIL TO VISIT HIS FRIENDS."

Florida Man existed to confuse me. "But why?" Florida Man also would never cease to amaze me, and despite everything, I laughed. "Don't tell me. Let me guess. Meth?"

"Bath salts with a twist."

"Did they let him see his friends when they arrested him? That seems important."

"Well, he got charged with some felony criminal mischief, assault against law enforcement officers, and driving while under the influence, so assuming they put him in the same prison, I'd say so. Florida Man has taught me many important life lessons."

"Don't do drugs comes to mind." I shook

my head. As always, my doubts surfaced. When I'd up and left home, anger over my brother's callous words had done a good job of making certain I followed through with my impulsive decision to change my life. Time did what it did best, casting doubt on my choice. "Do you think I'm being stupid, Rick?"

"No, not at all. Everyone has limits. When you hit your limit, you got yourself a car you like, you secured a better job for yourself, and you moved somewhere with more opportunities. I don't think that's stupid at all. Impulsive? For certain—but according to Mat, you're so meticulous most of the time that something like moving to a new city just isn't something you'd do. Too much could go wrong, and you're all about making sure nothing can go wrong. Mat's wedding is a perfect example. You prepared for every contingency."

"I needed to, too." I sighed. "I'm going to be in debt forever repaying favors."

"What do you mean?"

"I thought I had already told you she lost the deposits for most of the vendors she picked because she cancelled some, pissed the others off, and otherwise made a mess of everything."

"I think you had mentioned something about it, but truth be told, I was more concerned about you having taken a baseball to the head. I hadn't clued in that meant you had personally taken on the debts for the replacements. I thought your brother would have paid for it. How significant were the losses, if you don't mind me asking?"

"If I start thinking about how much money she lost Mat, I will just get even more pissed off about this situation. With the exception of the caterer, which I'd handled, everything else became a bust. Basically, I bribed the entire replacement wedding staff to cover my ass after Amy screwed up all the wedding plans. I left the papers proving it for my brother to find along with the ball and chain."

"He was not happy about the ball and chain, by the way."

"Tough shit. Honestly, that's exactly why I'm here instead of back home doing the same old grind. I refuse to regret it."

Rick laughed. "I see you still have a healthy dose of resentment towards your brother—or his wife."

"Can it be both?"

"It can be both. For the record, I have the ball and chain in my possession, and I have plans for it. I'm making some modifications. I asked someone I know to evaluate the work on it, and he was really impressed. You really didn't skimp on that thing, did you?"

"Well, it had to be suitable for Mat's wedding, so I couldn't just go with any old ball and chain. It needed to be nice. The paint work cost me extra. I had it made custom, as

I wanted it to be heavy enough she couldn't move it but not so heavy I couldn't move it. Unlike her, who likely consumes air and water to stay thin, I did a lot of working out."

"It weighs eighty pounds. I know this because I paid to have it shipped."

"I am rather proud of my ability to lift that ball and chain at my leisure, although I'm retiring from the gym life and taking up a new career as someone who walks a healthy distance while enjoying a milkshake."

"With a cherry on top?"

"The cherry is the best part. Don't leave your cherry unattended around me, because I might even become bold enough to steal it."

At the rate Rick kept chuckling, he'd make it through the rest of his day with a grin plastered onto his pretty face. "I'll make sure to bring an entire jar of them. If I tried to lure you into my car with them, would it work?"

I snorted. "Just lure me into your car with your dog. I already told you that you could take me just about anywhere if you were delivering me to your dog."

"I see you have fallen helplessly in love with my dog."

"How could I not? I saw her picture. She's just a big, fluffy bundle of love. She chewed up your invitation so you wouldn't leave her. You should surrender your dog to me. If I can't take her with me, I'm not going. Well, if it's more than for an hour or two. Long enough to go to the grocery store and places where my dog shouldn't go."

"I don't leave her that often," Rick replied, his tone amused. "I'm not giving up my dog. Despite having cruelly left her to attend your brother's wedding, I do love her dearly."

"You would be a terrible person if you did not love that dog dearly."

"I can't argue with that. Do you want me to do anything about your brother?"

"No, but thank you. I can handle him."

"Through steadfast avoidance?"

"If he's not willing to put in the work to say his apology to my face, he can sulk with his wife. So far, you've done a far superior job of demonstrating a willingness to put in some effort."

"You're quite stubborn, I see."

He had no idea how stubborn I planned to be. "Well, you are willing to put in effort. He's willing to send me an email without a subject line. I didn't open it, by the way, because I deserve better than that."

"Yes, you do."

"If you talk to my brother, just tell him I've lost my mind and will be unavailable until I've found it again. It'll take a while. My new job will be busy, I think. I'm looking forward to it."

"I'll just tell him you're the end-game boss he has to quest to find, only to discover he needs special equipment and a fancy sword for any hope of defeating you."

I hadn't taken Rick to be a gamer, and I laughed. "The last time that happened to me, I wanted to throw the controller and console through a window. I haven't had a lot of time to play games. I'd go over to a friend's house to play them. I'm too boring to have a system."

"You should get one. There's little as fun as playing a game where you can die if you look at a boss wrong and you're unprepared."

"At least you didn't say relaxing."

"There's nothing relaxing about having my ass handed to me by a damned group of pixels. Once, I called in sick from work because I had to defeat the mob. I was going to tell everyone I had caught the flu because it took me a week to be able to finally defeat him, but my mother showed up and caught me yelling at my console. It didn't go over well."

"It didn't? Why not?"

"She had to fly in from London to do it."

Ouch. "Did you forget to answer your phone or something?"

"I deliberately turned it off so no one would disturb me and Annabel Lee. For the record, she loved my impromptu gaming vacation."

I bet she had loved every moment spent fawning over her owner. "You might be able to convince me to play a game and get a console."

"I'll email you with some recommendations, I'll give you a list of games I play, and when I can be found playing them. If you have a decent computer, there are some computer games we could play, too. Since I'm coming to the United States, it'll be easier to find a time to play together."

"I should get a better computer," I admitted. "I can afford it. I think. I hope. I don't know how much my apartment will cost each month. I have a date with a real estate agent to find a place early next week. The company is providing one."

"You'll be all right, Hope. Of that I have no doubt."

Well, at least one of us had no doubt. In any case, I'd fake it until I made it. It would be enough.

It had to be.

EIGHT

One of the company's accountants hired male prostitutes.

MONDAY ROLLED AROUND FASTER than I liked. Spending the weekend making good on my promises to friends and associates for ensuring Mat's wedding went well drained me. Next weekend, I swore I would grab a few minutes of peace for myself.

As directed, I went to the third floor of my new building, escorted by one of the security guards, who unlocked the elevator door for me. Garret met me in the reception, armed with a thick folder, a briefcase, and an access badge for the building. "I was hoping to give you today to settle, but there was an incident this weekend. After going over the staff, I shunted the original project I was giving you to someone else, and you're getting the new emergency."

Uh oh. That didn't sound promising. "What happened?"

Garret handed me the folder. "Follow me, and I'll brief you on the situation."

He led me through a maze of cubicles and offices to a small conference room with a sea of folders covering the table. The stacks, which needed a great deal of attention to restore to order, promised I passed through the gates of hell into an accounting nightmare. I regarded the piles with narrowed eyes. "This doesn't look good."

"Every accountant I showed this to said the same. A few of them even cried. Our lead auditor threatened to quit after I briefed her. She's taking over the load I hired you for, and you're her new favorite person. I reminded her you weren't really being given a choice on this one, but she ignored me. I think the relief was too much for her. Daisy couldn't keep a straight face during the briefing, and she absolutely hates when she can't maintain professionalism."

"She couldn't keep a straight face?"

"One of the company's accountants hired male prostitutes to work with her, and while they're intelligent, hard-working men, they lack the necessary qualifications to work as accountants. According to the company hiring us, criminal charges will be filed against the woman, but I'm unaware of what the charges will be. We were warned, as there will be an ongoing criminal investigation, and it will ultimately involve the information you will need to audit. We have been issued an entire copy of the accounting files, although the originals will likely be claimed as evidence."

Somehow, I kept my mouth from dropping open, but I couldn't stop my eyes from widening. "Excuse me, sir, but did you just say the lead accountant had hired male prostitutes?"

"Yes, I did. Having seen photographs of the men, I can easily see how an older woman like Miss Meltrew might find them attractive. We have also been asked to interview the men to find out if they have skill sets suitable for other positions, as the company's management doesn't wish to lose hard workers and had no idea the accountant had lied about their qualifications to Human Resources. You'll have to handle this as well."

I could understand why Daisy would want to run from the job. The last thing I'd expected from my Monday was to be in a position to interview male prostitutes for any reason. "I don't have a lot of experience interviewing anyone, but I will do my best."

"It should be simple enough. The folder you're carrying includes a list of requirements for all open positions at the company, so you'll just speak to each of the men and find out if they meet those requirements or can be easily trained to meet those requirements. None of those positions require certifications."

I could do that. "What's the scope of my work on this, sir?"

"You'll be doing a full audit of the marketing department, which is what this specific accountant was responsible for. Unfortunately, this firm does a great deal of advertising and marketing work, so there are a lot of files that have to be gone over. The other accountants will be able to work with you on anything overlapping with their work. They want us to have a non-biased look at the accounting records before the files are handed over to a new accountant."

"Do you want me to treat it as I would an IRS audit?"

"Ideally, yes. They are uncertain if there was any other illegal activity, so they want an auditor to go over everything and flag suspicious invoices and activity. With the fraudulent hiring of these men, they're expecting a full IRS audit, but one hasn't been scheduled yet."

Yet. With criminal charges being filed, it was only a matter of time before the IRS decided to get involved and see if there were any low-hanging fruit for them to snatch. "And the police aren't confiscating files yet?"

"They wisely copied all of the files before pressing charges."

"What are the nature of the charges, sir? I'm just an auditing accountant, not a forensics accountant."

"The charges are sexual in nature."

"Oh." I raised a hand and covered my mouth. "Oh. At *work*?"

"According to my contact at the company, these gentlemen were working hard for the money. At current, she is being accused of requiring sex work to maintain illegal employment. None of the employees are being charged, as Miss Meltrew has claimed she coerced the men through use of their employment."

"What would they be potentially charged for?"

"Prostitution, if they're charged. It's a misdemeanor. But should she continue to claim she coerced them, no charges would be pressed against the employees, and they would be treated as victims. There may not even be a trial. She's quite proud of her accomplishments."

Wow. "Is that all?"

"If only. Miss Meltrew apparently approached a young gentleman in the accounting department to bring him into her fold. He refused and reported the incident to Human Resources. That's where we come in."

"We're making sure the accounting work is legal," I guessed.

"Precisely. I have no idea what you're going to find in these files, and there are more boxes on the way. A lot more boxes. She's been an accountant with the company for three years, so you'll have to go over all three years of invoices, billing, and anything associated with her specific work. Unfortunately, as she was the primary accountant for the entire marketing department, her work is rather critical."

"Okay. I'll get to work on this right away, then."

"It's not that simple."

"Sir?"

"I need you to go to the company's offices today and interview the men, find out what work they were actually doing on the files, and poke around their digital records. The briefcase has a laptop in it for your use, and you'll have someone with you to help you get the digital records. These are only the paper records."

I reminded myself I was receiving a huge pay increase to deal with odd auditing and having to interview male hookers. Honestly, interviewing male hookers would be a highlight of my year, and I might change my mind about giving my brother the cold shoulder just so I could tell him I was having lengthy talks with attractive prostitutes.

So much temptation, so little time.

"All right, sir. I can go get my car. It's parked at the hotel, as it's a pretty nice day. Can you give me the address, and if there's somewhere specific I should park?"

"There's a parking pass for you in the briefcase, along with where you can park in the garage. I'll need you to give me a description of your vehicle for their security."

"I drive a silver Mercedes accented with blue glitter," I announced, unable to keep the pride out of my voice. Then, as I doubted he'd believe me until I showed him a picture, I dug out my phone and showed him my car. "She's my present to myself. She's used, but I took her to a body shop, and I liked the glitter. She has glitter accents inside, too."

"I find myself shocked to admit that looks really nice. Just don't tell anyone I said that."

"A gentleman friend of mine really likes the paint job, too. I think he's debating getting a car like mine for himself."

"I'm debating getting one for myself," Garret admitted. "Do you mind if I send the photo over so they can see the vehicle?"

"Number to send it to?" He gave me his cell number, and I sent him a copy of the image.

"I'll make sure security is aware of which vehicle is yours. Just report to the security desk when you arrive, and they'll send you to the right floor."

"Will my badge get me into the building after hours?"

"Yes, but if you're at their building until five, just go home. Today, get a feel for the job. You can do the serious number crunching tomorrow."

"Do you want me to take the laptop home with me?"

"It'll give you the freedom to work from home as needed, and you can sync any data you need to on your desktop here. The tech department is currently working on setting up the machine, and it should be ready for your use by this afternoon."

I refused to wonder how bad the audit could be. With a bunch of uncertified prostitutes doing accounting work, I expected there would be a lot of problems with the numbers, the recording of invoices, and so on due to poor accounting work. No matter what, I wouldn't laugh or cry. "That sounds perfect. If I'm at their offices until five or later, I'll go home and prepare to handle this in the morning. Will the conference room be closed off until I can start sorting through everything?"

"The documents will be moved into your office, which will be locked. The receptionist will have the key for you, and she will show it to you when you get in. That'll let us put everything you need in there so you can work efficiently."

I checked my phone. "I'll be able to work as late as six, but then I have to meet with the real estate agent anyway, so I'll just use that extra hour there unless I run out of things I can do efficiently there."

"Good luck on your apartment search. I have to get back to work, but if you need me, I'll be at the end of the hall."

I took that as a dismissal, regarded the chaotic mess of papers with resignation, and took the few minutes to familiarize myself with the folder, explore the contents of the briefcase, and otherwise brace myself for the oddest work day in my entire life.

IN THE HEART OF MANHATTAN, Tallont Marketing Services took over two floors of a skyscraper in dire need of renovation, and the elevator worried a few years of my life getting from the garage to the lobby. Getting to the third floor knocked off another few years, and I would do anything to avoid having to return to the decrepit building. With my heart rate in the mile-per-minute territory, I headed for the receptionist, a younger woman who regarded me with a concerned expression.

In her shoes, I'd be stressed, too.

"I'm Hope Kensingvale."

The woman sighed and relaxed. "The auditor?"

"Yes."

"Thank goodness you're here. It's chaos. Everyone's going nuts. The cops are here, half the accountants are about to have a meltdown, and they just said to wait for you to come to help us sort this mess out. I'm Jennifer. I actually work in marketing, but our regular receptionist had been hired by Miss Meltrew, so he's in the back with everyone else. I'll ask Nancy to take over the reception while I show you around." Jennifer hopped to her feet and hurried to the glass door leading deeper into the office. "William is the most senior of Miss Meltrew's hires, and they asked me to put you in touch with him first."

It would be an interesting morning, and I'd need a vacation before lunchtime, assuming I could spare the time to find something to eat. For some reason, I doubted I'd have the time. I hoped my smile would put the woman at ease. "That sounds fine to me. Do you have a private conference room or office I can use for today?"

"I've been told to take you to Miss Meltrew's office. You can use it. Everything has been unlocked for you. All of the files are in her storage closet, which is attached to her office. We had no idea they didn't have the qualifications." Jennifer wrung her hands together and guided me down a long hallway to a junction. She turned right and gestured to the open door at the end. "That's her office. It's pretty crowded in there right now, but everyone will clear out so you can talk to William."

Straightening her back, Jennifer stepped into the office. "Miss Kensingvale from Cercson Investment Group is here about the audit."

I followed the marketer into the office to find chaos. Twenty people, including a pair of amused cops, crammed into a space ten might be able to fit without sitting on each other. I pegged the only woman in the room to be Miss Meltrew, an elderly woman likely ready to retire at any day.

She looked me over, and she licked her lips. "My, aren't you a pretty one? You're going to make this a memorable arrest. How'd a sweetheart like you get suckered into something like this?"

Okay. I could handle the situation without becoming offended, annoyed, or laughing. "Thank you, Miss Meltrew. My business here is a private matter."

"Of course it is, sweetheart. You wouldn't make a very good auditing accountant if you sang like a canary to the person you're auditing. Don't you worry yourselves at all, my pretties. She'll tell you what I told you; your work is pristine, my work is pristine, and you're all as smart as you are handsome."

I allowed myself to glance over the men crammed into the room, and I couldn't fault the woman's taste in men; while some were dark and others weren't, they all brought some form of physical beauty to the table. One took bodybuilding to a rather extreme level, while others could easily play the part of an elf in some movie with little work from the makeup artist.

A few of them would give Rick a run for his money in the looks department.

They probably made a fortune as prostitutes, and I wouldn't blame any woman for wanting to cut one of them a check.

Hell, if I could afford a misdemeanor, I'd

consider cutting one a check. On second thought, I wouldn't. I'd just think about it.

Assuming I had the time for a man, I wouldn't share him, and I expected loyalty in return. Players or prostitutes wouldn't work for me.

The grinning cops would be my next obstacle, and with the amount of work piling up on my day, the faster I got them out of the space I needed to work in, the better off I'd be. "Officers, I need to speak with a gentleman named William. Do you require his presence?"

The two, seasoned if I judged them by their age and worn appearances, exchanged looks. At a subtle nod from the darker haired one, the other replied, "Not at all. If you'll come with us ma'am, we'll handle the rest of this at the station."

"You should cuff me."

Somehow, I kept from laughing. I concentrated on my breathing, counting to ten while wondering what had made the woman snap so hard she wanted to take on the entire NYPD.

"Please come with us, ma'am."

"I see you're going to play coy. We can talk about it in your car," the old lady announced before striding for the door. I stepped to the side to give her plenty of space and stay out of her reach. Some types of crazy I didn't need in my life, and hers counted. If I could have a fraction of her crazy, in the form of a dedicated, hot man, I'd accept, but until the day I snapped in earnest, I'd keep my nose clean and my hands off the local prostitutes.

New York sure did have some nice prostitutes, though. Damn.

I waited for the cops to leave with Miss Meltrew before turning to the gathering of men, all of whom watched me with open curiosity. "Well, then. Which one of you gentlemen is William?"

The bodybuilder dressed in his rather tight suit smiled and raised his hand. "I'm William, ma'am."

Jennifer escaped while she could, and after a moment of thought, I closed the door behind her. "I was told you'd be the best person to talk to about the audit, and I was asked to speak with you alone first. Is this all of you?"

I wondered how they'd interpret my question.

William chuckled. "If by all of us, you mean Lana's hires, we are. She warned us this would happen when there were changes in HR and an HR audit."

Ah-ha. That explained a lot. "That exposed your lack of the proper certifications to work as accountants."

"That's right, but we didn't do much of the accounting work. Lana did it all. We just did what she told us to. It worked well. She handled the accounting, and we made sure everything was nice, neat, and orderly. You're not going to find any issues with our part of things."

"Well, I've been asked to find out what you're good at and pass recommendations on. They wanted a non-biased individual handling the interviews. Unless you go to school and pass the various tests, you can't legally act as an accountant. That's really the issue here. You'll probably have to take your original hiring agreement with HR and discuss it with them, but considering I was asked to figure out what you are good at, you're valued employees. Really, I'm just an accountant, but I'm good at solving problems and working with numbers."

I had a few questions for Garret, which I'd ask tomorrow, assuming I survived my meeting with a room full of hot male prostitutes. Given an opportunity, I bet the group could catch the attention of every damned woman in the city.

William glanced at the other men, who either shrugged or nodded.

I needed more friends I could communicate with without saying a word.

"We didn't do anything we didn't want to do," William announced.

Well, that was more than I wanted to know about their relationship with their now ex-boss. "I'll let HR worry about that. My job, right now, is to make sure each of you shine in terms of your actual skills. So, what do you gentlemen bring to the table?"

WILLIAM BROUGHT ATTENTION TO DETAIL, extreme flexibility, an insane amount of strength, and a wicked sense of humor to any table he was invited to. The rest of the men gave me very similar answers. After thirty minutes wasted on innuendo, explanations of sexual positions I couldn't evict from my head, and more enthusiasm over updating their resumés than I could readily handle, I determined Miss Meltrew had groomed a sexy army of meticulous secretaries who could count to ten without help and could handle even complex spreadsheets.

Given an opportunity, enrollment in the appropriate school, and some time, they'd likely make excellent accountants.

Once they figured out I meant to help them, they swarmed over the computer, worked on updating their resumés to be accurate, and regaled me with tales of life in the marketing department.

They also regaled me with tales in which marketers couldn't keep their numbers straight or their purchases legit. That gem came from William, who did most of the talking for everyone. Not only did he provide the gem, he pulled out the invoices he thought seemed weird.

I read over the invoices, my brows furrowing. "Why would an entertainer such as yourself view invoices for sex toys to be weird?"

"We market advertising for vanilla stores."

Vanilla? I frowned and regarded the invoice, wondering what sex toys had to do with vanilla.

"Non-sexual or plain sex. Nothing kinky. Those toys are rather kinky. We sometimes handle advertising for adult companies, but never anything physical. There's no reason for there to be those kinds of invoices here."

I checked the amounts; a firm the size of the one I audited wouldn't miss a thousand dollars, but fraud was fraud was fraud, and illegally using company funds for explicit purchases tended to fall into the no-no category. "Anything else like this?"

"There are some with unusually high spend compared to the other marketers."

After an order from William, his team divided and conquered to locate and present all questionable invoices.

Not only would they make excellent secretaries, they'd make marvelous general assistants. I set the invoices in a pile and patted them. "Please put everything you believe to be questionable here with a note explaining why you believe it's questionable. In the meantime, I'll go have a talk with HR. Can you point me in the right direction?"

"I'll take you there myself," William replied, heading to the door. "Thank you for helping us, Miss Kensingvale."

I smiled. "You're welcome."

Armed with their resumés, I ambushed the manager of HR, notifying her I'd been asked to gather and review the resumés of Miss Meltrew's employees. The woman, one Mrs. Thomasson, confirmed they'd made the request to help mitigate potential bias, considering the situation.

The entire company seemed in dire need of a shakedown if they were looking at an auditing firm to fix their mess from top to bottom. Bracing for the worst, I said, "They all seem very competent individuals with strong resumés, especially for assistant or secretarial work. They're also good candidates for proper schooling in accounting, if your company sponsors continuing education. They were taught to look for red-flag situations, and they brought them to my attention."

"They did?"

"Yes, they did."

"Are they…?"

My job had taken such a strange turn. "I don't believe they were at all coerced, and from what I understand of the situation, they all had relationships with Miss Meltrew prior to being hired."

"And prior relationships don't violate our company handbook, as long as they don't interfere with their ability to work," the woman muttered. "All right. This is a shock to all of us, Miss Kensingvale, which is why we asked for advice from your firm. You were recommended as someone who is practical, skilled at managing complicated and strenuous tasks, and otherwise flexible."

I wasn't as flexible as any of the men waiting for me in Miss Meltrew's office, that much was for certain. "Does wedding planning count as complicated and strenuous?"

"I would rather do an audit of the entire employee base of the company on a deadline," she replied.

"Well, if your company is in need of skilled secretaries and assistants, the gentlemen Miss Meltrew had hired will deliver. They're organized, they're observant, and if I were in your shoes, I'd be asking about sending them to night school to be groomed for higher positions."

"You've figured that out from that short of a time with them?"

"I helped them organize their resumés and talked to them. After I'm done here, I will get copies of the digital records and photocopies of any odd invoices they're currently gathering for me so I can focus on those first. Who should be my primary contact about the auditing results within your company?"

"Mr. Sactrin. He's in charge of the marketing department."

"Is there another individual I can discuss matters with, who isn't directly involved with the questionable accounting?"

The woman blinked. "Oh, yes. Of course. I'm certain the CEO would speak to you about such matters. That's Mr. Waltsen." While her expression remained puzzled, she dug through her desk, found a scrap of paper, and wrote down their names, phone numbers, and email addresses. "I do hope there aren't serious problems."

Oh, there were going to be problems. I already had a sex toy problem, and the last thing I wanted to do was inform a company one of their employees had been making odd purchases. How the invoices had gotten through accounting in the first place flummoxed me.

The good firms required approvals before invoices were paid, and there was no way in hell someone could have missed an order for sex toys.

"My job is to find any and all issues so they can be corrected," I replied, offering a smile. "That your company is handling this before it has reached the IRS is good for you, as it'll make certain you can file any corrections needed in a timely fashion. You'll also have everything organized to streamline the process, as it's my job to make sure you're ready for the possibility of a real audit."

"Which is looking pretty probable at this point." The woman heaved a sigh. "Thank you for your help, Miss Kensingvale. Please don't hesitate to reach out to me if there are any problems or if any of the staff don't cooperate with your auditing efforts."

"I'll contact you if there are any issues," I promised.

After exchanging pleasantries with the woman for a few minutes, I returned to Miss Meltrew's office to get all of the information I needed to make sense of the situation. With a little luck, I'd identify how much trouble the company would be in if the IRS came knocking at their door in the morning—or if the company had a bigger sex scandal on their hands than a bunch of male prostitutes livening up an accountant's work life.

Laughing over the absurdity of it all, I texted Rick with a clue he might even be able to follow should the scandal reach the news: DEVELOPING STORY: NEW YORK WOMAN SLEEPS WITH ENTIRE ACCOUNTING DEPARTMENT.

A few moments later, my phone rang, but as I had a situation to contain, prostitutes to reassure, and numbers to wrangle, I silenced my cell, put it in my purse, and went to work.

NINE

An army of prostitutes gave me a copy.

ARMED WITH A BOX of invoice copies, a complete digital record of the marketing department's accounting, and in possession of most of my sanity, I returned to my new place of employment. Garret intercepted me in the lobby, and his takeout bag implied he'd just raided the fast food joint next door for lunch. "You're back a lot earlier than I expected."

"An army of prostitutes gave me a copy of every invoice they deemed questionable, loaded my laptop with the accounting files in record time, and my blitz call to their accounting department for their total matched what they gave me, so I have enough to start the real work now."

My phone rang, likely Rick's relentless attempt to learn more about my headline. I ignored my purse, pressing the up button to summon the elevator.

"You have an hour lunch, so you can take that call if you want. If you want something ordered in, just make sure you give the delivery company our suite and floor so it gets to you. We have a no peanuts, no fish, and no shellfish rule on our floor because one of the secretaries has severe allergies. That means no Thai food, Vietnamese food, or Chinese food as a general rule."

"No Chinese? Why no Chinese?"

"Fish oil is a common ingredient in Chinese food, and it's safer to just ban it all. If you have Chinese food, you need to air out for at least half an hour before coming up on this floor. Her allergy is truly severe."

I couldn't imagine trying to survive in any city with that combination of allergies, especially one that was on an island and reeked of fish when near the water. "That's horrible. That poor woman."

"Let's just say the receptionist has emergency services on speed dial in case there's an issue. Most everyone does their best to avoid her allergies, but you'd be surprised what contains peanuts without people realizing it —or fish. The fish oil used in Chinese food surprised pretty much everyone. She learned about that by unfortunate mistake."

"I'll make sure to avoid any allergens," I promised.

"Without overstepping my bounds, can I ask about the army of prostitutes?"

"The allegation that Miss Meltrew hired male prostitutes is true. They're good workers from the looks of it, and they gathered everything I needed within an hour. They also had a good understanding of what constitutes as an accounting red flag. Those files are in this box, and I'll be doing a full audit of this marketer's work first. According to the gentlemen, they didn't do much accounting work, instead handling other tasks so Miss Meltrew could do the actual accounting while they kept operations smooth. I recommended that their HR department invest in their schooling. If they don't, you may wish to look into hiring them. They made a good impression."

"Beyond the accounting hiring fraud."

"That's not their fault. I believe Miss Meltrew is the one who falsified their qualifications, and HR didn't vet her selections. Since nothing seemed amiss, no one investigated. I helped them with their resumés, turned them in to their HR department, and went back to work on the audit. Until I have a better idea of what I'm working with, I don't need to get any more documentation from them. I loaded all of their digital recordings onto my laptop, so I can work from home as necessary."

"We'll try to keep you from working from home as much as possible, although it'll happen. Your office is this way." Garret led me to a surprisingly spacious office with a desk and a couch, enough filing cabinets to keep most accountants happy, and a dual-screen setup I'd appreciate once I started doing side-by-side comparisons of files. "Come see me down the hall if you have any questions or find anything important."

"I'll do that. Thanks."

Garret left, and he closed the door behind him. My phone rang again, and I dug out my cell to discover Rick's number gracing the display. Laughing over his persistence, I connected the call and said, "I never said I was the New Yorker, you know."

"Well, that's a relief. I was trying to figure out what I'd tell your brother—and I'd have questions about how you managed to seduce an entire accounting department in such a brief period of time. Where did you get that headline? I searched online and but couldn't find anything."

"It's a clue. If a similar headline shows up online, you may be able to narrow down my location."

"I find myself grateful for your generosity, and I will be making a point of checking New York for interesting headlines. Your brother claims I have delicate and easily offended sensibilities. For the sake of these sensibilities, might you give me a little more information to work with?"

"An older woman hired a bunch of male prostitutes to work for her at a company. That's all I can really say."

"Let me make an educated guess. Your company was hired to do an audit because they can't trust the work done. The prostitutes aren't legal accounting hires, I presume?"

My brows raised. "Do you have a mole at my workplace, Rick? The accuracy of your guess makes me think you have a mole at my workplace."

"No, I've just seen weirder things happen in the business world. I just tried to deduce what would create a headline like that with the information you gave me."

"I have to give that old lady credit, Rick. She picked really pretty men, and she liked all types, apparently. Also, she hit on me while she was being escorted out by police."

"I see she was an equal opportunity employer."

My mouth dropped open. After spluttering for a moment, I replied, "I suppose she was. The last I saw of her, she was trying to seduce the cops."

"You've had an interesting day. I thought you would like to know that we are now officially in the same time zone. My dog and I have successfully infiltrated the United States with the appropriate documentation to reside here for business purposes."

"And what job position does your precious Annabel Lee hold?"

"Wrangler of Humans. It's a distinguished title."

"Humans is plural. How many humans is she currently wrangling?"

"Two. You and me. She's plotting how to

lure you into her furry clutches as we speak. Should I be truthful about the situation, she's asleep on the couch, as she had a very long flight. She was required to fly in cargo, much to my disgust, but she made it safe and sound. I made her crate as comfortable as possible within their standards. The couch belongs to your brother. There's something particularly naughty about talking to my friend's missing sister while lounging in his living room with my dog. I'll be headed to New York tomorrow, after we've both had a chance to recover from the flight."

"Taunt him for me."

"If I taunt him, he will know I'm actively communicating with you."

"I don't see a problem with this, Rick. You're going to have to convince me there's an issue with this."

"I see you're still feeling rather ruthless towards your brother."

"Yes. You could convince me to relent should he acquire me a puppy, one who gets along well with your Annabel Lee. A puppy would go a long way towards convincing me he isn't an asshole."

"Oh, he's an asshole. I had a few words with him about his treatment of you upon arrival. He was appropriately chastened, but I'm not of the opinion you should let him off easily."

"But a puppy, Rick. I'd forgive him for a puppy. I really would." I had finally reached the level of adulthood I could have a puppy. I could have before, had I been a little more willing to defy everyone's expectations.

"Why don't I go to a shelter and introduce Annabel Lee to some puppies, and then I will tell you where the shelter is so you can meet the candidates? Then you can pick a puppy that gets along with you and Annabel Lee."

"This sounds like a horrible way to make a long-term arrangement for a new family member, truth be told."

"But you'll be happy, Annabel Lee will get to meet puppies, and I will be able to lure you to a known location. I will, upon your selection of a puppy, secure your person. I'll even be a gentleman and permit you to drive your vehicle and new puppy to my chosen location."

Had I not figured out Fredrick classified as a ridiculously nice person who wouldn't actually do that, I might've worried. Well, having invited him to do just that alleviated most of my concerns on that front, too. I grinned over his honesty regarding his tactic to locate me. "That might have worked if you hadn't exposed yourself," I confessed.

"I will take you on a search for the perfect puppy as soon as I locate you."

"That's a good incentive for me to accidentally reveal my location. That has to count as some form of cheating."

"I suspect you're only saying that because

you've reached your threshold for absurdity for one day."

I eyed the box of invoices, one of which involved sex toys. "You're probably right."

"Don't spoil your location, and if you would like to get yourself a puppy, ask to be matched with one that likes other dogs, as you want your puppy to go on play dates with other dogs. That will solve your problem. The only person Annabel Lee doesn't like right now is your brother, and that's only because we're arguing."

"It's okay if you let my brother off the hook, Rick. I'm sure he'll want to cry on your shoulder before I'm done with him."

"I'll keep that in mind."

SOMEHOW, I survived my first day of work. I spent most of my time organizing files and getting a feel for what I would be doing on Tuesday, which would dump me straight into the depths of hell. My tentative explorations had already revealed discrepancies, as Miss Meltrew's collection of handsome men kept immaculate records of their meetings, along with a spreadsheet dedicated to received, expected, and missing invoices. The missing invoices intrigued me, as they included the expected amount, when it should have been paid, how long overdue it was, and the advertising campaign the invoice was associated with. In some cases, the missing invoice sheet also included when an invoice exceeded the expected expenditures.

Before I left to meet with my real estate agent, I went to my new boss's office and knocked on his door.

"Enter," Garret answered.

I slipped inside his office, which could fit two of mine with room to spare. "I've done my initial evaluation of the files I received, and should the gentlemen at that firm be fired for their manager's actions, you would be wise to hire and get them certified. They have exceptional record-keeping skills. They've basically done the majority of my work for me, as they have an entire spreadsheet dedicated to suspicious invoices, missing invoices, or invoices that exceeded expected or allowed spend. I'm going to start the complete audit researching those invoices and see where it takes me tomorrow, but I think this is going to be a great deal easier than anyone believed. Maybe they aren't accountants, but they kept their records organized."

"I can tell when an accountant is happy, and you sound happy with that development. Good. Honestly, we'd been pitched a hell job, but if you can finish that job early, there's a lot of work for you to do, including the McCarthy file. I don't think you'll have much difficulty with the McCarthy file, but with their household changes and the legal elements involved, they wanted a good accountant to audit their finances. Are you willing to do paid overtime on the weekend? They work at legal firms on weekday hours, so it's difficult for them to make appointments."

"Assuming I'm not moving, I can handle a weekend appointment to help them. Tomorrow, I'll have a better idea of how long it will take to do a complete audit. If it takes longer than expected, I'll handle their audit on the weekends as well. A month of extra work isn't a problem. I can get settled afterwards."

"I don't want to stress you too much."

"You're certainly paying me well enough to deal with the stress, Garret."

He chuckled. "We have noticed well-paid employees tend to perform better and are more willing to deal with the shitstorms when they roll on it."

"Is anyone paid well enough to handle a shitstorm?"

"I'm assuming plumbers. That's part of their daily job, isn't it?"

I shuddered. "With that in mind, I don't think plumbers are paid enough."

"Same with the guys who clean the sewers or septic tanks. Wondering how they get into that sort of work keeps me up at night. I can't even imagine what it's like doing maintenance on a sewer line."

"I'm starting to think I'm going to need a puppy to help me sleep at night now."

"I have a cat and a dog, and they own my

bed. They allow me to sleep on it sometimes, but only if I serve as their bed warmer and offer them affection. Should I fail to pet them sufficiently, they try to sleep on my face. My dog is a golden retriever, and she really might suffocate me one of these days."

"Do you ever bring your dog to work?"

"I'll bring her tomorrow, and I'll ask my sister if she would mind me taking one of the puppies off her hands for tomorrow. She breeds Korean Jindos, and she has a litter that'll be going on sale soon. They're not all that popular here, but they're loyal, smart, and classify as guard dogs. They're pretty active, but they love interacting with people and animals. They're really trainable. I'll probably get a Jindo after Keekee passes away. Keekee is pretty old."

"Your dog is named Keekee?"

"My daughter named her, and she wasn't quite clear on the differences between cats and dogs when we brought Keekee home."

"Keekee as in kitty?"

"Yep. She now knows better, but she'll call the cat our puppy just to screw with me and my wife. Lindy is now a teenager, and she's determined to drive us mad."

Huh. Garret was a lot older than he looked. "Obviously, I need to take lessons on how to judge someone's age by their appearance, as I never would have imagined you are old enough to have a teenaged daughter."

"Good genes. My wife enjoys my youthful

appearance. I also enjoy telling our friends how I got caught by a cougar."

I bit my lip so I wouldn't laugh. "It sounds like you have a lovely wife. I'd love to meet the puppy, but I was figuring I'd adopt from a shelter."

"I'll let my sister know. She volunteers at the local shelters, and if she can find a good animal, she'd be happy to help you out. What are you looking for in a dog?"

"He or she must love other dogs, as I have planned dates with a friend's dog. I'd also like to bring my dog to the office. I'll need to be trained on how to be a good dog owner, though. My friend's dog is named Annabel Lee, and she's big, white, and fluffy, so I want my dog to be able to get along well with her."

"I'm absolutely positive she could help you out with that. I'll talk to her, and if she has a suitable puppy to keep you company tomorrow, I'll bring it in."

Good paycheck, easy access to dogs, and a flexible boss made my new job ideal, but I couldn't help but wonder what ugliness the beautiful veneer hid. I'd learned that lesson well enough from Amy.

Beautiful things often hid thorns, and only a fool would fully trust in picture-perfect opportunities. It hadn't stopped me from being a fool and taking the dive into my new work, but only time would tell the truth. To hide my worries, I grinned. "That sounds great."

"The rest of the office is going to love you tomorrow, because knowing my sister? She'll send the entire pack in with me, hoping to find good homes for everybody. As far as breeders go, she's a weird one."

"She is? How so?"

"She doesn't care who buys her dogs as long as they're going to good homes. If you don't plan to show them, she'll take care of having them fixed, and if you do plan to show them, she'll help coach you on how to do it. The shows only allow intact dogs. She keeps the best of the dogs to continue her bloodlines, but she tries to get dogs in from Korea to partner with hers to keep the bloodlines as true and healthy as possible. Since there aren't as many Jindos in America as there are golden retrievers or other popular breeds, it can be hard. Only mainland dogs can be exported out of Korea. They're pretty territorial, but my sister works hard to train them to be territorial under direction. It can make owning one a challenge, but they're a fun breed. My sister is one of the few registered breeders in the United States, and she only has them because her husband is Korean, and he imported his dog when he moved here. It's really interesting trying to prevent inbreeding with their dogs because there are so few of them in the United States. Unless showing, all of her males are fixed except one, and the males are sent to live with a reputable breeder to prevent accidental breeding. Usually, they're fixed."

I recognized an enthusiast when I saw one, and I found it fascinating my boss had a passion for his sister's work. "That's amazing."

"I think so, too. I thought it was really weird she wanted to breed dogs, but once I met her dogs, I couldn't help but fall in love with them. I'll probably take one of her males after Keekee passes and show him in case another breeder with a different bloodline shows up in the United States and wants to cross lines with my sister's. Intact males are a handful to handle, but it's worth it to preserve the breed here. They aren't shown at the most prestigious shows, but that's how these things go. These dogs aren't good around cats or kittens, though. They have a reputation with small animals."

I grimaced. "They like to hunt them?"

"They are hunting dogs. It's in their nature. But as long as you're aware of the dog's limitations and strengths, they're fantastic animals. But they're considered primitive. I tell potential owners if they can't handle a husky, they probably can't handle a Jindo."

"I'd feel pretty terrible if my dog killed some small animal," I admitted.

"And that's okay. A Jindo probably isn't for you, then. My sister can keep an eye out at the shelter for a good dog that'll fit better with you. I'll still bring in one of the puppies for a meet and greet. It'll be fun, and it'll make your workday nicer. You have viewings tonight, right?"

"I do." I checked my phone, which informed me I needed to leave within ten minutes to get out the door in time. "We're checking out five units tonight, as far as I know. There was the possibility of more if the agent could find anything."

"Keep me in the loop. As soon as you have a signed lease and move-in date, we'll arrange for the movers to bring your stuff to your new home."

"Thanks, Garret."

"Glad to help. Drive safe and let me know how it goes."

I took that as my cue to leave, exchanged pleasantries, and headed off to the next leg of my adventure into New York City and everything it had to offer.

TEN

That was a cockroach, wasn't it?

MY REAL ESTATE AGENT, Margaret Donner, met me outside of her office a thirty-minute drive from work thanks to traffic. All things considered, it might have been faster to walk. Rather than contain or straighten her hair like many black women did in professional environments, she styled hers in an afro, and I appreciated her lack of conformity to society's standards. I held out my hand, offered a smile, and said, "I'm Hope. It's a pleasure to meet you. I love your hair. It suits you."

She grinned in return, giving me a firm handshake. "I like what you've done with your car. Garret tells me you're from the land of politicians?"

"Unfortunately. Give me the bad news first. How bad is the rent going to be?"

"It'll be bad but affordable. As affordable as Manhattan gets, that is. I have a selection of apartments to visit today in the same area. I haven't been to the first we're going to before, but it is the cheapest of the lot. I don't have high hopes for it, truth be told. The pictures were misleading."

"Misleading? How were they misleading?"

"There is no picture of the bathroom, the kitchen pictures are taken at odd angles, which implies there is something they don't want prospective renters to see, and there's a lot of missing information on the unit. It's a new listing, so sometimes information gets missed, but the price was good, the neighborhood is pretty safe, and it's somewhat close to your work, so I thought it would be a good candidate to look at. My favorite is the second unit we'll be looking at, which is in walking distance of your work, has an underground garage, good security, and a good view. I've been told it's small, but it's tolerable for one person. That said, the landlord didn't tell me the square footage, and his definition of small doesn't necessarily match mine. It allows pets. Garret had mentioned you might wish an animal but don't have one yet."

"That's right. I'm thinking about a dog."

"I don't know if the other units I want to show you today allow dogs, but we'll find out when we talk with the leasing office. Some do, some don't. They change the rules all of the time. And some that don't necessarily allow dogs will if the price is right."

"And the ones that do are going to charge me a fortune in deposits and a monthly rate to have one," I muttered.

"That's usually how it goes. I'm hoping that if I show you a good spread of apartments, you'll be able to set your expectations for the rest of the viewings. I've found most people new to the area get a shock when seeing the apartments for the first time. Most are small and expensive. The penthouses that are showcased in the movies cost millions and are hard to get a hold of. The economy matters, though. A few went up for sale recently, though one sold in a matter of hours."

"Is that normal?"

"When it's on the top floor of one of Manhattan's premier buildings, it is. The last time it was on the market, it lasted less than a day."

Wow. "Well, I don't have millions to spend on a home, so I guess show me what else Manhattan has to offer."

On the drive to the first apartment complex, Margaret regaled me with cautionary tales of the city, including the classic warning to be aware of yellow ice on the sidewalks, a common enough problem near my old place. According to her, it would be more of a problem in Manhattan, especially as there tended to be a lot of dog owners who would take their pooches to the nearest place with grass available.

"Watching where you walk seems to be important here," I said, chuckling at the thought something as mundane as walking down the street could be a shoe hazard. "I've heard things about the subway. Terrible things."

"Once, a dude in a speedo decided to make himself sandwiches on the Q. A client wanted to see what the commute to his potential house would be, so we did a run to his work and back. Don't ask what he did with the sandwich. I'm scarred for life from that one."

"Did the incident show up in newspapers like the New Yorker version of Florida Man?"

"If only. No, he just decided the best place for his sandwich was in his speedo."

I opened my mouth and blinked, unable to think of a single reason why someone would make a sandwich only to stuff it in his underwear. "Did your client buy the house?"

"Yes, but he swore he would drive to work, and that was only after having to take the L to test what his commute would be if he picked his second choice. The L is a disaster of a ride on a good day, and it's in dire need of an overhaul. There's been talks about shutting it down and repairing it, but every time they go to do it, people freak out because they need the L to get to work, and there aren't enough busses to cover the load. When they do shut it down, it'll be for two years, and it'll make traffic that much worse. It's bad enough."

"So, you're basically telling me I probably want to pick a place close to work."

"If you can afford it, and I were in your

shoes, I would pick the more expensive place close to work. If you don't mind a bit of a hike, all of these places are close to your work or a short bus ride away. All the complexes have a bus stop nearby, and there's one right outside of your office building."

I could work with that. "Anything else I should know?"

"Read the lease carefully. Every landlord does things a little differently, and there are some clauses that'll drive you insane—or cost you a fortune if you try to break your lease early. One client didn't listen to me when I warned her she'd have a huge bill if she terminated the lease, and she had to pay out almost ten thousand to the landlord. She tried to take it to court, and she lost, too. Leases are legally binding, and landlords will take you for everything you own when they can. So, you have to play smarter than them. If you're aware and willing to pay the fines for leaving early, that's one thing."

"That's good to know. I was up for renewal when I left anyway, so I just notified my landlord and packed my bags."

"That's how it should be for everyone, but real estate here can be brutal."

"It sounds like it."

It took Margaret twenty minutes to find a parking spot several blocks away from the apartment, which I viewed as a bad sign. "Does this place include indoor parking?"

"If you want to pay three hundred a month for it, yes."

I winced at the amount. "I'll definitely want to see the parking spot before I sign anything on that one."

"Smart woman. The next unit I'm going to show you is more reasonable; the first spot comes included with your rent, and you can get a second for two hundred a month extra. The garage has security there at all times, so your car will be safe. There's a guard at the gate, and someone checks on the vehicles every hour. Your rent is expensive, but the landlords make sure the building is secure."

I could work with that. "What's the downside for the second place?"

"The price. This is the cheapest I could find, the next one is among one of the more expensive units on my list. I wanted to show you both ends of the spectrum."

"This is going to be an adventure, isn't it?"

"Oh, yes."

WHOEVER OWNED the disconcertingly old brick-faced apartment complex liked cranking the heat, and an old, rusted indoor waterfall transformed the lobby into a sauna. Within three steps of entering the building, I sweated.

Then, because my day was out to kill me, a

cockroach smacked into my face. The flying demon bug smacked into the wall next, and without missing a beat, Margaret put an end to the winged menace with one smack of her briefcase, which she cleaned with a tissue. "Heat and humidity spell palmetto bugs, and it seems this landlord is keeping some as pets. Lovely."

"That was a cockroach, wasn't it?"

"Yep."

"It flew."

"Yep."

"As I'm not usually a quitter, I will see this apartment, but there's no way in hell I'm renting something with lobby cockroaches."

"I can't say I blame you. I've seen worse. Unfortunately. The leasing office should be this way." Margaret gestured to a glass door at the other end of the lobby.

"Does it make me less of a person if I'm afraid of what we'll find in the unit?"

"As I'm afraid of what we'll find in the unit, not at all."

That was something. We went into the leasing office, where we were greeted by an older man in worn jeans and a t-shirt that had seen better days. I assumed the landlord wasn't paying the guy jack shit for his work. As a general rule, I tried to be kind to those who were underpaid for what they did. It wasn't their fault they weren't valued, and why would anyone give their best when they weren't valued? I bet he couldn't afford to pay much for business clothes. Hell, I hated having to pay for business clothes. My agent introduced herself, and without much more than a nod, the man retrieved a set of keys and waved for us to follow him.

I wanted to go back to my hotel and hide, but I refused to be beaten by a scary apartment building.

Instead of taking the elevator, the leasing office employee guided us up three flights of stairs, which creaked in places and showed signs of crumbling in others. At the rate my heartbeat was going, I wouldn't need to exercise for a week.

Under no circumstances would I run away.

The leasing office employee grunted, opened a battered door at the end of a hallway in dire need of a coat of paint, and gave the keys to Margaret. "Bring them back when you're finished."

Margaret nodded, and he left without a single care in the world. At the rate my mouth hung open, a cockroach might fly into it. I snapped my teeth together at that thought. "I'm scared," I confessed.

"Me, too. It's never a good sign when they leave the keys with me and run away. That means there's something horrible inside."

I straightened my back, lifted my chin, and pushed the door open. The carpeted main area seemed sane enough, with the window boasting a view of the neighboring building. I worried the tan would become white with a good washing, but I could hire someone to fix that disaster if I could bear the thought of being ambushed by flying cockroaches whenever I came home, which I couldn't.

"Too cheap to replace the carpet after a tenant left," Margaret observed, sticking her foot into the apartment far enough to toe the carpet. "I'm not even sure what color it's supposed to be."

I drew in a deep breath, wrinkled my nose at a rather musky odor, and took the dive, stepping through the door to discover what other horrors waited for me. To my immediate right, a bathroom invaded the kitchen, and the toilet, standing out in the open not far from the stove and refrigerator, stunned me so much I pointed at it, unable to say a word.

Margaret's eyes widened, and she covered her mouth with her hand. "Oh. Holy Mary, Mother of God."

That was one way to put it. "Why is the toilet in the kitchen, Margaret?" On closer look, what could only be a ceiling shower promised to rain hell dangerously close to high-powered appliances. "Why is the shower in the kitchen? What's going on here? Why would anyone do this? This is wrong."

I wanted to run back to her office, get in my car, hide in the back, grab a comfortable blanket, and suck my thumb for a while. I didn't even care what sucking my thumb would do to my teeth. Biting my lip, I retrieved my phone, took a picture of the disaster waiting to happen, and dared to step closer to investigate.

Everything went well until I reached the stove. The floor squished, and before I could adjust my weight, my foot punched through the cheap linoleum. I yelped, went down like a ton of bricks, and somehow kept my cell from taking flight at the cost of my knees and ankle, which twisted as the hole refused to release me.

Margaret spewed curses that'd make a pastor faint, dropped her briefcase, crouched beside me, and went for my ankle, grabbing my leg to hold it still while surveying the damage. "Your foot's caught on the flooring. Give me a sec, and I'll get you out of there."

"It's wet, Margaret."

"It looks like their creative bathroom scheme has sprung a rather unfortunate leak."

Gross. "I'm looking at the bright side. I didn't break my phone." I braced my weight on one palm and a throbbing knee, holding the device out to her. "Please take photographs of this monstrosity."

She obeyed. "I'm taking a few pictures, too. I'll call the front desk and have them document their shitty maintenance. I'm going to hold these jackasses liable for this bullshit."

With her help, I freed my foot and stood. My ankle made its unhappiness known, but I'd sprained my ankle enough over the years to recognize how I'd managed to hurt myself. Sighing, I took a picture of my foot near the hole, and as I felt sorry for myself, I texted it to Rick with a notice a New Yorker headline would be in the works.

Within moments, my phone rang. Blinking, I answered, "Hello?"

"What happened?" Rick demanded.

"Wait, you're awake?"

"I'm at your brother's place, Hope. He's glaring at me, as I told him I was talking to you, just as you requested. He looks like he wants to try to take the phone, but Annabel Lee growls whenever he approaches. I'm not in the mood to correct her about it. I'm not in Japan anymore, although if I were, it'd be nine in the morning there."

Oh, right. He had been crashing out on my brother's couch with his dog. "I forgot. This may have triggered memory loss. Sorry. I'm about to send you another picture. You can help me figure out the headline for this one. I'm apartment searching." Careful to keep from hanging up on him, I sent him the pictures of the bathroom-kitchen horror show. "There. I just sent it."

"Don't rent that apartment would be my first recommendation. What am I looking at?"

"The future electrocution of a tenant, who won't be me. The floor ate my foot."

"So I saw. Are you all right?"

"A mild sprain probably. I'll survive." I regarded the hole with a scowl. "You can show my brother the pictures, and you can tell him if he hadn't been an asshole, I wouldn't have put my foot through the floor of some dingy apartment building. As my brother is there, is his wife there, too?"

"She's off visiting some of her uncles north of my current location. I'll show him the pictures. Anything else you'd like to get off your chest?"

"Give me a second. Hey, Margaret? What's the rent on this place?"

"Just under three thousand a month," she reported. "It has higher than normal square footage for this area."

"It also has a bathroom in the kitchen," I muttered. "That's just highway robbery."

She nodded. "It really is."

"Sorry about that, Rick. Apparently, this wonderful place costs just under three thousand a month. A cockroach flew in my face when we got here. I'm going to the nearest pharmacy, buying a gallon of hand sanitizer and a cheap pair of shoes, and disinfecting my foot. Give me a good headline for that. I'll call you back in a few hours, assuming I survive my apartment search."

Before Rick could get a word in edgewise, I hung up, silenced my phone, and shoved it into my purse. Rick's warning that Amy was north of his location bothered me. "Where is the nearest pharmacy?"

"Right down the street not far from where I'm parked. Will your ankle be all right?"

"If not, I know exactly who I'm sending the bill to."

"Should it come to that, I'll be happy to stand as a witness and provide all documentation from our scheduled appointment." Margaret huffed and glared at the rotten hole in the floor. "Would you prefer to wait in my car while I have a discussion with the gentleman in the leasing office? I can bring it around and find another place to park."

While I appreciated the courtesy, I shook my head. "Thank you, but I'll take my chances with the flying cockroaches in the lobby. At least there'll be another witness if he tries to do something stupid."

"He won't, not unless he's been hitting up some drugs or something, but I doubt it. He looked disinterested more than anything else. He could be stoned out of his mind, though. Stoners are mostly harmless."

Moving to New York was turning out to be more of an adventure than I'd expected, and all I could do was pray the next apartment wouldn't try to kill me, too.

AS PROMISED, the next apartment complex was located near my work, and it was a mix of apartments and condominiums, with the condominiums taking up the upper ten floors of the skyscraper and the apartments taking up ten floors beneath that. Several businesses occupied the lower floors, with a clubhouse offering a limited buffer between the commercial and residential floors. To give me a better feel of the area, Margaret walked me around the building, showing me where the grocery store, coffee shop, and bookstore were before giving me a rundown of the building's history. "I didn't know they mixed buildings like this."

"In New York, anything's possible with enough money. This building is an oddity, but it works out well. The landlord was required to install soundproofing between the residential and commercial floors, and the commercial floors have certain restrictions and a different zoning than the residential floors, but it works. There's odd stuff like this all over Manhattan, but they're all odd in different ways. Don't ask."

"Oh! Like those stores in the basement of townhouses I saw driving in?"

"Exactly. You'll see a lot of that here. This building is pretty nice, as the landlord keeps everything maintained. Pricy, but you get good service for what you pay. There is a commercial entry on the other side of the building, but this is just for residents. Remember that condominium I told you about? It's on the top floor of this building. The penthouse owners have their own entrance and a private garage, too."

"That is really cool. Can't let the riffraff mingle with the rich and famous, right?"

Margaret chuckled. "Right. The apartment entry is this way. The condo entry is right around the corner, so sometimes you'll cross paths with your other neighbors, but that won't be often. They usually use their private garage and elevator rather than share space with the apartment dwellers. But don't feel too badly about that. You get a similar security team and concierge. You'll have to check in any guests or have them on an allowed list, as it's a part of the requirements for leasing here. This property is touted as one of the safest in the area, and they do a background check of all tenants. A criminal record won't bar your application, but they are rather picky about who they will accept. They will not allow anyone who has been convicted of a violent crime of any sort to rent a unit, and being found guilty of a violent crime is grounds for lease termination."

"That's legal?"

"It is. The Federal Fair Housing Act doesn't bar landlords from denying tenants guilty of violent crimes. A landlord can't realistically bar someone with a single conviction from a decade ago necessarily, but they have a lot of leeway if they think the tenant might bring violence to other tenants in the building, as the landlord does have a base responsibility to provide a safe environment for residents. He's particularly strict regarding domestic violence, and he has evicted tenants for violence to their partner in the past. That's actually why this apartment opened. The tenant beat his girlfriend, and he was evicted as a risk to others and for breaking the terms of lease, which strictly bars violence on grounds. He provided an attorney for the young woman, as the incident happened in an elevator and had been reported by security."

Damn. "That's terrible. Is she okay?"

"She's fine. The landlord moved her to a different complex he owns and has made a renting arrangement for her, as she was the boyfriend's dependent."

"But why were you told about this?"

"There's some repair work that will need to be done, as the resident decided to take his fist to the wall after it was over. The unit just opened. It hasn't even been listed yet, but I'd given him a call to see if he had apartments available, and as we've worked together before, he offered an advanced viewing. That does mean there'll be some renovation work right before you move in, but he'll work to your timetable or around you as needed."

I could handle some renovation work being done, especially as I'd be working long hours for a while. "That won't be a problem."

"That's great. This could be a really good home for you. It should be large enough for you to be able to have two dogs or three cats. He limits to two dogs because they tend to need more room than cats do. There is a rooftop dog park available for your use as well. That's shared with the condominium owners. One of the perks is a dog walker if you need to leave your dog at home, too. They'll come by three times a day to walk your pets. You can even get them to play with your cats. It's thirty dollars a day for that service. They'll even give your pets medications if needed, included in the fee."

My brows shot up at this. "Is this a pet heaven?"

"Basically. Pet owners love this place. The landlord? He runs an animal shelter as a charity. It's a no-kill shelter, and he only euthanizes if the animal absolutely cannot be saved."

I hadn't met the man, but I loved him already. "Who is this man? He sounds too good to be true."

Margaret laughed. "Oh, he's an interesting fellow. His name is Jacob, he's half Italian, and he cracks jokes about not paying any protection rackets because his uncle is a crime lord and likes him the best. Nobody knows if he's serious, but nobody cares, either."

I bit my lip so I wouldn't giggle. "That's different."

"It sure is. Just don't let him invite you to his office for a drink. He has one on the clubhouse floor, and that's how you get drunk and need security to escort you home. It won't be the first or last time a tenant has needed to be helped back to their home after being invited to the leasing office."

Okay. I could work with that. "How does one get an invite, and should I bring a bottle of wine as a gift?"

"I see this idea doesn't bother you in the slightest."

"Margaret, he sounds absolutely *hilarious*. I'd be drunk and laughing my ass off. What's there not to like?"

"I never thought an honest warning about the perils of being invited to the landlord's office would be a selling point," she admitted.

"What can I say? It's been a long life."

ELEVEN

Sensible landlords exist?

GLASS, steel, and marble collided in a mix of new and old, and the pair of security guards keeping an eye on the lobby would have gotten hired at Chippendales without question. Unlike the first apartment building, they wore classic suits, the kind my brother liked as they made him feel professional and worth his keep. That kind of suit had lured Amy right to Mat's doorstep, I bet. Mat's friendship with Rick, who seemed like the kind to have millions, had likely factored, too.

Maybe Amy wasn't a gold digger, but we wouldn't be playing sisters anytime soon, not after her stint as a bridezilla and losing so much of my brother's money, money he couldn't really afford to throw away for nothing.

We didn't have a million bucks, but my brother certainly looked it when he decided he wanted to impress somebody. Sometimes, I wondered if Mat's tendency to make friends with the rich and famous had drawn Amy to him. If his wife expected a life of riches and leisure, she'd be in for a nasty surprise.

He'd only had the money for the wedding because he'd worked hard to save for it. I'd always found it charming he'd wanted a fairytale wedding as much as most women. Despite everything, I hoped it would be a fairytale marriage rather than the prelude to a nightmare. Maybe Amy would change. Maybe she wouldn't.

Mat would do everything he could to turn any nightmares into fairytales. That was what Mat did when he got backed into a corner. When he got it into his head to be ruthless, he could take that to extremes as well.

His next move would be to recruit our parents to do his dirty work, and I had a harder time telling them no. They'd taken us in when no one else would, and they'd kept us together. I remembered being told there were good chances we'd be separated. Too many families had only wanted one child or a younger child. I would've been easier to adopt than my brother, as I'd still been baby-cute and well-behaved, where Mat had understood our parents had died and they wouldn't be coming back. If we had other blood relatives, none of them had cared enough to even meet us.

The entry to the apartment complex would stir a lot of memories every time I stepped through the doors, but after a moment of thought, I decided I appreciated the reminders of everything I'd gained and lost over the years.

"I'll show you the lobby floor first, which has some amenities for guests. After we take the tour, we'll meet with the representative. I don't know who we'll get. Sometimes, the owner decides he wants to meet the tenants at the viewing, and since this one isn't quite ready for habitation, we might see him today." Margaret gestured to the far wall, which had a bank of elevators. "You can't see them well from here, but there's a doorway back there."

She waved at the security guards, who gave her a nod and a smile.

"Do you come here a lot?"

"With surprising frequency. The condominiums are in high demand, and when they sell faster than my clients can buy, they often ask to see the apartments because they like the building. Because Jacob treats the apartments with as much care as he treats the condos, he will make arrangements to have a prospective future owner rent from him until there's an opening at one of his buildings. He just bought another complex not far from here that he's fixing up to be half apartments and half condos. If he follows this model, he'll put in an office complex below the units. That'll take work on the zoning, but he runs a tight operation and rarely has issues with the rental board. That's a good thing for you. He does raise rent yearly, but his increases are reasonable. He doesn't want to lose good tenants. He'll do the max increases for tenants who break his rules, though."

"Sensible landlords exist?"

My real estate agent laughed. "Shockingly, yes. So, the lobby floor has a few interesting offerings you might like. First, if you've notified the front desk you're having a guest coming to visit you, security will let them into the lounge, where they can grab a drink, watch television, or just enjoy the fireplace. Not all apartments or condominiums have fireplaces, so residents will come and enjoy the fire, especially in the middle of winter."

"There are apartments with fireplaces here?"

"I don't know if the unit we're visiting today has a fireplace, but some of them do, yes. It costs an extra two hundred a month for the fireplace, as the extra rent goes to specifically maintaining your fireplace. You also get a supply of wood or slow-burning logs as a part of the rent. If you go the slow-burning log route, you'll get enough to burn one log a day as part of your rent."

"No kidding?"

"No kidding. He buys them at a major discount and distributes them to residents, as he finds it allows him to control the amount burned. He'll even help provide and store the wood, as he is very picky about what sort of firewood comes into the building. He does a lot of work to keep pests out of the building.

He even will have security come and remove spiders. He has them taken outside or to other places spiders are encouraged to live rather than in the units."

Unable to help myself, I laughed. "My rent will include spider removal?"

"He hates killing innocent wildlife, even spiders. Jacob's a weird one, but he's a good man."

"It sounds like it. Just hit me with the damage. What is the rent going to cost me a month?"

"I was pitched $6,202.02, but it's negotiable due to the damage in the unit. He usually charges a little higher for the units, but it's a reasonable rate for what you're getting. He's all about making the rent worth the bill. Don't get me wrong, he'll be making a tidy profit off you, but he prefers when his tenants feel they're somewhat getting their money's worth. Jacob likes the number two, and he makes sure it's present at least once in every number he's involved with. I've seen him lower invoices just so he could have a two in the bill. As I said, he's a weird one."

Margaret led me to the elevator bank, and she tapped a number into a keypad. While the intercom activated, the door buzzed and unlocked. "If you forget your card key to get in here, they'll let you in with a code or escort you themselves. I have a code since I'm here so often doing tours with prospective buyers."

Beyond the door, a luxurious lounge filled with couches, a fireplace, a full bar and a bartender, and two pool tables filled a sleek white-painted room with dark hardwood floors and stone accents. "I could just move in here, right?"

She laughed. "That's what most say when they see this. Jacob set up an entire pool hall upstairs because these tables got used so much. The bar in here is pretty cheap, too; Jacob only charges at cost for the drinks, but the bartenders keep a close eye on intoxication levels. If you feel a need to get drunk, tell the bartender why. They'll make sure you make it back to your unit safely. Jacob is all about making sure his residents are secure."

"Okay. What's wrong with this place? I mean beyond having rent that will cost me more than six thousand a month."

"That's the downside. The rent is lethal."

"How much extra will it be for my dog?"

"Good question. I did mention you were interested in pets, so it may have included the pet rent. We'll find out when we talk to the representative. Can I tempt you into a drink?"

"If I'm going to be signing a lease with rent that much, I'll need one," I muttered.

She laughed. "We'll be here for more than an hour, so let's get something to calm your nerves. Hell, I need one after that last unit. Is your ankle doing all right?"

"It's doing okay. I'll be limping for a while, but it feels like a sprain. I've gotten those enough times to recognize what they feel like. I'll take it easy tonight and the rest of the week, and it should be fine."

"How does a Cosmo sound to you?"

That would work. If a Cosmo couldn't turn my day around, little would. "I'm game."

"Excellent. You play pool?"

I eyed the table. "I do now, apparently."

"I'll get us some sticks and we'll do a round. The representative will likely come get us from here, as the bartender will tell them we're having a drink and playing a game."

"Is the bartender also security?"

"Basically." Margaret went to get our drinks, and I hit the nearest table, racking the balls and setting them up for our game. I'd played enough times with my brother and his friends to hold my own, and I'd even won a few of the more competitive games. I liked math, I liked geometry, and I enjoyed the satisfying thunk of the balls hitting each other. By the time Margaret returned with our drinks, I had everything ready.

The bartender brought over the cues, a bridge, and chalk. "Have a good game, ladies," he said, lining them up against the wall. "Should you move here, there's a good pool shop a few blocks down the way, and you can get your own cues."

"Thanks. I'll keep that in mind." I lifted my glass to him in a toast.

"I see you've played before. Or you've

been put to work setting up games for people in the past." Margaret set her drink on the nearby table and pulled a quarter out of her purse. "Flip for break. Call it."

I nodded, and when she gave the coin a toss, I picked heads.

Tails won, and rubbing her hands together, my real estate agent grabbed a cue and went to work.

The last time I'd been run around the table, my brother had gotten it into his head I had no business getting a single shot in, and Margaret must have taken lessons from him. With systematic ruthlessness, she sank every last ball, and she took her time with the eight to make it clear she knew what she was about.

Damn. I wanted to be like Margaret if I ever grew up.

I eyed the table, chalked my cue, and gave a nod to the rack. "I see how this is, Margaret. If you're half as ruthless on price negotiations, I'm hiring you when I buy a house. Running the table is just mean on the opening round."

"I prefer allowing the competition to know exactly what she's in for. To be fair, I play this a lot. I couldn't help myself."

I chuckled. "Rack it. My turn."

I'd run my brother around the table once, and I meant to give Margaret a taste of her own medicine if I could. It'd been a while, but as long as I got a good break, I could make it happen, assuming the break didn't bust me and create a bad setup for a run.

A little competition and a lot of motivation did me a world of good when playing pool, and I'd played enough I could goose serious players who underestimated me. Running the table took a lot of skill, and I'd spent a few too many hours trying to learn the trick of it so I could put my brother in his place in front of his friends if he got too uppity.

The break favored me, and if I played the table just right, I'd only have to do one damned jump draw to run the table. Damn it. I'd learned jumps to spite my brother and his billiards buddies, but I'd never tried it in a serious game before. I did a walk around the table and turned to the bartender. "Hey. Do you allow jumps on your tables?"

Instead of replying, he bent over and retrieved a new cue from below the bar and walked it over. "Try not to damage the felt. These are the only tables we allow trick shots, as we replace the felt every other month. There's no jumps on the upstairs tables unless you're cleared by the boss and have the right cue."

Sweet. Life was looking good, and I accepted the jump cue, setting it aside until I needed it. "Thanks."

"Anytime."

I toasted Margaret, took a drink, and set my Cosmo aside, giving myself a good shake before I took my time and went to work.

As I'd planned, the jump draw happened at the end of my run, and if I did it just right, my cue ball would be in position for a light tap of the eight to win me the game. If I did it beyond perfection and called it, I might even be able to finish right off the draw. While I played, my real estate agent watched, her brows raised right up to her hairline.

Hell. I only lived once, and it was better to fail than to not try at all. "Jump to the six corner pocket and draw to the eight side pocket," I announced, tapping the intended pockets. The damned obstacle course of striped balls could easily make a mess of my attempt, but fate and geometry had decreed if I wanted to finish in one fell swoop, I'd have to make the jump for better or worse.

"If you make that shot, I'm taking you out to dinner and introducing you to the operator of my league."

"You play league?"

"Yeah. I'm a member of the American Pool Association. I play the amateur circuits, but I've had an invite to pro."

"Well, I'd hope you'd be invited to play pro with your ability to run the table."

"Maybe you should be the one who is invited to play pro. You're skunking me."

I laughed at that. "Unless the stars align and the universe pays me back in karma for spraining my ankle in a bathroom-kitchen nightmare apartment, I'm going to miss this shot."

"Hope, you're trying the shot. This is the sort of play that professionals use during trick-shot demonstrations. If you get anywhere near making the shot, I'm calling it your victory. You even knew to ask if they allowed jumps on the table."

Well, that was something. "Missing could wreck the felt, and it looks like good felt."

"It's due to be replaced next week, so don't be shy," the bartender called out. "And if you make that shot, I'm buying you a drink myself."

Apparently, I could be bribed with alcoholic drinks. "You can even record my miss if you'd like as proof I'd tried."

The bartender grabbed his phone and took me up on my offer. "I'm Luke. Can I just say I hope I see more of you around here? We could always use another good player around."

"I see how it is. No pressure at all. All right, cue. Don't fail me now. I have a drink to win. I'm going to need alcohol to sign over six thousand a month."

My real estate agent laughed. "I know your salary figures. You can afford the six thousand a month. Your base salary fits your zone of comfort for rent payments, and while on the high end, it is in your proposed percentage bracket."

Oh, right. I'd been rather meticulous over providing her and Garret with my budget. I *could* afford the six thousand a month. I'd still grimace over the money spent, but the pool tables and at-cost drinks might make it worth my while. I'd be needing a stiff drink after the hell audit. "Margaret said I'd have to inform you why I'd be drinking, and can I say I'm an auditing accountant going over a hell job?"

"That sounds like you need two drinks and someone to drive you home afterwards," the bartender replied.

"Unfortunately, my car is parked at her work."

"Margie?"

"If you give someone the keys, they can bring the car back here. Won't be the first or last time Jacob's sent someone from security to fetch somebody's vehicle. I can drive someone back to your car if you drink too much."

Two drinks and a ride home after viewing apartments sounded like a plan if I could land the damned shot. I took another sip of my Cosmo to steady my nerves—or ensure I'd miss and be laughed right out of the lounge. Either worked. "After the day I've had, going to work hungover might be worth it."

"I'll call Garret and tell him the last unit attacked you, and that I'm responsible for the alcohol if you show up to work a little worse for wear."

Allies made the business world go round and round, and I toasted her with my glass before setting it aside and taking another walk around the table to make sure I picked my mark just right. Math was my friend. Ball spin wasn't, but as long as I calculated the trajectory and rotation just right, I could pull off the shot. I'd worked a table for hours once trying, damaging the felt beyond repair to learn it. I hadn't even felt bad about the felt; the owner had it scheduled for replacement and it'd already seen better days, and he hadn't minded me putting it out of its misery to convince his wife it really needed to be redone.

All delaying would do would be to make me more nervous, so I chucked my last fuck into the fireplace, grabbed the cue, and gave a few test strokes before I jumped the cue ball over the obnoxious striped balls, landing it at the six, which went into the pocket just as planned. Things went sideways when the ball drew back and cracked into the eight with a hell of a lot more force than I'd intended. My angle was good, and it went into its pocket as planned, but the cue bounced off the bank and created chaos on the table as it crashed into Margaret's balls and sent them scattering over the felt.

I held my breath, keeping an eye on the cue ball. If it dropped into a pocket, I lost. I didn't give a rat's ass what happened to the rest of the balls on the table, but damnit, I didn't want to lose because I'd gotten overenthusiastic.

The cue ball, along with the rest of Margaret's balls, remained on the felt where they belonged.

I grabbed my Cosmo and knocked it back. "And that's how it's done."

"Yeah, I'd say. Why aren't you playing professionally?"

I blinked at her. "That's an option? Really?"

"You ran me around the table and did a high-end trick shot to make it happen. Yeah, it's an option. Can you do that all the time, or did I get you on a good day?"

"I play with my brother and his friends, and sometimes, I like to win. But they're good, so I have to work to win. But most of the time, I cheerfully lose so they don't feel badly about themselves."

"Luke, can you send me a copy of that video?"

"Sure thing. I can probably get security to get a video of both games, too. I'll ask the boss."

"Please do."

An older man dressed in a clean-cut black suit, an Armani from the looks of it, with salt and peppered hair swept into the lounge, and he came armed with a bottle of wine and three glasses, which he held up in salute. "Margaret, my darling!"

"And that would be Jacob, armed with more alcohol." My real estate agent laughed and shrugged. "I'm going to need someone to drive me home, too, Luke. And to take us to the other viewings tonight. We'll probably need the alcohol to deal with those. They're on the lower end."

"You got it, Margie. Hey, boss man. They've got other viewings tonight, so you can't drink them completely under the table. The lady here just ran Margaret around the table and used a jump draw to do it."

"Please, call me Hope."

"And you're getting a discount on your rent for putting this evil woman in her place. It's a pleasure to meet you." Jacob put the wine and the glasses down on the table with our Cosmos, popped the cork, and tested a sip before pouring a round and handing me a glass. "You need a little wine before we see the unit. I was just up there, and they've started repairs, so it's more of a mess than I like, but I really wanted to give Margaret first crack at it, as she always brings over the nice tenants."

"You can give me my owed drinks another day, Luke, but I'll accept the offer of someone driving my car back to the hotel. It's been a day."

"You got it, Miss Hope."

"What's this about a jump draw?" Jacob asked.

Luke wasted no time showing his boss the video he'd taken of me making the shot, including the subsequent chaos on the table afterwards.

"In my defense, I hit the ball too hard, I

meant to nudge the eight in, and it was damned luck and luck alone that it actually worked."

"You made the shot, Hope. I couldn't," my real estate agent replied. "I wouldn't have even tried, because the last time I tried a jump shot, I ruined the felt, and it was the high-end tournament felt. I ended up paying out a thousand dollars to replace it. I didn't have to, as I had permission, but I felt guilty I'd busted the table. At least my thousand got next-day replacement."

"She barely left a scuff, and nobody is going to care about yet another scuff on this one," Luke replied. "That shot was something else, wasn't it? Margie ran her around the table, and this was Hope's revenge."

"I will bribe you to run every damned league player in my building around the table, Hope," the landlord announced.

I liked bribes, especially when the bribes involved playing a game I liked and could openly do well at. "What sort of bribe?"

"Free pet rent a year for each tourney player you run around the table."

"Any bonus points if I run them around the table and they did the break?"

"I'll figure something out. How often can you run someone around the table?"

"I've done it a few times. I usually target my brother when he annoys me, as there's nothing quite as enjoyable as running him around the table in front of his friends. I usually try to lose a few times to give a surprise factor, too."

Margaret burst into laughter. "You're a pool shark!"

After thinking about it, I realized I really was. "I don't take money for doing it, though. I just take payment in their pricked prides."

"That's just beautiful. What other tricks do you have up your sleeve? Do you play any other sports?"

"I like tennis, but I suck at it. I like to bowl, too, but I don't have anyone to teach me. I want to try fingertip bowling, but I don't know anyone who does it," I admitted.

"I have a bowling alley in the building several blocks away, and I can definitely find someone to teach you the finer points of bowling." Jacob took a sip of his wine. "Margaret told me you moved here from Washington?"

"Yes. I needed some fresh air, and New York has a lot of opportunities for auditing accountants. I just started my new job today, and I'm at a long-stay hotel down the street for the moment. This is really close to work."

"That would put you at the Cercson Investment Group building if you're an auditing accountant who works nearby. It's a ten-minute walk on a bad day. The drive is quick, since the garage lets out right onto the main street, but you'll have to battle the lights, so call it ten minutes either way. Most go around the block so they don't have to try to make the left. It can be done, but it's a lot faster just to come around the back and turn right onto our street and into the garage."

Damn. Jacob knew his business well. "That's right."

"Good outfit, and they treat their employees pretty fair. You should like it, and the lack of commute will be what you need after a hard day. Has Margaret gone over the perks?"

"Some of them," my real estate agent replied. "I figured I'd show her the lounge first and save some of the perks as a surprise when we went to the clubhouse."

"Great. Let me show you the apartment first and give you a rundown on the renovations that will need to be done. There's a lot, as the previous tenant made a mess of the place, but once it's done, you'll find your rent to be well worth it. Enough was damaged I'm giving the place a complete overhaul. It'll be two weeks until you can move in, and even after then, there'll be work that'll have to be completed. Three solid weeks will put the work at mostly done, with a few small tasks to be completed."

I could handle living in a hotel for three weeks. "I can deal with the hotel life for three weeks. I don't have any pets yet, and the hotel does allow pets in their rooms if I decide to get one before I move in. I'm looking at a dog possibly. Do you allow dogs over limit if it's a visiting pet with a friend?"

"Absolutely. The limit is only on the animals permanently staying in the apartment for more than a few nights. If you need to babysit someone's dog for a week, I don't have a problem with that, just let the leasing office know there's a temporary resident so we can register the animal. We keep a log of all animals in the building in case of a fire, as we try to make sure all residents are able to be rescued, including the pets. We can't do anything for the fish, but if we can grab cages or other pets during an emergency, we will. Having a roster helps us make sure everybody got out, too. We do require all guests, including delivery staff, to check in at the front desk. If we have a security guard available, delivery staff are escorted to the appropriate apartment. If it's non-food deliveries, staff make a round once a day to apartments unless it's something you've flagged as time sensitive, in which case they'll give you a call when your package arrives."

When something sounded too good to be true, it usually was, but I couldn't figure out what was wrong with the landlord or the building. I'd already been warned the entire place would be under renovations, which was a major downside, but I could live in a hotel for three weeks. "That sounds great. Do you have pictures of what the apartment should look like when it's finished?"

"I have something better. I'll take you to one of the apartments that has been renovated. The tenant is moving in this week, so it's currently empty, although I did get their permission to take you into it so you can see what yours will roughly look like after renovations. Their apartment is smaller than yours and doesn't have a fireplace, but you'll get a feel for it at least."

"Mine has a fireplace?"

"It will when the renovations are done. The unit already has chimney access, but I hadn't installed the fireplace before the previous tenant had moved in. That's why it will be three weeks for the renovation. The fireplace needs to be inspected and verified before I can allow you to move in. The fireplace itself is already in place, so you can see where it will be and how much space it will take up, but there's renovation debris still inside."

I could definitely wait three weeks for an apartment with a fireplace, and I would feel a great deal better about paying the rent with a cozy fire I could sit in front of every night while reading a book. A dog warming my feet would make things even better. Rick's dog warming my feet would be perfection.

As I couldn't help myself and he kept doing nice things for me, Rick warming me would be beyond perfection.

Damn it, I needed to get over him and quit giving myself the run around on an impossibility. Rick was my brother's friend, he was getting married to someone, and I had no business liking someone I couldn't have. I could be friends with him and nothing more.

I'd need to read a lot of books in front of a cozy fireplace to get over him.

"That sounds great." I took another sip of my wine. "I think I am properly fortified with alcohol to see some renovation debris."

"Then please follow me."

I found it amusing Jacob took the bottle, as though believing I'd really need some more alcohol to handle a little dust and debris.

I NEEDED MORE alcohol to deal with the apartment, but not because there was dust or debris, but because it was larger than I expected, had a view I might kill for, and there was a balcony overlooking the city with little in the way of obstructions. Manhattan twinkled, and while there were a ridiculous number of cars on the road, we were up high enough the sounds of the city soothed more than it annoyed. From my understanding of the building's layout, the condominiums were on the next floor up, and I could easily understand why someone would pay more than six thousand for the place.

The apartment ventured into the surreal category. The fireplace was fashioned of stacked stone to give it a rustic feel, the hardwood floors throughout would warm nicely beneath the feet, aided by a subfloor heating system, and the marble bathroom featured a jet tub I could lose many an hour in.

My e-reader was waterproof. When I wasn't warming myself beside the fire, I could soak my cares away. Who needed a pool table when I could have a jet tub?

"Margaret, what's the average rent in Manhattan?"

"$4,200, give or take a few hundred."

All right. While two thousand over the average, I could see the apartment costing so much. "You could move me in tomorrow and I wouldn't have a complaint about the renovation work." I pointed at the tub, which would comfortably fit two. "I can live in the tub for three weeks without any complaints, and take-out exists."

Jacob laughed and topped my glass of wine. "I hear that a lot for some reason. It's amazing what a little extra investment into an apartment does for a tenant's willingness to pay extra rent. Your extra two thousand a month gets you good mileage. Since you're an accountant, you'll get this. My profit margin isn't nearly as high as you might think even with charging this much. On average, I'll spend four thousand a month of your rent on the extras, and then I use a hefty chunk of that into future investments, so I don't pocket much as profit. Make no mistake, I make money—and I make decent money—but it's a snowball rather than a waterfall. A slow, gradual build of profit is more my speed than gouging my tenants. It's not perfect, but I try to make sure you have a comfortable, safe home." Jacob set the bottle of wine on the tub's ledge and pulled out a folded sheet of paper from his jacket's pocket. "The lease period is for one year, and for your first year, I will waive your pet deposit and pet rent. It's usually a hundred a month per pet, as accidents happen and flooring often needs to be replaced. The pet rent and deposit cover the so-called security deposit most landlords charge."

"You don't charge a security deposit?"

"I don't charge a security deposit. I also don't charge first and last. Your first month's rent will be due when you move in, and your rent will be due on the first of every month. If you have something barring you from paying rent on the first, contact the leasing office. Arrangements can be made, especially in case of an emergency. Rather than charge you a security deposit, my pet rent is higher. The pet deposit is poorly named, as it's not really a deposit. You won't get the money back. The deposit covers emergency pet care, rounding animals up if there's a fire, and boarding them in case something happens with the building. If your pets can't be in the unit while there are renovations or during an emergency, your deposit covers that as well. We audit every year, and if the deposit wasn't used in full with a quantifiable service, you're refunded the difference. There's also the optional daily services we offer that are outside of the rent."

"What types of emergencies do you count for late rent payments?"

"Medical emergencies, a death in the family, or the paycheck just happens to hit on Friday and rent is due on Thursday. I do not like charging my tenants late fees on rent, and I've lived paycheck-to-paycheck often enough to understand that life isn't kind to most. If you give us your payment schedule, we can make notations on the months this happens to you. We'll send an automatic notification we're aware your paycheck happens immediately after rent is due and do an automatic extension of three to five days depending on your bank and their payment processing. In the case of the first being on a weekend, we automatically check payments on the Monday, as some banks don't process over weekends."

"Okay, what's wrong with you or this apartment?"

Jacob laughed. "I view myself as living perfection, so there's absolutely nothing wrong with me or my buildings. In reality, expect maintenance to take up to two days to handle non-critical problems, although if you spring a leak, you can expect someone within ten minutes. But because of that, the little things might sit for a while. The fixtures are also a pain in the ass and require maintenance to replace, but as I'm already scalping you for six thousand a month, I don't charge for the lightbulbs."

"Small miracles," I muttered.

"Do you want to see the finished apartment before you decide?"

"I do, but only because I'm curious. If the bathroom is any indication, I can't imagine there being a dealbreaker for me here unless the utility bill is lethal."

Paying so much in month a rent would suck, but I'd given my maximum as a soft maximum, and the apartment was below my threshold. In reality, I could afford up to seven thousand a month all in.

"Utilities are included, as I'm a lazy bastard who hates dealing with the utility companies more than necessary. You're on your own for the internet, but that's it."

Yep, the apartment fit my budget even with the pet rent included. "What's the yearly pet deposit?"

"Five hundred per pet."

Ouch. That wasn't far from the norm, and that he refunded what wasn't used made a difference in my willingness to deal with the fee. "Breed restrictions?"

"In your apartment, there are no restrictions, but we ask that you pick your pet wisely. An energetic dog needs a lot of care and space. The roof park does offer the space, and we have some agility equipment for training and play, but you should pick a breed that fits your lifestyle and their needs. I don't ban by breed, but I will require a tenant to remove any aggressive animals from the property. I scrutinize the owners more than I scrutinize the breed. If you want something like a pit bull, talk to me about it. I know some reputable breeders who take care with preliminary training, and I know some rescues that have good animals."

"I was thinking big, white, and fluffy with a love of other dogs and people," I admitted. "My friend has a dog like that, and I want to steal her. I figure I just need to get one of my own. I haven't even met her in person, but she's so pretty, and she obviously loves her owner."

"I will ask that you don't steal your friend's dog, but if big, white, and fluffy is what you're looking for, that is friendly with people and animals, may I recommend a Great Pyrenees? You'll need to train the dog, as they take large to extremes, but they're a good breed, and you won't get much bigger or fluffier than that, although many have other colors, too. There's also the Samoyed, but those are very energetic. What are you looking for in an animal?"

"A lot of love, cuddles, and an enjoyment of reading books with me near the fire."

"Try the Great Pyrenees first, although I'd definitely recommend looking into the Samoyed. Either dog will be a loving member of your family. Just know both are a lot of work."

"Anything worth having is a lot of work," I replied.

"Keep thinking that way, Hope, and you'll go far. Now, let me show you the other apartment. It's smaller than yours and on one of the lower floors, but I think you're going to like what you see—and it'll help you think about something other than the renovation materials taking over the place." Jacob retrieved the bottle of wine and lifted his glass in a salute. "You won't regret picking this apartment, and I trust Margaret to show you why when she takes you to the rest of her stops tonight."

After the floor had attempted to eat me at the other unit, I had no doubts I'd find everything else on Margaret's list would come a distant second, but a wise woman took the time to look at the other offerings first, even when the final choice seemed obvious.

TWELVE

Apparently, I'm adopting a dog and a kitten today.

A WISER WOMAN would've waited to sign the lease until seeing the other offerings, but after my impulse purchase of a car and meeting my new bathtub and fireplace, I'd abandoned any wisdom I'd accumulated over the years. Add in the short hike to work and a secure garage to keep my Mercedes, and I couldn't see many downsides to my situation beyond a deep-set need to never lose my job.

My savings would only last so long if I joined the ranks of the unemployed.

After sharing the bottle of wine with Jacob, neither Margaret nor I could drive, and Luke played chauffeur, making certain we made it to the other viewings scheduled in for the night. While the places had middle of the road pricing, they reminded me more of the nightmare apartment than the luxury Jacob offered.

Sure, I would pay a ridiculous amount per month for it, but I deserved a little luxury and better than settling for the absolute minimum.

The next morning, rocking a hangover I wouldn't forget, I took a cab to work so I wouldn't crash my car into something or puke on the sidewalk trying to walk. Garret intercepted me on the way to my office, and he came armed with a tiny white puffball of a kitten and a monster of a white dog with a charming black splotch over its left eye.

I'd seen a dog just like it before: Annabel Lee.

"What breed?"

"The kitten is a ragdoll, and the puppy is a Great Pyrenees. Your new landlord gave me a call last night, warned me you'd be coming in possibly still drunk, apologized for giving you so much wine, and shared a video of you crushing Margie at pool. He really, really wanted me to ask my sister about pets for you, but the shelter only had one big, white, fluffy dog, and that's this old, tired man. They were found together abandoned, and the old man here doesn't like when anyone takes his kitten away. So, they're a matched set. I stole them from the shelter this morning, and you get to pet sit today to see if you like them."

Well, I now had an old dog and a kitten, as I abhorred when people dumped animals because they were old and tired. "Apparently, I'm adopting a dog and a kitten today."

"I have been asked to tell you that if you don't take them, Jacob will. He's a sucker for old animals who won't get a chance at a good life. But that's where the bad news comes into play."

Uh oh. "What's the bad news?"

"His food bill is terrifying."

I regarded the dog with a raised brow. "There's a lot of dog there, so I expect so. How old is he?"

"He's nine. His breed usually lives to be ten to twelve. He's in good health for his age, but he isn't a puppy anymore."

Poor old man. "Does he have a name?"

"He wasn't collared or microchipped, but he was well-socialized with humans and knows a lot of commands and tricks. The shelter tried to locate his owners and ask if anyone had lost a big dog, but no one claimed him. He's been in the shelter for three months."

"How old was the poor kitten?"

"Too young to have been separated from her mother, but they had a foster mother at the shelter who was willing to nurse her. Apparently, he whined the entire first few weeks the kitten was with the foster cat, and he settled down when they were reunited."

Ugh. My boss had my heartstrings in a firm grip, and the more he talked, the tighter his hold got. "Did they name the kitten?"

"Neither have names."

My office would be a little crowded with a big, fluffy dog, but he checked off every one of my boxes, and I couldn't ignore his sad eyes—or the little kitten mouthing at my boss's knuckles. "I'm hungover, and I apparently need to buy pet supplies and beg the hotel to let me have two pets."

"I'll handle getting the basics for you and tell Jacob you'll be bringing home the old man and his kitten."

"You don't have to do that. They're going to be my responsibility."

"Consider it an employee perk. If you're worried about making sure your new rescues are taken care of, you won't be able to concentrate. Then again, with a hangover, you're going to have a tough time concentrating. Honestly, I should have known you'd have trouble today. Margie was involved with your viewings. However, I can't help but notice you're limping. What happened?"

"The floor of the first apartment we looked at attacked me. Someone had put the bathroom in the kitchen, the bathroom had sprung a leak, I guess, and the floor had rotted. I stepped in the wrong spot and sprained my ankle. It'll probably be all right, but I'll be limping for a few days."

"I'm sorry, but did you say there was a bathroom in the kitchen?"

"I did." As I still couldn't believe it myself, I showed him the pictures of the monstrosity of an apartment.

"That's horrible."

"It really is. They wanted to charge me an arm and a leg for it, too."

"From the looks of it, they almost got your leg before you even decided if you'd sign a lease."

"No kidding." The old dog seemed happy enough to follow Garret around, and someone had added a furry rug onto the floor, which the animal flopped on. Garret placed the kitten on the fluffy dog's back, and she settled in for a nap. "Her litter box is in my office, but I'll bring it in along with their water dishes and food bowls. My sister gave me a list of good vets in the area so you can have them examined if you want, and I got their registration forms so you can get them licensed."

Well, caring for a cat and a dog would keep me busy. I pointed at the old man and said, "His name is Edgar Allan Paw."

My boss stared at me with his mouth hanging open.

"Did you just turn your dog's name into a pun?"

"My friend's big, white, and fluffy dog is named Annabel Lee." I pointed at my new kitten. "Her name is Lenore."

Garret groaned. "That's terrible yet somehow wonderful."

"They are both loved masterpieces, which is exactly what they deserve."

"Just don't buy a bird."

As I was hungover and needed to spread the misery around a little, I replied, "Come on, Garret. Raven would be a great name for something like a parakeet."

"I am putting a sign on your door that warns people that you will weaponize words in punny fashions."

I needed to write that one down and send Rick a text notifying him of this truth around the same time I introduced him to Edgar Allan Paw and Lenore. "Make it a nice sign, please. You may as well add a little white-board to it so people can record when I last landed a successful word weaponization."

"That sounds like a plan. Swing by my office if you have any problems, drink a lot of water, and make sure you take time for lunch."

Apparently, I had a hover boss, which was a pleasant change compared to managers who didn't give a damn. "Is water a euphemism for coffee?"

"Today it can be, but tomorrow it's not."

That would do. "As my new co-workers are already slacking on the job, I'll get to work and try not to fawn over them too much during the day."

"Fawn over them as much as you want. They could use a little extra love."

Some orders were easier to obey than others, and rather than start tackling my work-load, I sat on the floor and introduced myself to my new pets. The animals didn't seem to mind me, and I even got Edgar Allan Paw to lick my hand after a few minutes. Lenore ignored me, burrowing in her buddy's fur to take a nap.

Once satisfied they would be all right without me petting them, I took a picture and sent it to Rick.

My phone rang, and I grinned at the man's inability to just text me back. Rather than play coy and dodge his call, I answered with, "The dog's name is Edgar Allan Paw, and the kitten's name is Lenore. I couldn't say no. My boss brought them in and the big boy had been abandoned, and he's an old tired dog."

"Edgar Allan Paw?" Rick asked.

"Well, your pretty girl is named Annabel Lee, and this big old baby is a boy, so he's Edgar Allan Paw. Lenore was the only other Edgar Allan Poe lady I could think of offhand, so she's Lenore. They were abandoned together a few months ago, and he cries if he's separated from his kitten."

"You're a sucker for animals, aren't you?"

"Yep. The instant my boss said they'd been dumped together, I couldn't send them back to the shelter. But in good news, I have an apartment that welcomes animals, and they'll even pet sit for a small fee if needed."

"Well, in good news, I like cats and so does Annabel Lee. Cats don't usually like her, and that breaks her little heart."

"Lenore seems to be rather fond of Edgar Allan Paw. You can't have my kitten, so you'll just have to get your own."

Rick laughed. "All right. Everything okay?

Your voice sounds odd."

"I'm hungover because my new landlord insisted on pouring wine down my throat last night. He got my real estate agent drunk, too. He thought we needed it after the other apartment attacked me. It was so bad that my new landlord called my boss and said I might come to work still drunk. I'm not still drunk, but I'm definitely feeling it today."

"Your new landlord got you drunk?"

"I think he's part Italian or something. I went to the viewing, he brought the wine. But I kicked my real estate's ass in a game of pool."

"You did? Mat said you weren't all that great at pool."

"He can kiss my ass for sparing his weak little ego and pride. I'll fucking run him around the table next time, just like I ran my real estate agent around the table, and I had to do a fucking jump draw to do it."

"What is a jump draw exactly?"

"There's a video. I'll get a copy and send it to you. The bartender owes me drinks because he didn't think I could do it, and my real estate agent wants me to join her pool league. Last night was a good night. Also, we need to talk so I can plan your wedding." Reminding us both he had a wedding upcoming would do me a lot of good.

I could be friends with him. Everything else was strictly off limits, and I would make sure I kept reminding myself of that.

"My cousin seems to want a church, but she's open to other ideas. As in, she doesn't want anything to do with the actual planning of the wedding, and she just wants to show up, get married, and go on the honeymoon. This is creating a rather large issue for the family, as there's so many of us, and she wants to bring the family, the family friends, and their friends, and I don't think we'll all fit in a church. That means your family will also be in attendance, as you'll be present. Unfortunately, that includes Amy."

Oh, well. "There are plenty of large parks that'll allow a wedding party, I think. I'll have to think about the reception, though, if there are that many of you. How many of you are there?"

"Too many. At last count, including you, your brother, Amy, your parents, and a bunch of your friends, there's a guest list of potentially five hundred."

Okay. That put the wedding at substantially larger than my brother's. In any case, I would not panic. I'd just think about panicking. "How many bridesmaids and whatever the hell you men are called?"

"That's where things become even more complicated. My cousin saw your picture and wants you in the wedding party. She thinks you're adorable."

Uh oh. "But I'll be coordinating the event, Rick."

"That didn't stop you before," he countered in a rather smug tone.

Damn it. "Okay. She's the bride, so she gets to decide. If that's what she wants, I'll go along with it. How many in each party?"

"About seventy-five per side."

We'd have to take over a mega church if we wanted to cram in that many people. "I recommend a park or garden for the entire thing, and I think a garden would be easier to arrange a picnic or something for that many people. We might need a freaking stadium with a guest and party list that big. Or an entire yacht."

"A yacht could be fun, then there could be no runaway brides, grooms, or the targets of proposals."

"We'd need an entire cruise ship if we wanted to do that." A cruise ship might allow anyone dealing with a proposal to hide somewhere on board. In the target's shoes, I wasn't sure if I'd run, faint from mortification at being the center of attention, or wonder why the hell anyone would do something so elaborate to try to get me to marry him when I'd probably just cave at the first sincere and interested man who didn't trip one of my mother's triggers.

My mother had a good eye for people, but Mat had opted to ignore her advice.

Love did crazy things to people.

I needed to do better at being a supportive sister, but damn it, I hated how much money she'd cost him. And me.

I also needed to get over my jealousy issues, and identifying I resented the thoroughbride had run off with my brother helped a little. Why had I gone along with it, anyway? All I would've had to do was forgo the ball and chain threats and let her climb out the window.

If Mat didn't find happiness with her, I'd spend most of my free time crying over my mistakes.

Rick made a thoughtful noise, drawing my attention back to our conversation. "The budget won't be an issue. If it's possible to get an entire cruise ship, she would really enjoy that, I think. So would her groom. They love the ocean."

"And what about your bride, Mr. Fredrick?"

"I'm thinking more along the lines of staging a proposal, which has been already okayed and encouraged by my cousin, rather than trying to spring a marriage on her. I figure the lady I'm proposing to might want a say in our wedding, assuming she accepts."

Huh. I hoped the woman Rick liked recognized how much work he meant to put in with his scheme, and I'd spend a lot of time trying to balance his cousin's wedding with his proposal. "That's sensible. Just have Annabel Lee deliver the proposal. It'd be impossible to say no to your dog. She's really that cute."

Rick chuckled. "I see you are in love with my dog, and you haven't even met her yet."

"She's really that cute. My new old man is that cute, too. I think they're the same breed. But even if they aren't, I don't care. He's my old man of a dog now. I made the mistake of telling someone I wanted a big, white fluffy dog." I scratched Edgar Allan Paw behind his ears, patted his head, and sat at my desk so I could get started on my day. On my first break, I'd be giving the hotel a call, notifying them I had two animals, begging them to ignore my pets along with giving promises to pay whatever outrageous fees they'd charge for having them in their room.

"I'd say you should refrain from making any more impulsive decisions, but honestly, if someone came to me and told me the old dog I had to look in the eyes had been dumped, I'd be going home with an old dog, too."

"Yeah, I couldn't say no after looking him in the eyes. Honestly, I'm thinking this is for the best, because I would try to adopt the entire shelter and cry at all the animals I couldn't take home with me."

Rick chuckled. "There's nothing wrong with having a soft heart, Hope. I got Annabel Lee because she isn't suitable for showing, needed medical care, and the breeder wasn't sure what she'd do with a dog that can't be bred, can't show, and would eat a fortune in dog food."

"What's wrong with Annabel Lee?"

"There's a lot wrong with Annabel Lee. She has hip and elbow dysplasia, and she's the runt of the litter with some resolvable birth defects. The other puppies in the litter were flagged low risk, and the breeder is really good about trying to prevent health problems in her dogs, but Annabel Lee drew the short lot. She isn't sure why she has so many issues, but she does. I adopted her because the breeder was considering putting her down; she needed a lot of medical care early in her life. I got lucky with Annabel Lee, though. After the first few rounds of treatments, we got everything under control, so she's able to lead a happy life. She's now a very spoiled and beloved member of the family, but part of my contract with the breeder was to make sure she was spayed so the genetic faults she developed wouldn't be passed down. When I asked why she had problems and the other puppies didn't, she just shrugged and said it happened sometimes. I got a really good deal on her, though."

"You did? What's a really good deal for a sweet dog with medical problems?"

"Her feed and medical bills, mostly. She hates putting a dog down, and since I was willing to play ball with her medical bills, she gave her away for free. She's a good woman, and she'd never sell a sickly dog to someone. She's been trying to get me to take her to show where they allow altered dogs, but I think it would be too stressful on her, so I refuse. If it wasn't for her health issues, she'd be a beautiful example of the breed. Her temperament is perfect."

"I see you're a sucker for animals, too."

"You've caught me."

"I'm just glad my new job and apartment will be friendly for my big old boy and his pet kitten."

"I like how you've already accepted that Lenore is your dog's kitten rather than yours."

"I just hope we coexist in the same space without problems. Right now, she's sleeping on him."

"I'm sure it'll be fine. I'll pitch the cruise ship idea to my cousin and see what she says. I'll mention the park and gardens, too. Honestly, she wants some chapel in New York City, but getting the approvals to do everything would be quite the process, and it has to be booked a year or more in advance. She's already made arrangements for the Pre-Cana should they decide to go the church route."

My grandfather on my adopted mother's side of the family was Catholic, and he'd wanted Mat and Amy to go through their Pre-Cana, which they'd agreed to in order to keep peace in the family despite having been married in a non-Catholic church. "Your cousin is Catholic?"

"The church is. Technically, we're Protestant Anglican, which isn't Catholic. And I say technically because almost nobody in the family is actually religious. I can't remember the last time I went to church that wasn't for a wedding, truth be told. Well, my parents go, but they go to keep peace in the family. I moved to Japan to get out of doing a lot of the family activities, and I only come out of hiding when I absolutely must."

"That sounds complicated."

"It really is. In good news, most of the family doesn't care what I do, so I get to handle my business how I see fit without family drama and politics getting into it. I'm only getting involved with this wedding because my cousin is a good person, and I happen to like her groom. Anyway, I must get Annabel Lee loaded up, as we are going to a car dealership today to pick something, and it's important I pick a vehicle she likes."

I laughed at how his dog ruled over his entire life with an iron paw. "Good luck with that. Don't let her run you around the dealership, Rick."

"I'll try not to. I'll be heading to New York in a few days, so if you want to start thinking about your first real clue, I'd appreciate some form of hint to help keep my weekends and evenings interesting."

"You got it. I'll send you a text. Have a good trip to the dealership." I hung up, set my phone aside, and cracked my knuckles.

No damned hangover was going to stop me from getting through the audit, and come hell or high water, I'd have a good day.

THIRTEEN

Why does this company have such a huge prostitution problem?

HELL MANIFESTED as a set of invoices registering the purchase of adult company under one of the marketer's accounts, a rather illegal activity in the state of New York. The high water came along in the form of my boss flipping his lid on the hiring company. Within an hour of my unpleasant discovery of the acquisition of prostitutes for clients on the company's dime, the cops showed up to claim the evidence, and they brought several employees from the company with them. I wasn't sure why, but I decided against questioning the cops about it.

The invoices, which had been in the unsorted pile from the not-quite-accountants and only a few days old, cleared them of wrongdoing; they hadn't even had a chance to see the damned things before it'd gotten into my hands. I could do without the cops leering at me, and I bet my entire face would be burned permanently red before I got through the job from hell.

Garret, still fuming to the point I expected smoke to roll out of his ears, paced around my office and made disgruntled noises while waiting for the entourage to finish clearing out.

"Prostitutes!" Garret grunted, flung his hands into the air, and resumed pacing. "And they weren't even that Meltrew woman's prostitutes. They were a marketer's prostitutes. Why does this company have such a huge prostitution problem? How is this even possible?"

A professional remained calm in any situation, but I suspected my boss's patience had finally snapped due to the unexpected illegalities. Embezzlement and other financial crimes tended to crop up often enough in our line of work, but the hiring of prostitutes was a new one.

While technically prostitution counted as a class B misdemeanor and offering prostitution services counted as a class A misdemeanor, the invoices didn't indicate the age of the prostitutes, in which case the employee —and possibly the company—could face a class E felony.

Ugh. I remembered way too much about the various sexually oriented crimes that a company could get dinged with if their employees developed certain tastes. Assuming I escaped from my current assignment unscathed, I'd take the time to do something fun, such as enjoy evening strolls with my dog. I'd have to see if I could train the kitten to walk with my dog, as I didn't want Edgar Allan Paw to have to deal with separation from his best friend again.

"I'd say I'm sorry I found that, but I'm really not. I suspect Miss Meltrew may have bailed while she could, understanding there'd be trouble around the corner. These invoices were in the pile that hadn't reached her collection of assistants. They don't have any of the notations her assistants used when checking them, nor were they registered in their spreadsheet yet. I was inputting them into the system for auditing when I noticed the line items."

"Who is stupid enough and audacious enough to openly write that the invoices are for prostitutes? They even used their stage names on the invoice." Garret groaned and flopped onto my couch. "This is a nightmare. How are Edgar Allan Paw and Lenore settling in?"

"They seem okay so far. Neither hate me, and I'll take that. I'm seriously considering taking my lunch break to look into buying them a lot of toys and things for the apartment. I'll need a bed for them, as I don't want his old bones having to deal with the hardwood floor, but they're heated in the new apartment, so maybe that'll be good for him. As for the nightmare, it isn't all bad. The accounting itself, except for this one individual's illicit acquisitions, seems to be mostly in order. I don't know why this person thought it was okay to use company accounts to make these purchases."

"To pass guilt to the company in revenge? This is going to cause them a lot of problems."

If the employee took the fall rather than the company, it would create some scandal and some news, but I doubted it would do much damage to them—assuming they did a good job mitigating the fallout. "Well, their accounting will be sorted otherwise. If you hear me laughing later, it's because I'm working through the varying stages of acceptance about this job. I now understand why the other accountants ran away."

"Yeah. Every now and then, we get something weird. I hadn't expected the weirdness to spread, though."

"I guess the marketer decided if Miss Meltrew could hire prostitutes, so could he."

"That's a frighteningly plausible thought. You deserve lunch for putting up with that. How does pizza sound?"

"Pizza sounds good. I'm just going to hope I don't find anything else unique in these invoices. I did check through all of that one's outstanding invoices, so it would be for a new marketer if something crops up."

"Hopefully without literal crops."

I snickered. "Hopefully not. If I do find

any invoices for literal crops, I will hope there's an associated employee perks party involving a stable. Riding crops could be justified in that case."

"Hell, if that marketer had been smart, he would have disguised his prostitutes as rides at a local stable for client enrichment."

Huh. My boss had a good point; that would be a decent way to hide illegal activities, especially if the marketing department did enrichment activities with their advertising firms often. "Don't give any marketers bad ideas, Garret. I might have been caught by that one. It's not unreasonable for companies to do weird things like that to build corporate relationships."

"I have an entire list of weird things we've found that were used to hide illegal activities. No one has actually used the stable idea yet, though. But after one of the accountants pitched it during a brainstorm, we're all on the lookout for oddball invoices that might be hiding illegal activities."

"When I became an accountant, I never believed there'd be so many unique perils associated with my job."

"Well, you'll appreciate the McCarthy file. It's fairly normal, although there are a lot of medical receipts that need to be checked over. Honestly, I don't think you'll find anything, but they were worried it was complicated, and they'd rather file the corrections before they get audited—if they get audited."

"They're anxious about their taxes, aren't they?"

"They are. They don't want any financial surprises."

I read between the lines, assuming that the couple was particularly worried about their taxes. "Would they like to do the initial meeting with me tonight after work? As long as they don't mind Edgar Allan Paw and Lenore settling in and a possible trip to the pet store, I don't have anything else planned for tonight. If the animals like car rides, I can go pick up the files."

"They can bring the files to you, I'm certain. We already have the digital copies, but they also have all the paper records, too. I'll give them a call and see if they want to move the timeline up. If they have an early night, it wouldn't surprise me if they take you up on that."

"How do you want me to proceed should I find any other unwanted surprises in this audit?"

"Call me over and warn me I'm going to need a stiff drink after work tonight," he replied before hopping to his feet. "I will futilely hope for no more surprises today."

"Please send me that list of oddities, please. For some reason, I think I'm going to need it."

ACCORDING to the introductory paragraph of the file Garret sent me, several bottles of alcohol, twenty accountants, and a bad shift had resulted in a brainstorm session of frighteningly plausible methods in which someone might hide illegal activities. It amused me that the file openly acknowledged alcohol had been involved in the creation of a work document with a disclaimer that it had been after hours.

Some of the entries, including the stable visits for a ride, left me a giggling mess. From falsely increased invoices to unusually expensive trips, the brainstorm session read more like a guide to skimming money from a company. As accountants could be trusted to cross every t and dot the i while they were at it, the guide included links to the expected costs of various goods, services, and trips.

To my relief, I plowed through all of the unregistered invoices but found nothing else questionable at first glance. With a little luck, the rest of the audit would be mundane and boring and lack sex workers, adult toys, or bedroom activities unsuitable for public places.

As promised, Garret brought pizza along with offerings for Edgar Allan Paw and Lenore, who warmed up to me enough to shuffle closer to my feet rather than sticking to the bed set out for them. When my dog wanted to go out, he heaved a sigh, stood up, and shuffled to the door and stared at me with sad eyes.

Lenore wanted to go, too, and she cried when I clipped Edgar Allan Paw's leash to his collar.

That sent me to my phone to call my boss asking how I could possibly take the cat on a walk, and he showed up with a harness and leash for the kitten, which she wore without much protest. Rather than make her try to keep up, I carried her in the crook of my arm while I led the old dog to the elevators for a stroll to the park down the street so he could do his business outside.

To my delight, Lenore limited her protests over going outside to the occasional whine, and once I had them at the park, I discovered she would ride on Edgar Allan Paw's back.

My unlikely pair drew attention, including the owners of other dogs giving their pets a chance to stretch their legs. My old man handled them with skepticism but grace while Lenore hunkered in his thick fur and hid.

To keep from stressing them more than necessary, I waited until Edgar Allan Paw lost interest in sniffing around the park before leaving, taking care to make use of the nearest trash can to deposit his odiferous offerings. To keep from trailing muddy prints all over the lobby, I cleaned his paws, which he tolerated with a flick of his ear and no other sign of being annoyed by my activities.

I praised him for being a good boy, took the pair back to my office, and out of curiosity, I moved the dog bed closer to my desk to see what would happen.

Edgar Allan Paw approved of my decision and opted to use my foot as a pillow.

Life was good, and I meant to enjoy every minute of my enslavement as his provider of walks, treats, and affection. If I lost my foot, it would be a worthy sacrifice. I churned through the majority of the outstanding invoices, breathing a sigh of relief that none of them seemed to be infected with any form of insanity. A knock at my door stirred the sleeping beasts, and Edgar Allan Paw issued a low growl. I reached down and scratched behind his ears to convince him there was no danger. "Come in."

My boss cracked open the door. "Did I just hear the dog growl?"

"Apparently, this is his space now, and if you could bring him the appropriate sacrifice, he might forgive you for potentially being a threat to my office." I chuckled and gave him another stroke before giving Lenore a rub, too. "I think he's figured out I'm not going to hurt him."

Either he was satisfied Garret meant no harm or he decided it wasn't worth the effort, because Edgar Allan Paw resumed napping on my foot.

"Good. I'm glad he's settling in with you. Truth be told, if he wasn't going home with you, he'd probably be going home with me, and I have no idea how I'd deal with a second cat because my wife's mildly allergic, but she can't say no to rescues, either. Thank you for sparing me from having to tell my wife we would be having a kitten to add to her allergies to go with the cat we already have."

"It seems Edgar Allan Paw has a line of people wanting to take him home."

"Yeah, my sister has an eye for the suckers. I'm a sucker, Jacob's a sucker, and you're now a confirmed sucker."

"It's true, I really am. What can I do for you?"

"It was deceptively quiet in here, so I wanted to check in."

"I'm almost done with the outstanding invoices, and they look clean. I'll be sending the digital copies back to the firm today so they can be paid and give them instructions on how to record their payment status so we don't lose extra time dealing with them. Some of these will be due in the next few days, and I'd rather not disrupt their operations more than necessary. I don't usually audit in-process accounts, but I can work around it to make sure everything is correct."

"Yeah, I wasn't too thrilled that there were open invoices in the lot, but with your work history, I figured you could handle it. If you find any past due, please let them know right away so they can handle it. I was warned the accounting might be bad enough to have past due invoices."

"So far, everything has been really, really tidy. The issues aren't with Miss Meltrew's men, but rather with things outside of her control at this point in time. That doesn't mean I won't find anything questionable once I start going through paid invoices, but I'm starting to hope I might get through the outstanding invoices without wanting to cry, commit any felonies, or otherwise lose what's left of my mind."

"I like that you are openly acknowledging this job has resulted in at least some parts of your mind leaving the premises. To be fair, I'm pretty sure there's not much left of my mind following the general description of this job. While this isn't going to influence your work right now, it seems that there might be a bigger issue in that company that will need to be addressed."

"Please tell me they weren't operating an illegal sex operation of some sort. The inclusion of prostitutes and sex toys could easily indicate that."

"Not quite."

"Then what?"

My boss sighed and bowed his head. "I don't want to say it."

"Now I really need to know."

"Insider trading of publicly owned adult entertainment companies. So, technically, while it involves the sex industry, they're corporate firms operating legally, although there's the possibility of illegal activities."

"That would explain the prostitutes and sex toys, though," I replied.

"Unfortunately."

"There are publicly traded adult entertainment companies?"

"Yep."

I frowned, my brows furrowing. "But why?"

"Sex sells, and people have faith in sex selling, so they perceive it as a safe stock to invest in."

I considered that and shrugged when I realized that was a damned good reason for keeping stock in an adult entertainment company. "So, this is going to be even worse than I thought?"

"It's going to be even worse than I thought, and I went in expecting it to be pretty bad. The company management wants a good idea of how bad it will be on the accounting front so they can be prepared for any and all fallout. When you review the invoices, keep in mind there has been garnering of favor among some invoicing employees and insiders at the various associated adult entertainment firms. I'll be emailing you with a complete list of all known companies dealing with adult entertainment. I'll warn you. There's a lot of them."

"There are?"

"Sex sells really well."

"Someone should probably tell our client that while sex sells, they shouldn't be selling it without the proper permits and legal coverage."

"Or buying it."

I bit my lower lip so I wouldn't laugh.

"Go on, Hope. Laugh. I've been doing it all day. Every time I think this couldn't possibly get worse, it does."

"Instead of Debbie showing Dallas a good time, we have Meltrew taking over Manhattan, and it only goes downhill from there."

My boss snorted. "That's one way to put it. While I have you here, I did get ahold of Mr. McCarthy, and he'll be free as early as six tonight along with his wife, but there's a catch."

"What catch?"

"Unbeknownst to him this morning, his wife got a new pet, and she needs to bring it with her. It will stay in a container unless you want to say hi, but she'd need a place to plug in a heater for it, as it doesn't like getting too cold."

"What sort of pet is it? A snake? A lizard of some sort?"

My boss sighed. "It's a spider."

I frowned. "A spider?"

"It's a very big spider."

I could handle a spider if it was in a container. If it escaped or jumped at me, that'd be another story. "If it's in a box or something, I don't care. I'll try to make sure Edgar Allan Paw and Lenore don't bother it."

"That leads me to the next issue."

Uh oh. "Haven't we had enough issues for one day?"

"I made the mistake of telling Jacob about the spider."

While I had only met my new landlord once, I could guess how the rest of my night would work out, and it involved another hangover. "Jacob wants to meet the spider, doesn't he? Garret, he's not a reasonable man when it comes to pets. I figured this out last night while listening to the various perks he offers pet owners."

"He offered to let you use his office for the meeting, and he wants to meet your new dog and cat, too. Just smack him if he tries to adopt them."

Well, it wasn't far from my hotel, which would make everything convenient for me. "Okay. I don't have a problem with that. Parking won't be fun around there, but it can work. I'll try not to smack him, but I might growl menacingly."

"I have a difficult time imagining you being menacing, Hope. Jacob will let you and the McCarthys into the parking garage for the meeting, and he'll give you access to the clubhouse or the guest area on the lobby level if you want to get in some pool, too."

Even if he got me drunk and hung over

again, I decided I loved my new landlord. "I'm game if they are."

"I'll let them know, and I'll bring over instructions on what to tell the security guards when you enter the parking garage. Thanks for being game to take on so much at once, Hope. I think this is going to make the next few weeks hard on you, so if there's anything I can do to help, let me know."

I pointed at my new dog, who kept a close eye on my boss. "I did not have a dog yesterday. I have a dog today. As far as I'm concerned, everything is worth it. Thank you for bringing him in. I do appreciate it, and I think he's going to be perfect."

"And when he passes away, I'll talk to my sister about a younger puppy that'll match well with Lenore. She's a sucker for the old ones, and she didn't want to see him stay in the shelter any longer. A few months is a long time for an old man like him."

"Oh. Adoption forms. Aren't there adoption forms I should fill out? Isn't the shelter expecting them back?" I hesitated. "I really don't want to give them back or even take them anywhere near the shelter to handle the paperwork."

"There is, but it'll be easy. My sister will fill out the papers, you'll make sure they're right, and you'll sign. The shelter is aware Edgar Allan Paw and Lenore would be either fostered or adopted, and considering how much it costs to feed him, they're happy."

I bet. “Okay. I can work with that. Is there anything else I should know for today?”

“I think that about covers it. I’ll be back shortly with the directions for the garage, when Jacob will be expecting you, and the probable time the McCarthys will show up.”

“Sounds good.”

I waited until my boss left before regarding my new pets with a raised brow. “Things just keep getting weirder, guys.”

Edgar Allan Paw took Garret’s departure as a sign to return to his nap, and Lenore joined him. I returned to work to cram in every second I could before I needed to head to my future home to get the groundwork on my second accounting assignment started.

FOURTEEN

I considered running away from her pet.

ALICE MCCARTHY'S pet spider was larger than her hand, and it crawled up her arm while she cooed at it. The bright pink color startled me, and I gaped at the arachnid and its red-haired owner, astonished anyone could be so happy while a hairy beast from some spider hell crawled all over her. Her expression, soft despite the scars crossing one side of her face, implied she loved little more than having an eight-legged hairy beast exploring its way to her shoulder. The man with her seemed more bemused by her behavior and unconventional pet than anything else.

I couldn't decide if Jacob wanted to run away or cuddle with the tarantula.

Fortunately for me, my old man of a dog preferred lounging at my feet, and Lenore stuck to her fluffy buddy better than any glue I'd ever used. "You must be the McCarthys," I greeted, keeping a careful hold on both leashes so there wouldn't be a feline-canine-arachnid incident in the lobby. "That is one very large and pink spider."

"She's an old Mexican pink, and her previous owner passed away. She's really friendly, and she's used to being handled. She's been displaced, so I let her out for a few minutes since the lobby here is warm enough for her. You don't mind she's out?"

Unlike my new landlord, I absolutely would not reveal I considered running away from her pet. "As someone who is adopting an old dog because I couldn't stand the thought of returning him to a shelter, I fully understand why you wouldn't want to keep your new pet in its… cage?"

"I have a plastic tub for her with a heat pad and a mini habitat inside for her until I get her home. I put her in a carry tub when in the car, as that protects her. She might fall if she's loose in the bigger tub when we're driving, and she's old enough I'm not sure how well she'd handle a fall. One of my friends is at our place setting up her new tank now. She's huge for her species, so she's probably near the end of her lifespan. Lance is being a good sport. He even held her for a few minutes."

Lance winced. "I stood like a statue and tried not to whimper while she crawled all over me, Alice. That's hardly being a good sport, and I don't really call it holding. But she is friendlier than your devil of a spider Julian keeps coming over to visit because he misses her. You should just give that terror to him. Please put your new baby away. I'm terrified she'll jump and get hurt, and the last thing I need today is my wife crying because a spider was injured."

"Don't say such terrible things about Boomer. She's a great spider. And Ruby is being perfectly well behaved."

"Boomer wants to kill you, and the jury is still out on Ruby."

"Boomer wants to kill everybody. The only thing Ruby here would kill is her dinner. She's a perfectly sweet spider. You just need to move slow and keep to her pace is all." Alice took her time strolling across the lobby to the security desk, where a large, plastic tub waited. She eased her hand beneath the massive spider and transferred her to the container before securing the lid. "There, you big wuss. She's safely in her container now. Just because she's a little bigger than the others doesn't mean she's going to crawl over your face and eat you tonight."

"But are you really sure about that?"

"She likes bugs, Lance. You're not a bug. You're too big to interest her. She only cares if you plan to feed her bugs. Now, if you withhold her dinner, she might have a problem with you."

"Please feed your latest demon on time every day."

I bit my lip so I wouldn't giggle at the man's plea. "If my opinion matters, she's a very pretty spider. I had no idea spiders came in that color."

"She's huge for her species. They're usually smaller, which means this old girl has had someone taking very good care of her over the years. Lance isn't going to be happy about having to share his reading room with her, but it was the only place we could squeeze in a large enough habitat for her. Your dog is very pretty. What's his name?"

"Edgar Allan Paw, and his kitten is named Lenore. They came as a matched set, and they were found together. Lenore doesn't seem to like people all that much, but she has tolerated me as long as I keep her with her old man."

"That is so cute. What breed?"

"I think he's a Great Pyrenees, and she's a ragdoll. She's around three months old, and he's nine, so he's a tired old man. Honestly, tired old man is my speed for a dog right now, as I've never had one before. He's like a dog on training wheels for me, I guess. I've never had a cat before, either."

Jacob laughed, came over, and crouched near my pets, holding his hand out so they could decide if they wanted to make his acquaintance. "You took me as the kind who couldn't say no to an animal in need. When we're doing the floors, I'll make sure to get the best heating system I can for him, as he'll appreciate it. I have a litter box set up in my office in case she needs one."

"That's great. Thanks, Jacob."

"Come with me, and I'll get you three settled in my office so you can get your work done. I'll have someone bring up the boxes in a few minutes, but I'm sure you can discuss other matters while they're ferried upstairs." Jacob led us to the elevator and pressed the button to the clubhouse floor. "Can I get you something to drink?"

"Water or tea, please."

"Black, green, white, rooibos, herbal, or would you like me to pick for you?"

"Chai if you have it, and I'll take mine with no sugar or milk," I replied.

"I see you like to discipline your taste buds. For you two?"

"Water, please," Alice replied.

"And you, Lance?"

"Coffee, black. With extra darkness added if possible, as that's what it's going to take to get me through dealing with these taxes."

Alice rolled her eyes. "It's not going to be that bad, Lance. It's just a little complicated is all. That's why Garret sent Hope our way. He said she was qualified to handle this mess."

Messes I could handle, but I really hoped their taxes wouldn't be a mess. "I'll do my best to make sure everything is sorted, and if you need to file any adjustments with the IRS, I'll walk you through everything and prepare the forms so all you have to do is sign and send."

"That's the best news I've heard all day," Lance announced.

"Hey, I got Ruby this morning. That's the best news of the day," Alice protested.

"How happy Ruby makes you is the second-best news of my day, but having someone fix our tax disaster is better news. That means I don't have to try to make sense of the tax code."

Alice pouted, which made Lance smile.

Damn. If I had a man look at me the way Lance looked at Alice, I'd have it made. "Well, I can take care of making sense of the tax code, and if I don't know something, I work with a lot of people who do, so I'll make sure they're filed accurately. Don't you worry about that at all. My job is to make this as painless as possible."

Alice grinned. "I like the sound of that. Still, I'm sorry. I had no idea the lawsuit and getting married in the same year would make such a mess of our taxes."

"That seems to be as good a place to start as any. What happened with the lawsuit to make it a tax nightmare?"

"I was awarded a cash settlement in an assault case." Alice gestured to her scarred face with a shrug. "I opted against paying out the ridiculous amount for anything more than the basic reconstructive surgery and spent the rest on cars and our house. Then I was repaid for one of the cars and the house, and we have no idea how to handle the taxes as a result. The last tax person I gave the file to cried."

That didn't sound promising. "The government does enjoy getting every penny out of you as much as possible."

"Yeah, and we received extra to cover the taxes, which made it even more complicated. I think I overpaid our taxes, too. Well, I know I did. I got a hefty check back from the IRS, but that shouldn't be right."

Ah. When someone owed a lot in taxes, and they received a refund after paying, triggers were tripped, anxiety kicked in, and doubt usually won. "Did you happen to register all of the various health bills associated with your injuries as part of your taxes?"

Alice frowned. "Yes, one of the accountants did make me hand over all of the receipts, even the one I got while out west. I broke my stupid foot being stupid."

The elevator pinged and opened to the clubhouse level, and Jacob led us to his office, which had a few extra chairs and a card table brought in to offer extra room if his desk lacked sufficient space. Alice's spider was placed in the far corner, and she plugged in a mat, which she placed beneath the tub. "Don't worry, the mat doesn't get hot enough to hurt the plastic. It just makes sure she stays warm enough."

"Alice, stop fretting. Your spider is fine, nobody minds you have her here, and you're not going to burn anything down while you're in here watching the heat pad. Please relax. Please, I beg you. If you keep fretting any more today, I'm going to have a heart attack."

She scowled, and I recognized an old complaint when I heard one. As the last thing any of us needed was a bundle of anxiety fretting over taxes and her pet at the same time, I said, "It's okay. We'll keep an eye on your spider, and I'll make sure Edgar Allan Paw and Lenore don't bother her. Their favorite hobby is sleeping, although I expect the kitten will start getting into trouble soon. That's what kittens do. Or that's what I've been told kittens do. I've never had a cat or a dog before, so I expect the next few days of my life will be interesting."

"You're sure?" Alice asked.

"Absolutely. Let's sit down and start going over these papers so I can see if there's any obvious issues, and I'll take the lot with me tonight and get to work on it. I'll make sure all of the deductions you can claim have been claimed and close any potential audit risks to keep the IRS from poking its nose in your business. Of course, that won't stop you from being selected as part of the random draw for audits, but my job is to keep your audit risk as low as possible. If you are audited, my job also involves making certain you get through it as quickly as possible without incurring any bills."

"I thought an IRS audit automatically meant a huge fine," Alice muttered.

"There's only a fine if they find anything

wrong with your taxes. If it's discovered they overcharged you as part of the audit, they owe *you* money. They try to avoid auditing anyone that might result in them having to pay a refund."

Two of Jacob's employees brought in a stack of four boxes, which they placed on the desk. I raised a brow, making a mental note over how I'd need to add a few extra hours to every day for a while. "Is this all medical?"

"Honestly, I didn't know what I'd need, so I brought everything. The renovation payments for the house, the car registrations, the medical bills, the court paperwork showing how much I was owed and paid, taxes paid everywhere, charitable contributions, and that other thing Lance said we'd need."

Lance laughed. "Our W-2s, babe."

"Yeah, those."

I giggled. "How is this organized?"

Alice gulped. "It's not. I'm a secretary, and I should know better, but I got frustrated, I couldn't find a paper, and I made a mess of it, so I just shoved everything in the boxes, and then I kept shoving things in them I wasn't sure I needed, and now there's four boxes, and I don't even know how much of it you actually need."

Alice's admission made her husband smile even more. "You're such a mess, Alice. Anyway, we're sorry, Hope. She got flustered, and she didn't know if we'd done it right, and once she gets to that level of flustered, she becomes the equivalent of a toddler on sugar. While I think it's hilarious, she gets pretty upset over it. I put an end to the train wreck and hired your firm to handle the taxes before she went insane. If you could make a list of what we need to keep and what we don't need to keep to prevent future meltdowns, that would be amazing."

"I can do that. I'll organize the papers by what is actually needed, what isn't needed, and make any notations about anything that might be missing when I compare them to the tax documentation you have already filled out."

Alice pointed at one of the boxes, which had a black spider sticker on it. "That one has the tax documents in it. I put it in numbered envelopes because there are that many pages."

"That's normal when taxes become complicated. There are often a lot of supporting forms." I took the lid off the box with the tax documents, found the envelopes, and tried not to sigh at the six inches of hell waiting for me. Somehow, I succeeded. "While the tax code has been confirmed to break tables, I think you could turn your tax package into a lethal weapon. Someone should sue the IRS for weaponizing their documentation."

That got both of them laughing, and by the time Jacob returned with drinks, the pair relaxed enough to give me a better feel for them and their financial situation. Helping good, funny people get through a tax hell appealed to me, something I hadn't gotten to do at my old place of employment.

Silver linings helped me get through the rough times, of which there would be many in the upcoming days. If I could turn their tax woes into a victory for them, it would console me when my personal and professional life went from weird to miserable.

And it would. The shine of the new and interesting couldn't last forever, especially when auditing a company with twisted morals.

IT TOOK until midnight to get the basics of the McCarthy file situated, and I put an end to the discussion out of worry for them, as both yawned and seemed barely able to keep their eyes open. A single glance at Jacob got the man to send a pair of his employees with them to make certain they got home in one piece.

I accepted his offer for the same, although the older man who drove my vehicle back to the hotel would walk back to work rather than partner up with someone else. Settling my new pets took longer than anticipated, as Edgar Allan Paw whined if his bed was too far from me, which transformed my hotel room into a maze. Lenore insisted on staying with her friend, and she allowed me to pet her.

Morning came early, with a hungry dog and a kitten both pawing at me in a demand for a walk and their breakfast. It amused me the pair had figured out I would be their provider, and I fed them first before taking them into the hotel's miniature yard so Edgar Allan Paw could take care of his morning constitutional at his leisure rather than mine. To spare the old man from walking to work, I herded them to the car and drove them in, laughing over how my initial plan to avoid traffic and get exercise hadn't even lasted a week.

Working without a hangover did me a world of good, and despite the oddities of my assignment, I discovered I could settle into a routine and gain back some control over my life. Over my lunches, I both amused and tortured myself with planning a wedding for Rick, narrowing the field to one old church, several potential yachts, a cruise liner willing to host a wedding if we could plan for it eight months in advance with an upfront payment for the use of the ship, and several parks and gardens suitable for wedding photography.

Some of the yachts reminded me of miniature cruise liners, and they took luxury to excess—as did their operational costs. One yacht, with a maximum capacity of over seven hundred, would cost a hundred thousand to rent for the wedding, including rehearsals, catering, and entertainment. I particularly liked that yacht, as it oozed luxury and would sail anywhere within six hours of port, resulting in a party nobody would forget anytime soon. The cruise liner would be willing to take the entire party anywhere they typically sailed at standard cabin fare plus an additional fee for the wedding itself.

I worried that the rich and famous might even bite on a week or two adventure for the entire wedding, as that seemed something the excessively wealthy would indulge in.

I wondered if my boss would let me take a week or two off to go to a wedding.

On Friday night, I headed to the hotel with my pets in tow, braced for a conversation I'd ultimately hate and love at the same time, and called Rick.

"I was wondering when you'd call me," Rick answered. "How is everything going?"

"I survived my first week of work, and I have a weekend of helping a couple with their taxes ahead of me. One of the clients has pet spiders, and I'm pleased to report there were no fatalities from the spider. I'm not sure her husband is convinced he's going to survive sharing a home with his wife's pet spiders, but he seems to be a good sport about it. I did find some time to work on the wedding, and I had some questions."

"I may have answers, and if I don't, I know who to ask."

"There is a cruise liner that would be willing to allow you to book the entire ship to any of their regular destinations for the standard cabin fare plus a fee for the wedding. With the numbers you were tossing around, you almost have enough to fill almost the entire ship, hitting the liner's minimum to sail. There are some pretty big yachts out there, but they run the same price as the cruise liner if you have a big enough guest list, which you might."

"We can make the guest list larger if the ship can host the entire wedding party. We were limiting it due to space restrictions. My uncle is handy with technology, and we were going to record and distribute for those who couldn't come anyway."

That sounded like my personal hell in the making, but I would figure some way to survive through the planning.

Focusing on the perks of using a cruise ship for the wedding might help. "It's a pretty big ship, but I expect the deck would be crowded if we tried to cram that many people in one place at the same time. I can ask if they have places on the ship where we could spread the gathering. It would be extra planning to account for several celebrations happening at the same time, but it could happen. Depending on the total size of the wedding, yachts are an option, and there are some really nice ones that sail out of New York. The yachts usually max out at no more than six hundred guests, so if you want a bigger wedding, you might want to go with the cruise liner. They have cruises ranging from a week to an entire month, although they'll do a one-day event if you book the ship before they establish their schedule. They essentially make the ship available between official cruises, and they charge a fee for doing it because they'll need so many staff on board. But you have to book it far in advance either way. If you take the whole ship, they have to schedule everything."

"That's tempting. If we use a week-long cruise, most should be able to get the time off, and I would have sufficient time to make my plans. That said, what about our dogs?"

"I have no idea. I didn't ask if they'd allow dogs on board. I can ask them next time I talk to them."

"Please do so, as I think that'll matter. I'd rather not leave Annabel Lee for a week."

"I wouldn't want to leave mine, either, but I have a good pet sitter in mind if it's necessary."

"For some reason, a cat on a cruise ship seems to be a recipe for disaster."

"So are a bunch of dogs, but it might be viable. Lenore doesn't seem to mind her harness if it means she gets to stay near Edgar Allan Paw."

"Ask the cruise liner if they'll accommodate cats and dogs, what the extra fee for it would be, and what their room cleanup fees would be afterwards. Annabel Lee loves boats, so she will adapt nicely, but you may want to take your old man on a test cruise to see if he does okay on the water. Some dogs don't. Some cats don't, either."

"I'll do that, assuming I can find someone with a boat willing to take me out. It won't be a cruise liner, though. Aren't they different from one of the smaller boats?"

"Somewhat, yes. If they can't handle a small boat, I'd be worried about them on a cruise liner."

Where would I find time to take my pets on a mini cruise to see if they liked the ocean? I added it to my list of things to do. "All right. I'll see about that as soon as I have some time. What is the timetable for this?"

"Honestly, once I tell my cousin about the cruise liner and a week on the water, it will be as soon as you can get one booked. She doesn't even need a destination port. She loves everything about the ocean. Her groom likes the water, too, though not as much as she does."

"And you?"

"I very much like the idea of having a week to work on the target of my affection, even if I don't get to ask her during the actual wedding ceremonies. That'll let my cousin shine at her wedding too, despite her willingness to have me encroach on her turf."

"You told me it was basically a family tradition to double up on these things."

"She's willing to accept a proposal instead of me trying to toss a woman into a wedding gown on a whim. Members of my family and the family friends are used to that sort of thing, but it might be a harder sell this go around."

Interesting. "So, you're willing to double up but you don't think the woman you like will be willing to double up?"

"I wouldn't say that, I just don't want to spring it on her without giving her a chance to think about it. I'm not the kind to force someone to give me a yes or no with an audience, so I figure I'll be sly about it. She can decide without an entire cruise liner watching and waiting for her answer. If she wants to double up, I'm sure my cousin would be happy to toss her into something and drag her along for the ride. And if she *is* interested in that sort of thing, I get a chance to stick it to my parents and the other intermediate members of my family who have ideas about who I should be marrying."

Ah. Poor Rick. "They want you to do one of those alliance marriages, don't they?"

"Precisely. I'm trying to teach Annabel Lee to tell my mother no, but my mother has charmed my dog too much for it to work. Her inability to speak English also hampers with my attempts to have her tell my mother no."

I laughed. "That would be some trick, though."

"I tried telling Annabel Lee that, but she doesn't listen, and she insists on adoring my mother even when she's being a pain in my ass."

"Just tell your mother you're happily dating someone, pass on her kind offer to be set up with a woman, and go about minding your own business. You'll have to be sneaky with when you see your lady until the cruise, but that's a small price to pay for some peace, right?"

"I'm not sure my lady will like being treated like she should be hidden from sight, though."

"Have you asked her?"

"Not precisely. I'm trying to figure out how to convince her I shouldn't just stay in the friends category."

Ouch. Poor Rick. Poor me, too. Damn, we were good at making messes for ourselves. "So, it's less of a proposal for marriage and more begging for a chance to be her boyfriend?"

"That is sadly accurate. I figured if I proposed, she'd know I'm serious about a relationship."

"I'm probably the exact wrong person to talk to about relationships, because I totally made certain my brother got married to a bridezilla, and I'm still not convinced she has his interests at heart, but he really wanted to marry her, so I went with it. I'm thinking this might make me a bad person."

"I'm thinking it makes you a smart person,

really. I did have a question about that, if you don't mind."

"I don't mind. What's up?"

"Did you vet the services she wanted to use?"

"Amy picked, and Amy would not tolerate other suggestions. I went behind her back on the arrangements that were actually used. Why?"

"I found something interesting when I was going through the invoices."

I scowled. "I vetted the invoices before Mat paid them. They were legitimate companies, and they had good reputations. Amy was the one who drove them off, deliberately if you'd like my opinion on that."

"Ah, yes, but were you aware that they are all owned by someone related to or working with her mother?"

I frowned. "Pardon?"

"I was curious, so I started doing some research on each of the businesses, and with some poking, I found out that they're all owned by people Amy's mother works with in some fashion or another."

Ugh. Great. "Mat is not going to be happy if he finds that out, especially when accounting for how she's run at the altar how many times?"

"It gets better."

That didn't sound good, especially when his tone of voice promised there was nothing actually better about the situation. "All right. I'm ready. Hit me with it."

"Her mother owes all of them money, in similar amounts to the lost deposits."

Fuck. Fuckity, fuck, fuck, fuck. "Are you implying that she was using Mat to use the deposits to pay off her mother's debt, Rick?"

"Basically. And because she actually married Mat, the odds of this being exposed are rather high. Amy went off somewhere for a week, apparently for a business trip, and Mat isn't really sure where she's at. He's started doing some investigating of his own. I'm concerned."

My initial knee-jerk reaction involved popping the bitch in the mouth for using my brother like that, but instead of saying so, I took a few steadying breaths. "Okay. So, she may have done that. She still got married to my brother, even though I did catch her trying to climb out the window. Then there's the issue of the baby."

"That's the only thing going right. Mat's excited, Amy's excited, and they're probably going to end up with a functional marriage because they both want that baby. Don't ask them if they're sure they want a baby so early. They will go for your throat. It's nobody's business other than theirs, by the way. They're tired of the question, and they don't appreciate anyone being nosy."

"Did you make that mistake?"

"No, that honor went to your father."

Oh, boy. "I'll call Mom tomorrow and see about playing peacemaker."

"That wasn't why I told you. You don't have to do that."

"I'm definitely contributing to the problem, and as such, I can solve the problem easily. I'll just show up, yell at people for a while, and snarl at them until everyone behaves."

Rick stayed quiet, and in the background, I heard his dog give a quiet woof. He chuckled, and a moment later, he grunted. "Sorry about that. Annabel Lee gets sad if I don't pay enough attention to her. That sound was her vocalizing how her heart is breaking because I haven't paid attention to her for five whole minutes."

"She has a convincing argument."

"She usually does. So, that's the current situation with your brother, and it annoys me that I somehow became the bearer of bad news."

"Well, view it this way. My brother hasn't completely written you off if he's dragging you into this mess. That's something."

"That's true. I have a much better understanding on why you would just pack your bags and go. I'm glad I'm already on the way to my new residence, as I don't think I'd be able to deal with the family drama for much longer. Your family's drama is almost as bad as my family's drama. Oh, I have another bit of insider information for you."

"You do? I'm not sure I can handle any

more information today, Rick. All the information you've given me means I'm going to have to find time in the next week or two to go down there and knock some heads together. Also, I'm inviting you to the festivities, and it doesn't invalidate our scavenger hunt. You can't use my tags to get my address, though. You can't use anything that happens during this gathering against me."

"I find these terms to be acceptable. Amy's father had been trying to get her married off for a lot of reasons, including the preservation of his personal reputation. Her tendency to flee her weddings has lost him a lot of business. This was creating problems between Amy's parents, and it would not surprise me if there's a divorce in their future. With how much debt her mother's accrued and how much business her father has lost, it doesn't hurt her father too much to get out of the relationship now. He is confident he can restore his businesses if Amy and her mother aren't in the picture. That leads to some other interesting issues."

On Monday, I'd make certain to be far more grateful for the limited insanity my current work project brought to the table. "Dare I ask? I'm not sure I should ask, Rick."

"I'm telling you only because I don't know what Amy's main objective is—and if she is the kind to get revenge on someone. By someone, I mean you. Everyone knows you're the reason she made it to the altar and the reception, and she's not the kind to take that sort of thing with grace."

"I feel like we should be saying something nice about Amy at this point in time. She can't be that bad of a person."

"I'm sure she has good traits, otherwise Mat wouldn't want to make a marriage with her work. What are those good traits? I don't know. All I've seen from her lately has been petty jealousy."

I considered that. "Maybe she's just jealous I have a good relationship with my brother when he's not being a jerk?"

"That wouldn't surprise me at all. She's definitely the type. I don't like that type," he admitted.

"Neither do I. She might be one of those people who can't stand when her partner has a friend or loved one of the opposite gender. If that's so, I think that's really sad. I have a lot of male friends, and it'd be a deal breaker if my partner couldn't handle that. I'm not giving up my friends for a relationship. I'm totally willing to move away to get a better job and take control of my life, but that's a different thing."

"It is. As soon as you think Mat has been properly chastised, you may want to invite the lot of them to visit you, as they're upset you moved away. That said, they're not upset about why you moved away. They just like you and miss you."

"You've been cornered by them, haven't you?"

"Yep."

"I'm sorry."

"Don't be. I had your favorite milkshake, and I was given the extra cherries."

I laughed at the well-aimed tease. "I really do have a problem with those cherries. I think those will be my first grocery store purchase when I move into my new apartment."

"That sounds like a plan. Still, just keep your eyes open and be careful. I don't want Amy to do something stupid—or Amy's mother, if what I've been researching proves to be the truth."

Money could make good people do terrible things, although I believed Rick worried unnecessarily. Amy annoyed me, but she didn't seem that vindictive. "I'll keep an eye out," I promised.

"Good. Now that the unpleasant business is out of the way, how are you liking your new job?"

"Well, I can say this much. I don't think I'm cut out to be a criminal, business owners probably hate me, and I'm not sure how I managed to get this far in life being a strait-laced accountant. Also, being a good accountant is a lot more work, and while I appreciate the paycheck, I have some regrets right now."

"I think you'll be all right."

"If I'm not, I'm blaming you. Mat can deal with you then."

Rick laughed. "For a straitlaced accountant, that was a potent threat."

"Was it? Mat's still in the doghouse, and I've decided he's not allowed to share doghouses with either Edgar Allan Paw or Annabel Lee."

"That's absolutely ruthless."

"Putting him in a doghouse with either of our babies would be a reward."

"That it would be. How do you want me to handle your brother?"

"Don't. I'll take care of our family mess. I'll give Mom a call tomorrow and figure out when I can head down for a visit to set everybody straight."

"I'm pretty sure you threatening to set everybody straight will be sufficient to take care of the situation."

"If only."

FIFTEEN

It's the naughty daughter calling.

WHILE I NO LONGER ATTENDED CHURCH, MY parents did, so I busted ass through Sunday morning until two in the afternoon, which would be late enough for them to have attended service, grabbed something to eat with their church friends, and return home. Then, because my parents liked having their afternoon tea in peace, I waited for an extra thirty minutes before calling their house line.

On Sundays, their cells counted as the devil's tool, and they wanted nothing to do with technology.

"Hello?" my mother answered, as she also viewed her answering machine and Caller ID as the devil's tools, too.

"Hey, Mom. It's the naughty daughter calling to inform you that word has spread through the grapevine Dad said something stupid to Mat, and I am required to stage an intervention and go through familial repair protocols. I will be bringing a friend, his dog, my dog, and my cat, and I will expect all furry members of the family to be treated as though they are visiting dignitaries from a faraway land."

My mother sighed. "Are you drunk, Hope?"

"No. I was drunk early this week, though. My new landlord is a very nice Italian gentleman, and he celebrates new lease signings with wine. As it would have been rude to refuse the wine, I enjoyed some. My new apartment has heated floors, a jet tub, and space enough for myself and my two new pets."

"You got a new job and moved so you could have animals, didn't you?"

"That plus Mat was mean to me, so I decided to teach him an important lesson, but it seems Dad tried to teach Mat a lesson or two and created a family meltdown. Dad should have known better."

"Your father should have known better, yes. He's working his way around to apologizing, so an intervention may not be required."

I faked a gasp. "No! Dad might actually apologize without requiring an intervention? This isn't acceptable, Mom. That's not allowed in the family rule book. He can't break the family rules."

"You just want to stage an intervention."

I shrugged. "You tend to feed me when I'm

required to stage an intervention, and I'd like you to meet my dog and cat."

"Very well. I'll tell your father he needs to maintain his grumpiness levels with your brother until you can come visit. What would my little girl like to have for dinner?"

"Roast beef, please. It'll probably be two to three weeks, as I have to finish getting settled here first, but I might be able to wing next weekend if I finish a work project early."

"Don't rush through your work to finish it early. You know how badly you stress if you feel you've rushed your work. Two weeks is fine. That'll give me plenty of time to call the butcher for a good roast. Can you accept prime rib?"

Could I? I snorted at that question. "Only if you let me pay for it. I got a substantial raise at my new job, so I can afford the splurge. That can be my penance for taking a job offer without warning."

"I'm proud of you, but a little warning next time would be appreciated. How do you like your new job?"

I smiled, and I sharpened my various weapons in my arsenal of parental torment. "I got to work with male prostitutes all week."

"I was unaware prostitutes needed accountants."

"These ones do."

"Male prostitutes?"

"My work this week has been stunning, and their preferred outfits are suits."

"Have you been enjoying the scenery at work, Miss Hope?"

"Absolutely. It's strictly look but don't touch, but the two days I've had to run to the client's building have been very pleasant. They're polite gentlemen. You'd like them."

"But they're prostitutes."

"They're exceptionally polite prostitutes, hard workers, and smart. Honestly, I'm doing them a favor and not telling the single women of my new home state they're available. They'd be swarmed."

"What did I do to deserve to be taunted today?"

"You let Dad say something pretty mean to Mat, and while I'm still planning appropriate payback against my brother, that was *really* mean."

"I'll make sure your father knows he is going to be thoroughly scolded so he can prepare the appropriate forgiveness bribes."

I laughed, as that meant Dad would come to the family mediation meeting armed with milkshakes, extra cherries, and a chocolate cake for my brother. The parental forgiveness bribes had worked from the day we'd been adopted, and it would likely work for the rest of their lives. "And however much some of us are annoyed with Amy, we will be polite to her. She's pregnant, and as such, you will come with everything a mother-to-be requires for her torturous journey towards delivery."

"I'll keep that in mind."

"And we'll pretend that they didn't spill the beans about this before the generally safe window to do so. You will also offer to take her to any doctor's appointments she may need, as I have the feeling that her parental situation may bar much support from her family."

My mother sucked in a breath. "I see."

"You're good at the parent thing, so while I want to shackle Amy at times, do the parent thing and pretend she's just an extra one that wandered home with Mat. However much I want to shackle Amy at times."

"You're still upset with Amy."

"Yep. I took a baseball to the head for her, and all I got out of it was a headache and a hard time from my brother. He found out about the ball and chain."

"We have heard all about the ball and chain. We have also heard that the ball and chain has a new owner, who happens to be one of Mat's best friends. You should know better."

"The other option was to just let her get cold feet and run out on Mat. It only took threatening to use the ball and chain once to get her to the altar. Once she got there, she did fine, and everything I've heard so far indicates they want that baby, so I am expecting my mother and father to be the perfect grandparents for that baby, even with whatever other issues Mat's wife may bring to the table."

"I see you have decided to become assertive."

"Damn straight I've decided to become assertive. So, you are going to be hosting two very big, white, and fluffy dogs along with one fluffy white kitten. Edgar Allan Paw is quite old and will probably just want a cushion to rest his tired bones on. Lenore will stay with Edgar Allan Paw, and I have no idea what Annabel Lee will do, but I hope it involves putting Mat in his place."

My mother stayed quiet for long enough I worried I'd broken her. "That means Fredrick will be coming to our family dinner and bringing his dog."

"Yes, the one big dog is Rick's. He's been putting up with Mat's issues, so he deserves to be fed a good prime rib."

"Did you say your dog's name is Edgar Allan Paw?"

"Yep."

"And your cat's name is Lenore?"

I grinned. "I'm thinking about a parakeet, and should I get one, I'm naming it Raven."

"I see you are pursuing your love of animals now that you've flown from the nest and found an apartment that permits them."

"I met a spider earlier this week. Her name is Ruby, she's huge and old but not cranky. I wasn't brave enough to hold her, but her owner, one of my clients, had her out of her container. I never knew spiders could be pretty, but Ruby was nice for a spider."

"Please do not get a pet spider. I would have to visit your home and be forced to like a spider."

I considered if my apartment could handle a spider, if I wanted a pet spider, and what I might name one to fit in with my plans to theme my pets around a literary genius. "I'll think about it."

"I'm interpreting that to mean you're thinking about getting a spider."

"You're so smart, Mom."

"I suppose I should be grateful you didn't hit your rebellious stage until after you moved out of the house."

I thought about that, my eyes widening as I realized my mother made a good point. "This is like a rebellious stage on steroids, isn't it?"

"It really is. I hear you got rid of your old beater, too."

"I am the proud owner of a glittery Mercedes. I'll show it to you when I visit. It's a great car, it's really comfortable, and Edgar Allan Paw really likes rides in it. I didn't realize this when I got it, but the back seats are heated, which is great for him, as he seems to appreciate warm places. He'll even sit in the front seat, and he's been taught to tolerate a seatbelt, but it's not as comfortable for him as the back. It does mean I have to clean the interior a few times a week, but he's worth it."

"Why did you get a dog so soon, though? It's not like you to jump into that responsibility so recklessly."

"He's old, he's been living in a shelter, and he was up for adoption. My boss brought him in and had me babysit him and his kitty friend. I couldn't let them go back to the shelter, so I adopted them. I even have their signed papers and everything. They were dumped when Lenore was really young. But she's warming up to me, probably because Edgar Allan Paw loves to keep me company while I work. You will be required to love both Edgar Allan Paw and Lenore unconditionally."

"I can meet that condition without any complaint. You know the only reason you didn't have pets was because we all knew you wouldn't care for them."

I shrugged as she spoke the truth. "I am now a responsible adult. You should be utterly ashamed of yourself for raising me to be a responsible adult."

"I would like to take this moment to remind you that you had to have your brother remove spiders because they scare you. You would not enjoy having a pet spider."

I thought about Ruby, who was pretty for a hairy, eight-legged arachnid who might eat me in my sleep. "Ruby might convince me to change my mind."

"No, Hope. You do not need a spider in addition to your dog and cat."

"I can get a spider if I want to, Mom."

"Your brother will not rescue you from your pet, nor will your father. There's no way I'm going to."

I giggled. "But you'd visit me even if there was a spider in my apartment, wouldn't you?"

"Unfortunately, yes."

"I probably won't get a spider, but it's fun thinking about it. So, I'll plan on visiting two weeks from now, assuming Rick is available. If not, I'll find the first weekend everyone is free. Also, I'm planning another wedding."

"But is it yours?"

"No, Mom. Rick's cousin is getting married, and she was really impressed with Mat's wedding."

"You did a great job with Mat's wedding except for the baseball incident. Mat was disappointed you didn't want him at the hospital."

"Not on his wedding day!"

"Hope."

"What? It's true. After putting all that work into planning his wedding, he was attending it, as were you and everyone other than Rick, and Rick refused to go away."

My mother laughed. "Okay. That's fair enough. How is your head doing?"

"It's fine. I had a headache for a few days, but I otherwise escaped intact."

"And how are you getting along with Fredrick?"

"We're getting along fine, I guess. He's

been giving me information about what his cousin would like for the wedding, and I've come up with some good ideas. I think it'll be nice, although I'm concerned it's going to be extravagant—far more extravagant than Mat's."

"I'm sure you'll do a great job. So, two weeks, then?"

"Unless Rick can't make it, in which case I'll give you a call back in the next day or two. I'd rather not ruin your prime rib order. Try not to bankrupt me."

"Oh, I'm going to go after your wallet for worrying us. Prepare yourself for the bill, little girl."

Damn. When my mother got payback, she did it in a way I'd have to accept with good cheer and a large hit to my bank account. "All right. I guess I'm buying the best prime rib money can buy. I recognize when a cause is lost."

"Good girl. Do you want me to put your father on the phone? He's grumpy."

"Because of Mat?"

"You would be right."

"Just tell him I love him and will fight him for the extra cherries. I'd rather not interrupt his brooding."

"He needs a good brood every now and then."

That my father did. "Love you, Mom. Try not to annoy Mat until I'm there. Also, tell

Mat if he doesn't show up, I'm going to be very annoyed with him."

"As far as threats go, that's a good one. Are you very annoyed with him right now or just slightly miffed?"

"Slightly miffed."

"I'll inform your brother of the sliding scale of your wrath so he can make an informed decision."

"Please let me crash in my old room with my pets, as it's a long drive home and I'd rather not try to drive while stuffed on prime rib."

"Of course. Rick will be invited to spend the night as well. It won't take but a few minutes to get the guest room ready for him."

We exchanged pleasantries, and after I hung up, I rubbed my hands together and considered how best to implement my plan. First, I needed to call Rick and confirm if he would be available. Then, I'd let the pieces fall together as they would. Rick seemed like the convincing sort, so I'd recruit him to make sure my brother showed up, with or without Amy.

I brought up my contacts and tapped on Rick's name.

As always, he answered by the second ring. "Hey, Hope. What can I do for you?"

"Family intervention the week after next. Care to join my family for some prime rib and witnessing disaster?"

"I do care to join you and your family for

some prime rib, as a matter of fact. What's the catch?"

"You'll have to bring your dog, sleep in the guest room, and convince my brother he better show up. Preferably with Amy, but I'll accept just him if necessary."

"I'm confident I can do that. Will you be bringing your dog and cat?"

"As a matter of fact, yes. I have also reserved my childhood bedroom for the night, as I will be too full to drive back to New York following dinner."

"I'll need directions on how to get there. My car should be ready by then, but it'll be a little questionable. I ordered mine custom, and it takes a few weeks to get it in from the factory, and then I need to have it sent to a body shop for its new paint job."

"I could be talked into picking you up from a neutral location that completely hides where both of us live or will be living within two weeks. You might have to catch a cab to said neutral location, but I don't mind driving you to and from my general state and leaving you somewhere somewhat convenient for you."

"I have someone who can drop me off and pick me up from such a location. Will it bother your parents if you show up with me?"

"Not at all, especially if I tell them it was on the way. They like when I try to be a decent human being, and saving gas makes me a decent human being. Hopefully, our pets like each other. I think the back seat should be large enough for both of the dogs."

"Annabel Lee often prefers the floor-boards, as she's a weirdo."

I chuckled. "Edgar Allan Paw prefers the back seats because they're heated and he can stretch out."

"I see you got an upgraded model. I had to pay extra for the rear heated seats. Well done on picking a good car."

"I'm pretty sure some politician bought it, got tired of it, and dropped it at a loss, and the dealership was willing to wheel and deal with me for it. It was expensive but good for its make and model and perks."

"Maybe I should take you car shopping with me next time I go."

"You just got a new car. Unless you break that one, you don't need a new one for at least five years, unless the one you bought doesn't fit things like an unexpected wife, kids, or dogs. This is good life advice, and I intend on following it. Honestly, I intend on running my car into the ground, as I tend to remain chronically single, and I'm not sure I can handle more than one dog and a cat at time, although I am really considering a parakeet because they're cute. I've decided I probably shouldn't get a spider, no matter how nice Alice's seemed to be. In that she didn't attack, bite, or eat anyone during our meeting."

"That sounds like an excellent choice, although I'm saying that as a man who has run away from a small spider. It startled me. I relocated it outside where it belonged when my heart rate lowered to something tolerable."

"I used to make Mat deal with any spiders, but I figure I'm screwed if I have to deal with any now. Or I'll be that awful tenant who asks the building staff to rescue me from a spider. Actually, I don't like bugs all that much, especially since I've recently learned there are cockroaches that can fly."

"Cockroaches can fly?"

"I didn't know this until one flew in my face at the cursed viewing. In good news, my ankle is fine, but yeah. It was in the same building with the bathroom-kitchen monstrosity."

"Ah, that reminds me."

"Reminds you? Of what?"

"I am fairly confident I have identified which city you live in due to the reference to the bathroom-kitchen monstrosity. I began doing searches into real estate that followed this trend, and it's fortunately uncommon except in a few locations. There are only two locations in New York I have found where this trend seems to exist, and only one of those locations has the population required to support numerous male prostitutes. You're somewhere on Manhattan Island, Miss Hope."

Damn. "You literally deduced that based on my exposure to a bathroom in a kitchen?"

"I may have requested the aid of a real estate agent, as I had trouble believing this could possibly be a trend anywhere remotely civilized. My agent confirmed it, and I think he even directed me to the complex you had viewed. I was even going to have a look at it, but it was undergoing repairs. That is why I am confident in my thought I have your position nailed down."

Damn. Rick meant business, and I appreciated his ruthless approach to the hunt. "And here I thought you wanted to drag out the hunt."

"I'm debating if I'll continue to narrow down your location, have you confess your location, or just show up one day, tap you on the shoulder, take you off somewhere, and make it clear I'm the true winner here."

That would be quite the feat, especially when I kept my general activities limited to work, walking the dog, and staying at the hotel. Once I moved into my apartment, I would likely only leave to walk the dog and go to work. "I already said you could get away with a lot if you bring your dog and use her as bait, but you'll have to accommodate my pets now, too. I'm changing that rule because he's an old man who doesn't need to be displaced again."

"I'll make sure Edgar Allan Paw is the happiest of dogs while you're in my custody."

"I get terrible wine hangovers, so don't let me have wine. I learned my lesson after my landlord plied me with extra wine. It didn't help I'd had a Cosmo before the wine, but we won't discuss that. I had intended to only have the Cosmo, but then he offered wine and showed me the tub. Waiting to make use of that tub is awful."

"I see you're highly motivated by a good tub. Tell me. What is your dream tub?"

"Apparently, it's the one in my new apartment. It's really nice."

He laughed. "Well, I hope you enjoy your new tub when you get moved in."

"I also plan to enjoy my new fireplace, too. It also has heated floors. Basically, I'm paying a ridiculous amount to live in heaven, and I'm all right with this."

"As long as the amount you pay equates to the happiness you get out of it, that's great."

I blinked, as I'd never heard the issue of high rent put quite that way before. "How about you? How is your foray into real estate going?"

"I found a really nice place, it did some damage to my investment accounts, but I think it'll hold its value well over the years, and I'm hopeful it'll make a good family home for the area I've chosen. I won't know if I had the right idea until I ask the woman, of course, but I'm feeling confident right now."

Lucky woman. "And if she doesn't like it?"

"We'll go house shopping until we find something we both like."

I needed to yell at my brother for having perfect friends that'd make perfect husbands, especially as edging in on my brother's turf likely counted as rude. "Well, if you think the value will hold, then it's a good investment either way, even if she doesn't like it and you need to move."

"Moving is such a pain," Rick complained.

"Isn't it, though? I haven't technically finished my move yet, and I'm already done with having to move. I'm just glad work is paying for the actual movers, because I'm not sure I could deal with the stress on top of having to pay more money out."

"Unpacking is atrocious. It should be criminalized."

"Try packing in a hurry. I didn't have time to properly label everything, so I'm going to be box surfing for months."

"Well, that part is okay on my end. I had to inventory everything to bring it into the United States. Let me tell you, that was a pain in the ass. Fortunately, the movers handled almost everything, but I had to pick what would stay and go. I donated a lot of things to charity, as it wasn't worth importing into the United States. I may have donated too much stuff, but buying new furniture isn't nearly as bad as moving the old stuff overseas."

"I'm still impressed you managed to get a visa to be here."

"Money talks. It talks especially well when I can make my money talk in other countries instead. It's amazing how quickly money can talk when you have a damned good immigration lawyer who knows who to talk to in the government about getting the right forms processed promptly. Making my money talk in this case is going to work well, because it'll mean a lot of job openings as I open a proper branch of my business here. My main operations are still overseas, but I can do the mandatory work for them anywhere. I take a rather untraditional approach to my business."

"I hope untraditional also means legal."

Rick chuckled. "Perhaps I'll hire your firm and demand you're in charge of making sure the accounting department for my American operations are properly legal and set up efficiently."

"Did you know that's how you flirt with an accountant, Rick? That's how you flirt with an accountant, especially a nitpicker of an accountant like me. You shouldn't be flirting with me."

"I was more thinking I value competence in the workplace, but I consider myself educated on how one might flirt with an accountant. I had no idea tidy, legal paperwork could possibly count as flirting."

"If you saw what I have to do during a bad job, you would understand that tidy, legal accounting is equivalent to an elaborate marriage proposal. Some of the accounts I've had to do have been that bad."

"I am making a note to have all of my operations properly audited, and then I'm going to buy flowers for all of my accountants, and I may also give wine, chocolates, or whatever other edible vices the accountants need to get over any accidental cruelties I've subjected them to."

"Can you burn the tax code while you're at it?"

"If only."

"Bummer. So, can you get on the phone with Mat and make sure he knows he can't miss our date with prime rib?"

"I'll make sure he's there," Rick promised.

"I need to get back to work, so we'll talk about where I'm picking you up from later, and we'll go from there. I'll call you sometime this week?"

"Sounds good. I'll give you a call if your brother puts up a fight."

"Inform Mat baseballs to the head really, really hurt, and if he puts up a fight, I'm coming armed with one so I can beat sense back into him."

"I will warn your brother that you are ready to wage war for family peace."

"When you phrase it like that, my mediation efforts sound somehow violent and contradictory."

"Hey, I'm not judging. If it takes a baseball to the head to make things work out, it's a small price to pay. Mat's head is hard enough to handle it."

I considered my head, how I'd gotten rather lucky all in all, and wondered what would have changed if I hadn't gotten smacked with a baseball. "I did get to skip the reception because of a baseball. Does that count as working out?"

"It was a good start. I've got to run. I'll let you know if there are any problems with Mat, and I'll shoot you a text as soon as I know either way."

"Sounds good. I guess I'll see you in two weeks."

"I'll see you in two weeks."

Rick hung up, and I considered my phone through narrowed eyes. Threat? Promise? Something about his tone conveyed there was more to it than met the eye, but I couldn't figure out what.

Whatever. I'd think about it sometime after I played the family mediator and kept the little fights from turning into big explosions.

SIXTEEN

I loved snuggling up to my old man of a dog.

MAT AGREED TO COME, he somehow convinced Amy to go along with it, and I worked every waking moment to make certain I finished with the McCarthy file before I was scheduled to pick Rick and his dog up from an associate's home in Hell's Kitchen. Before he'd told me where he'd be, I hadn't heard of the neighborhood, and I wanted to know why anyone would want to live in a place with such a weird name. A little research online indicated the place was gradually gentrifying, budding actors tended to live there, and it was fairly close to Broadway, drawing in those who enjoyed the arts.

Armed with everything my pets would need for the weekend, extra supplies in case Annabel Lee needed them, and enough room in the trunk for anything Rick might have with him, I braved the roads and headed for the address, discovering a nice row of townhouses with a larger house on the end, the sort of place a young couple might move into to build their family.

SUVs dominated the driveways, and I only found the house because there was an available spot for my car, something Rick had promised would be waiting for me to spare me the headache of trying to find a spot on the street. Considering how busy a Friday night could get in Manhattan, I appreciated the courtesy. I wasn't sure how dinner and staying the night had turned into a weekend-long affair, but I didn't look forward to the four or so hour drive to reach my parents' house before I could crash out for the night.

At least I'd enjoy sleeping, as I'd enticed both of my pets to join me in bed. Edgar Allan Paw needed help to get onto the mattress, but some prices were worth paying.

We kept each other warm, and I loved snuggling up to my old man of a dog.

I debated my options, as my old dog didn't like getting in and out of the car much. Giving him the choice would make things easier, so I killed the engine, got out of my Mercedes, and opened the door for him. Edgar Allan Paw considered his options, gave a low woof, and oozed out of the vehicle, stretching his old bones while Lenore sniffed the asphalt. I kept a firm grip on their leashes, waited for them to go through their investigatory routine, and clicked my tongue to indicate it was time to go.

After two weeks of effort and a little help from my boss's sister, I'd taught them to heel at a single click, and the pair walked with me to the front door. It opened before I could ring the bell, and Rick grinned at me. "Come on in. My hosts want to meet you, and Annabel Lee is begging for treats. It'll be good to introduce the animals inside, too, so we can see if I need to sit in the back with one of the dogs while the other has the front. I brought a seatbelt leash, and I have a spare if you need one."

"I have three seatbelt leashes, as I'm vain and need my dog to be appropriately colored depending on my mood. I also have a seatbelt harness for Lenore. Edgar Allan Paw is a little tired today, so don't be surprised if he flops somewhere and takes a nap. Napping is his favorite hobby."

Rick crouched down to introduce himself to my dog, and after a few sniffs, he earned a lick from my rescue, and even Lenore allowed him to pat her head. "Have you had a vet do his labs and diet?"

"I got the information from my boss's sister, who is a dog breeder and was working at the shelter where he lived. I have a lot of vet paperwork from her, but I don't know what any of it actually means. He goes again in six months, and I was told as long as I followed the instructions, he'd be fine. I also got a list of things to watch out for, but that's been okay so far."

"Well, he looks healthy as far as I can tell, just old."

"Yeah. That's what everyone has been saying. He's a really good dog."

"Spoken like a true, biased dog owner. Well done, Edgar Allan Paw. You have successfully enslaved your owner."

"I have to help him into bed, and he starts crying if I leave him on the floor. I'm whipped."

"There's nothing wrong with being whipped by an old dog. Come on in before we slaughter their electric bill. Are you hungry?"

"I was figuring we'd grab something on the way," I admitted.

"I like the way you think. Road trips are the only time I get to eat quality junk food, so I hope you're not on a special diet."

"I am on a seefood diet. I see food, I eat food. Mom makes amazing prime rib, but she's making me pay for it as retribution for running away from home with minimal warning."

Rick led me into a spacious kitchen, where an older man and woman showered Annabel Lee with their attention. I smiled at how the large dog soaked in the love. She was a little smaller than my dog, and sat with picture perfect patience, obeying commands to shake, lie down, and other basic tricks I hadn't tried with mine, as I figured he'd earned being lazy.

"Juliette, this is Hope. Mr. Carter, if you would kindly stop keeping your first name a secret, it would make introducing you so much easier."

"You got a letter out of me once. If you want the other letters that make up my first name, you'll just have to figure it out yourself," the man replied with a smile. He strode over and held out his hand. "It's a pleasure to meet you, Hope. Everyone calls me Mr. Carter, and while I'm sure I have a first name, I seem to have forgotten it."

"It's a pleasure to meet you, Mr. Carter. I hope this isn't an inconvenience."

"It's not. My wife needed to lure Rick over for a fitting anyway and discuss the matter of wedding apparel."

My eyes widened. "We're wedding planning, Rick? You didn't tell me we were going to be wedding planning. I left my notes at the hotel."

"I was wedding planning. You're just here to pick me up. Juliette is a fashion designer, and my cousin has decided only a custom Carter gown will do for her big day. As I happened to have worked with Mr. Carter in the past, I thought I'd reach out since I was in the area. Somehow, that turned into me being fitted for a new suit. I'm not actually sure how that happened."

"Pretty men who enter my home must be fitted for a suit," the woman announced, giving Rick's dog a final pat on her head before rising. "Pretty women who enter my home must also be fitted. It's a rule. I just made it up. Come along, lovely lady. It's time for your fitting."

"Juliette, you can't dress up Miss Hope today. They have a long drive ahead of them."

The couple squared off to fight, and I glanced in Rick's direction.

He shrugged and grinned. "I had no idea Mrs. Carter was so much fun, but when I came over, she announced I was being kidnapped, and if I could cooperate until you arrived, she would be very appreciative. Mr. Carter just sighed, so I figured everything was okay. I need a few new suits, anyway."

"You came here so I could pick you up, and you were ambushed into having a fitting?"

Juliette dodged her husband, snagged me by the arm, and dragged me out of the kitchen with surprising strength. "It'll take twenty minutes, and I'll return her unharmed and in possession of some random object from my closet. You were complaining it's too full again, darling. I'm helping to empty it."

I gasped, staggered but caught my balance, and went with her flow, as I had the feeling she could—and would—drag me across the floor otherwise. Dropping my pets' leashes put me in the bad pet parent category, something I'd feel guilty over later.

Laughing, Rick contained both animals

and pet Edgar Allan Paw. "Don't worry, old man. She'll be back in a few minutes."

Juliette hauled me to a sewing room, closed the door behind us, and rubbed her hands together. I recognized the manic gleam in the woman's eyes; I'd been around enough energetic, obsessive people to understand I'd captured whatever quality made the woman tick.

Surrendering would make the whole thing end faster. "What am I being fitted for?"

"Clothes."

Uh oh. "What sort of clothes?"

"I'm thinking about that. You'll need a wedding dress, as he told me you're coordinating his cousin's ceremony. You'll also need business attire, I'm sure. Casual clothes. Lingerie. You know, the usual. Do you like black?"

"I like black."

"Blue?"

"I guess?"

"How about orange?"

"I can't say I've ever tried wearing anything orange before."

"Purple?"

"Are you trying to turn me into a rainbow?"

Juliette giggled. "I wouldn't make you wear all the colors at once, but I do enjoy bright colors. You have to put up with that scamp in the other room for a long car ride, so you deserve a purse and a nice pair of boots. Do you like heels?"

"No higher than two inches, but I sprained my ankle a few weeks ago, so I've been sticking to low heels or no heels at all."

"Two pairs of boots, then. Maybe a runner. One with heels, one without heels. Excellent. All right. Strip down and let's see if your bra fits."

When I made it home, I would have to thank my mother for having acclimated me to scrutiny in the dressing room, and after a moment of thought, I did as told, folding my clothes and setting them on her sewing table until I stood in my less-than-appealing cotton bra and underwear.

"You're practical and enjoy comfort, but you're wearing the wrong cup size. You're supposed to contain your breasts, not strangle them within an inch of their poor lives." Juliette tested the shoulder strap, made a thoughtful noise, checked the tag of my bra, and whipped out a measuring tape. She measured me head to toe, taking notes in a journal while muttering to herself. She spent a disconcerting amount of time poking and measuring my feet. Once done, she eyed my bra like she wanted to burn it. "Wait here, don't get dressed, and if you get cold, grab a robe from the rack. I'll be back within five minutes."

As I wasn't cold, curious over what horrible offense my bra had done to her, and doubtful I could realistically afford whatever rates she charged for her apparel, I waited as told.

She returned several minutes later with a large box overflowing with clothing. "One of these days, my husband will learn he can't tell me I need to clean out my closet again. When he tells me that, I grab innocent people, usually young, pretty women, and I have my way with them. It's a deep-set character flaw."

Dumping the box onto the table beside my clothes, she rummaged through it until she located a lingerie box, which she handed to me. "He said one lingerie box only, but he didn't say I couldn't cram as many sets into the box as possible, which is what I did."

More bras and underwear than I currently owned competed for space in the box, and my brows shot up. "This is a fortune in lingerie."

"If my husband hadn't cruelly forced me to clean my closet, I wouldn't be just handing out lingerie at my whim." She turned to the door, made a face, and hollered, "You hear that, you wretch? Cruelly forcing me to clean my closet! And then to dare restrict me on what I can do with my closet? Rude!"

The woman's husband chuckled from somewhere nearby. A moment later, he said through the door, "You have ten minutes, but they do need to get on the road, Juliette. You're only getting away with this because she showed up a few minutes early."

I did hate being late. "It's okay, Mr. Carter.

While this is weird, I don't mind. But shouldn't I pay for this?"

"No," the Carters replied.

I considered the situation, and while accepting random charity baffled me, I could do so with grace. "Thank you, then." I picked through the bras and lifted one out. "This is so much prettier than what I would have bought myself," I confessed.

"There are a few of the more practical ones in there for your enjoyment as well. I've worked with your type before. You'll appreciate expanding your lingerie horizons down the road, and when it comes time to replace them, you'll be knocking at my door with your credit card in hand. I know what a good bra does to a woman."

Clever. "You're just securing future sales."

"And I have to make you a dress for the wedding anyway. It works out for all of us. Get changed while I decide what you're wearing out of here. I tossed in some pajamas, too. They're flannel. Every woman deserves a nice pair of flannel pajamas. They're extra good at catching dog fur, and I can't help but notice you have a nice, big dog to cuddle up with at night."

I grinned. "He does have a lot of fur, he is big, and he's very nice. He's only recently become a cuddler, but he needs help getting in and out of bed."

"Invest in a ramp for him at the foot of your bed. That'll help, and it'll spare your back trying to lift that much dog. You probably have fun lifting him into your car."

"Fortunately, he doesn't need too much help getting in, although he gets up on the floorboard before getting onto the seat."

"Since you're driving a long way, you get jeans, a blouse, and a leather coat. You get a puppy blouse because I say so." Juliette plucked a silky blouse from the box, gave it a shake, and showed me. The cream color would match with a lot of what I wore, and it had a pocket over one breast with the picture of a cute puppy peeking out over the pocket. "I was told I couldn't just make a puppy pattern, and that I had to limit myself to one puppy on this one."

"But why would anyone limit you to one puppy? That seems cruel."

"That's what I said. Those mean people stood their ground and demanded I stick to one puppy only."

"They weren't being mean, Juliette. Stop filling Hope's ears with nonsense, finish dressing her, and get out here. They do need to go. Long drive," Mr. Carter said.

"Cruel!"

"I'm not cruel, I'm just not letting you keep her all night long when her family is expecting her. You also can't keep Fredrick or the dogs or cat."

"Extra cruel," Juliette complained.

"Did your assistant forget your medications again?"

"I made my assistant transfer to design, where she belongs. I have been assistant free since five this afternoon."

"Juliette Carter, you did not transfer your assistant!"

"I most certainly did. She deserved it! She had it coming to her, doing all sorts of good design work. Don't you tell me how to run my company, you jerk."

I changed into one of the cream-colored bras and matching underwear before taking the shirt out of Juliette's hands and putting it on. "Jeans, please?"

"The darker pair is best with the jacket and that shirt," Juliette replied. She abandoned me to the box and stomped her foot near the door. "She deserved it, Mr. Jerk!"

"Please finish with Hope and come take your medication before you break the house again."

"Just because I bounced off a banister too hard once doesn't mean I'm going to break the house."

"Except you did that twice this month."

"Why are you so mean to me?"

"I'm not being mean, but I'm going to make sure you have an assistant that makes certain you get your afternoon medications without being lured away to a different position in your company. Your assistant is there to make your brain stop being broken. Your brain is broken right now, Juliette. Take the pills that fix it."

I put on the jeans, pleased with how well they fit me. The black leather jacket I located fit me a little too well, and I worried I'd be knocking at her door sooner than later to buy more clothes. At the bottom of the box, I found two pairs of running shoes, three sets of kitten heels, a pair of calf-high leather boots, and two pairs of slippers. The running shoes tempted me, but I went with the boots, pulling them on and tucking my jeans into them before lacing them. "Okay. I think that's all I need," I announced.

Juliette whirled, looking me over with narrowed eyes. "Purse. Most Evil Spouse, I will agree to your terms if you locate a good leather purse. In black. Make it a big one. Put a little one with a gold chain inside the big one. Should you do this, I will do as you ask."

"The only reason you're getting away with this is because I told you to clean your closet."

The woman smirked and flipped her middle finger at the door. "Don't tell the jerk this, but I love him very dearly even when he's trying to tell me no."

I could tell, and I smiled. "Are you sure you don't want me to pay you for this? There's a lot of clothing here."

"I'm sure. They're prototypes, and I keep a lot of this stuff in my closet for people who come over. My husband has figured out I can't help myself, so he lets me keep a closet I can just give stuff away from. They've already served their purpose, so it's time for them to go to your home and be loved until they're worn out. Then you should light them on fire. Lighting old things on fire is a lot of fun. I volunteer my fire pit. Bring the scamp with you. We can roast marshmallows. It'll be fun. Just don't tell that mean husband of mine I'm planning on burning things again. It upsets him for some reason."

"Is it safe to come in?" Juliette's husband asked.

"You can come in."

The older man cracked open the door, peeked to confirm it was actually safe, and entered, carrying a blue, a red, and a black purse, and judging from the chains peeking out of all three bags, he'd joined his wife in being excessive. "She may take all three of these home, as I have noticed that your purse closet is overfilled. Again. Purses attacked me when I opened the door, Juliette."

"Damn it. I worked so hard to train those attack purses to only go after unknown entities. They weren't supposed to attack *you*."

Mr. Carter thrust all three purses into my arms. "I will grab your box and help you take that to the car. Please take these things from my house. I'm begging you. If she doesn't get rid of some stuff, I'll end up sleeping with her purses. Again."

"I'm not that bad."

"You really are, Juliette." Mr. Carter kissed his wife's cheek. "I'll get your pills as soon as I get her things taken to her car. If you're good, you can invite her over to our house again to play later, but you have to let her go visit her family for now. Remember, you can't adopt young ladies or gentlemen because you're lonely. Julian, Chloe, and the baby will be over tomorrow morning. You'll last that long, I promise."

"But are you sure? Are you really sure?"

"I'm positive. Now, shoo. Go say goodbye to Fredrick and Annabel Lee so they can get on the road. They have a long drive ahead of them, and you'll worry if they're out too late. March, woman!"

Juliette pouted, but she obeyed.

"Please forgive her," Mr. Carter said once his wife left. "She gets excited, and when she's off her medications, things can get weird. She's mostly harmless, I promise."

I could believe mostly harmless, a lot of fun, and possibly the victim of a great deal of sugar. "It's okay, Mr. Carter. She seems really nice."

"That she is. She just gets excitable is all." Mr. Carter picked up the box and nodded towards the door. "With luck, I'll have you on the road in a few minutes. Just have Fredrick give Juliette or me a text when you get in so she doesn't worry. The last thing I need is to have to go on a long drive so she can visually confirm you made it safely."

For some reason, I believed she'd make him do just that—and he'd be willing to go with it because he seemed like the type, too.

"I'll make sure he texts. Thank you for the new clothes and the purses."

"You're welcome. And yes, they really are just taking up space in the closet because she no longer needs them for design, so please don't worry about it."

I decided I wouldn't worry and just enjoy her gifts. "If there's anything I can do in exchange, please let me know."

"I'll let her know—after you're safely out of her clutches."

I had a feeling I'd appreciate that later.

ANNABEL LEE and Edgar Allan Paw took to each other well enough they crammed onto the back seat together and opted to take a nap, leaving Lenore to decide which dog to sleep on. She sniffed Annabel Lee warily, flicked an ear back, and claimed her throne on Edgar Allan Paw's back.

I envied Rick, who could twist around and watch our pets whenever he wanted.

Escape happened later than I'd liked, with Mr. Carter catching his wife by her waist and dragging her indoors while waving a farewell with his free hand. I took the opportunity to lock the doors and pull out of their driveway before she could escape and delay us longer.

"You know the strangest people, Rick."

He laughed. "I knew Juliette had a reputation, but had I known how fun she could be, I really would have concocted an excuse to visit sooner. I wasn't expecting her to corner you, but I find it difficult to be sorry. I got a bill. You got a box."

"She probably took you for all you're worth and felt your purchases had paid for her generosity."

He laughed harder. "You're probably right. I ordered a ridiculous amount of clothes while waiting for you to get here. It worked well, since you'll have a great dress for the wedding, although apparently, I have to pay for it."

"I can pay for my own dress."

"You should ask how much the dress costs before saying that. I know how much the dress costs. Just don't ask how much the dress costs. My cousin is going to regret wanting Carter gowns when she gets the bill. And yes, my cousin *is* paying for the dresses. Since they're Carters with minor variants, she'll pay for the design and the materials, which is cheaper than if she were to buy them individually. They're still not cheap, though."

"Oh, so my dress will be one of those?"

Sighing, Rick bowed his head. "Probably not."

"Why not? She wanted me to be part of the party. You cousin did, right?"

"Elizabeth does, yes. That's my cousin. I'm not sure I've said her name before. But yes, she does. The problem is, I told Juliette you were planning the wedding, too. So, you get a dress all of your own, and since it's my fault, I'm paying the bill. Juliette has opinions about wedding planners."

"She does? Are they bad?"

"Oh, no. Juliette loves planning weddings. But the planners usually get a slow screw, and the only person who will be dressed better than you will be the bride and groom."

"That sounds worrisome." At the first stop sign, I tapped the nav panel and activated the drive instructions to get to my parents' house. The car informed me we would be on the road for almost five hours thanks to traffic. "How will everyone else react to it?"

"It will be glorious chaos, as you'll be surrounded by the rich and famous, and you are neither rich nor famous. I'm going to have a great time watching them try to figure out how to handle you. Since Elizabeth determined you're planning her wedding *and* you'll be in the party, nobody will want to piss her off, but they aren't going to understand why she wanted an American. They're already having kittens that I've moved to the United States. They had kittens when I moved to Japan."

"Where are you supposed to be from, anyway?"

"I was born in Dover."

"England?"

"Yep. My mother was visiting Dover castle when I decided I was done with being carried around. She appreciated my escape plan, which was done within an hour. She didn't even get to leave the grounds before I showed up, much to her disgust. I showed up two weeks early, ready to conquer England. Then I decided I liked business and international affairs more than appropriate, and I started my business ventures at sixteen. She thought I was working on a hobby rather than making some serious ploys to start my own company. By eighteen, she realized I had more business sense than half of the family combined. I started with stock management, had some really lucky hits, and then I moved into other business ventures. Dad says I have a horseshoe crammed up my ass. When I started heavily investing in Japanese companies, I moved there to be close to work. I've gotten those ventures stabilized, so here I am."

"And then you told Elizabeth you were interested in someone."

"Yep. That's got the entire family riled up, too, as I refuse to inform them of the subject of my interest. If I tell them, they'll ambush her, and I'd rather she have plenty of warning. I'll talk to her about it eventually. When I work up the nerve. Someday. Hopefully soon."

Poor Rick. "Good luck with that. It sounds like you're going to need it."

"I really will."

SEVENTEEN

I got dragged into a woman's sewing room.

WE MADE it to my parents place a little before one in the morning, and my brother stormed out of the two-storied house. According to his expression, we were dead and didn't know it yet.

Edgar Allan Paw didn't approve of my brother's body language, jumped out of the car, and gave a big woof, which stopped Mat in his tracks. My dog sat down and gave a self-satisfied huff. I rewarded my old man with a head pet and a kiss on his nose. "Good boy."

"That's not Annabel Lee. That one is even bigger than Annabel Lee. What have you done, Hope?" my brother complained.

"I invested in my personal security. Okay, he is just really old and had been dumped, and I couldn't let him spend the rest of his life in a shelter. This is Edgar Allan Paw, and his kitten is Lenore. Yes, he's bigger than Annabel Lee, but he's usually a good, quiet boy. Come over nicely and say hello. Without being cranky. Why are you cranky, anyway?"

"You were supposed to be here two hours ago."

Oh. Right. "I got dragged into a woman's sewing room. Sorry. She was too nice to say no to."

"Juliette Carter got her hands on Hope. I had gone to get fitted for suits, and when Hope showed up, Juliette dragged her off, and Mr. Carter said to just let it be. I think Juliette had a few hard days at work and wanted something positive to do. And there was something about medications. Oh. Juliette is the fashion designer doing El's wedding. Hope needed to be measured anyway, so it worked out. I texted you we would be late. That reminds me. I need to text Mr. Carter so Juliette doesn't worry."

Rick sounded as tired as I felt, and I expected I'd be rambling within a few minutes, too. While Rick handled texting Mr. Carter, I introduced my brother to my dog, and as I wasn't a complete bitch, I gave him a hug. "I'm still mad at you for saying stupid shit, but I'll let it slide for now."

"How long are you going to let it slide?"

"You'll have to figure out where I live on your own, and I'll only give you clues if you're nice to me and my pets."

"Harsh but deserved. Amy did come, and I think she's mostly forgiven you for the ball and chain. On a condition."

Uh oh. “What condition?”

“Should any man ever decide to propose to you, she’s showing up with the ball and chain, and she’s making certain you can’t run away from any embarrassing overtures he might subject you to. She will also attend your wedding, and she will be prepared to use the ball as necessary. She might insist you just wear it and be hauled to the altar on a cart. Your groom can walk down the aisle, as you’ll be incapable of doing it in a dignified manner.”

Wow. There was harsh, and then there was flat-out revenge. “That’s mean.”

“I thought so, too, but Rick decided he’d loan his ball and chain for the cause, as the idea made him laugh.”

I turned to Rick, put my hands on my hips, and narrowed my eyes.

Rick grinned and shrugged. “It seemed like a good idea at the time, and she was willing to forgive you if she could have a turn with the ball and chain. She even admitted it was a little funny you’d gone that far to make sure she married Mat. And since you were trying to play peacekeeper, I thought I’d join in, too. That said, don’t let Mat know if you find any men interesting. He’ll demand the ball and chain, and I’ll be forced to offer it to him.”

Double wow. “That’s ruthless. Utterly ruthless. I’m not sure either one of you deserve Mom’s prime rib.”

Rick held his hands up in surrender. "I was surrounded, and they were issuing ultimatums. But at least I'm warning you, right?"

"There will be rules. First, should the ball and chain be used, the victim will be in good health, there will be a safe word in case of panic, and it will not be used should it potentially cause risk to life or limb. There will be no ball on board the cruise liner, as the ship could rock, the ball could roll, and those in the ball's way could be severely injured. You may bring the chain and only the chain on board the cruise ship, and you will not use it without the bride's permission. Actually, you need the groom's permission, too. I'd normally say the wedding planner's permission, but it seems I'm being vetoed. Second, you will make sure the manacle can be removed without the key, so you'll have to replace that part. I got it as a threat, not as something to be actually used. Third, you will make sure that all targets of the manacle are sized appropriately for it, as it is iron and will cut off circulation. You will have soft padding to prevent injury to the victim. Fourth, you will not break any laws while using the ball and chain."

With that list, I might dodge it assuming I ever found a man eligible for marriage. As Rick already had his eye on someone, I expected I'd dodge the ball and chain. I narrowed my eyes. "Fifth, you will not hire male strippers or prostitutes to pretend they're interested in me for an excuse to make use of the ball and chain."

Rick covered his mouth, but I heard him snort in an attempt to contain his laughter.

My brother's mouth dropped open. "Why do you think I'd hire male strippers or prostitutes?"

"They're gorgeous and make a good bachelorette gift? Have you ever met a male stripper before, Mat? Or a male prostitute?"

"I can't say I have."

"I have, and should I ever be put in a position where a ball and chain might be warranted, well, the groom will have a fantastic night after I've been looking at hot men for several hours the night before the wedding."

Rick choked on his laughter, went down on his knees, and buried his face in his dog's fur.

I smirked.

"You're doing this to get back at me, aren't you?"

"Absolutely. That said, you don't have to actually hire any strippers, as I'd probably get upset or jealous if my husband-to-be was drooling all over other women without me. What can I say? I'm the jealous kind."

"You are?" Mat raised a brow. "I thought you were the chronically single kind uninterested in marriage."

I scowled. "Just because I haven't expressed interest in specific men does not mean I'm not interested in establishing a permanent relationship with one. I just have a busy job, and it wouldn't be fair to the poor man who has to compete with my current schedule. Maybe in a few months I will look for a suitable partner. And if I stay too busy, maybe I'll just hire a male prostitute."

"Please don't," Mat begged in a strained voice. "If our parents find out, I'm a dead man for not keeping a closer eye on you."

"You're a married man who needs to keep an eye on his wife, not on his wayward sister. Anyway, I'm old enough I can hire male prostitutes if I want to. I'm even old enough I can snag some random man off the street and take him home with me if I want to. No matter what I decide, you get to have zero say in who I date or take home with me."

"Hope, please."

I engaged in a glaring match with my brother, and I prodded his chest with a finger. "If you can pick any woman you want, I can pick any man I want." I considered pointing at Rick and making a comment about the man who technically no longer classified as an eligible bachelor, but I decided against it. "Have I made myself clear?"

"You've made yourself clear," my brother replied. "Please don't make use of a male prostitute. I'll do whatever you want, but please don't go there."

"Anything I want?"

My brother heaved a sigh. "As long as it's legal and within reason."

"I'll get back to you on that. Is the guest bedroom ready for Rick?"

"It is."

"You can carry my box of stuff to my room while I show him where the guest bedroom is and get him settled in for the night. This doesn't count as your owed favor, but I haven't gotten to sleep in for weeks, so I'd appreciate if you convinced our parents I should be allowed to laze about in bed until after noon if I want."

Mat chuckled, kissed my cheek, and went to the back of my car. "You got it. I'll keep them off your back."

"Come on, Rick. I'll show you to your room. As you're a guest, you do not have to get out of bed before noon unless you want to. Mom and Dad will just expect me to play hostess, so with my luck, Mat will cave and get me up no later than nine."

"I'll really try to keep them from bothering you until noon."

Rick chuckled and snagged his bag out of my trunk. "I'll keep them busy while you sleep, Hope. That's the least I can do as thanks for driving me here."

If Rick kept being nice, I'd be a depressed mess at his cousin's wedding, aware I was trying to prepare a perfect day and the start of a new life for him and his partner. While I wouldn't make use of any male prostitutes, I would begin with doing my best to cure myself of my ill-timed, ill-fated crush. I did give myself credit.

My heart had picked a good man.

"Thanks, Rick. If they give you problems, just pick a fight with Mat. They'll forget I exist until you two are all nice and friendly with each other again. Or grab a deck of cards and play Euchre."

"I know how to play Euchre. That actually sounds like fun. If Mat and his parents play, we'll have four. Does Amy play, Mat?"

"No. Amy prefers to watch television and relax, usually with a book. I can't tell if she's reading the book or watching television, but I figure if that makes her happy, it's no skin off my back."

I hadn't taken Amy to be the type to read while watching television, but while I still had some misgivings about the woman, I would reevaluate my stance with that in mind. "We're going to bed, Mat. You can play Euchre with Rick tomorrow." I meant to grab my bag, but my brother slapped my hand and shooed me towards the house. Shaking my head, I headed to the walkway. "After you, Rick. My old man picks his own pace, which is typically a dignified waddle. If he has trouble on the stairs, I'll give you directions."

Rick chuckled. "If he has trouble on the stairs, I'll carry him."

Bye, bye, heart. I didn't need the damned thing anyway. It just insisted on getting me into trouble.

TRUE TO HIS WORD, Rick carried my old man of a dog up the steps, and he insisted on putting Edgar Allan Paw to bed first. Both of my animals settled on the bed while I showed Rick the guest bedroom, but Annabel Lee whined and huddled against my legs.

"I think she wants to cuddle with her new friends," Rick admitted after five fruitless minutes of trying to convince his dog to go into the guest bedroom with him while my brother moved my box into my old room.

What was one more dog in my bedroom? As far as I was concerned, I'd stumbled into doggy paradise. "She can stay with me if she'll survive being separated from you for that long."

"I think she'll manage," Rick replied in a rueful tone. "You weren't kidding about charming my dog, were you? You can't take her home with you. I love her too much. You can visit her as often as you'd like, though."

I took Annabel Lee's leash, and sure enough, she followed me without hesitation. "I won't steal your beautiful girl, but I'll think about it often."

"If she becomes a bother, come get me, and I'll carry her over and deal with the whining. It's probably a ploy to get extra attention. She lives for attention."

I could believe that. "Sleep well, Rick.

Don't let anyone in my family talk you into doing anything you don't want to do. If you're not careful, you'll end up helping Dad in the garden while Mat becomes Mom's slave."

"How about you?"

"I usually end up in the garden because I like it," I admitted. "I have old pairs of sweats here just so I can play in the dirt."

"I did bring spare clothing, so I'll be all right even if I get saddled into doing yard work. Sleep well, Hope."

"You, too."

Annabel Lee heeled until I opened the bedroom and unclipped her leash, and then she jumped up on the bed with Edgar Allan Paw and Lenore, curled up, stuck her nose against my dog's side, and crashed out. I regarded the bed with a sigh, wondering how I'd fit without disturbing them.

Oh, well. I bothered my kitten long enough to remove her harness, and I changed into the flannel pajamas Juliette Carter had given me.

With a little work and curling up, I got into bed without dislodging either dog or the kitten. Had I been home, my cramped state may have prevented sleep, but the long drive worked in my favor. I passed out within minutes.

Sharing the bed with two dogs and a cat was one thing, but waking up buried beneath a pile of animals was another. One of the dogs had their butt in my face, and I spit out long white strands of dog fur. Lenore batted at my nose whenever the dog moved its tail.

One of them was licking my toes, and I wanted to scream and kick my feet, but I restrained myself, as I didn't want to hurt my dog *or* Rick's.

On second thought, I doubted I'd be able to kick, as a dog had decided to use my legs as a bed, and the weight did a good job of pinning me in place.

Lenore pawed at my nose, I spit out even more fur, and I sighed.

"While you said you wanted to sleep until noon, are you sure?" Rick asked from somewhere nearby. "Are you still alive? Please tell me you're still alive. You're completely buried under our dogs. Hope?"

"I'm not dead yet." Speaking came with a problem. The instant I opened my mouth, I ate fur, which I had to spit out. Again. "A dog is sitting on my head."

"That would be Edgar Allan Paw. The rest of him is covering your chest down to your knees. Annabel Lee has claimed the rest of you. Hold on, I'll get her to stop licking your toes." A moment later, he clucked his tongue and the torture of my feet stopped. "Sorry about that. That's how she gets me up when it's time for her breakfast. It's effective."

I bet. "What time is it?"

"Save you from being eaten by my dog o'clock. She would have started nipping your toes next. If that hadn't worked, she would have tried the same on your ear. It seems I've been replaced as her food provider. She wants you to get up, feed her, and take her on a walk."

"Your dog has betrayed you," I muttered. "I can't get up until they're moved. I'm too tired to move them."

"There's coffee downstairs. Save you from being eaten by my dog o'clock is a little after ten in the morning by human reckoning. Mat checked in on you about an hour ago to find this general same situation, except the animals were still asleep, too. Then I got recruited, since Mat is scared Annabel Lee will try to eat him."

"She wouldn't hurt a fly."

"She'll definitely hurt your toes. She'll lick the flesh right off before she nibbles, though. I've been trying to convince her nibbling is not a good habit, but unfortunately, it usually gets the result she wants along with a morning scolding. Her response? Lick for longer. I just can't win."

"Well, you shouldn't have been late with her breakfast, you terrible, cruel human."

"You're probably right. Your mother is making breakfast, as I've been told you're just as grumpy as my dog if you're not fed."

"Just because I bit my father when I was four or five for not feeding me doesn't mean I'm still a monster in the morning."

"It's better to be safe than sorry." Rick

hauled his dog off me first, and she hopped off the bed without further encouragement. He took more care with Edgar Allan Paw, easing him to the floor so he wouldn't jar his old, tired bones. Lenore mewed, and Rick grabbed her harness from the nightstand and put it on her. "You need to teach your cat she doesn't have to be harnessed all the time."

"She associates the harness with staying with her dog, and while I take it off at night, she gets upset if it's off during the day."

"Are you sure she's actually a cat?"

"I'm questioning her status as a cat," I confessed. Without the pets weighing me down, I crawled out of bed, regarded my rumpled pajamas with a resigned sigh, and grabbed the leashes so I could take care of the dogs. If someone wanted me in real clothes, they'd have to pick a fight over it. "Thank you for the rescue, although it was the sweetest of imprisonments. Has Dad roped you into yard work yet?"

"We distracted him with Euchre for a while, but it appears yard work is in the cards as soon as you're up and ready to tackle some weeds. Apparently, the back corner has been taken over."

Ugh. Mint. I'd warned my father about planting the herpes of the plant world in the back, but he'd loved the idea of having fresh mint around. "He thought it was a good idea to plant a weed. The weed insists on taking over and choking out everything in its domain. I keep telling him he'll have to dig a trench and make sure he gets every last bit of root to get rid of that contagion, but he never listens to me."

"Contagion? What does he have growing back there?"

"Mint." I wrinkled my nose and headed for the door, and the dogs and cat followed me. Edgar Allan Paw didn't seem to mind the steps going down, although he took them at a slower pace than Annabel Lee. To keep Rick's dog from knocking us all down the steps, I released her leash, and she danced in place waiting for us to catch up. "Your dog is very excited for breakfast and her walk. Which does she get first?"

"Walk, else she might explode. After her walk, she will dine like the dainty little princess she is, and then she'll want another walk within a half an hour to an hour. It keeps my mornings interesting. She'll take her time on the second walk, as she knows I will have to go to work, and she wants to usurp as much of my time as possible."

I didn't blame her for that. "Edgar Allan Paw does about the same, but his morning walk is more of a morning limp to the nearest patch of acceptable grass so he can have his breakfast. Unfortunately, it's a hike, but he's a good sport about it. I need to take him to a vet and see if there's anything I can do for his achy bones."

"It depends on the cause. I've done some

research, but I've discovered there isn't any cure for growing old, much to my dismay."

I nodded my agreement, and while I could have gotten away with letting the dogs run loose in the quiet neighborhood, I kept the animals all leashed, as there were a few kids around scared of dogs. The last thing any of us needed was to listen to their terrified screams at ten in the morning—or deal with the neighbors, who would pitch a fit if their kids were scared.

Once we started the yard work, the dogs could run around unleashed, although I'd keep Lenore tethered to something to make sure she couldn't run off.

Then, because the last thing I needed was fleas in my hotel room or new apartment, all three animals would be getting a flea bath and a thorough brushing to check for ticks. I'd gotten the combs and shampoos for that purpose, as I hadn't liked the idea of putting flea collars on my animals.

I liked giving myself more work than necessary.

In what I counted as a miracle, Rick volunteered to take the dogs and cat on their second walk so I could have breakfast and get changed, and I nursed a cup of coffee between yawns. Mom and Dad swooped in, sat at the table with me, and to prevent complaining over a morning ambush, they provided food. In their early sixties, age was just starting to catch up with them, and my mother's hair had gone more salt than pepper, and my father had a lone gray streak in his otherwise dark hair. As always, it amused me he kept his badger stripe, and I wondered why his gray hairs had showed up all in the same spot.

I bet I had something to do with it.

As I would endure a lot for waffles topped with fresh fruit, I thanked them properly and dug in, waiting for them to drop whatever bomb they intended to smack me with.

They didn't leave me waiting long. My mother cleared her throat and said, "I think you should explain your rationale for investing in a ball and chain and subjecting your brother's wife to it."

I raised a brow, finding their choice of opening volley interesting. "If you need me to explain my rationale, you haven't been paying attention. Next?"

My parents stared at me as though I'd flung a basket full of copperheads onto the table and let them slither over my breakfast unchecked.

"But—"

"I'm an adult and can make my own decisions and mistakes as I see fit, and I don't have to justify those decisions or mistakes to you. I love you both, but that's not how this works anymore. Mat didn't have to justify his choice of wife to you, either—nor should he. It's his choice to make, for better or for worse." I took another bite of my waffles, chewed, and swallowed. "Just like I don't have to justify adopting an old dog from a shelter and opting to adopt his kitten at the same time despite not really knowing what to do with a cat beyond clean her litter box, feed her at the appropriate times, and pet her when she seems interested in being pet. And provide toys, of which she's collecting many and uses few."

My dad huffed before leaning back in his chair and crossing his arms over his chest. "And bringing your brother's friend with you last night?"

"He asked me to help plan his cousin's wedding, and it was convenient to have him come along for the ride. He's also Mat's friend, and it is good for Mat to spend time with his friends. I was being efficient."

While he narrowed his eyes, my father accepted my reply with a nod. "And this wedding?"

"I guess I did a good job, and his cousin wants someone with a proven track record of doing a good job. It's more complicated than Mat's wedding, but I think it'll be fine. It'll be a challenge, but it should work out all right. And if it's too challenging for me, I'll recruit help. I've found people will do a lot to secure free help with their taxes."

My mother frowned. "His dog slept with you."

"My dog is an old bundle of joy, and it was inevitable that Annabel Lee would want to cuddle up with someone of her own species. I woke up buried in dogs, though, which made getting out of bed difficult. After I've eaten my waffles and the hungry beast is tamed, I'll get changed. Did the mint take over again?"

"It took over again," Dad confirmed.

"Gasoline and a match will solve that problem for you."

"But I like my mint. It just gets a little rambunctious is all."

"How much of the garden has it taken over this time?"

He grimaced. "More than it should have."

I rolled my eyes. "Come on, Dad. You have to stay on top of the mint or you're just going to have mint in your yard rather than vegetables, flowers, and grass. We've talked about this before."

"But it's a lot of work."

"And that would be why I suggested you not get mint in the first place."

"But I like mint."

I rampaged through my waffles, glaring at my parents for having turned their once-pristine garden into a disaster area. "You two are something else."

"Pot meet kettle," my brother announced behind me. "You only have yourself to blame for this, Hope."

"How do you figure?" I demanded.

"You moved out of the area, so you can't visit whenever they get lonely. I stayed in the area, as I'm a good son."

Like hell he was. As bickering with my brother would get us both in trouble, I finished off my waffles, grunted, and did the dishes so I wouldn't earn a scolding to go with my meal. "I need to get dressed, then I'll deal with the disaster that is the garden."

EIGHTEEN

They took ruthless to a whole new level.

LIFE RARELY WORKED out as planned, and my parents' garden did a good job of reminding me of that simple truth. I toiled on it the entire day, taking a break only to eat the promised prime rib, which I paid for in cash to my father, as my mother tried to refuse to accept payment for the ridiculously expensive dinner. Rick and Mat had a better time than I did, and even Amy seemed to warm up to the family chaos, although we kept our interactions with each other to cordial nods and little else.

The next morning, I returned Rick to the Carters' home, barely dodged a second clothing session with Juliette as she was working with a client, and dove into the rest of my life. Planning Elizabeth's wedding would be my last obstacle before I could enjoy what I'd worked so hard to gain, but I could survive through a year of extra work.

I'd done it every single year between

moving out of my parents' house and venturing to New York. One more year wouldn't hurt me. Much.

Probably.

The move into my new apartment went better than I expected, and Edgar Allan Paw didn't mind the walk down to the lobby and to the section of yard dedicated to pets needing to do their business. The security guards always had treats for him, which helped convince the old dog he wanted to make his ventures outside several times a day. I took to bribing him on our walks at the office, too.

The tub and fireplace proved to be my saving grace, offering refuge from my work. The wedding planning, as expected, turned into a nightmare, as every damned guest on the list outside of my immediate family had some special request, Elizabeth had a difficult time saying no, and I had to ultimately put my foot down and remind the woman, using Rick as my delivery method of choice, that she was the one being married, not her mother, not her aunts, not her uncles, not her cousins, and not any one of her friends, all of whom thought they knew what she wanted more than she did.

Three weeks into the venture, I wanted to quit, but I refused to give up without a fight. I'd thought Amy had been picky, but she'd been a mere blip on the radar.

I had to, much to my disgust, completely

ban dogs, cats, and any other pets from the cruise ship, which meant I'd have to board Edgar Allan Paw and Lenore for the week. Fortunately, Jacob offered to watch them, however much I hated the idea of leaving them for a week. I considered staying on the cruise only long enough to see the wedding go off without hitch. I could, with a little work, arrange for a pickup—or jump overboard and swim for shore.

After the edict barring all animals from the cruise ship, Rick avoided me, not that I blamed him.

Since I'd banned animals, Elizabeth's family and friends wanted to hire their specific caterers, to which I said no. In what most wedding planners would consider the suicide of their careers, I sent everyone on the guest list a sternly worded reminder that the wedding was for Elizabeth and her groom, and as guests, they were to show up and enjoy the festivities of *their* choice.

Then, as I had a death wish and faltering patience, I put a hard limit on one request per household, which included allergies, personality clashes, and preferred cabin assignments.

All other requests, unless it came from the bride or groom, would be ignored.

In one email, I earned the wrath of everyone and began a wedding-wide war aimed in my general direction.

It beat the guests feuding with each other,

as I'd learned Rick hadn't been kidding about the oddly combative relationships the family 'friends' had with each other. One by one, the requests came in, and when it came to seating, I'd have to play a masterful game of chess to keep the bloodshed to a minimum.

No wonder Rick had wanted to keep his woman a secret from everyone.

They took ruthless to a whole new level.

I could also understand why Rick had fled the country to get away from them. When emailed threats to cooperate didn't work, I started receiving letters with demands, which I put into a box after reading to check for anything important, including allergies and possibilities of bloodshed should they be placed near an enemy. I found nothing overly obnoxious, and while a few guests had allergies, most refused to have anything dealing with shellfish, something I found odd but easy enough to accommodate. From clams to lobster to shrimp, I banned it all, made sure none of the stocks or other ingredients contained any of it, and made arrangements with the caterer Elizabeth had liked the most who was willing to work a cruise ship for a week.

The bill had shocked me, but she'd paid the deposit without hesitation and would pay the balance a week before the ship set sail.

After the caterer came the fittings, and while the caterer's bill for the event had about floored me, Juliette Carter went for Elizabeth's purse ready and willing to kill. I freaked after seeing the cost per gown and suit, and she'd gotten something for everyone. Elizabeth put her foot down, dictating that the guests would wear what Juliette gave them or they would be uninvited to the wedding.

I hadn't even spoken directly with Elizabeth more than three times, but the entire tone of the wedding planning changed with her single display of authority. The guests fell into line, and none of them dared to peep and find themselves removed from the bride's list of those allowed to board the cruise ship.

The groom, who I learned was named Edward only because of the wedding invitations, went with what Elizabeth wanted with a very important catch: when he decided something wasn't happening, no force on Earth could move him.

My most ruthless stunt of the entire wedding was to declare that if both Edward and Elizabeth didn't agree to the changes made towards the finalization of the plans, it wasn't happening.

The weeks slid by, and while I'd regretted upsetting Rick with the no pets policy that made a mess of his plan to use his dog to secure his future wife, I stood by my decision, although I did remind people about the importance of why.

A cruise ship was not a safe place for a lot of animals, and while there would be a doctor on board, cruise ships weren't equipped to take care of sick animals. Elizabeth and Edward backed me on it, as none of the guests had service animals and they knew it.

Two months before the wedding, I gathered up the courage to send Rick a text, consisting of a predictive headline claiming a New York wedding planner might be tossed from cruise ship deck by stubborn guests.

After months of not a single word from him, it startled me when my phone rang. According to the display, it was Rick, but I hesitated for a few rings longer than normal before I answered, "Hope speaking."

"While my family can be quite brash, none of them would actually toss you over the rail. They might complain enough you'd consider flinging yourself overboard and swimming for shore, but none of them would actually help you over. They might break a nail or wrinkle their suits."

According to Rick's tone, he had as many issues with the guest list as I did. "They were not amused when I brought Edward into it."

"That's because Edward doesn't at all care about what any of them think, and they all know it. This would count as a peace-making marriage if the bride and groom hadn't decided they wanted to marry for love sometime after the initial marriage negotiations went through. That's half the problem right there. How dare they interrupt old traditions? Frankly, it wouldn't surprise me if the bride and groom decided to start tossing wedding guests overboard at this point. Good job on putting an end to the stupidity, but you've earned zero friends."

"Not my problem, Rick. I'm here to make sure the wedding happens, not cater to their delicate and bruised sensibilities. If they want someone planning the wedding around their whims, they should get married and hire their own wedding planner."

"Yes, they are horribly dismayed to discover their usual tactics for bringing a wedding planner in line simply doesn't work with you."

"And it must annoy them even more that I refuse to accept bribes to change just one little thing for them. How dare I have ethics, Rick?"

"Yes, how dare you have ethics, Miss Hope Kensingvale?"

"I've been very bad. Also, now that I know how much Juliette Carter's clothing costs, I've developed a complex. I can't tell if I want to wear the clothes every day until they are held together by scraps of thread, if I should limit each one to no more than once a month to make sure they last, or just crawl into my closet and cry. I grew the courage to check how much those purses sell at retail. The cheapest one was two thousand dollars."

"According to El, they are the best purses, made by a woman for women, and they'll last forever if you treat them right. If you don't know how to treat them right, talk to Juliette.

She'll help you. And if one needs to be repaired, she can handle it. If it can't be repaired, she will hold a proper funeral for the purse and help you find a replacement."

"That I can afford," I muttered.

"Relax, Hope. You've been doing great with the wedding planning. You gave those busybodies an opportunity to get the majority of their complaining out of the way, and you drew lines they aren't stupid enough to cross. Ed is pretty damned happy with you, and Ed is a tough one to please. By setting him as the final line, fewer people are bothering El about the wedding, and since everyone has figured out you're not going to say yes after you've said no, it's going to go a lot better than most of our weddings."

My brows shot up at that. "You have got to be kidding me."

"Hope, the last time we had a wedding, we went through five wedding planners in the first three months before my aunt found an old goat who was deaf in one ear and didn't speak English to handle the preparations. When only the bride could speak the wedding planner's language, things went far more smoothly. It turns out the old goat could actually speak English, but my aunt had told her to play dumb to stop the bullshit. That wedding turned into a double wedding, because who wants to go through that sort of nightmare more than necessary?"

"You have double and triple weddings because the guests are demons disguised as humans, don't you?"

"I'd be offended, but it's really true. My family instigates because they have opinions, and they think their birth rank entitles them to have their opinions listened to. You're great because you literally don't give a shit about the circumstances of their birth. El loves it. You have the entire guest list, and you don't even care who they are."

"They are a number on a card that I sometimes match with their actual name, because dealing with numbers makes things easier," I confessed.

Rick spluttered. "You gave everyone on the guest list a number?"

"Yes. And I reference their name with their number, but when I'm handling most of the arrangements, I just work with the numbers. Numbers are easy. People are hard. When I'm working with just numbers, I don't tend to think about which guest was a jerk, and it's easy to keep things fair. I'm very careful to make sure the numbers are properly matched, and the important issues are dealt with. None of the dishes have any actual allergens, don't ask me what we went through to make sure Guest #278's Celiac disease doesn't create an issue, and there's no dairy because of Guest #426's daughter."

"You really know them by number!"

"Why do you sound so surprised? I'm an

accountant. I made Mat #666 at his wedding because he's the devil."

Rick snickered. "And my number?"

"*Sore wa himitsu desu,*" I replied.

"Since when do you speak Japanese?"

"I don't. I picked it up from an anime I watched. I thought it was hilarious, so I'm parroting it to you."

"Why is my number a secret?"

"It's more fun that way." In truth, outside of the bride and groom, I'd randomized everyone in the wedding party and picked their numbers before doing the same with the guests, and as I wasn't a fan of torturing myself, especially when he'd gone off on his own as was proper for a man getting ready to propose, I'd ignored his number as much as I could.

"Come on," he whined. "Tell me."

I rolled my eyes. "You'll have to do me a favor if you want your number."

"Okay. What favor?"

"Can you handle Guest #354? Of the lot, she's really sweet, but she's going to drive me crazy, Rick. She has so many questions, and she's reasonable, and it's hard to tell her no all the damned time, but I have to because I can't make exceptions for her even though she's really nice."

"I'm going to need more than that to go on, Hope. Does she have a first name? That might narrow the field a little."

"Loretta."

Rick sighed. "That would be my mother. I can talk with her."

Crap. "She's your mother?"

"Alas, it is true. I'm the child of a horribly sweet woman who tries to be reasonable but really just drives everyone around her crazy. She has developed a rather annoying tendency to want to offend no one because offending someone means that everyone will get on her case, so she tries really hard to be friends with everyone. She's probably asking questions because she wants to pack her bags perfectly with zero risk of breaking one of your rules."

"I'm not sure what to say," I confessed.

"Well, considering my mother is as sly as she is sweet, you're doing just fine. Just keep telling her no on anything that pushes one of your lines, don't make exceptions without an okay from El and Ed, and keep doing what you're doing. It's probably the first wedding our family has been involved with in at least twenty years that hasn't churned through wedding planners. And most of the actual planning is done, isn't it?"

Much to my relief, it was. "I still have to coordinate the decorations, but the cruise liner is handling most of that with the help of the catering staff. Elizabeth requested eco-friendly decorations, so everything will be edible or biodegradable, including the settings. The settings might kill me."

"What's wrong with the settings?"

"Nothing, except the caterers and cruise staff have to clean everything because the intention is to send home a place setting for every guest as part of a gift basket Elizabeth insisted everyone should receive. Those might really kill me."

I had to customize every damned basket to match the guest, but Elizabeth had provided a list of what she wanted in each one, which left me with buying everything and giving her the bill.

"She's going overboard."

"She absolutely is *not* going overboard in a reversible dress that cost a quarter of a fucking million dollars!"

Rick snickered. "I didn't mean it literally."

"Quarter of a million dollar dress, Rick."

"I know. I've seen the dress. It's beautiful. Not as beautiful as your dress, but it's still beautiful. El even agrees with me. Your dress is superior."

Shit. "That's not good. That breaks the rules, Rick. *Nobody* can have a prettier dress than the bride's."

"The bride has dictated you get the prettier dress. Don't worry about it. Her dress is stunning, but yours is better only in that you're wearing it."

I scowled. "You are now yanking my chain, aren't you? Elizabeth hasn't even met me in person."

"But she's seen your picture, has spoken

with you on the phone, and has a good eye for clothes and people. Your dress is better."

Oy, oy, oy. "I'll talk to Juliette about the dress."

"No, you won't."

"Yes, I will. It's Elizabeth's wedding day, and my dress cannot be better than her dress."

"Rules are the rules and the rules say nobody can complain about their Carter apparel. That's your rule, by the way. You made that rule so nobody would bother Juliette. Juliette is kissing the ground you walk upon for that rule, as she has full design control and can do what makes every guest shine for the wedding."

Fuck. I had made that rule. "The bride's dress having to be prettier trumps the Carter apparel rule."

"It really doesn't. Sorry. You're stuck with the prettier dress."

"I can't be prettier than the bride, Rick. They'll toss me overboard!"

"Nobody is going to toss anyone overboard."

"If I show up outshining the bride, they most certainly will. That's how this works. There are hundreds of them, and there's one of me. One of them will definitely toss me overboard. I suck at swimming, so I'll drown. I've been thinking about learning how to swim better because the odds of a vengeful guest tossing me overboard is fairly high."

"I think you're overreacting, Hope. They're not going to throw you overboard."

"Have you seen some of these emails?" I complained. "According to them, I'm ruining the entire wedding, the bride will cry because she's so unhappy, and I'm the worst wedding planner to exist."

"Hope, they're haughty, overly wealthy Brits who genuinely believe they were born superior."

"I've met Brits. They're nice. Sure, their curses threw me for a loop at first, but once I figured out their words don't mean the same as American ones, I got over it."

"Ah, the fabled c-word in America. It basically just means idiot for those of us who live overseas."

"Yeah. The first time someone from England whipped it out, I was stunned into silence."

"Whipped what out, precisely?"

"The word. Nobody whipped anything literal out at me." Thankfully, especially as it had been over the phone, I'd been talking to Edward, and I'd been so shocked he'd gone on for another five minutes before he remembered I was American, laughed, and explained how the word worked in his country. "And I was talking to Edward."

"You got him to cuss at you on the phone?"

"Not at me."

"Hopefully not at my mother. I could see

her testing his patience that much. She's really sweet, but she's *really* persistent."

"No. It was one of the guests from hell. Again."

"Ah. Aunt Carolina."

I sucked in a breath. "How did you know?"

"She's usually the one responsible for driving the wedding planners into quitting. Dad's side. Her birth rank makes her particularly snooty."

"I'm not sure I want to know."

"Hope, you've been dealing with the invitations."

"I don't particularly care if Elizabeth wants to lord or lady people on the invitations, Rick. I thought it was cute."

"They're actually lords and ladies, Hope."

My mouth dropped open. "Could you repeat that?"

"They're actually lords and ladies. Aunt Carolina is a duchess. Don't ask of what. Elizabeth banned the full titles and decreed everyone was going to be a lord or lady, even the ones who technically aren't either, as she will not have any of the typical posturing when the family gets together—or the extended family. Or the friends of the family, who also have titles. Not all of us are British, so that complicates things, too."

Okay. I could handle the realization that the lord and lady titling on the guest cards and invitations was serious. I could do so without embarrassing myself, too. "Your aunt is a duchess?"

"Yes, she is. There aren't actually many dukes or duchesses in Britain, but any child of a duke or duchess is a lord or lady. There are a lot of lords and ladies because of being the child of someone with the appropriate title. That includes barons, viscounts, earls, and marquesses. Most of us fall into one of those categories or the other, with some of the family friends lacking a title or the heritage to be a lord or lady. So, El is breaking the rules a little, but she doesn't care. Since they're not getting married in England, she feels she can break the rules if she wants to."

I swallowed. "You're basically telling me that I'm dealing with an entire boat of nobility, and I've been sitting here like a dictator telling them what they can't do, which is everything they want to do?"

"And you're doing so fabulously. Keep doing exactly as you are. Mother's having a grand time with it."

"Dare I ask if your mother has a title?"

"She absolutely does have a title."

"That means you have a title or are some little lordling."

"I'm not too fond of that part of things, but you're right."

Well, screw me with a stick sideways. "And you're positive nobody is going to throw me overboard?"

"I'm positive."

"I really should call Juliette about the dress." Damn it. It was one thing to annoy a bunch of rich people, but to annoy a bunch of rich people with actual titles? I bet every last one of them could find a way to make my life miserable until the day I died.

"I'm putting my foot down on this one. Don't call Juliette about the dress. Your dress is beautiful. Stop worrying. Nobody is going to be upset about your dress."

Like hell nobody was going to be upset about my dress. I was upset about the dress. I couldn't goose the bride.

It was her day. If my day came around, I could strut around and be the pretty one.

Taking a few deep breaths, I calmed myself the best I could. "I bet Juliette could make me a beautiful potato sack, and I could wear that to the wedding."

"While I'm confident she could make you a beautiful potato sack, she already made you a gown. Just relax. There's nothing wrong with your dress. It's pretty."

"It's too pretty!"

"It's not too pretty. Please don't call Juliette about the dress."

I scowled, but as I knew where she lived, I could drive over after work one night. Doing so without calling would be rude, but I could text her that I wanted to talk to her in person. That wasn't the same as calling. "Fine. I won't call her about the dress."

"Good. I'll talk to my mother and suggest

that she should keep being sweet but stop making requests that stress you out because you have to say no. I'm not sure I can stop her from bothering you, but she tends to fixate, and when she fixates, she wants to make everything perfect for everyone."

"Thank you. You're not upset?"

"Hope, my mother drives me crazy most days because she's sweet but determined to be involved in everything. I will admit I was sad I can't take Annabel Lee on the trip, but I found a good dog sitter for her, and she'll have a great time. She'll be sad for about ten minutes, after which she'll realize the dog sitter will have a dog she can play and cuddle with. I'll get her back exhausted and played out."

"I hope Edgar Allan Paw will forgive me for leaving him."

"He will. He's a good dog."

That he was. "I hope so. I don't want him to think I'm abandoning him."

"He won't, but you're not going to believe me until you're back from the cruise and he greets you with sloppy dog kisses, are you?"

"I'm really not. Sorry."

He chuckled. "Don't be sorry. We'll make some time to mope about missing our dogs on the ship. It'll be therapeutic. That said? You made a good call, because a lot of my family has obnoxious ankle biters that are devils in the flesh the instant their owners look the other direction."

"Well, that makes me feel a little better about the pet ban."

"I need to go, but I'll take care of my mother, and I'll get on the phone with Aunt Carolina and give her a few reasons to reconsider her poor behavior."

My brows rose at that. "What are you going to do to her? Oh, and since you're taking care of your mother, you're #666 since it's your fault I'm the wedding planner," I fibbed.

"Really?"

"No, not really, but I thought it was funny. I'm withholding the number until I have a confirmation about your mother. Are you sure about dealing with your Aunt Carolina?"

"If I have my way, she'll be an angel for the rest of the wedding."

"That would take a miracle, Rick. She's awful."

"Care to make a wager on that?"

Uh oh. His tone implied he would do anything necessary to win said wager if I was foolish enough to challenge him. "If it involves you making headlines, no."

"I will endeavor to avoid any negative or outrageous headlines," he promised.

I sighed. "All right. Hit me with it. What kind of wager do you want to make?"

"Should Aunt Carolina behave herself until after the wedding, you will owe me one favor. Should she fail to behave herself until after the wedding, I will owe you one favor."

Favors made the business world turn, and they could also give me a dog sitter when I needed some fresh air. "What is the limit of the favor?"

"Anything within reason. I promise I won't ask anything of you that would hurt your career, but I can't promise it wouldn't make you take a day off work to help me with something. The favor I have in mind isn't monetary, but it could take some time."

A day off work doing his bidding wouldn't bother me much, and I could think of a few things I could ask for my favor, including taking care of my pets or going on a road trip to protect me from my family. "Okay. We have a deal, then. I'll try not to punish you too much when you lose."

"I appreciate that. Call me if anyone gives you trouble. I'll set them straight."

I huffed at that. "The only reason I couldn't handle your mother was because she's too sweet. Don't worry about the other ones. I can handle them. I just don't want to be killed through kindness right now is all."

Rick laughed. "I'll keep that in mind."

Long after Rick hung up, I stared at my phone, wondering how I'd managed to make a mess of things from being afraid of talking to him. If I judged by the call alone, every problem had been in my head. After I spoke to Juliette about the dress, I'd put some thoughts into my unfortunately human nature.

On second thought, I'd be grateful for the lesson learned at little cost to anyone other than me.

Talking solved more problems than they made, and I'd do well to remember that.

NINETEEN

One day, I would admit I spoiled my pets rotten.

ON FRIDAY NIGHT, I drove to Juliette's house and braced for the battle of a lifetime over the issue of my dress. I pulled into her driveway, parked my car, and gathered the courage to face off against the wickedly nice and energetic designer. Over the months, I'd taught the animals the routine, and they both waited for me to open their door, leash them, and unclip their seatbelt harnesses before they tumbled out of the vehicle to go on their next adventure.

According to Edgar Allan Paw's tail, he expected the best of adventures and a lot of treats.

One day, I would admit I spoiled my pets rotten.

Before I made it halfway up the sidewalk, Juliette bounced out her door, hopped down the steps, and kissed my cheeks. "Fredrick warned me you'd threatened to call me about your dress."

That man lived to vex me. "As you can see, I am not calling you about the dress."

She laughed. "I wisely didn't mention he hadn't barred you from texting or showing up in person, although I'll make sure he's educated on the errors of his ways, as you're not someone to give up so easily."

That I wasn't. "I'm sorry to bother you."

"I'm not bothered. You're a good person, and good people worry about things like this. Come on in and set the beasts loose. I put a litter pan down for Lenore in the entry, so she'll be able to figure out where it is without help. I've learned that it's just wise to prepare the necessary things for any sort of pets clients might bring over."

I followed her into her home, and once she closed the front door, I released my pets and let them wander as they wanted. As expected, Lenore followed Edgar Allan Paw, who found the living room rug to be a tolerable place for a nap. Mr. Carter glanced up from the book he read and waved. "Good evening, Hope. If you're going to help her empty her closet, go after the boots. She's hoarding them again."

"It's not my fault my employees do not acknowledge my genius for boots."

"You only need so many styles of classic black boot, Juliette. You do not need a thousand variations of a singular boot style. If you're going to insist on playing with black boots, add more designs to the stitch work."

"But then they wouldn't be classic."

"Six months, Juliette. No more black boots unless they're a whole new design that can be distinguished from the many other variants of classic black boots you've convinced your employees to sell over the years."

"Cruel!"

"Juliette."

"You're still cruel. You're siding with those meanies."

Mr. Carter shook his head and stared at me. "Hope, there's nothing wrong with your dress. It's beautiful, and it's not your fault there are biased people who forget they can't think you're prettier because they like you more than they like the bride." Mr. Carter frowned. "Have I covered the fine points yet? It would be a shame if I had to interrupt my reading to continue setting people straight tonight."

"You're still in lawyer mode," Juliette complained.

"Well, I am a lawyer, and I only got home about ten minutes ago to find out my wife was planning on holding a wedding planner hostage for the entire weekend."

My eyes widened. "Wait. What? The entire weekend?"

"Oh, right. I set the guest bedroom up for you, and I've picked some beautiful clothes to dress you in this weekend. Kidnapped victims get to keep the clothes I give them to wear. I even got everything you need for your pets. It took me a little work to get to your landlord and figure out what they eat and if they needed any medications, but I triumphed."

I lifted my hand and pinched the bridge of my nose. "Maybe you should be planning this wedding rather than me."

"Nobody on this sweet Earth could afford my rate to plan that disaster. Frankly, you need to charge them quadruple for doing it."

"Quadruple of zero is still zero, Juliette. I'm doing it as a favor to Rick."

Both of the Carters stared at me as though I'd lost my mind. To be fair, I likely had.

"What did you do to owe him a favor like *that*?" Juliette rested her hands on her hips and glowered at me. "You can't let them get away with that. It's worse than murder, especially considering how much of a nightmare they're putting you through."

"I wouldn't quite say they're putting me through a nightmare," I protested.

"I would. Fredrick is very up front about how the planning is going."

"I volunteered to do it."

"And you should be paid for your hard work. How many hours, precisely, have you spent on that wedding?"

"I've been doing it in the evenings and on days off."

"That doesn't mean you shouldn't be paid for it."

"But I volunteered."

"Still doesn't mean you shouldn't be paid for it."

Mr. Carter sighed and set his book aside. "Obviously, I need to remain in lawyer mode. I will make a few phone calls, and I will return with a proper payment offer for your work. They can afford to pay you properly for your work, Hope. And while I realize Fredrick is a friend, that doesn't mean he should take advantage of that work."

"It's not taking advantage if I volunteered!"

"It's taking advantage," the pair chorused.

"But Fredrick—"

Juliette raised her hand, and I snapped my teeth together. "Fredrick would have assumed his cousin would be paying the bill for your work, as she has been the one handling the payments although her groom is likewise contributing to the effort. Edward wouldn't have figured out the planner needs to be paid, and Elizabeth would have assumed Fredrick would be handling your pay. It's a simple miscommunication that my lawyer of a husband can resolve within a few minutes. Get her a fair rate, darling. Fair does not mean rob them blind however much you think Hope deserves to be paid millions for putting up with that disaster of a wedding."

"I'll get it sorted. Since you're insisting on kidnapping her, you have to feed her dinner, make sure she has everything she needs, and quietly do whatever it is you wanted to do with her for the weekend."

"Dress her up, obviously. It's not my fault my client cancelled this weekend because of an emergency. I need something to do, or I will become bored, and because I had an appointment this weekend, you decided to cram in some overtime."

"I'm cramming in overtime because I want to enjoy the cruise without work getting in the way. That is how this works. I have several large projects I need to be finished before we leave."

Juliette pouted. "That's not fair."

"It is fair. That's how this works, and pouting isn't going to change that. I already caved and agreed you could kidnap Hope for the weekend. You still have to obey the rules. If she wants to go home, you need to let her go home. If someone else wants to take her home, you can wage war with them, but no property damage. Behave yourself. And yes, you will be expected to take all of your medications on time because it keeps your brain from staying broken. I will recruit Hope to help with your medications if you decide against using your alarms again."

"Dictator!"

"When it comes to your health, yes. I am, indeed, a cruel dictator who will not accept no for an answer. Hope, she's already had her medication for this evening, but I'll leave a list of times and what she needs so you can keep an eye on her. She becomes quite the handful when she's off her medications, and she's been notoriously bad about it the past few weeks."

"I'll keep her in line," I promised.

"I wish you the best of luck with that."

"Well, if she wants me to stay and pose for her, and continue the argument about the dress, she needs to take her medications. Otherwise, I'll have to attend to something at home, and that would be a tragedy, wouldn't it?"

Juliette slumped her shoulders. "She's as cruel as you are."

"Go have your argument over the dress while I take care of the bill for the wedding planning. Hope, I'll negotiate an appropriate rate for you for the level of work you're doing. It's not the first time I've had to help a planner out on a high-end wedding, so I have a pretty good idea of what you should be paid for this."

As I couldn't see a way to reject his help without turning myself into an asshole, I surrendered with a quiet sigh. "Thank you, Mr. Carter."

"Have fun, and take however many pairs of boots you can get your hands on. After this weekend, you deserve them, and she really does not need that many pairs of black boots eating away space in her closet. You can keep three pairs for emergencies in her size, babe."

"Three?" Juliette wailed. "Why only three?"

"Because you do not need to keep twenty pairs of black boots in every size in the closet."

That sounded like a ridiculous number of boots, and I wondered how any one closet could fit them all. "But how do they all fit?"

"They fit?" Mr. Carter asked before rolling his eyes and striding out of the room and disappearing down the hallway.

"They really don't fit," Juliette confessed. "It's my fault because I submitted a lot of different designs all at once, and we do one pair in all sizes for each design to make sure we see how they wear. I've also been working on designs for women with wide calves, and I have a few for women with narrow calves, too. It's a lot of boots. And they're all black, because I was trying to design the perfect boot. But they accepted five of the designs for upcoming releases."

"Out of how many?"

"Twenty-nine."

"And they're all black boots?"

"They're all black."

"You could just change the color of the leather and use the designs for different colors. They don't need to all be black."

"They took two to make into red and some other colors, but they're all of a more classic design, and they yelled at me. They want me to use more bling. But I don't want to use more bling. I want to make the perfect classic boot."

After months of planning a wedding, I began the tedious work of solving the first problem, which involved the woman's fixation on the perfect black boot. "For every five designs of different shoes with bling or whatever other criteria your employees need, you may make one new black boot design. That way, you are still working on your other work and can still try to make the perfect black boot. Everyone is happy that way."

Juliette considered me, her eyes narrowing. "Three."

"Five."

"You're not going to budge, are you?"

"I am absolutely not going to budge. I've gotten so used to telling rich people no that I can do this all weekend without even having to think about it."

She heaved a sigh. "Fine. Five."

"If you complain about it, I'll up the number to ten."

"I'll behave."

With that problem out of the way, I wrinkled my nose. "Now, to deal with the problem of my dress."

"Your dress isn't a problem, the bride has seen the dress, and she agrees it is perfect for you and wants you to wear it. The bride likes her dress, and she has confirmed the design. The groom likes his suit design. Nobody else gets a say at the wedding, so everything is going to plan and on schedule. You don't get to whine because you're getting a pretty dress."

"I'm sure the dress is pretty, but it can't be prettier than the bride's."

"It's not prettier than the bride's. They're equally pretty dresses designed specifically for the woman wearing them. If you put a supermodel in a dress and have her strut her stuff, the dress will appear to be prettier on the supermodel than it does on the average woman who may also wear the same dress. You're the one who is making the dress stunning. The bride is the one who is making her dress beautiful, too. Now, you should just accept that you're going to be beautiful in your dress, as I enjoy making beautiful things for beautiful people. I could put you in just about anything and have you look pretty."

"A potato sack."

"Marilyn Monroe did that. She was gorgeous in the potato sack. You would likewise be gorgeous. That said, I'm not making a dress like that, as I don't have any canvas potato sacks in stock, nor do I particularly feel like making one or finding one. You'll just have to deal with the dress I've designed and made. As I've heard about the disasters you've been dealing with as part of the wedding planning, I am also going to make you a cocktail dress for the reception. Every woman needs a black cocktail dress, and I've decided that I'm making yours. That's why you're being kidnapped this weekend, as the perfect cocktail dress takes time to design. I have brought home a selection of cocktail dress styles I'll need you to try on so I get a better eye for what dresses work best for your figure. You're a challenge, and I need a challenge."

"I'm a challenge? How so?"

"You can wear numerous styles, and I'm not sure which one will look the best until I put you in them. I'll design the cocktail dress based on which prototype fits your figure best."

"Okay. Is that the only reason you're kidnapping me?"

"I'm putting some serious thought into making Fredrick rescue you and grovel for daring to forget you deserve a paycheck."

Mr. Carter marched into the living room and pointed at his wife. "You will do no such thing!"

"Why are you eavesdropping when you're on the phone? Don't eavesdrop. It's rude."

"While I'm an evil lawyer, you're the devil of the design world, and I'm onto your trickery, woman."

"I was only going to make him come get her and apologize in person."

"Juliette."

Juliette wrinkled her nose at her husband. "You're on the phone, deal with the person on the phone, not with me."

"Fredrick is on the phone, and he is laughing. As you're shrieking worse than a banshee, he can easily hear you. He wants to know why you're kidnapping Hope."

After stomping her foot, Juliette stole the phone from her husband. "Keep her amused. Don't let her escape while I deal with this man." She headed off down the hallway and began muttering something I couldn't hear.

The Carters redefined weird, and I found I enjoyed their special brand of crazy. "I'm sorry for the inconvenience, Mr. Carter."

"You're not an inconvenience. The instant her work called that her weekend client had canceled because of a family emergency, I realized I would have my hands full with her. Your text gave me an easy solution to my problem, as I do need to get work done this weekend. Basically, I'm hiring you to babysit her, and I'm paying you in boots and whatever other clothes she forces on you."

Considering how much her clothes cost, I made off like a bandit for doing some babysitting of an adult woman. "That seems fair."

"That it does. I told Fredrick that someone had overlooked paying the wedding planner, and he started snarling curses and promised he'd take care of it, so that's dealt with. As I thought, he'd assumed Elizabeth would have been on top of it, as all he did was hook her up with you after you'd done a good job on your brother's wedding with an intractable bride."

"She's still intractable, and there are still issues," I muttered.

"What sort of issues?"

Crap. I bowed my head and sighed. "Please don't let this spread around, but I'm fairly certain she played my brother to help pay off her mother's debts. Fredrick had looked into it, but I'd thought something was fishy considering how *everything* except the venue had gone wrong. There was only a wedding because I made so many contingency plans. Now there are problems between Amy's parents, and it's a mess. But it's not all bad. I think Amy and my brother are working on having a legitimate marriage, even if I do think she started out trying to use him."

"People can do awful things in the name of love, and sometimes, that love is a daughter for her mother. What are you going to do about it?"

"Nothing," I admitted. "Unless she comes knocking at my door and brings trouble with her, I don't think it's worth creating even more problems because of it. My brother knows she lost all the deposits, and he knows I made other arrangements. After Elizabeth's wedding, I'll be working triple time paying back all the favors I called in, but that's on me. I made the offers to secure the backups. I have backups lined up for this wedding, too, but it's less of an issue since we're renting a cruise liner, I'm the only one with direct access to the vendors, and the bride put an end to most of the nagging."

"Does that make you happy?"

I took my time considering that. "Generally, yes. I don't want to create more trouble, my brother will have to handle any problems with his wife on his own, and I gave him the invoices of the lost contracts, so he knows they were lost and that I made arrangements for backups. Amy's parents are having their problems, and the only thing I'm guilty of is preventing Amy's mother from having access to her thoroughbride again for yet another wedding. And honestly? If she hadn't married Mat, I figured she would've lost it all anyway. Even men who like challenges would be aware that someone with so many counts of running from the altar will be a problem. And the only reason she hadn't run from the altar from my brother was because I threatened her with mass humiliation."

"I have a hard time imagining you humiliating anyone."

"I had invested in an eighty-pound ball and chain, I had it painted white, and the bridesmaids were willing to help me haul her to the altar with it. She wouldn't have been going anywhere with that thing manacled around her ankle."

"Okay. That surprises me. I thought marriage to my wife for so many years had made me immune to such things, but I had not thought you were the type to invest in a literal ball and chain."

"I thought that was what it would take to get them married, and Mat really wanted to marry her."

Mr. Carter chuckled, and he glanced over his shoulder. "She might be a while talking to Fredrick. She quite likes him, and they're probably arguing over your status as a kidnapping victim. She'll either try to kidnap him or taunt him into trying to rescue you."

I raised a brow. "Why would he try to rescue me?"

"He's stubborn. I've grown accustomed to being surrounded by stubborn people. My wife is very stubborn."

That she was. "Should I be apologizing for the inconvenience now?"

"Only if he invades and refuses to leave until Juliette has finished with your design and fittings. She just decided you're getting the time because she didn't have any easy clients she wanted to bump up to take the slot. If Fredrick annoys her, she'll just send him a bill, tell him she would have done it on the house if he hadn't annoyed her, and keep battling with him until she's satisfied."

"I'm concerned for Rick's wallet."

"He can afford it."

I figured, although I believed he could afford it through hard work and building his own businesses rather than using family funds. "I have trouble believing anyone can afford her prices," I muttered.

"Her affordable line of clothing has been doing exceptionally well. Per item, the profits aren't all that much, but in volume, her company is making a fortune. They're still in the testing phase, but that's part of why she's been designing so many boots. She's trying to make an environmentally friendly vegan option for faux leather boots. It's a challenge, as the plastics used in boots aren't recyclable at current, and the biodegradable plastics aren't suitable for footwear yet. She's toying around with a material made of plant fibers with a coating of biodegradable plastics. If she can get the fiber base to work well, she can set up a facility to renew the biodegradable plastic coating for customers as needed. She needs the plastics to last a minimum of twelve months of hard use before she's willing to sign off on that, though. If it works, it'll be an excellent alternative. She doesn't like non-recyclable plastics, and a lot of shoe material, while vegan, is destructive if it's thrown away. And since the recycling challenges bar the materials from being reused, she doesn't like it. It's a challenge for her, and she needs a challenge."

"That sounds really cool, though."

"It is, but it's a going to drive her crazier than she already is."

"That sounds like a problem."

"It won't be too bad, and the affordable

line will pay for the research and development. If she cracks a good formula for a biodegradable shoe with a year lifespan or longer, with a renewable coating, it'll be a money maker.. A lot of people are concerned about their carbon footprints now. That's part of why she does so much of her work locally. It cuts down on a lot of her company's carbon footprint. She does still have some leathers sourced from overseas, but she tacks on a surcharge for environmental charities when she uses them. She gets as many supplies as possible from close to home."

"And for her, it's not about the money," I guessed.

"Precisely."

"And this whole kidnapping thing?"

"She gets lonely when I have to work weekends, so she plans a weekend design fest with her favorite clients. There wasn't enough time to schedule a new client, so she took advantage of your text. It'll be all right. She'll let you go home if you ask, so don't worry."

"It's just a little weird," I admitted.

"Since when is something my wife does *not* weird?"

"Good point."

Juliette walked into the living room with a wrinkled nose. "Hope? He's being mean and wants to talk to you."

I took the phone, put it to my ear, and said, "Hello?"

"How did she get you in her clutches? She'll never let you go now, and I'll have to come over. Then she'll end up with another pet human to do with as she pleases. You've doomed us both to captivity."

His plaintive whine amused me. "Apparently, I'm getting a little black dress, and as she views you as a guilty party, she's making you pay for it."

Rick fell quiet. "Could you repeat that?"

"I'm getting a little black dress, and as she views you as a guilty party, she's making you pay for it."

"How little are we talking about?"

As that was a good question, I regarded the fashion design through narrowed eyes. "How little is the black dress, Juliette?"

"If you want a nightie, I can have one made free of charge to go with the dress. The little black dress will likely need a slip, so that part can be particularly little if you'd like. The perfect little black dress also comes with the perfect lingerie. It's a rule. I just made it up. The little black dress can be as little as you're comfortable with."

I giggled. "Which part of the little black dress are we talking about, Rick? Apparently, there's little, and there's also particularly little."

"I'll be over in an hour. Don't let her steal your clothes." Rick hung up on me, and I rolled my eyes at his reaction.

Shaking my head, I returned the phone to

Mr. Carter. "Apparently, he'll be over in an hour. He thinks you're going to steal my clothes."

Juliette snickered. "Well, yes. You told him you'd be prancing around in basically nothing. He knows how fittings work, and he knows what a little black dress is. It works out well enough. I've an extra guest bedroom, and your dogs will enjoy keeping each other company, as I can't imagine he'll leave his puppy home alone. What's an extra body in the kidnapping count? I'll be extra amused this weekend, babe. I can dress them both up."

Mr. Carter returned his phone to his pocket. "Good. Remember, you need to eat, they need to eat, and I will be expecting you to take your medication right on time, even if you need to interrupt a modeling session to do it. I will recruit both to make sure you take them."

"Dictator!"

"As I am a most benevolent dictator, if you don't miss any of your doses by the end of Sunday, I'll take you out for fast food."

Juliette sucked in a breath, and her eyes widened. "You promise?"

Mr. Carter smiled at his wife. "I'll even tell your doctor I used it as a bribe for good behavior and negotiate fast food for good behavior as a more common occurrence."

"You're *evil.*"

"I am. Now, be good and get her changed however you want before he arrives. He said an hour, which means he'll probably be here in forty-five minutes, ready to rescue his wedding planner only to fall into your clutches."

"I'm so good at luring young men into my lair and refusing to let them leave. It's a talent." Juliette rubbed her hands together. "This is going to be so much fun. How is our cookie stash doing? I feel he's going to need cookies to accept his cruel containment as my guest for the weekend."

"You know full well Chloe bribed you with an entire batch to make sure she got a weekend alone with Julian and the baby."

"I don't see what she has against free babysitting!"

"She doesn't have anything against free babysitting. She just wants to take our son off somewhere with their little one and have some fun. It's much harder for them to have a family outing when you're stealing the little one. We've talked about this before."

"I know, I know. And they don't need any more clothes until next year."

"Chloe promised she would take pictures, so you'll have to amuse yourself with Hope and Fredrick. Remember, you *do* need to let them leave if they genuinely want to go home. Other than that, do whatever they'll allow you to do."

"I'll behave. For the most part."

According to Mr. Carter's expression, he

had his doubts. "Hope, if she gives you any problems, call me."

"But you'll be working."

He heaved a sigh. "I see she's already gotten to you. It may be too late. Try not to let Fredrick likewise fall into her clutches."

I laughed. "I'll try to prevent him from falling into her clutches."

"Well, I tried. Have fun. I'm going to read my book from the safety of my study. Try not to damage the house, Juliette. You're dressing them up. You're not renovating the place."

"Your rules cramp my style."

"My rules make sure we don't have to spend the night in a hotel until a repairman can fix what you broke. Try to behave, Juliette." Mr. Carter kissed his wife before heading deeper into the house to escape the insanity.

"Well, we have forty-five minutes. Let's toss you in a cocktail dress and work some magic on Fredrick."

"How is me wearing a cocktail dress working some magic on him?"

"You'll see."

TWENTY

Sleep is a requirement, Rick.

IT TOOK Rick fifty minutes to show up, and Annabel Lee led the way, dragging her owner to the front door. From my place near the window, wearing one of the seven little black dresses Juliette had me try on, he took the tired from a long day at work thing a little too far. One jump from his dog might knock him flat and keep him there. "He looks exhausted."

"He works hard for the money, and like my husband, he has to get everything ready to take a week off for the cruise. A lot of his business ventures are doing well, so he doesn't want to abandon them at a bad time. That said, it will be an early bedtime for him for sure." Juliette bounced to the door and opened it before he could reach for the doorbell. "Come on in and set your puppy loose. Her best friend and his cat are in the living room sleeping off their hard day at work."

Rick unclipped Annabel Lee's leash, and

sure enough, she bounded to Edgar Allan Paw, woke him up, and gave him a rather thorough tongue bath before turning her attention to my overgrown cat.

As Lenore seemed to enjoy the dog's attentions, I left them alone. "Sleep is a requirement, Rick."

He grimaced. "There was a work emergency in the middle of the night, so my day started early. It's resolved, but today was less than ideal. I'm really sorry. I had no idea Elizabeth hadn't handled your payment or given you a proper contract. She's usually on the ball when it comes to that sort of thing."

I waved him off. "And I had volunteered to do the wedding as a favor and didn't expect any payment at all. Am I the only one who doesn't have a problem with this?"

"Yes," they replied.

Oh, well. I should have known better. "Well, I am not upset over this, I went in not expecting payment, and with a few exceptions, I've been enjoying the work. I already thought getting one of Juliette's dresses was overkill for the work I'm putting in."

Juliette grinned at me. "You have no idea how much a wedding planner typically charges for an event like this, do you?"

"Why would I? I'm not rich, and I don't care what rich people want to do with their money. I mean, I know how much work my brother's wedding was to plan, especially when I had to account for his bride's running tendencies, but it wasn't that bad."

Rick glanced at Juliette. "Do you want to tell her, or should I?"

"Oh, I want to fully enjoy her expression, so you should totally be the one to tell her what your family typically spends on a wedding planner."

Rick scowled, drew in a deep breath, and let it out in a heavy sigh. "My family is made of clusters of demons and demonesses with a few devils tossed in for good measure. We pay the wedding planner a hundred thousand to put up with our bullshit, and depending on how well the planning goes and the event itself, we also tip. Worse, the various clusters of demons and demonesses will individually tip. We had one wedding planner get tipped by every family for putting up with us at our worst. That there was a wedding at *all* in that case was well worth the amount he took home with him."

"Tell her what the tip is," Juliette prompted.

Rick heaved another sigh. "Up to twenty percent of the entire wedding's fee."

My mouth dropped open, as I had seen the insane bills for everything from chartered jet flights to get the family to the United States, the cost of the cruise, the catering bill, the cost to give the catering crew rooms aboard the cruise liner, and the various fees to use the brand-new ship on its maiden voyage. "And each family did this?"

"It was an awful wedding, and everyone was that grateful it happened at all. We're monsters at times, but we're monsters who recognize we're monsters. That's something, right?"

"Maybe you should tell your family they should try a little harder not to be monsters, although that explains a lot. They're expecting me to earn that paycheck. I'm still telling them no. I really don't care how much they want to pay me, but the answer is still no. Elizabeth's wedding is not up for negotiation."

"If all wedding planners went that route, we'd have easier weddings every time, but they're all afraid of being fired."

"I really don't care if I'm fired, but I wish Elizabeth luck finding someone who can take care of this with only a couple of months before her wedding date."

Rick grinned. "I told my mother that, and she was horrified at the idea she might actually scare off a wedding planner from being overly nice. I told her she should keep being nice, just not to ask anything of you, because you'll have to tell her no, and that makes you sad."

"I don't suppose that you can use that logic on your aunt, could you?"

"If only. I took a more direct route. I told her I'd chuck her overboard if she upset or scared you off during the wedding. I also gave her an outlet."

Alarm bells rang in my head. "An outlet?"

"I was solving a few problems with one stone. That the stone happens to be my aunt, well, I would feel guilty if it wasn't deserved."

"What did you do, Rick?"

"I pointed her at Amy and her parents."

My eyes widened, and I sucked in a breath. "You didn't."

"I may have accidentally sent her a copy of the invoices from Mat's wedding along with the various bargains you'd struck to make sure Mat's wedding went well, and then I may have accidentally made some commentary about my concern our rather productive wedding planner might become stressed if Amy's family were to become upset over the probable use of lost deposits to pay back a debt. Aunt Carolina loves setting wayward Americans straight, and while she tends to drive wedding planners up the wall, losing one because of an outsider is unacceptable. I'm expecting trouble."

I groaned and bowed my head. "Really, Rick? Why would you do that?"

"It was the only way I could make sure Amy's problems stayed Amy's problems rather than becoming your problems. Or, more accurately that her mother's problems stay her mother's problems. Considering the evidence that Amy had used the same staff for the wedding with the same loss of deposits because she'd run from the altar, it could become a severe issue quickly. Compared to the other weddings, Mat's was pretty cheap."

I frowned. "Amy didn't want it too expensive."

"That's probably because she actually wanted to marry him. That's my guess at least. So if she kept the wedding on the fairly cheap side, the losses were relatively mitigated. Comparatively, it was a cheap wedding. Ironically, it was the nicest of her weddings. But I believe she thought about running because of the general fear of retribution. You weren't accepting no for an answer, and I think she knew it."

I lifted my head at that. "Really?"

"Really. I suspect Amy's mother pressured her into it. She owed a lot of money, and if she could get that money using Amy, I could see it happening. It's a common enough ploy among the rich and famous. Hell, my family has been guilty of that crap more times than I care to count. Elizabeth refuses to play that game, as it turns out she genuinely loves Edward. I won't play that game, either."

"Thus the subterfuge about who you're interested in. Have you told anyone yet, or will it remain a great secret of the universe?"

Juliette snickered. "I know."

Of course she did. "That's because you're really good at cornering people and making them share their secrets," I muttered.

"I really am. So, Fredrick. How do you

like this little black dress? I'm debating on the style, but this one is conservative enough she has the freedom to bend over without offering everyone a show of her lingerie, but it's modern enough to satisfy the nitwits who think women should show off their legs."

"I was concerned when Hope mentioned particularly little, but it's a very pretty dress. Is it for sale?"

"It's in the fall line for this year, and it'll be coming out just after the wedding. I figure I can make a riff off this basic design, match it with a nice pair of knee-high boots, and send her on a mission to kick ass."

"It's a cocktail party, Juliette. High heels, not knee-highs."

"Don't you ruin my fun with rules."

"That's the party dress code."

As I'd been expecting to discuss the wedding, I'd loaded the actual rules onto my phone, which I referenced. "There's no shoe requirement for the cocktail party or the reception beyond a ban on flip flops and bare feet. Business casual is the requirement for all dinner functions with the exception of the gala on the last night of the cruise, which is formal. I will be hiding in my cabin for the formal dinner party."

"No, you won't," Fredrick and Juliette replied.

I scowled. "I don't have any formal wear, and it's an optional gala." Flagging that one as optional had been intentional so I could avoid attending.

"You will have a proper gown, and you're going." Juliette rubbed her hands together. "Fredrick, don't let her escape. I was not aware I needed to provide formal wear for the wedding planner, so we are going to have our work cut out for us this weekend. Darling? Darling? I need you, my darling!"

A weary Mr. Carter came into the living room. "What's wrong now?"

"She doesn't have a formal dress for the gala the last night of the cruise. Nobody told me she didn't have a formal dress."

"That party is optional," Mr. Carter replied, and his brows furrowed. "Why is it a problem if she doesn't have a dress? Did you ask her if she wanted to go to the gala?"

"She needs to go to the gala."

Technically, I needed to organize the damned thing, which meant I would only get to hide in my cabin after it looked like the show was on the road and no longer needed me to keep things rolling smoothly. "I will be at the gala among the staff—"

"I am conspiring with Elizabeth. You'll be attending the gala," Juliette announced. "I absolutely need to design you a formal gown. If I don't, I will die. Dramatically. They will be discussing my death in social circles for years."

Mr. Carter raised a hand and rubbed his

temple. "I think your medications need to be adjusted again."

"My medications are fine. I just stole a few cookies and washed them down with a coke."

"You rampaged on sugar? Juliette!"

"I needed it. My client had to cancel, and I'm sad because of why. I needed that sugar."

"I'm so sorry, Hope. She's supposed to limit her sugar intake, or she becomes rather uncontrollable." Mr. Carter sighed. "You can't force her to go to the gala, Juliette."

"Like hell I can't. I have cards. I'll play them. Watch me."

"Okay. Let me rephrase this. Why is it necessary she goes to the gala?"

"Presents. It's listed as optional, but the bride has presents for everyone, and she will be upset if she can't give Hope her present at the gala."

Crap. As upsetting the bride went against the rules, I would be attending the gala. "It would have been nice if the bride had told me this so I knew to not bother making the gala optional. I do have to arrange for catering for it. And while the caterers are in charge of that, with limited exception, I do need to tell them if the numbers are changing. It's not like they can just go to the store while we're floating in the middle of the ocean."

"It'll be fine. When you give catering the final numbers, just tell them they have to feed everyone on board. They'll take care of it with the help of the cruise ship. Fredrick, tell her it isn't a big deal!"

"It's probably not a big deal, especially if you tell them they have to feed everyone," Rick said, and I caught him grinning before he smothered it for a more neutral expression. "There's not even going to be assigned seating for it. Elizabeth has told me what she wants for the gala. It's chaos. She wants chaos."

"But how will she distribute the presents if she doesn't have assigned seating?" Presents added a whole new level of complexity, and I'd be driving myself insane if I had to help make arrangements for the gifts. "This is a disaster. Again. Another disaster."

"It's not a disaster. Elizabeth has handled all those preparations. She ordered the presents herself, she delegated to trustworthy members of the family to take care of the wrapping, and we just need to load them onto the ship. They're in safe keeping, so that's not going to be an issue. I've already hired a moving company to get them to the pier and loaded onto the ship on the wedding date."

Well, that was something. "It's still a disaster."

Rick grinned at me. "It's only a disaster because you didn't coordinate it."

Busted. I nodded. "Obviously."

"It'll be fine."

"Do you know what those are, Rick? Those are famous last words. Don't use those words when it comes to planning a wedding, because that's when things start going wrong."

"I will do my best to make sufficient backup plans so nothing goes wrong."

I narrowed my eyes at him. "I suppose that's a start. Also, had I known the gala wasn't actually optional, I would have gotten a dress."

"The invitations say optional, but it's really not. Just tell the caterers how many will be on board, and that'll simplify your life. I'll also give you a list of everyone's favorite foods so the caterers have ideas of what sort of things to serve."

Rick's offer elevated him to the greatest man alive, and I wanted to worship the ground he walked on. "Really?"

"I'll even give you a list of the foods Aunt Carolina hates above all others. She'll see them and recoil—and possibly hiss. It'll be great entertainment for everyone. I always recommend we have one of her most hated foods at every family gathering. Usually, I get away with it. As she's been particularly rude to you, I'll have you put her top three out. Elizabeth loves those foods, too."

"It seems reasonable that the bride's favorite foods should be present in a buffet setting."

"That's what I thought. Edward likes some of her other disliked dishes, too."

"It is also reasonable that the groom's favorite foods should be present in a buffet setting." I giggled. "Who knew indulging in pure evil could be so much fun?"

"We're just beginning," Juliette promised.

EVERY WAKING minute of the weekend went to clothes, and my head spun over Juliette's cheerful ambition. The bribe of fast food to take her medications worked like a charm, and after loading my car with more clothes and boots than I needed, plus loading Rick's car with even more clothes and boots than I needed, she evicted us so she could get her hard-earned dinner. I barely had room to fit. Even my poor dog and cat had to share the back seat with boxes, and I'd spend most of the night ferrying stuff to my apartment. To make matters worse, Rick went home with me as he had half of my stuff, and he took over the delivery spot by the doors while he waited for me to park. I wouldn't remind him I'd lost the bet, not that we'd had much of a chance to pursue clues.

To my dismay, Rick recruited help from the lobby desk in the time it had taken me to get my car in its spot. My landlord grinned and waved. "If you'll give me the key to your car, I'll bring it around and have it unloaded before returning it to your spot."

Oh, well. It would save me a lot of trips. "Thanks, Jacob." I unclipped the fob and tossed it to him. "I'm so sorry about the fuss."

"Nonsense. You hardly ever ask for a thing, and having taken a look in the gentleman's car, you have a lot to take upstairs. Your closets won't feel lonely after tonight."

My closets did have a tendency to stay mostly empty, as I didn't buy more than I needed. I wouldn't need to buy clothes again at the rate Juliette kept using me as an excuse to empty her closet. "That's one way to put it."

As I refused to be a layabout, I scurried to Rick's vehicle and grabbed one of the boxes while juggling my pets' leashes. "I really wasn't expecting her to try to give me her entire closet."

"I'm pretty sure Juliette's middle name is Excessive."

"Juliette Excessive Carter sounds weird but accurate." I giggled, shaking my head at the insanity. "The lengths she was willing to go to, to make sure she got fast food for dinner tonight, was the truly excessive thing. I thought Mr. Carter was going to faint from shock when he realized he could control his wife through her desire for greasy food."

"I expect that is going to become a tactic of his, making sure she takes her medications on time. She's been a handful because she keeps churning through assistants. According to Mr. Carter, every time she gets one, she finds 'a better place' for them in the company. She's missed a lot of her doses lately."

"That's not good."

"That's what I said. Mr. Carter is looking for a new assistant for her. I expect he's going to pick someone who has zero interest in the fashion world beyond wearing clothes because clothes are necessary. Personally, I think it's a disaster in the making, as Juliette's assistant does need *some* knowledge about clothing design."

"That's going to be interesting."

"But effective. I think. I told him I might have an employee who would do a good job, and it would be a good deal for her. She does fit the bill about being completely uninterested in anything to do with fashion, but she's as stubborn as they come, so if she can't survive Juliette, I'm not sure anyone can. And she really needs a capable assistant. Any CEO needs a capable assistant. We are lost without them. I have three, and they're all a pain in the ass, but they do good work."

"But are they accountants?"

"Some days, they consider making me pay for an accounting degree for them because so much of my business does involve money."

"Some days, I regret becoming an accountant," I confessed. "Especially days when I'm in a room full of male strippers who are getting a briefing on what it's like to be an accountant so they can go to accounting school. I'm glad that company is doing right by them, but they keep coming to my firm asking for advice from me, so I keep having to run to their office building despite having finished their auditing job. My boss thinks it's cute how determined they are to keep their jobs and be good accountants. I tried to warn them, but every time I warned them about the downsides of being an accountant, I somehow encouraged them."

"Accounting is tough work, especially when you're dealing with a tax code capable of breaking tables. Half the time, my accountants want to go hit the liquor bottles because they genuinely believe the latest rules were implemented by drunks."

I've felt that way a time or two. "If I didn't get wretched hangovers, I'd probably be one of those accountants. The hangovers do a good job of convincing me to avoid most alcohol."

"Hangovers are the worst, and they're definitely not worth the liquor that creates them. Unfortunately, every damned time I go to a business meeting, I'm expected to drink something, so I nurse a small glass of Scotch to appear sophisticated. It usually works. A few glasses of water before bed helps me dodge the worst of it."

I held the elevator until we filled it to capacity before hitting the button for my floor. Somehow, we ended up the only people on the first trip, and it would be entertaining ferrying everything to my door. "In good news, my apartment isn't a disaster. In bad news, my apartment is about to become a disaster, but you're welcome to come in and enjoy my fireplace if you'd like. I'm sure Annabel Lee will appreciate the heated floors, which I'll turn on as soon as we get in."

"Heated floors are the best."

"They really are, especially when they're in the bathroom. My bathroom is my favorite place in the whole apartment. I love the tub. I'll show it to you if you want!"

"Sure. I've always been curious what makes a perfect bathroom."

"Well, mine isn't quite perfect, but it's as close as I'm getting on my income. I looked at houses in the area, and I can't afford those. As long as I keep my job, I'm living here for life."

Rick chuckled. "I see you like your apartment."

"I do. I was worried about the price, but I really do feel like I get my money's worth. It's expensive, but it's worth it to me. My pets are happy, and it's a really nice space to unwind in."

"Hey, as long as it makes you happy, that's what's important."

Rick helped me ferry my boxes, bags, and loose boots into my living room, and he set the animals free. I turned on the heated floors, which I'd appreciate for a few hours before I went to bed and got ready for yet another grind mixing work and wedding planning.

By the time the wedding rolled around, I'd be on my last leg, I'd likely catch every virus known to man thanks to a stress-compromised immune system, and I'd regret having dealt with the devil in the form of Rick's family. Some prices were worth paying, although I hoped by the time the dust settled and I learned more about Rick's perfect woman, I'd be able to like her. Still, I refused to regret being his friend.

He proved there were men in the world worth chasing.

Had he not told me he'd been interested in a woman and wanted forever with her, I would have chased, too. That was something I could live with. No matter what and no matter who, I would be happy for him and give him his best chance at a perfect future.

After the wedding, I'd go look for my happily ever after, too.

I deserved one.

That thought made me smile. All I had to do was survive the wedding from hell to take the next step towards living life on my terms.

TWENTY-ONE

The chocolates helped.

THE NEXT TIME someone asked me to plan a wedding, I would run away, dig a deep hole, bury myself, and refuse to emerge until the risk of becoming a wedding planner went away. While Rick managed to somewhat tame his mother, the rest of his family viewed me as a challenge to overcome. How could someone like me, some American broad with a stubborn streak stronger than theirs, properly plan a wedding fit for nobility?

The more they attempted to micromanage me, the harder I dug my heels in. The only one happy with the situation was the bride, who viewed my struggles with her family as the ultimate form of entertainment. Her groom kept sending me apology cards, chocolates, and baskets of dog and cat toys as an attempt to make up for his family's contribution to the chaos.

The chocolates helped. My pets enjoyed their new toys, and at the rate I was going, I'd need a new apartment to contain their belongings.

More than once, I considered quitting and leaving the noble assholes to fend for themselves for the seven-day cruise, but quitting meant walking away the loser, and I wasn't going to let a bunch of overly rich egotistical so-and-sos beat me. I lost the war with Juliette, and she punished me for having dared put myself down in any fashion, foisting an entire set of new clothes onto me for the cruise. From bathing suits to lingerie to dresses to jeans and blouses, she included everything I might need to take the ship by storm.

I figured I'd get the last laugh, as I'd instructed the cruise ship to put me in the least convenient cabin in the entire ship, somewhere on the lowest deck away from the most popular spots. I'd get a lot of exercise when I emerged, but I had a stockpile of new books to read and a determination to stay out of sight and out of mind most of the time.

I'd even gotten some tips from the ship's captain where I might be able to find a nice, quiet spot on deck to enjoy reading if I found my cabin too cramped for my liking.

Had I been able to get away with it, I would've taken a spot in the crew's quarters to escape the guests, something I'd admitted to Captain Wellans, who'd laughed and admitted being able to escape after shift was one of the perks of being part of the crew.

At least he'd been quick to side with me, as my refusal to make unnecessary changes simplified matters for everyone.

I still struggled to believe I'd gotten lucky enough to book the maiden voyage of a modern luxury cruise ship.

I also struggled to accept how much Elizabeth and Edward spent on their wedding day. Despite having worked with profitable companies, the number stunned me. What was life like with over two million dollars to spend on a wedding, a week-long cruise, clothing for the entire guest list, and gifts? The gifts took a hefty chunk of the budget, and it was one of the reasons I refused to quit on the wedding planning even when tempted on a daily basis.

Elizabeth cared. Edward cared, too.

It showed every time she called me, worried about one of the unnecessary changes a relative flung at her. Edward's involvement kept the concerns to a minimum, and the only changes to slip through were the ones he wasn't certain about.

The day before the wedding and ten minutes from a complete mental breakdown, the confirmations came in one by one from the vendors, the caterers, and the cruise liner. One cake had fallen prey to an accident, but one of my uncountable backup plans had saved the day on that one; with Elizabeth's wishes, I'd ordered extra cakes from other vendors with instructions to make them magically appear at other weddings happening throughout New York City if they weren't needed.

There would be at least ten weddings with various surprises showing up, including cakes for the first civil union at the courthouse the bakers could find and more flowers than I cared to think about, although I'd suggested the majority go to hospitals rather than other weddings. I feared we'd wiped out most of the floral shops of plants, as Elizabeth had opted for the majority of the display flowers to be potted rather than bouquets. Every bridesmaid had a bouquet of some sort to match her dress, and the groomsmen had single flowers to be tucked into the jacket of their suits.

The morning of the wedding, I showed up at the pier shortly before dawn, dragging my suitcase with me. The dress would be on board in the care of Juliette and her twenty chosen minions who would enjoy the cruise when they weren't busy addressing any wardrobe disasters. Mr. Carter would help me keep cranky nobility in line at Juliette's suggestion, as it was one thing to tango with a wedding planner and another to get in the face of an attorney who could go from patient to irritable at the drop of a hat.

I hadn't yet witnessed Mr. Carter lose his temper, but if he decided to tear verbal chunks out of Aunt Carolina, I'd enjoy the show and place my bets on the attorney.

As planned, Captain Wellans greeted me at the pier. He saluted me with a tip of his hat and took my luggage from me. "This isn't the first time the company has allowed a full ship to be used for a wedding, but so far, this has been the best of the lot. So, on behalf of the crew, thank you for keeping this from becoming a circus."

"We still have roughly eighteen hours for this to become a circus, but once we get past the exchanging of the vows, I think we'll survive. After the reception, with limited exceptions, it's just another cruise, right?"

"And that's why this is working so well. We're doing the job we're familiar with, and everyone is seasoned at this, as this ship is going to be a star of the cruise line. That we get to have her maiden voyage on a planned event is unusual, but considering how much money the bride and groom are throwing at making this happen, I think we're all walking away happy."

I could only hope we would. "Have all of the service providers checked in?"

"The caterers are on board and working with the regular ship staff now, and the kitchen is fully stocked. We bordered on being over capacity, but we made use of a few staff refrigerators and freezers until we're through the reception. We've made a list of the overflow, and one of my permanent staffers is making sure nothing is misplaced. Too much is better than not enough. The flowers are on board and in position, the bouquets are in my cabin until they're needed, the wedding gifts are all accounted for and in their appropriate places. The gala gifts are in storage and are all accounted for, although the bride called me and indicated she wanted to move the gala gift distribution to during the reception. I cleared that with the staff, who liked the idea, but I said I would clear it with you."

Hooray! If the gala gift distribution happened during the reception, I could show up for the gala for all of ten minutes in the dress Juliette had insisted on making for me before fleeing back to the safety of my room. "I love it. That'll also make it easier on your storage."

"Which leads to the next surprise and the reason the bride wanted to move the gifts to the reception."

Surprises were bad. Surprises were very bad. Surprises meant I would have to plan around said surprises. "I'm afraid to ask."

Captain Wellans led me to the gangway to board the ship, gesturing for me to go first. "It's nothing bad, and it'll make for a good time during the rest of the cruise. There's a prime snorkeling destination four days into the cruise, and she inquired about whether it was possible to stop there before we returned to New York. While we hadn't been initially planning a stop, I was able to make arrangements. The bride took care of most of the work, and I assisted her with the rest. She thought we might break you if she added something on the spur of the moment. She handled all of the snorkeling equipment, and after the wedding, it will be donated to schools local to where we'll be snorkeling. A few local tour guides will be accompanying everyone. The hardest part will be doing the head count of everyone who leaves and boards the ship, but that's something we're already accustomed to doing."

Okay. I could only foresee a thousand things that could go wrong with the unexpected snorkeling stop. No big deal. I could handle it. "What do you need from me to make it happen?"

"If you fail to show up in appropriate swimwear, I have been instructed to make you walk the plank."

I paused in my walk up the gangway and regarded the distance from the lowest visible deck to the water. "That would probably hurt."

"I told her I wouldn't allow any plank walking from the ship because of the chance of injury, but there is no reason you can't be forced to walk the plank from one of the sailing ships that will be accompanying the group during the snorkeling trip."

Great. I could see Elizabeth making me walk the plank for fun, and I'd probably cooperate because it sounded like a good time. "What counts as appropriate swimwear? I have like seven different swimsuits with me.

Which one is the right one? I mean, if she's going to be holding a sword and acting like a pirate queen, I have zero problems with walking the plank as long as there are no sharks in the water."

"There are rarely any sharks in the snorkeling area, and there'll be plenty of small ships for the wedding guests to use should one be spotted. There'll also be rescue divers on hand should there be any issues."

Captain Wellans led me on board, where I was greeted by a startling number of the crew, who wore black suits marked with the ship's logo on the shoulders to distinguish them from the guests. Men and women alike wore slacks and bowties, which amused me.

I loved bowties, and wished more people wore them.

"This is Hope, and she's the wedding planner for the event. While we've discussed this before, should any guests attempt to make changes, you are not to implement anything without Hope's approval. The guests will begin boarding in an hour, so go over your final preparations. We have a three-hour window to board all guests before we set sail. Don't worry if the boarding process takes longer than normal. We do have up to four hours to set sail if necessary. I don't expect any problems with this part of the boarding process. If a guest has forgotten their invitation, confirm their attendance using an identification card or passport. Any questions?"

I figured the captain made me visible and offered the opportunity to question me to keep his crew at ease, and everyone seemed rather cheerful for the wretchedly early hour. To my amazement, nobody spoke up.

"Come with me, Hope. I'll show you to your cabin. The bride demanded you have one of the state rooms, but I had an extra cabin on one of the lower decks set aside for you. As such, she believes you will be in the state room, but you will be able to retreat to the smaller cabin at your leisure. I figured you would need some peace and quiet after dealing with the ceremony and reception. There are a total of ten empty cabins available should a guest also need some privacy during the cruise. I have one of those cabins reserved for anyone who happens to become particularly seasick, as it's in one of the best places to mitigate rocking and allow for them to get their legs under them or undergo treatment."

Seasickness was something I'd worried about from the day we'd confirmed booking the *Pearlescent Star.* "Hopefully we won't have many who get seasick."

"With the number of precautionary measures you've taken, I think it'll prove one of the better voyages for that. The weather has checked out, although there'll be one afternoon of potentially rough seas. Fortunately, the rough weather will be at the end of the voyage, and we'll clip it on the way back to port unless something changes."

The weather could be a fickle mistress, and I did my best to ignore the one problem I couldn't do something about. "Thank you, Captain Wellans. If there's anything I can do to make this go smoothly, please let me know."

"At this point, I believe you've done all you can. After tonight, it should be smooth sailing for the rest of the trip, with the exception of the dinner party on the last evening. Knowing the crew, there won't be any significant problems. You'll find them to be excellent at their jobs."

I hoped so, or I'd have a mess on my hands.

BOARDING EARLY GAVE me a chance to take a tour of the cruise ship and confer with the staff handling the wedding and reception. The wedding itself would take place on the largest of the decks, and while a tight squeeze, those who couldn't fit could watch from one of the other decks on a large-screen television. According to my list, half of the guests had opted for watching from afar.

The strategically placed open bar had something to do with that.

Unfortunately for me, I was to stand at the

very end of the bridesmaids, and as such, I would be wearing a dark red dress, as I was one end of the rainbow. The maid of honor, one of Elizabeth's closest friends, would be wearing a purple dress with the rest of the bridesmaids filling in the rest of the rainbow. While I wasn't the only woman wearing red, I had the darkest of the dresses. The groomsmen endured the same brutal color scheme, with the white of the bride and groom forming the central piece of the wedding.

Elizabeth loved the rainbow, and Juliette had enjoyed the challenge.

I couldn't help but notice the cruise ship lacked suitable holes to hide in to get out of participating in the wedding. While the wedding guests boarded, I hid in my state room, which had a splendid view of the water from the top cabin deck. While I'd heard that some of the larger cabins connected to each other, I hadn't expected to get one of them. A balcony would make my reading adventures particularly pleasant assuming no one came to bother me. I wouldn't hold my breath for that, but I'd try to enjoy as much reading time as possible.

While I'd escaped the general boarding process, I hadn't dodged a gift. The 'basket' was numerous baskets, a few boxes, and a ridiculous number of smaller bags, all in the same color of my gown. I couldn't scold the bride for going overboard, and I'd learned enough about the woman to know she'd ask me if I'd liked what she'd gotten me, eliminating ignoring the excessive number of presents as an option.

Heaving a sigh, I grabbed the largest basket, put it on the king size bed, and glared at the opaque red metallic paper preventing me from getting a preview of what lurked within. As Elizabeth had a rather dry sense of humor, I could see her inflicting one of a hundred harmless pranks on me. Bracing for confetti, glitter, or something equally heinous, I untied the red ribbon holding everything together, peeking inside.

A fortune of chocolate piled into a basket waited for me along with the box for a new e-reader, a high-end model I'd been drooling over; it boasted waterproofing for poolside reading and could hold tens of thousands of e-books for my enjoyment. I abandoned caution, tore into the basket, and grabbed for the box.

Someone had tied the damned thing to the basket along with a note, and I scowled at the obstruction. Pulling the wrapper away, I flipped open the folded note, which informed me I needed to investigate the rest of the basket before I played with my new e-reader and possibly miss the wedding due to being caught up in my latest read.

One late-night call with Edward had exposed my book-hoarding tendencies, and I assigned blame to him for the well-aimed note and gift. I freed the basket from the wrapping paper and obeyed his orders, checking out my excessive collection of chocolate that would likely last me through the entire cruise and quite possibly until Christmas. As the note implied I should check everything out, I obeyed, sorting through my candy until I discovered the tricky bastard had buried more things beneath my chocolate.

To go with my sweets were a collection of hard sausage, a knife to cut them with, and a note informing me that there were cheeses in the refrigerator for my enjoyment. Beneath the sausages I found a red-wrapped present. As the basket had yet to bite me, I tore into it to discover a new collar and leash for my dog and a new harness for my cat, who might never stop growing.

My vet had promised she'd stop growing eventually. I didn't believe him.

One last thing waited at the bottom of the basket, a rather thick envelope, which I pulled out to discover the e-reader's string was attached to it. I separated it, flipped the envelope over, and opened it. Several gift cards, including one meant for the online bookstore, tumbled onto the bed along with a card depicting a kitten playing with a puppy.

Inside, a short note informed me that Elizabeth and Edward had reviewed the application for a new furry addition to my household, which they had approved. I furrowed my brows, wondering what had gotten into them—and why they would be even considering furry additions to *my* household.

I had a dog and a cat. I didn't need another dog or a cat. However, should a dog or a cat fall from the sky and land on my lap in need of a good home, I doubted I could say no. Edgar Allan Paw adored other dogs, and Lenore was a dog trapped in a cat's body.

The soon-to-wed couple was about to goose me somehow, I just knew it.

I would just have to surrender and accept a new pet in my life. Such tragedy.

I hated being played, especially when I understood I would be played in a way I couldn't refuse. My apartment had enough space for another dog, and my landlord would love yet another furry tenant.

Jacob loved animals more than life itself, and I bet he campaigned to spoil my pets. Spoiling them wouldn't take much work, as I went out of my way to make them the happiest of animals, providing them with attention on demand, sharing my bed with them, and even taking them on car rides on the weekend because they expected to go to work every day. Instead of work, I took them either to the beach for some time outside or to a park.

When the weather didn't cooperate, we walked through the apartment complex, I drove them around the city for a while, and I went to one of the bookstores that welcomed dogs but allowed my cat inside when they realized she was a dog who'd been born the wrong species.

They loved the trips to the bookstore, as they always got treats from the staff. Trips to the bookstore also meant I spent time reading by the fireplace, which they both enjoyed.

I missed my dog and my cat.

To amuse myself, I set up my new e-reader while I still had reception, plugged my gift card into the site to discover some insane person, likely Elizabeth, had given me a thousand dollars to read through.

Well, then. If she wanted me to stay in my cabin most of the voyage and read books, I would. I lost thirty minutes buying every book on my wish list before tearing through the new releases to find a good variety to keep me occupied. Once done, I put my new toy in my purse so I could grab every spare minute escaping from reality as possible.

After returning everything else to the basket and setting it on the floor, I went for the next package in line, the second of six baskets.

It contained a bottle of red wine, a nice one from the looks of it, a pair of wine glasses, a bottle opener, and a book, which offered the clue that Elizabeth believed I was in dire need of help to catch a man. According to the sticky note attached to it, I needed glasses and to read the book several times.

To add insult to injury, although I couldn't

help but laugh, Edward left a note, too, which supported his wife's claim while also offering a talk if I needed help figuring out how to have a love life.

Then, because the pair couldn't leave me alone, the bottle of wine came with a condition: I needed to pop it open with someone of the other gender. I would earn bonus points and their favor if I allowed the gentleman I lured to my state room to feed me some of my chocolates.

Shaking my head and giggling at the insanity, I returned everything back to its basket and fetched the next one. Continuing the theme of adding inches to my waistline, the basket contained crackers, jams, jellies, dried fruits, nuts, and everything else a woman might need to nibble on while reading books. I assumed the basket was one of the base presents given to most guests, although I'd appreciate the easy access to things to eat without having to deal with people.

A knock at the door prevented me from discovering my other treasures, and sighing, I opened it.

A grinning Rick waved at me. "The captain told me you'd escaped to your cabin, so I thought I'd come visit before everything went to hell. I come bearing a gift."

More gifts? Sure enough, he held a small gift bag in his hand, and it followed the red scheme of my other gifts. I laughed and held open the door for him. "Come on in, but be aware of the various traps on the floor."

"Traps?"

I pointed at the open baskets.

"Ah. I see you are exploring your gifts. They refused to tell me what they'd gotten you, and Elizabeth caught me on the way in and told me I had to give this to you. I have no idea what's inside, but she seemed really concerned it hadn't gotten sent to your room already. As such, to prevent the bride from having a fit on her special day, I agreed to play the delivery boy. My cabin is next door, but I haven't been to it yet." Rick held the bag out, and when I took it, it didn't weigh all that much.

If it contained more gift cards for the bookstore, I would not complain. Using the bag, I gestured at the connecting door. "That one?"

"That one," he confirmed.

"If you don't hear from me, I'm probably reading a book. They gave me a new e-reader and a nice gift card to go with it, and I intend to enjoy some quiet time with a good book. If you could drive away unwanted visitors, I'd appreciate it."

"You are welcome to read on my balcony if the visitors become too numerous for your comfort. They probably will. You're the wedding planner they haven't conquered, which is a first in my lifetime. My family understands if they bother me without a good reason, I'll get snappy with them. You can come hide out in my cabin whenever you need a break. Honestly, I expect to be doing a lot of hiding, too. It's bad enough I have to wear a red suit. I got a consolation prize, though. Juliette made me a black one in the same cut so I'd stop sighing. I look like a bloody pigeon in a red suit. The only benefit is that we match, since we're both at the end of the line. I can't believe Juliette made bridesmaids match groomsmen. Worse? Most of us are still single, so everyone in the family will get ideas. You'll likely get off lightly because you're not British."

My brows shot up at his admission. "Are you serious?"

"Yeah. I didn't know my suit was red and matched yours until about thirty minutes ago. That was when Juliette found me and had fun at my expense."

Poor Rick. Poor me, too. "To be fair, I had no idea who would be on the groomsmen side of things. We had separate rehearsals."

"That was Elizabeth being evil and wanting to keep the pairings secret. She didn't like having to do two sets of rehearsals, but she wanted her secrets badly enough to do it."

I shrugged. "I just thought she liked spending even more money, honestly. Because two rehearsals cost her twice as much."

"That, too. She's having a little too much fun attacking her father's wallet for the wedding. Edward has done his share of attacking his family's wallet, although he's paid for most of it himself. His family only contributed out of familial obligation."

"Familial obligation?"

"They viewed it as shirking their time-honored tradition to help pay for the wedding. The groom is usually supposed to pay for the wedding, but Elizabeth wasn't having any of that. She hates being traditional."

I could easily see that, as very little of the wedding was technically traditional. As a whole, the bride and groom used the structure of a traditional wedding, but beyond exchanging vows and having a reception, they did most things backwards. While they would accept wedding gifts, they wanted to be the gift givers. They wanted a celebration, but they wanted the focus less on them and more on the families and friends being together for their union. "Were you aware of the snorkeling venture?"

"I found out about it last night. I took the liberty of scolding my cousin rather fiercely over the inevitable heart attack she'd give you springing a snorkeling trip on you out of the blue."

"The captain informed me I would be walking the plank if I resisted attending. Honestly, I want to walk the plank, preferably if Elizabeth is dressed up as a pirate and is putting her wedding planner out of her misery. My misery. I am questioning why I am the wedding planner right now. I don't know how I'm going to survive this week."

"You're going to be fine. Remember, you can hide in my cabin. The boarding was going smoothly when I was there, and I'm pretty sure everyone is accounted for. While they like to push your buttons, they believe you'll leave without them without hesitation, likely because you're capable of telling them no without caving under pressure."

"I swear they're worse than children," I muttered.

"They really are. Is there anything I can do to help?"

"Don't be late for the final preparations for the wedding. I'm already expecting to be herding bridesmaids and groomsmen. It'll be chaos."

"I won't be late," he promised. "If you need anything, I'll be next door until it's time to get ready."

I needed to jump overboard and run away, but rather than dodge the final stage of my job as a wedding planner, I went back to work so nothing would go wrong with the wedding or the reception.

TWENTY-TWO

Wait. She decided who you should be dating?

DRESSED in a red gown that transformed me into a bloody swan, I did my rounds. First, I checked with the boarding staff to make certain all guests had made it onto the ship. They had, although the nefarious Aunt Carolina had tested her luck and barely squeaked onto the gangway before they closed it. She'd gotten in with seconds to spare, and to my delight, the staff had spent twenty minutes scolding her, reinforcing if she'd been any later, the ship would have left without her.

The thought of the woman dealing with criticism amused me. On the main deck, where the wedding would take place, everything went precisely to plan. The quartet of photographers took glamour shots of everything before the guests could make a mess of it, the cakes were on display and guarded by the catering staff, someone had set up a red rope to prevent anyone from getting too close until the appropriate time, and the reception, which was spread out across the entirety of the ship, only needed a few finishing touches to be ready.

Unlike with my brother's wedding, everyone hired showed up, did their jobs, and followed my instructions to refuse any special requests from the guests unless they were cleared by the bride and groom before being brought to me. As the bride and groom were busy being prepared for the ceremony, I got to enjoy a quiet morning. Chaos engulfed the afternoon in the form of a buffet style luncheon on one of the lower decks to appease hungry guests while waiting for the ceremony to begin.

I dodged the luncheon by returning to my cabin and attacking the sausages and cheeses on my balcony while indulging in a new book.

Wedding planning went best when I didn't have to do anything at all.

Thirty minutes before my scheduled time to join the wedding party, I did my final sweep of the preparations, dodging the more persnickety guests so I wouldn't be tempted to toss some noble-born so-and-so overboard. Thanks to Rick, I even had a picture of his most annoying aunt so I could avoid her.

Going for a neutral color scheme consisting of whites, creams, and tans had mitigated Juliette's riotous choice of colors, although the bride held some responsibility for the prismatic display of people. The guests took their seats, which had been left unassigned with a few exceptions involving the immediate family of the bride and groom, who got the first two rows to themselves.

I joined the herd of bridesmaids and groomsmen, muttering curses over how I'd been partnered with Rick, which meant we'd take photographs together, sit together at the reception, and otherwise be expected to keep each other company for the entire day. Part of me liked the arrangement, as I'd have pictures with him. I ignored my other concerns, as we hadn't had a choice in the matter. If the lady Rick liked had a problem with our pairing, I'd worry for his sake.

By the end of the week, I figured I'd find out one way or another.

"So far so good," Rick commented while we waited for the musical cue to march down the ridiculously long aisle and take our places as a living rainbow flanking the bride and groom. Edward, dressed in his white suit, waited patiently alone at the white and gold altar, something the pair had imported from England. It had created a nightmare of paperwork, as it was a registered antique with an insurance value of over a million dollars. I didn't envy them getting it back home, but the paperwork was their problem rather than mine. "I almost wish Aunt Carolina had decided to wait until after the boarding cutoff to test her luck. She's been complaining that you're not letting anyone get away with anything today."

"Well, I told the staff they weren't to let anyone get away with anything."

"That amounts to the same thing. And after witnessing Aunt Carolina be scolded by the staff, everyone decided it's probably a good idea to behave and keep their complaints to themselves. That, plus Elizabeth made it rather clear she'd toss anyone who ruined her wedding overboard."

"Would she?"

"Nobody knows, which is why everyone decided it's a good idea to behave and stay quiet if something doesn't suit them."

I loved when my planning and a little help from the bride resulted in miracles. "I'm afraid to ask how the gifts went."

"Fine as far as I know. I've opened a few of mine, and I may need to tell Elizabeth she shouldn't be playing matchmaker at her own wedding. She's decided who I should be dating, and every gift she gave me was a rather blunt hint about how I should be spending the rest of the cruise. She took pity on me, though. She gave me an e-reader and a gift card to get new books, too. I'm going to join you in hiding, I think."

"Wait. She decided who you should be dating? But…"

"As I have kept my mouth firmly shut about any and all women I have ever been interested in, the family believes I am hopeless and will never marry. As such, they have determined I'm not actually interested in anyone, using my claim as a clever ploy to get them to leave me alone."

I giggled at the thought of his aunt tormenting him because of his status as a chronically single man. Then I shook my head, putting together the basic pieces of the puzzle. "As she instructed Juliette to put us in same-colored attire, she must be trying to set you up with me."

"That thought had crossed my mind. The potential couples do happen to be wearing the same colors, and she's set everything up so the pairs will be forced to spend time with each other. I don't mind this arrangement, as it means I get to have good company for most of the cruise. As we both enjoy reading books, we can just hide on our balconies and get in some rest and relaxation time. Should we wish to share a balcony, well, we have connecting doors and can do just that."

"Edward and Elizabeth are probably convinced I'll starve to death, as they put more than a week's worth of hard sausages and various types of cheese in my cabin. I skipped lunch and had sausage and cheese just to avoid the wedding guests."

"I had wondered where you'd gone. I was worried you hadn't eaten anything at all. The luncheon went over really well, though. My family couldn't find anything to complain about, which is exceptionally rare."

"Your list of favorite foods helped, and I only put out one thing your aunt loathed."

"I have a video of her discovering the eggplant parmesan, and it is priceless. I also liked the sign with it naming those who shouldn't have it because it contained dairy. That was a nice touch, especially the fine print claiming my aunt would love the dish. I'll be sending a copy to the photographers for the wedding video collection."

I grinned. "That was Elizabeth's idea. I just implemented it. You don't mind being stuck with me?"

"I absolutely don't mind at all. The only thing I'm annoyed about is my idiot family making it so our dogs had to stay at home for the week. I'm sure our dogs will forgive us. I'm not sure about your cat, though. Do cats ever forgive anyone who has slighted them?"

I hoped Lenore would forgive me. Over the past few months, she'd grown into a cuddling lap cat, and I enjoyed when she graced me with her attention. "Here's hoping."

The music, played by a small orchestra, put an end to our conversation, and began what I hoped wouldn't become my living hell.

UNLIKE MY BROTHER'S WEDDING, which classified as short, sweet, and to the point, we got a sermon from a priest who enjoyed gushing over the joys of marriage, the responsibilities of a wife, the responsibilities of a groom, and the challenges couples faced in the modern world. The wedding guests handled the lengthy discourse better than I did.

I wanted to run and hide, but my job was to stand at the end of the line, look pretty, smile until my face wanted to fall off, and keep a general eye on things. Nobody protested the union, a good thing in my opinion, as I would've lost my temper and rampaged had anyone decided to be an asshole without a damned good reason. I figured most of the guests had worked out their need to be assholes in the months leading up to the wedding.

As planned, the bride and groom left the ceremony first, and the pairs of bridesmaids and groomsmen followed in their wake. For the next four hours, we would be subjected to taking photographs on the uppermost deck, which had been transformed into a garden paradise for the cause. The potted, flowering plants added to the colorful chaos, and the newlyweds had even gotten a few trees to offer some shade and add some natural beauty to their pictures.

Rick nudged me with his elbow. "Baseballs were banned from the ship, so you should be safe. I am concerned there are other things someone could hit you with, but I would happily volunteer to keep you company should something try to crack your skull again."

I laughed, startling everyone near us.

Coughing to regain my shredded dignity, I replied, "Can I pass on anything hard encountering my skull today?"

"Do you have another method we could use to escape the reception? I feel like we should be trying to get out of going. The photographs are going to be bad enough, but do we really have to go to the reception?"

Right. Rick had an allergy to receptions. I grinned, as I would have liked to be able to escape from the rest of my job, too. As I couldn't be in two places at once, the guests were being watched over by various staff members from the crew and catering team, and if there were any problems, they'd find me with the main wedding party.

In addition to the main quartet of photographers, I'd hired three more to get pictures of the wedding guests on a different deck, and I'd given them instructions to keep everyone amused for as long as possible, allowing varying group shots only after everyone had at least one picture taken with the bride and groom.

The happy couple blitzed through their first round of photographs, including one group picture, a picture with every pairing, and pictures separated by gender. Once they left to take their photos with the rest of the wedding party, I relaxed. As the end couple, we'd go last for our private pictures, which meant we could sit down at one of the little tables scattered over the top deck and relax while waiting for our turn.

Rick leaned back in his chair, staring out over the ocean. "Well, I do have to say the view is spectacular. I bet Elizabeth put us at the end of the line so you wouldn't be running around the cruise ship today keeping an eye on everything. She's forcing you to stay here for however long she sees fit, and she's getting away with it because you won't interfere with any of her requests."

"In this case, I do not mind being manipulated into sitting in one place for an extended period of time. At this stage, I'm here to fix anything that goes wrong, and I've layered together so many contingency plans that I'm only going to be approached by the staff or caterers if I didn't provide enough alternatives to cover all the possibilities. If something does go wrong, that means it's really, really gone wrong. I figured the staffers were hired because they were skilled and good at their jobs, so I'm letting them do their jobs without getting in the way. As long as Elizabeth and Edward are happy, I'm happy."

"They looked pretty happy to me. The ceremony itself went smoothly. They'll toss the bouquet and garter at the reception, and don't be surprised if those cretins aim them at us as part of their scheming. Hell, knowing Elizabeth, she's just going to turn around and hand it to you."

"If she throws the bouquet at me, I am

going to let it hit me in the face." I grinned at my oddball threat. "It might let me get out of the rest of the reception."

"While clever, don't let that thing hit you in the face. I held it for a few minutes this morning, and that thing is heavy. If it hits you, it will hurt."

"But will it hurt more than a baseball to the head?"

"I would certainly hope not."

"It might make for a good excuse to retreat to the cabin and read a book," I muttered.

"I'm pretty sure Elizabeth is on guard against either one of us making a break from the reception. While she obeyed the no ball and chain rule, she has handcuffs that match our clothes, and I've been told she's not afraid to use them. What I don't know is how many pairs of handcuffs she has or how she intends on using them."

"We should have her handcuff us to the nice chairs on the balcony so we can read in peace."

Rick narrowed his eyes. "That's a pretty good idea, actually. But we'd be easy to find."

"That's definitely a problem."

"We'll just have to endure through the reception."

While the reception would test my patience and worry me from start to finish, I could think of a few things we could do to make use of our time. "We could make up headlines about your aunt in the tradition of Florida Man."

"And my day just got a tenfold better at the thought of that. What sort of mayhem would she create should she follow the Florida Man tradition?" Rick asked.

"FLORIDA MAN LIGHTS CRUISE SHIP ON FIRE AFTER RECEIVING UNWANTED GIFT."

He shuddered. "She really would. Elizabeth spent the longest on her gift so Aunt Carolina wouldn't have her delicate sensibilities overly offended. Alternatively, FLORIDA MAN SINKS CRUISE SHIP."

"More dramatic than just lighting it on fire, although I question how Florida Man would sink an entire cruise ship."

"It would become a mystery of the world," Rick replied in his most solemn tone.

"FLORIDA MAN DEFENESTRATES RAINBOW-CLAD WEDDING PARTY DURING JEALOUS FIT," I predicted.

"I'm not sure the windows in the cabins are really big enough for a proper defenestration."

I considered the cabins. "The ones in ours are."

"She'd have to have a really good toss because the windows lead out onto the balconies, so she'd have to clear the railing while defenestrating our family and friends."

As I already considered Aunt Carolina a force of nature on par with a rather large hurricane, I could see her managing to throw a body far enough to clear the railing. "I feel like I should be watching my back and locking my door now."

"She won't actually do anything to you. She'll just think about it. Honestly, she probably likes you."

I raised my brows at that. "How do you figure?"

"She didn't deliberately make herself late. She just pushed her luck. That means she takes you seriously, which is an accomplishment as far as she's concerned."

"Has anyone told her that she can be quite the asshole, Rick? I feel like someone needs to tell her this."

"Oh, we have. She just doesn't care. She figures if you can't handle her at her worst, you don't deserve her at her best. And to be fair, her best is pretty spectacular. She just makes you earn it first."

THE EXPECTED trouble began at the reception, as alcohol tended to make people do stupid things. Most of the trouble remained harmless enough, with the various disgruntled factions within the family tossing barbs at each other when the bride or groom wasn't looking. Then, because rich people competed with each other, they made bets among themselves as to who would get the best present from the couple—and who had bought the best presents for the couple.

"I didn't bring them a present at all," I confessed to Rick. Somehow, we'd gotten one of the smaller tables meant for two, which were scattered throughout the various decks to offer privacy to those who couldn't handle larger groups of people. Thanks to the changes to how gifts were being distributed, the bride and groom had reserved some places and let everyone else fill in the blanks. To keep things somewhat organized, each guest, with the exception of those who'd been assigned a seat, retrieved their name card from staff members on the top deck along with a generic small gift bag meant to keep busybodies occupied while they waited for their real gift.

I'd gotten more chocolate, a gift card to a local bookstore, and a warning I would live to regret it if I skipped out of the reception early.

Rick's bag contained similar items, except instead of chocolate, he'd been given a fidget toy to keep his hands busy and click at anyone who annoyed him. I found it amusing that he rolled the toy around in his hands while we waited for the first of the real disasters to begin. The dinner, a rather elaborate buffet, took over the entire cruise ship, with Rick and I enjoying the upper deck while the sunset illuminated the ocean.

While he fidgeted, I debated heading for

the nearest bar for a drink to take the edge off. I opted against it, as when something went wrong, I needed to be able to think clearly. I sighed my frustration.

"What's wrong?"

"I can't drink myself under the table because I have to be accessible. That's what's wrong," I complained.

"You're a lightweight, aren't you?"

"I can do a glass and make it home. After a glass? I'm done and worse than hungover. I mean, I'm hungover on a single glass, but at least I'm not a menace to myself."

"There's no reason we can't make off with a bottle of wine after the reception and smuggle it to our cabins and share it. I'm avoiding alcohol for the same reason. And I'm foolishly waiting for after the first round rush so I won't be tempted to toss some of my more annoying relatives overboard."

"I see your patience with the reception is shot already. Elizabeth put us in the corner so we wouldn't be as tempted to leave early."

Rick set his fidget toy on the table. "My family has mastered the art of senseless small talk, and they're usually more concerned about talking about each other than anything interesting. And they can't even be funny about the senseless small talk."

"Florida Man headlines are rather amusing. I bet the gift card is for a ridiculous amount, and we'll be forced to spend hours in the bookstore trying to decide what we want to get. That's the real tragedy here. We're being forced to wait to go to the bookstore. Had I known I was attending a torture session, I would have contracted some sort of plague the night before the wedding and made someone else do the work."

"You wouldn't do that, not knowing how hard Juliette worked on your clothes."

Damn. He had me dead to rights. "I can think about it, right?"

"Absolutely. I considered it, too. Alas, we're stuck here." Rick straightened, his attention focusing on something behind me. "The bride and groom are headed our way, they have red-wrapped presents, and my mother is with them. Ah, my father is, too. It seems he's being used as a mule. They are being excessive again."

"Which they? The bride, the groom, or your parents?"

"All of the above."

"Aren't people going to be upset there are so many gifts?" I turned in my seat to confirm the size of the disaster approaching our table, and everybody had at least a few presents in hand, which would make it difficult to get everything back to the cabin without help. "That's an absurd number of gifts."

Elizabeth grinned at me, and she deposited her armload of gifts beside my seat. "It is an absurd number of gifts, but Aunt Carolina made a bet we couldn't get you to accept them all, and it has become a wedding-wide event. We come bearing gifts, and if you accept them, Aunt Carolina owes me a week in the Bahamas."

"I am accepting your gifts only because it serves her right to owe you a week in the Bahamas," I replied. "I will likely regret this decision when I see what's inside, but I couldn't possibly sacrifice your week in the Bahamas at her expense. The number of times I had to tell her no completely justifies this."

Rick snickered, and he got up, kissing his mother on the cheek before exchanging hugs with his father. The pair, who barely seemed old enough to have a son Rick's age, stood at ease and regarded me with interest. "Mom, Dad, this is Hope, our most esteemed wedding planner and the owner of Edgar Allan Paw and Lenore."

As I had gifts practically on my shoes, I offered a strained smile. "I'd get up, but I'm trapped. It's a pleasure to meet you."

"It's a pleasure to meet you, too," Rick's mother replied. "Thank you for accepting the gifts. It will be amusing notifying Carolina she has lost yet another bet today. She was convinced the wedding would be a disaster because all of her precious recommendations were ignored, and she was certain the reception would be a disaster when it's everything but. Also, thank you for including the deviled eggs. She screamed when she saw them."

"She screamed? But why? They're just deviled eggs." I would spend at least an hour wondering about the woman and her problem with food. "They're fancy deviled eggs, though. I thought the caterer would cry when I asked for them to be included until I mentioned who disliked them. For some reason, they became a favorite dish after that. I can only presume she kept annoying the staff."

"Of course. That's how she operates. She just isn't satisfied unless she tests every limit possible. As for the eggs, I have no idea what goes on in her head. She's got a problem with eggplant, too. I swear, every time she checks out one of the buffet tables, she finds something to start screaming about."

I covered my mouth so I wouldn't be caught giggling over my payback for being a pain in the ass. "How interesting."

"It's like someone gave the wedding planner a list of Carolina's least favorite foods." Rick's mother raised a brow and stared at him.

Rick grinned, and he held up his hands while he shrugged. "We were allowed to make one request each, which would be considered for inclusion. I just happened to use my request to make certain the wedding planner knew what Aunt Carolina loved and hated. It seemed like the gentlemanly thing to do. If she hadn't bothered the wedding planner so much, I'm sure more of her loved dishes would have made an appearance."

"You are a terrible boy. Who raised you to be so bad?" Rick's mother scowled.

With his grin still in place, he pointed at his mother.

"Where did I go wrong with you?" Rick's mother transferred the packages she carried to her son, who had to put them on the floor because they wouldn't fit on his lap or on the table. "There are a few in there for you, Rick, but the rest are for her. She has earned them. All you've earned is coal, and I'm very disappointed Elizabeth insisted on proper gifts for you."

"What did I do now?"

"First, you moved to Japan. Since Japan wasn't bad enough, you moved to America. You don't write, you don't come home for visits. No, you do whatever it is you want to do."

"I don't write because I call you at least three times a week. I do come home for visits, I just don't come home every weekend like you want me to."

"It would be nice if you would."

"The jet lag would kill me."

"Don't be such a baby. It's just a little jet lag."

Edward laughed and added to the pile of presents surrounding my chair. "Thank you for your hard work on the wedding, Hope. You've done a spectacular job. You're officially off duty, and I told the staff to come to me with any problems—and that I wouldn't be happy if anyone came to me with any problems, and that I'd be taking my unhappiness out on the requester. That should let you enjoy the rest of the evening. The staff has everything under control, and when I inquired, they reported that everything was minor hiccups that nobody really cares about, in that they didn't want to have to explain their problem to you and thought it wise just to accept they weren't getting their way. One of my cousins apparently doesn't handle being at sea well, but I was told you'd reserved a cabin in the best place in the ship for that sort of thing, so he's been moved there."

I grimaced. "The captain told me there's usually a few, and I can probably make arrangements for another cabin if there's more issues."

"I already spoke to the captain, and he'll take care of it if it is an issue. Also, avoid the deck two levels below us unless you want Mrs. Carter cuddling with you. She's our first victim of overindulgence, supervised by Mr. Carter, who just shrugged and said she only gets to let loose once a year. He'll keep her contained. In good news, she's a very happy drunk."

"Most people on the ship are going to be drunk within the next two hours," I warned. "We literally have a plan for how the staff should deal with the overly intoxicated and do cabin checks with various hangover remedies in the morning. Anyone who gets too drunk will have a staff member keeping an eye on them and be cut off."

Edward sighed. "I wish I could say it won't be a problem, but it really will be. I don't think anyone on my side of the family will be able to move before noon, and even then, they'll believe they're dying."

I decided I would be passing on the alcohol, as there was little more amusing than being the only person not hungover following a party. "Try not to join them, you two. Thank you for the presents."

Elizabeth leaned over my gifts and gave me a hug. "Thank you for being such a good sport about all of this. Rick, keep a close eye on her. My brothers have been drinking."

"Your brothers are not nearly as talented at flirting the skirts off ladies as they like to believe," Rick grumbled. "That said, I'll keep a close eye on her. Please note that we are protesting the throwing of the bouquet and garter, and we may toss ourselves overboard should we be forced to attend that portion of the reception."

The bride giggled and waved her hand. "It's happening on the same deck with Juliette in thirty minutes, and I'll pretend I didn't hear you claim you'd miss it—and I'll even act like I thought I saw you there. You can just assume you caught it. You're next."

Without waiting for his reply, Elizabeth turned and left, and her groom followed, leaving us with Rick's parents. They waited for the pair to turn the corner before Rick's mother rested her hands on her hips. "And why are you skipping the traditional toss, Fredrick?"

"The last time anything was tossed or hit at a wedding, it collided with Hope's head. I am preventing that from happening by barring our attendance. That, plus I want to eat when everyone else is crowding a different deck and I have the entire buffet to myself." Rick pointed to the buffet tables, which were being refreshed by the caterers. "Speaking of which, the first wave is over, and that is my cue to get dinner. Would you mind guarding Hope's hoard of presents while we partake of the offerings? Aunt Carolina might try to add something wicked to them while we're gone."

"Well played, Fredrick. Well played. We'll watch your gifts. When you're ready to retire for the night, flag somebody down to help carry everything to your cabins. Elizabeth warned the staff this morning you'd have a lot to handle and would need the help."

When opportunity knocked and fresh food was waiting, a smart woman took advantage. I rose from my seat, stepping carefully around the gifts so I wouldn't trip, fall, and break my neck—or fall overboard. "Thank you, ma'am."

"No, thank you. This has been the most entertaining family wedding we've been to yet, and hardly anybody is drunk yet. The fun's just starting."

TWENTY-THREE

Is your aunt someone you'd toss overboard?

RICK and I stayed at the reception long enough to eat dinner and make off with several glass bottles of water before staging a retreat to our cabins. Three members of the crew helped us carry everything over, and we used my cabin to determine which gifts were mine and which were his. As warned, I got the lion's share of the presents, leaving him with a gift bag and a single box.

"Do they like you?" I asked, frowning at the ridiculous number of boxes, bags, and baskets taking over my cabin. "They don't know me well enough to like me this much, Rick."

"They adore you. You gave them their dream wedding without any of the headache we normally go through. You even have contingencies if anyone else wants to get married during the cruise. Really, I'm considering trying to figure out how to hire you away from your company. Your project management skills borders on the insane. Are you sure you're an accountant? You handled the planning like it's your main job. Honestly, I've seen professional planners be less thorough."

"Professional planners probably have a set method they use to plan a wedding, and they stick to their method, where I made it up as I went to keep things from being taken over by the various friends and family determined to have the wedding suitable for them rather than the bride and groom. Absurd, really. If they want to attend the wedding perfect for them, they should go get married."

"Well, a lot of them tried to do that, but they kept driving the wedding planners away."

"That's their own dumb fault, then."

"It really is. I expect my gifts are either pranks or taunts, as both have taken up annoying me as a hobby. I think Elizabeth has sided with my mother, indulging in a vendetta for moving abroad. I mean, she was already on my back for having moved to Japan, but moving to the United States? I have brought shame to the family name."

I snorted at that. "But didn't you move to work on your little empire?"

"It's not quite little, but it still has growing pains from time to time. The new branch in the United States is already doing better than I initially thought it would, but it helped I was able to get a good core employee base. Good employees make or break a company. That's one thing I learned while in Japan. They work exceptionally hard, often at high personal cost to themselves, so I got a lot of first-hand experience managing and preventing burnout. I am hoping to top employee satisfaction in the area while also building a good profit margin. I've been doing a lot of investing while the market is low, and I'll be reinvesting my profits into growing my business efforts. I'm branching into new fields, including banking, so it's going to be a challenge. Starting a new bank is particularly difficult, although I have enough global infrastructure to pull it off. The banking effort started because I had too many employees in the United States struggling with their banking situation, so I got the banking insurance sorted, and I eliminated the elements making it difficult for my employees to maintain an account."

"But how?"

"No overdrafts are permitted through my banking institution as a starter. If the person doesn't have the money in the account, the transaction is declined. That prevents the overdraft fees, which is a huge financial barrier. I don't require good credit for them to have an account, either—nor do I charge monthly fees. I make the money back by not offering interest on the checking accounts, and the interest rates on the savings accounts are tolerable but lower than competitors. It's been working so far, especially as a lot of the banking clients couldn't otherwise get accounts at all. Bank security is a beast, though—but that was one of my first business ventures. One of my companies is specialized in software that monitors for fraud, and we've come up with an app that lets banking users manually authorize each transaction using the app and their phone's camera. It adds an extra step when paying for something, but people like the security, and it prevents card readers from skimming the credit or debit cards and being able to withdraw or use them. If you don't have the physical card, the phone, and your special code generated at the time of purchase, you can't process any transactions. Keeping call center staff available to help is expensive, but we save a great deal of money preventing the fraud from happening in the first place. Users can also call in, verify their identity, and have their cards unlocked that way."

"And when you don't have much money, losing any money to fraud is a big deal."

"Exactly. I figure my real fortune will be made from that security system, if I can make it secure enough hackers can't readily bypass it. So far, my fraud numbers are exceptionally low, especially for such a new institution. Frauds piss me off. If I could tie thieves and con artists to the cruise ship and drag them through the wake while chumming the water for sharks, I really would. And I'd discourage the sharks from eating them for at least an hour to make sure they got in adequate suffering time. Those assholes steal from people who usually don't have enough money to cover the basics as it is—and then the big bankers finish the job off charging them overdraft fees instead of just preventing them from paying for something they can't afford in the first place. Maybe I should drag the big bankers behind the ship."

I giggled at the thought of Rick tying a bunch of bankers to the cruise ship and feeding them to the sharks. "Is your aunt someone you'd toss overboard?"

"Sometimes, I consider it. She's not that bad, but she definitely lacks a general connection with the rest of the world. Elizabeth forgets the value of things, too, but she's sweet enough to make up for it. Hell, I forget, too—that's why I invite my lowest-earning employees for a chit-chat and discuss their financials with them. Things change year after year, and what worked one year might not work the next. I do a handful of such meetings every month, and I usually target the employees that the managers tell me seem to be stressed. Money usually stresses people, so I evaluate the situation and figure out how to provide for my employees. It's been a challenge."

I bet. "I see you have a deeply ingrained need to be as busy as possible. Do you hate sleep, Rick? Because all of those challenges you're making for yourself make it sound like you hate sleep."

"What is sleep?"

"It usually happens in a bed, and in my case, there's usually two furry beasts who join me and try to serve as blankets. There was one incident where I became a bed for three furry beasts, and I didn't mind at all. Sleeping isn't easy when the dogs decide to sleep on you."

"It seems you were plenty content to sleep with the dogs on you. You didn't budge the first time someone tried to wake you up. You can't trick me. You're a sound sleeper. Would you even notice if I stole away your dog in the middle of the night? He'd warm my bed nicely."

I sat on the edge of the bed, grabbed one of the baskets off the floor, and picked at the ribbon securing the wrapping paper. "Did I give you the key, or are you breaking and entering to get to my dog?"

"You would be offering me the key, of course."

I laughed. "The only way you're getting to my dog is if I have equal and easy access to your dog. If you're going to try to steal my dog, I'm going to try to steal your dog. I have no intentions of losing. Both dogs will be mine. And you can't have my cat, either."

"If you steal my dog, I will be forced to visit her daily, as she's my dog. I have to go where she goes. That's a universal rule of dog ownership, except when I'm going places she can't go."

According to the contents of the basket, Elizabeth and Edward believed I needed to spend more time reading, as there were more gift cards to various bookstores around New York City, a throw blanket, several book-themed mugs, and a book light if I decided to try to read printed books in the dark. I showed Rick one of the mugs and the collection of gift cards. "I think they just gave me a hermit's starter kit. Do I need to leave my apartment ever again after I finish buying more books?"

"That's a very good question." Rick pulled up the chair from the cabin's desk and sat nearby. "As I know where you live, I feel I need to check in on you at least once a week, else you might never leave home unless you're going to and from work."

"But why would I want to with so many books to read, a nice fireplace, and a great tub?"

"I find your point very difficult to argue against. Honestly, I'm in a very similar situation at home. It has been a definite improvement. I've learned a lot about what my future homes should have, assuming I move again. If my parents have their way, I'd move back to England where I belong."

"Well, upon learning you're a lord or whatever, there's a reason for that."

"I literally want to throw up every time

someone calls me Lord Fredrick. I really do. It's awful. They also hate how I've convinced a lot of the family to start using nicknames. They're all about the formality. El was the first I corrupted. I got her to call me Rick along with a bunch of our mutual friends. I don't have the time to deal with stiff formalities."

I set aside the basket and eyed the selection of gifts. "Do you think she wants me to open the reception gifts first or the boarding gifts? I'm concerned she has more presents stashed away on this ship somewhere."

"I'll go grab my collection, and we'll open them together. We'll pretend it's Christmas, and we can make fun of what we got. I'm sure there will be pranks in here somewhere." Rick hopped to his feet, went to the connecting door, and headed into his cabin, returning a few moments later with a few gifts, which he piled on the floor far enough from my presents we wouldn't mix them up before making his next trip to fetch more boxes, bags, and baskets. Like me, he'd been gifted with a ridiculous number of presents.

"This is way too excessive, Rick."

"They're good at being excessive. I'd peeked into only one of my baskets, which had my e-reader in it. That made me happy enough I figured I could wait for the rest." He sat on the floor and rubbed his hands together. "This is more fun than Christmas. I don't have to put on a show when I open these. For some reason, people expect me to be happy with whatever gift they give me. Last year, Aunt Carolina gave me several books on dating, the ugliest sweaters I'd ever seen in my life, and a rugby ball. I'd be utterly destroyed at rugby, and I have no desire to inflict pain on myself. I've watched enough rugby matches to understand that way leads to concussions and pain."

"As someone who has experienced a concussion before, I heartily recommend avoiding them."

Rick grinned at that. "I agree. On the bright side, we got through the photography session without any incidents."

"I'm amazed we made it to the reception without anyone needing me for anything."

"I have no idea how that happened with an entire ship full of my family and our family friends. It's a recipe for disaster, yet we have been completely devoid of disasters."

"Bite your tongue before a disaster happens!"

"There will be drunk people within the hour. Hundreds of drunk people. The disaster is already beginning, and there's nothing we can do about it beyond hide behind locked doors and open presents."

"Good idea." I picked a larger box, which weighed enough I grunted setting it on the bed. Inside, a game console and a collection of car racing, action-adventure, and role-playing games waited for me. I frowned, furrowing my brow. "I guess I'm a gamer now, Rick."

"For when you need a break from books, I guess?" Rick tilted his head to the side, regarding my new collection with interest. "That must be from Edward, as he enjoys gaming and thinks everyone else does, too—they just need to be given a gaming starter set to discover the joys of pixel-based destruction. In good news, I recognize a few of those titles, and they're multiplayer, so you can entertain guests with it. I hope you have a television."

I clicked my tongue and refused to look him in the eyes. "Maybe."

"You don't have a television, do you?"

"I guess I'm going to have to get one. I'm sure I can find a place for it in the apartment. Is it bad if it doesn't get used much? I have a lot of new books to read."

"Just keep it around as a way to entertain guests. If you mount the television to the wall, it's basically a nice decoration you ignore unless you have guests who need to be amused."

"Good idea. I'll do that." I set the console and games aside before grabbing the smallest of the reception gifts, a tiny bag barely large enough to hold a gift card or a few pieces of chocolate. "This is really cute. I'm not usually the kind to keep gift bags or wrapping paper, but I might have to keep this one."

"It's definitely diminutive."

Like the other bags, it was tied off with a ribbon, which I removed and set aside. Inside, I found a gift card and a folded slip of paper. My brows shot up, as it was for one of the more high-end adult boutiques in the city. "Well, someone wants me to have a good time." I turned the gift card so Rick could see it, and like me, his brows shot up.

"I'm not sure I want to know what the note says. Isn't that the sort of gifts Elizabeth was supposed to receive at the bachelorette party she didn't have so she wouldn't receive such things?"

I laughed, as I'd dodged a lot of headache not having to deal with either a bachelor or bachelorette party. "She could be confused."

"That's entirely probable. The wedding planning, even though she dodged the worst parts of it, definitely rattled her brains. She went flat-out psycho over the snorkeling. She got it into her head we needed some form of activity, but she absolutely didn't want you to be burdened with planning it so she went crazy making sure it could happen. I didn't know it was possible to get the supplies needed in such a hurry—or charter enough smaller boats to take us all to the spot. She's lost her mind. The stress of somebody possibly ruining her wedding must have gotten to her."

I laughed and set the gift card in my purse to deal with later before opening the note, which informed me I had their permission to take Rick home with me, as nobody would miss him. "Apparently, you must have annoyed the bride and groom."

"I did? Wait, what?"

I handed over the card, and laughter bubbled out of me. "A rather inappropriate gift card with a permission slip to take you home with me. Your mother must have been lying about missing you, as the bride and groom say otherwise."

"My mother really would," Rick muttered, taking the note and reading it over. "Wow."

"I think you were just sold into slavery."

Rick narrowed his eyes, considering the note for a long moment before handing it back to me. "I'm now slightly concerned what else is in her gifts—and what is in mine. She already gave you a hermit's starter pack. She might have given you other starter packs, too."

I retrieved the gift card and held it up. "I saw how much she put on a gift card for books. I've learned we are not dealing with reasonable people here. This would be the starter pack. For what, I'm not sure."

"Tripling the population of New York?"

I snickered and tossed the gift card at him, which he leaned over to dodge. It skittered across the carpet, and he flopped over to retrieve it, setting it on my console's box.

Rick snickered, and he collected his two gifts from the reception, untying the ribbons.

"Okay, maybe she means for you to practice the skills required to triple it."

"It's rude to get revenge on the bride, isn't it?"

"Usually, although I'm sure you can make her walk the plank when we go snorkeling. I was told I would be attending under threat of death. Considering that note, I do believe my cousin is trying to play matchmaker."

"Yet here we are in my cabin gossiping about her matchmaker ways."

"I could either be here or out at a reception getting unholy drunk, which is not one of my favorite activities. Hangovers? Another hated activity. I'm highly amused right now, and if you're okay with this arrangement, I'm okay with this arrangement."

Huh. "But you were sold into slavery. I mean, you weren't even sold. You were just tossed to the sharks without pay. I'm the shark right now, and I'm okay admitting that."

"That does hurt a little. She should have at least tried to get some money out of you. I'm a good purchase. She shouldn't be giving me away for free."

"Here's the important question: do you come with your dog?"

"Let me think about that for a second." Rick paused, and with zero evidence he'd thought about it at all, he announced, "Yes. Nonnegotiable."

"It's not kidnapping if I have a permission slip, right?"

"Technically, it would be kidnapping, but you do have a permission slip, and it's rude to tell the bride no on her wedding day."

"It really is, isn't it?"

"Definitely."

"Do they make beds big enough for two people and two huge dogs and a cat?"

"They do. I happen to own one, as I'm spoiled. It's an oversized king, and it was custom made. There are steps at the foot of the bed for Annabel Lee. Edgar Allan Paw would definitely appreciate the steps."

Damn. I couldn't even tell if the man was serious, if he'd been leading everyone on about having a woman he was interested in, or if he was just humoring me. The only way to find out was to ask, but the answer scared me, because no matter what his reply was, everything would change. Change could be good. Change could be bad. But change would come, and I didn't want to lose the friendship I'd managed to salvage despite the several months we hadn't talked at all due to my general cowardice.

"What am I supposed to do with a slave? There's no handbook." I frowned. "Wait. Maybe there is a handbook. There are more presents. She would include a handbook for this situation in here somewhere. I don't know her that well, but she really would."

"The only way to find out is to open everything."

"We'll take turns. I got a slave, so it's your turn to open something."

"I don't have a little bag. This is now really disappointing. You got an entire person from a little bag."

I shrugged. "You could have planned the wedding and gotten bequeathed with an entire person. I'm just being fairly paid. And I didn't just get an entire person. I got an entire person and his dog."

"Maybe they gave you the game console to keep me entertained when you want to read a book by your fireplace?"

I considered that. "Do you play games?"

"Sometimes. If I've been reading all day at work doing business research, I'll play games instead of reading. I sometimes watch movies, but not often. I'm guessing you don't watch movies, as you don't own a television."

"I've been working so much I haven't had time. I don't mind movies, but I'd rather read a book."

Rick selected his next basket and opened it, revealing a collection of Scotch bottles, glasses, and a decanter. Shaking his head and laughing, he lifted out one of the bottles. "This one would be Edward's contribution, as he enjoys implying I should have been born in Scotland. He might also be thinking I need a stiff drink to survive this cruise. Hell, knowing him, in two or three days, he's going to be visiting me to have a stiff drink to get through this cruise."

"I'm hoping that's because of the sheer number of family on board rather than marriage to Elizabeth."

"Maybe Elizabeth set up the snorkeling event so she could get rid of the more annoying members of the family. Alas, everyone will be counted getting on and leaving the ship, along with a lot of precautions to make certain nobody is left behind or goes missing. Of course, my cousin is a trickster at heart, and if she thinks she can get away with something, she will."

"What could she possibly get away with while snorkeling?"

Rick considered, wrinkling his nose. "Abandoning us on an island or at a beachside resort and leaving us for someone else to pick up at a later date?"

"She better not, not without our dogs and my cat!"

He snorted. "I like how you're not against being abandoned at a resort, but you are if your pets don't show up."

"I miss them," I whined.

"Me, too. I'm sure they'll be fine without us. Truth be told, if I had brought Annabel Lee, the only time I'd leave my cabin would be to take her on brief walks, and I'm still at a loss of how we'd walk the dogs on a cruise ship."

"I was going to have big boxes with grass

set up on one of the decks for them," I admitted.

"That would have worked nicely. Annabel Lee isn't particularly picky."

"Neither is Edgar Allan Paw. And Lenore? Provide her with a litter box and show her where it is, and she's happy."

"I tried to teach Annabel Lee how to use the toilet once. It didn't go over very well. Apparently, she likes going on walks and resented my attempt to teach her a new trick so I could be lazy."

I laughed. "Walks are sacred, Rick. You should know this by now."

"They really are. I've opened a present, so it's your turn to open one."

"As the reception presents have been the most impressive, I think I'll do the largest of the reception presents now." I selected the large box, which weighed little enough to warrant suspicion. I joined Rick on the floor and unwrapped it. I'd been around Juliette Carter often enough to recognize the designer's lingerie boxes, and Elizabeth had crammed six of them into the larger box. At the bottom of the emptied box, I located a pair of red, fuzzy handcuffs. I hooked them with a finger and lifted them out. "Continuing the enslavement theme, it seems I have been gifted with a pair of cuffs."

"And some boxes."

"Those would be lingerie boxes, and judging by their weight, she emptied her closet of everything in my size again. Either she believes I'm only going to wear them once or I'll somehow destroy them."

Rick eyed the boxes like they might rise up and bite him. "I'm not sure how you could destroy them."

"Judging from the inclusion of the handcuffs, I'm sure they would have help being destroyed. While I am not currently involved with any men, I can verify that lingerie has a remarkably short lifespan when in the clutches of an eager gentleman."

"How is destroying lingerie gentlemanly? I've seen the price tags on those things. There's nothing gentlemanly about destroying a hundred dollars or more in lingerie."

"It's like elaborate wrapping paper, and I'm sure a proper gentleman assists in the acquisition of new lingerie to destroy."

"This morning, I did not anticipate lingerie becoming a legitimate peril in my life."

"It's only a peril if you're too cheap to replace what you destroy, and if you're handcuffed during the destruction process, is it really your fault?" I shrugged, twirled the handcuffs around my finger, and dumped them onto the console box with the gift certificate for the adult boutique. "I'm going to assume all of my reception gifts are expensive clues I should change my career from wedding planner and accountant to seductress."

"I guess that gift card counts as a seduction starter kit, doesn't it?"

"I don't feel I am at all prepared for this. Mat is comfortable believing I'm chronically single and incapable of drawing the attention of men. Well, straight men. I'm very good at having gay friends. I mean, they're great. They are usually cool people and don't treat me like I'm there for the potential benefits."

"No matter what I say, I'm going to say the wrong thing. Can I pass on making any commentary?"

I thought about that. "Being able to see your dog is a benefit."

"I don't think that's the right sort of benefit being discussed."

"While it's not, I'm just saying I'm already using you for the potential side benefits, which includes seeing your dog." I shrugged and pointed to the bag Rick had gotten at the reception. "You should open that one next. Maybe it's a starter kit for you of some sort."

"I'm concerned it might be. What sort of starter kit would she give me, though?"

"That's a good question. What could you possibly need a starter kit for?"

"Being a good slave, as I have not taken any lessons on being properly subservient. Honestly, I'm going to make a terrible slave."

"But you have a cute dog. That makes up for any other flaws you may have."

"I see my dog has thoroughly charmed you."

"She really has." Annabel Lee's owner had done some significant charming of his own, and I debated gathering the courage to be direct with him about it. If there was another woman somewhere, I hadn't seen any evidence of her, and well, if I could take her place without actually bothering someone who'd gotten to him first, I wouldn't have a complaint with that. "What counts as a good starter kit?"

"At this point, I really don't know." Rick opened the bag and revealed a large jewelry box. "I'm now scared to open this. The only jewelry I wear is a watch, and I'm not sure what else could be put in here."

I held out my hand. "I'll open it for you if it's that scary."

He handed me the box. "I hope it doesn't attack you."

"Would Elizabeth or Edward put something in a box that might attack me?"

"At this stage, I wouldn't be surprised."

"That would be a spectacular headline. BRITISH LORD MURDERED BY NEWLYWEDS IN GIFT-GIVING INCIDENT. You'd go down in history as the first to be murdered by a jewelry box."

"Now I'm wondering how someone might die from a jewelry box."

"Maybe you could be bludgeoned to death with one? It'd be a lot of work, though. That'd be a spectacular headline. NEW YORK WOMAN

Murders British Lord with a Jewelry Box."

"If you murder me with the jewelry box, you can't visit my dog."

"You're absolutely right. That's a good point. You're required to maintain my dog-visitation rights."

"Or you can invite me over to visit, and I would be inclined to bring my dog with me because she likes you and your dog. She even likes your cat."

"Annabel Lee is incapable of disliking anyone." Cracking open the jewelry box, I peeked inside. On one side of the dark velvet pad within lay a wristwatch, but instead of the expensive kind I expected CEOs to wear, it was a digital one meant to be used with a phone. On the other side was a pair of wedding bands and an engagement ring with a dark blue stone, and the worn, engraved bands implied they carried the weight of age with them. Uncertain of what to think of that, I closed the box and handed it over. "It will not bite you, but it is a starter kit of a sort."

"Of a sort?" Rick took the box and opened it, and his brows shot up. "This goes beyond issuing hints. My parents are not long for this world, and my cousin has provided an excellent opportunity to drown them both."

"Okay, I'm obviously missing something."

Rick set the box on his lap and retrieved the wedding bands and engagement ring, setting them on his palm so I could get a better look at them. "These are about five hundred years old and count as family heirlooms. In my family, the heirlooms are given to the eldest son of the family when being given approval to wed. While not everybody has traditions like this, it's been done in our family for, well, hundreds of years. My mother and father have such a pair of rings, although they never wear theirs and they were only used for the wedding ceremony. These rings are among the first. The stone isn't diamond—I think it's a sapphire. Anyway, the Romans came up with the whole idea of having wedding bands, and these were among the first ever used in my family. There are numerous sets of these in the family, but I like these ones the best," he admitted.

"Why?"

"As far as I know, every couple with these rings ended up having a happy marriage. Perhaps not always the most prosperous marriage in terms of wealth, but they were happy despite the challenges. That said, they are somewhat of a double-edged sword, as many of the marriages did have rough spots."

"Something worth having is worth fighting for."

"That it is. So, it appears my cousin got together with my parents, leaving me a rather strong hint."

I pointed at the boxes of lingerie, the gift card for the adult boutique, the handcuffs, and the note. "I think they've gone beyond mere hints."

"It's probably because I threatened to rain down hell on anyone who bothered you after we talked about how Aunt Carolina was driving you crazy. This is my fault."

"Or Mat told one of them that you'd spent the night at the hospital with me after I got smacked in the head with a baseball."

"Mat didn't have to. I opened my fool mouth and told her myself when I'd suggested you be the wedding planner."

"So, let me see if I get this straight. Your entire family has been tormenting me about this wedding, and after the wedding goes off without any catastrophes, your cousin conspires with your parents to give you an engagement ring and wedding bands, which are priceless family heirlooms."

"That sounds about right. The whole tradition of marrying family friends to stop feuds is an old one, but it doesn't exactly lead to happy marriages—well, some of the time. Some of the time it works out. But you'd count as an outsider to them, as you're not exactly standard bride material in my family line."

"No kidding. I'm about as common as dirt, and you have a pedigree."

"Common as dirt is better than a pedigree to me. If I had wanted a pedigree, I would've been married off the day I turned eighteen in as ridiculously elaborate of a wedding as this one. So on that front, they're right, as I've made it pretty clear I need more in a woman than the circumstances of her birth."

"I'd say I have pretty high standards for a man, but really, he needs to be nice and have a good dog."

"Interesting. How do I rank on the nice chart?"

"You do a decent job. It takes a pretty nice guy to introduce a lady to ridiculous headlines during an equally ridiculous hospital stay."

"Well, next time, don't catch a baseball with your head."

"I have learned my lesson. I will do my best to avoid catching a baseball with my head."

"And that leaves the issue of these rings and my nosy family. The instant they think I've opened this, they're going to start getting into our business. Obviously, they deserve some form of punishment for their meddling."

"I have enough sausage and cheese to feed us both for a week. We could hide on the balcony and avoid the entire lot of them. Conveniently, we were provided with a gaming console, there is television in this room, and we have new books. We can hide. Hiding is always an option, Rick."

"Until it's time to go snorkeling and my cousin comes barging in. And she will. She will get the crew to unlock the doors, and they'll drag us out on the snorkeling trip. Then there's the gala, and knowing her, she'll find another pair of handcuffs and use them on us until we give her what she wants."

"Has anyone told you that your family is insane?"

"Is it a good sort of insane this time?"

I took that to mean he'd heard about his family's possibly genetic-level insanity before. "It's potentially sweet, assuming she has good intentions."

Rick narrowed his eyes. "I'm concerned Elizabeth asked Aunt Carolina to be a pain in the ass now."

"But why?"

"Well, when Aunt Carolina isn't being a jerk because she doesn't like somebody, she's usually a good judge of character, and your ability to handle her really would impress most of my family. I mean, she's a walking disaster with a temper and a drive to get exactly what she wants when she wants it. You dealt with my entire family pulling that shit, and you handled them well. Honestly, I can't even express how impressed I am with your ability to put up with them at their worst. They certainly weren't giving you their best."

No, but when I thought about it, they may have been giving Rick their best. "Do they like you or hate you?"

"I thought they liked me, but now I'm not so sure."

I pointed at the one of his gifts, which was

a mid-sized box. "You need another present. It might be another starter kit of some sort, and honestly, I'm curious to see just how much they hate you. As they got you some nice presents when you boarded, they might not hate you completely."

"I am not responsible for what I find in this box."

"I would say the bride and groom are responsible for what's in that box."

"That's true, but after you received an entire human and his dog as a gift, I'm not sure I want to know what I'm going to get."

I giggled. "If you receive a gift of a human, does that mean the human belongs to me since you're now my property?"

"That's a really good question. I'm not really sure how this works. Do you have full ownership, or do you only have partial ownership? Do you own me when I go to work or only after hours? I feel like we weren't given adequate instructions on what to do about this situation."

"Maybe the box contains your instruction guide on what you do now that you're my property."

Laughing, Rick opened the box, lifted one of the flaps, and peeked inside. He snorted and shook his head. "I don't know which one of them came up with this, but I think they need a talk about reality."

"Now I really want to know what's in that box."

Rick pried open the flaps, lifted the box, and turned it upside down. A cascade of foil-wrapped condoms spilled out and piled onto the floor. "Is this an instruction guide on what I should be doing now that I'm your property?" He gave the box a shake, and more condoms fell out.

"There must be hundreds of them!" I leaned over, picked one up, and giggled. "This one is banana flavored." I set it aside and picked up a different one. "And this would be raspberry, and there's a blueberry, and honestly, I'm not sure I really want to think about how much time someone spent taste-testing these before selling them."

Rich set aside the box and picked one up. "And for any adventures to take place in the dark, this one glows in the dark."

"I'm having a very difficult time imagining Elizabeth or Edward picking out every variant of condom type on the planet to give to you at their wedding."

"I bet Elizabeth ordered them online, opened all the boxes, and dumped them in. She would, too. That said, I doubt she would have expected me to come to your cabin and open them with you."

I pointed at the card that declared Rick was my property. "Are you sure? Because honestly, I *could* see myself visiting you after opening that."

"Well, I would hope so. It's not every day you receive an entire human at someone's wedding. Had I gotten that card, I definitely would have been paying you a visit to learn more."

"Maybe we should run away to one of those resorts wherever we're snorkeling to escape the insanity. I'll even leave her a note telling her I have claimed my property and left while I could."

"She'd be upset if you missed the gala."

Damn it. "I think that's unfair. We went to the reception." I pouted. "I even planned the gala. That said, the dress Juliette made for me is very pretty."

"I'm not sure what my cousin is thinking, but I'm man enough to admit I'm not man enough to use all of these condoms. Do condoms go bad?"

"I have no idea. I can't say this is a situation I've ever encountered before."

"Is it bad that I'm so used to my work that I feel an almost compulsive need to tally the condoms and figure out how long it would take to use them assuming I had a partner for such activities?"

The accountant in me needed to know, and I abandoned my gifts to help him tally his new condom stash. "I'm sure there's a proper mathematical formula, but we're going to need some vital statistics on the performance of men and women to accurately determine how long it would take to go through them all."

"We better account for business trips resulting in separation, as those do happen, especially when the individuals in said partnering have their own careers."

I went to my luggage and dug out the pad of paper and pens I'd brought with me just in case. "On average, how often would you say a British lordling engages in sexual activity with his partner?"

"The correct answer is obviously as often as possible."

I considered the pile of condoms and the potential perils they represented. "How often would you say a British lordling realistically engages in sexual activity with his partner?"

"As often as possible still applies."

"And if you were to put a number to this figure, that realistically accounts for stamina, duration of sexual events, and time required for sleep, work, and other basic necessities?"

"Not as often as a British lordling would like."

I laughed. "There's so much disappointment packed into those little words. I will guess based on my schedule you are looking at a realistic two nights a week to indulge in any activities with your sexual partner, but I will give an allowance for enthusiasm, which suggests two incidents per available night, which becomes four condoms spent per week."

"This is sad. There should be at least one additional incident, which would bring the total up to five."

"Five seems like a reasonable number." I began counting condoms, and to make it easier on myself, I grouped them in batches of five. "It seems Elizabeth and Edward have decided you needed a lifetime supply of condoms."

"Or they want me to be prepared for any and all types of duty my new owner might have for me." Rick picked up one of the condoms. "There seem to be a lot of condoms marketing to women in here."

"How is a condom marketed to women?"

"Ribbed, patterned, fruity flavors, and with coatings meant to stimulate her?" Rick showed me the various kinds of condoms. While there were some standard kinds, most of them had some sort of bell or whistle. "And she went for the best brands, too."

"You're assuming this is from Elizabeth?"

"Edward would believe a condom is a condom, and as long as it does the job, it is a good condom."

"Right. That's not at all weird, Rick."

"Oh, it's definitely weird. This is not a hint. This is a shouted announcement from the rooftops. I'm not sure how I'm going to get all of these off the ship without everyone knowing I have a major stockpile of condoms."

"Well, you were the one who told your family you were interested in a woman."

"This is true. I see I have made some critical errors in my general plan to get them to leave me alone."

I grinned. "Now is the time you come clean, Rick. Was there ever a woman, is said woman interested in you, and what will you do now?"

"At the time I put this scheme together, I was hopeful there would be a woman, I have no idea, and I also have no idea, mainly because the woman I like might like my dog more than she likes me."

Well, I hadn't been eliminated yet, although I liked Rick in a completely different fashion. I eyed the condoms, wondering how many a couple could burn through in a week alone on a cruise ship. "That's a lot of women, Rick. Any woman with half a functioning brain cell is going to love your dog."

"Now that I think about it, you're absolutely right. Oh, well. I can probably handle being second place to my dog. She is that cute."

"You're sweet, you get along with my family, you can put my idiot brother in his place whenever you need to, and you have a cute dog. You're a decent bachelor on the market, and I see a lot of benefits to having ownership of your entire person." I counted out another set of five condoms, looking over the collection with a raised brow. "Maybe Elizabeth thinks you have exceptional endurance?"

"She'd have no way of knowing, as I'm very private about my relationships, and there's only been one prior that escalated to the point of needing condoms at all, but let's just say that didn't last long. She wanted more than I was willing to offer, and it didn't take me long to figure out she was after my money more than she was after me. My businesses could crumble tomorrow, and I don't want a woman who is only in it for the money."

"Well, you won't have to worry about that with me. I only care that I have enough money to feed my glutton of a dog and a cat, pay my rent, and buy books. I'm a voracious book reader."

"I'm spoiled," Rick admitted. "I've found that I do like spending more time at home than not, though. Fancy dinners and expensive vacations don't make up for the more important things in life."

"In that, we're agreed. I do like my few luxuries. My tub and fireplace are my favorites, but the heated floors come a close third. I don't need things like fancy dinners, although I really am not a fan of going hungry."

"I've done that a time or two. After I moved abroad and started my company, I had a few tight stretches. I got through them, but it gave me some important perspectives on what it means to be short on money. I mean, my family has had fortunes come and go, but several of my uncles and my aunt are all pretty savvy when it comes to the stock market and general investments. Elizabeth might not look like it, but she's got a good eye for investments and finances. She's considering starting her own firm, but I figure she'll wait a few years to see how things go with Edward, who is also into business."

"I figured someone in the family had to be good with money to afford this wedding. I handled most of the invoices on their behalf. This thing was terrifyingly expensive."

"I am very sorry they overlooked your initial pay. That was not my intention."

"I already told you that I had been intending to do it for free. I didn't even think about getting paid for the work. I am accepting her offer of an entire human, though. That's a pretty good deal for me." I allowed myself a smirk and lifted up one of the condoms. "The only reason I haven't dated much before now is because men don't often understand I actually care about my career."

"For the record, I do not have any intention of being one of those men who can't stand the woman of the relationship being successful. The way I figure it, two successful people in a relationship means everyone wins."

"But do you like long soaks in a tub with a book?"

"As a matter of fact, yes."

"Reading by the fireplace?"

"One of my preferred hobbies."

"Pool?"

"You'll kick my ass, and I'll accept my defeat with grace. I've seen the video of you playing. I will enjoy watching you slaughter your brother in future matches."

"He still thinks I'm a mediocre player, too."

"Reality is cruel, and I will enjoy watching him realize you've been playing him."

I grinned. "It will be pretty good, yeah."

"I feel I need to warn you I'm really not good at relationships. I'm oblivious half the time with my family and close friends, so if you want me to catch onto something, you're going to have to be direct with me. I'll do my best to be direct with you. I'm really bad at that, as I'm definitely one of those men who was brought up to never admit weakness or emotion."

"I thought you were upset with me over the wedding planning because we couldn't bring our dogs, so I had convinced myself you hated me for a good two months," I confessed.

"To be honest, I had wondered if I'd done something wrong."

"You hadn't. I'm just stupid." I continued to separate condoms into piles of five, marveling at the insanity of so many condoms. "There's literally hundreds in here. Hundreds of them! I had no idea you could fit so many condoms in a box that size."

"I'm amazed my cousin spent this much on condoms. Honestly, a standard package of condoms would have sent the same message."

I considered that. "I can't tell if she likes or hates you, Rick."

"I can't tell, either. I could figure out how to use a single pack, but how am I supposed to use so many of them?"

"You'll have to get creative." I continued separating them into piles with Rick's help and determined that his cousin had purchased three hundred condoms for his enjoyment. "There's over five *years* of condoms here if we assume you will indulge five times a week."

"At the risk of being beaten to death with my own condoms, how many do you think we could go through on a cruise?"

"You wouldn't be of much use if I beat you to death with your condoms. That would also be a huge waste of an entire human, and I might damage the condoms. Let's not be wasteful."

"I like the way you think. I just don't want to be offensive, and honestly, I've had no idea how to approach you. I didn't want to come across as one of those creeps."

"Well, this could make a good headline. NEW YORK WOMAN KIDNAPS BRITISH LORDLING FOR EVENING ENTERTAINMENT. I'll even let you go to work when we aren't reading, playing with our dogs, or keeping ourselves otherwise occupied. I'm no good at the whole flirting thing, either. That's probably why Juliette insisted on dressing me up in red and hoping for the best. The little black dress is as little as I'd let her make it. That was a battle, Rick."

"I don't want other men to see you in a little black dress. I have womanizing cousins, and I'd hate to have to murder them at my cousin's gala. Since we're confessing, anyway, my plan was to ask if you'd consider a relationship with me sometime during the cruise, but I am much happier that my cousin opted to give you the gift of an entire human. This way is a lot less stressful—and I was concerned the rest of my family would try to interfere. They already have, putting you through hell planning this wedding!"

"I just figured they were rich snobs and would annoy any wedding planner equally. I've dealt with rich snobs before. It's easy. No is a powerful word, and I like using it. And the more often I have to tell someone no, the more stubborn I'll get about it."

"I had guessed as much, which was why I was worried about asking you. I figured if I didn't ask, at least I could still be friends with you."

"Being friends is mandatory in any sort of relationship. But that was a good thought. I had similar. I will also admit I was jealous of whomever the woman was you were interested in."

Rick snickered. "You were jealous of yourself, then."

"Well, I guess I have a chance against the competition."

"That you do. I still fully intend to enjoy a lot of time reading on the balcony, and it'd be much nicer with you keeping me company." Rick examined one of the condoms. "And if we get tired of reading, I guess we have options, don't we?"

"That we do."

TWENTY-FOUR

I am a fierce dragon, and my hoard consists of books.

HAD I BEEN THINKING CLEARLY, I would have remembered I'd spent months overworking and not nearly enough time resting. After we took our time getting to know each other better, I barely had the energy to take a shower before Rick helped me into my pajamas and put me to bed.

A knock woke me, and I cracked open my eyes to discover my cabin had been tidied and there was no sign of my evening activities with Rick. Grumbling a curse, I got up, stumbled across the room, and cracked open my door to discover my brother and Rick, both bright eyed and ready for the day.

"I don't know what you want, but the answer is no." I considered shutting the door on them, but I stifled a yawn. "What do you want so I can tell you no?"

Rick grinned, and he looked rather proud of himself. Mat didn't seem to notice, and he replied, "It's time for breakfast."

"It's a cruise. I can eat when I want, how I want, and where I want. Go away. I'm going back to bed."

"Did you even drink last night?"

"No, I didn't, but I am still tired from planning the wedding." I made shooing motions with my hands. "I am going to hide in my room, eat chocolate all day, and maybe go through my stash of cheese, which was a gift from the bride yesterday. I have enough food in here to survive through a siege. Unless something is going wrong, I want to be left alone." Then, because I could use a little more tender loving care, I pointed at Rick. "Since he lives next door to me for the next few days, you can recruit him to bring me a plate. Just tell the staff why he's stealing a plate so we can return it without them panicking a plate and cutlery went missing."

Rick chuckled. "I have no problems with bringing you a plate on my way back. That'll save you a trip halfway across the ship, Mat."

"Mom and Dad want to see you."

"I'll go see them tomorrow or the day after." I pointed at the floor. "I am not leaving my room today. I am going to sleep. You hear me? I deserve sleep, and I will enjoy it. I have presents to open, too, because I was too tired to open them last night." I took a moment to look Rick over, made a note to add him to the presents I needed to unwrap, and resumed glaring at my brother. "Defend my rest. I will allow Rick to bother me if he's bringing me food. Anyone else will be sent away. And Rick's only getting away with it because he's my neighbor for the week."

"All right, all right. I'll tell Mom and Dad you're being crabby and need sleep."

"I'm also planning on reading a new book. I was given a new e-reader yesterday, and I will enjoy reading on my balcony."

"Ah, I see. I will tell them you have developed bookworm tendencies again."

"I am not a worm. I am a fierce dragon, and my hoard consists of books. Knock on my door at your own risk. In fact, Rick, please ask someone for a do not disturb sign. I don't want to be disturbed!"

"I'll take care of it." Rick grabbed my brother and hauled him away from my door. "Come on, Mat. I don't want to die today, and she looks ready to kill us both and toss us overboard. And she might bother to tell someone she dumped our bodies into the sea when she's done."

I closed my door and locked it. I then made certain the door to Rick's cabin remained unlocked before I went back to bed to enjoy some quiet time.

The next time I woke up, a weight on the side of the bed disturbed me. "I've brought you a plate. I waited until they refreshed the buffet so everything was nice and hot for you. You're missing a ridiculous number of hungover people complaining they're hungover, so really, you're not missing anything. I made sure nobody was out in the hallway to notice I took the plate into my room. How are you feeling?"

"Like it's the first time I got enough sleep in approximately six months," I admitted, yawning and sitting up. "Sorry about earlier."

"You looked tired, and I'd be grumpy too, if someone woke me up before I wanted to be woken up. He annoyed me first, and he barged into my room, which makes me really happy I hid our stash."

I grinned at that, got out of bed, and took the plate out to the balcony, which had chairs for two and a little table I could have breakfast at without getting crumbs in the sheets. Rick followed me. "Smart move. I'd noticed my room had been tidied. You didn't have to do that, but thank you."

"I figured someone would bother us, and having a lot of rather unique gifts sitting out would invite unwanted questions. In good news, I claimed I was going back to bed because I've been working too hard. Unbeknownst to them, my plans for the bed don't involve catching a nap."

The plate, which had enough food for two or three, would do a good job of sustaining me for a few hours. I stabbed some scrambled eggs and went to work shoveling breakfast into my mouth. "Do you think they'll leave us alone?"

"You have a do not disturb sign on your door, so I think there's a decent chance you'll be left alone for a while. They even gave me one, too. Before I came in here, I used a sticky note to inform people I had been working overtime lately and needed some quiet time. We'll just have to be somewhat quiet if we want our ruse to work."

"Why are we hiding what we're doing, anyway?"

"I want to see how far my family will go to remove me from the pool of eligible bachelors. That'll also teach them for getting involved in the first place."

"If your cousin demands a condom count, we're caught," I replied.

"There is that, but I think we're going to have to adjust our weekly averages based on what we learned last night."

I'd learned I could be convinced to abandon my books with little effort on his part.

Rick chuckled and relaxed in his seat. "I'm viewing it as a challenge to see how much damage we can do to our stockpile. I'm sure we'll both enjoy it. After we get back from the cruise, we can see what the boutique offers couples looking to add a little spice to life."

Well, I had no doubt Rick was an active and interested partner in our evening activities. "Game on, but after breakfast—and we'll have to make a friendly wager."

"About?"

"How long it takes my brother to figure out I'm making off with you."

"If he hasn't figured it out by the end of the cruise, he needs a lot of help and an appointment with an eye doctor, as I have every intention of educating my family if they take their pressuring too far, and they will."

"Unless they ditch us at a resort on their dime. That's not taking it too far. We just need to make sure they bring our pets to us. I'm sure I can get the extra days off work if I ask. I'm sure your boss will give you some time off work, too."

"I can probably arrange to give myself some time off work."

"Then it's game on, and our goal is to get them to give us some time off at a resort where they won't bother us. I think a week should be sufficient. How do we convince them we need time off at a resort?"

"Do independent things, steal occasional glances, and sigh sadly now and then? That's what I've heard is how people express being lovesick. I always thought it was weird they call it being lovesick. Honestly, I'm not going to do anything of the sort and act normal, which is oblivious if I listen to my cousin."

"I'm going to act normal, too, which is obviously oblivious. I really didn't think you were interested until you said so."

Rick grinned at me. "I became suspicious you were interested when you took a rather intense interest in the condom collection."

"I won't lie, it's true. Too much temptation in one little room for me."

"You won't hear me complain."

I giggled. "In good news, you already moved to the United States from Japan, and we live in the same city, so seeing each other will be simple. I'll even give you a key, but you can't steal my dog. You can steal me with my dog and cat, however."

"Do you want to be stolen?"

"At least once, yes. Please."

Rick laughed. "I'll ensure my theft of your person will be enjoyable for both of us. In case you weren't sure, I'm rather the slow, methodical type."

"When I decide I want to get married, if you are too slow, I will ask you. I don't want to be one of those couples who date for years without dedicating, but I'm happy to see how well we get along in close quarters. I don't want to find out any nasty surprises after marriage."

"On that, we're agreed."

"We can worry about it after we survive this cruise. There's still six more days our families could do us in. We better enjoy ourselves while we can."

THE THIRD DAY into the cruise, Rick's family conspired against us, coercing him into doing the many activities on the ship meant to entertain guests and keep anyone from getting bored. My family took advantage of the situation to force me out of my cabin and away from my books. The instant Rick's Aunt Carolina realized I was available for her amusement, she stalked me across the ship. Like before the wedding, she always wanted *something*. Most requests I could answer with a simple no, and the ones I couldn't, I sent her to Edward, which made her hesitate, but she ultimately left to go bother someone else about the matter.

On the tenth such visit in a matter of six hours, I considered tossing the woman overboard. "How can I help you?" I asked, already aware I likely wouldn't be helping her, as I would not be adjusting the ship's schedule to convenience her.

"What do you know about Fredrick's living accommodations in the United States?"

"Absolutely nothing," I replied, puzzled by her question. "He has a cute dog, and I got to meet her. He lives somewhere near me, but I don't know where. He knows more about my living accommodations than I do about his."

"Oh? Why might that be?"

"Because Juliette Carter ambushes me and puts too much stuff in my car, and when she runs out of space in my car, she coerces anyone she can find to do her dirty work. She has her claws deep into Fredrick's wardrobe, and he's often unwilling to tell her no. I don't complain because he brings his dog with him, and my dog likes to play with her. My cat likes Annabel Lee, too."

"Interesting. And it doesn't bother you that he knows where you live?"

"Why would it bother me? He's always a polite gentleman. And anyway, the building has really good security. The security desk doesn't allow anyone up to the residential floors who hasn't been authorized."

I would need to talk to Jacob about giving Rick open access to my apartment—and a set of his own keys.

"And you wouldn't say he's overbearing or otherwise obnoxious?"

"Him?" I blurted, astonished his aunt would think of him as anything other than polite and caring. "Why would you say such a thing?"

Mat snorted, and I kicked him beneath the table.

"He is a rather severe young man, much to our dismay. I wanted to ask if you might be willing to do me a favor."

I polished my favorite word in the dictionary and prepared to use it. "What sort of favor?"

"It would do little Fredrick some good if he could spend more time with people outside of work, and while your brother is a charming enough fellow, you live much closer than he does, and he doesn't find your presence offensive."

I would hope not, considering how much effort we'd put in attempting to decrease the size of his condom collection. "I have no problems spending some time with him if he needs local company. I can always use some company when I go to the bookstore, and there's one near me that welcomes dogs. Lenore has an exception because she's on leash, although they don't normally allow cats in."

"Excellent! When is best for you? I will go make certain he knows that you require assistance with your bookstore ventures. How many trips do you think you need? Little Elizabeth mentioned she was giving you gift cards to your favorite stores, and it would be gentlemanly of him to carry your purchases for you and help hold the leashes while you browse."

Who had taken over Rick's Aunt Carolina and turned her into someone deceptively nice? "I usually take Edgar Allan Paw and Lenore to the store when the weather sours. He doesn't handle cold, wet days very well because of his age, and he likes the heated seats in the car. So I suppose it would be the first Saturday or Sunday that has poor weather. There's a nice little park near the store we go to as well." In reality, the park was several blocks away through shit traffic, but Edgar Allan Paw didn't mind a longer car ride. "It can be quite the juggle trying to pick books while managing their leashes."

"That's just lovely. I'll go recruit him to help you. That's the least I can do after burdening you so much these past few weeks."

Months, but I smiled rather than correct her. "That's very sweet of you. Thank you."

"You're welcome." She left without a word, and my brother's eyes narrowed.

I could think of thirty rude things my brother might make a comment on, which would get us in trouble with our parents. "Don't say it, Mat."

"She's acting weird," he replied.

My parents nodded at that, and my mother said, "That woman has been a bloodthirsty harpy the entire cruise, and she's now playing nice. Your brother is right to be concerned."

"Don't say it, Dad."

"Why are you telling me not to say anything?" Dad complained.

"Because you will, and it'll be truthful, and because it's truthful, we can't protest, so if you don't say it, you may not be overheard, which saves us a lot of trouble later." I smiled. "We'll just leave it at that was weird and try not to worry about it. Should she bother Rick, well, he can hold the leashes while I buy some books, and it shouldn't inconvenience him too badly."

After we bought books, I could take him home and reward him for being a helpful gentleman, and we'd both enjoy it.

"Rick's usually busy," Mat muttered.

"And if he's busy, he can tell his aunt that he can't, and there's no harm, no foul. My feelings aren't going to be hurt if he's busy."

Well, mostly. My newly revitalized libido would be unhappy, but I could be a patient woman. If he played hard to get, I'd have to go on a hunt and figure out where he lived and come knocking at his door. I figured turnabout was fair play, and Rick knew where I lived. "If he isn't busy, I'll remind him that you need a great deal of attention or you feel lonely."

"Cute, Hope."

I grinned at him. "Juliette has worked very hard to make me cute, so thank you." Even my most casual outfits for the cruise did wonders for me. "She's very good for my self-esteem."

"I just don't want you to get your hopes up about Rick having time is all. It astonished me he was able to come to dinner, but I think that was because he was still settling in the country and hadn't restored his work schedule yet. He works too much, but I haven't been able to find a way to get him to take it easier. He's going to burn out one of these days."

Poor Mat. When he figured out I was pursuing a relationship with his friend, there'd be fireworks, and I had no idea if he'd be happy for us or not. "Well, if you think he's in trouble, you could always come to New York and storm his castle. Surely he's told you where he works or lives."

"He's renting a chunk of a skyscraper in Manhattan. I don't know where he lives in the area, but he said he bought a place. I'm trying to avoid thinking about that. Amy wants to buy a house soon because of the baby."

"Where is Amy, anyway?"

"She's enjoying the pool on the upper deck with some of her friends. She doesn't get to see them often, so she's spending most of her time with them. That plus she's worried about getting another tongue lashing from Dad."

My father sighed. "I already said I was sorry."

Ugh. More drama. "Do I want to know?"

"All I did was tell her she shouldn't be criticizing your work with the wedding without having yet attended the wedding. That was the day before we boarded," Dad reported.

I rolled my eyes. "I really don't care, Dad. Mat married her, not me. If she's too chickenshit to come have dinner with the family, that's not my problem. She'll get over it, or she won't—and I don't particularly care either way, truth be told."

My parents sighed, and my mother shook her head. "Hope, you should be nicer than that."

I stared at my mother. "Why?"

That drew her up short. "What do you mean by why? You should be nice."

"No, I was already nice. She had a nice wedding to Mat, they're going to have a child, and I've done my dues. The way I figure it, being a neutral party and not actively disliking her is me being nice. I just don't see a need to go out of my way to be friendly or social with someone who openly dislikes me. That's fine. Let her do what she wants. I'm adult enough to pay her no mind if we have to share space. If she can't do the same, that's on her."

"Hope," Mat protested.

"What now? If the woman wanted to be friends with me, she'd come be friends. She doesn't, and that's no big deal. We're in-laws. We can't all get along. We'd be obviously breaking some sort of sacred rule if we all got along."

"Ain't that the honest truth," my mother muttered.

"And now that we've gotten that out of the way, have I done my daughterly duties enough to be excused? I have a huge new collection of books to read while indulging in my natural introverted tendencies."

If Rick happened to wander into my cabin, well, I'd put my introverted tendencies away for however long I could get him to stick around. With a laugh, my parents shooed me away, and I took advantage of the opportunity for some hard-earned peace and quiet.

THE BRIDE and the groom were up to

something, and I could make a few guesses as to what. If the pair haunted my steps any closer, they'd discover my cabin neighbor and I had done quite a lot of damage to his condom collection, I hadn't gotten in much reading time at all, and I might require therapy to get over Rick if I couldn't convince him to stick around permanently.

With the snorkeling adventure right around the corner, I needed to either get them off my back or pack my bags and stage an escape. I regarded the ridiculous piles of gifts, many of which remained unopened thanks to Rick and his persuasive argument I should join him in bed rather than worry about what the bride and groom had offered me. Most of his gifts remained unopened, too.

Whoops.

A knock at my door annoyed a sigh out of me, and through the open door connecting our cabins, Rick snickered.

As agreed upon, I closed and locked it on my way by, and cracked open my door to discover the bride and groom waiting to continue tormenting me again. Worse, they carried yet another red-wrapped basket.

"I'm not sure this cabin has much more room for those things. Where did you get that one?"

Elizabeth grinned, bumped her hip into the door, and strode on in. "I had it in hiding, waiting for this very moment. I have more where this one came from. See?"

To my dismay, more boxes, baskets, and gift bags littered the floor outside of my door.

"You did this because you figured I'd try to refuse a tip in the form of a check, didn't you?"

"That didn't take you long to figure out. It's a lot harder to say no when I went through all this effort to wrap these just for you."

I gave up. Making the bride and groom happy mattered, as it was their wedding cruise. I could sort the mess out later—and hire movers to get everything back to my apartment. "I'm going to need several trucks for all of this."

"I've already made those arrangements, as I'm aware that you came with what would easily fit in a taxi." Elizabeth set the basket near my pile of other unopened gifts, and Edward went to work ferrying the gifts inside. As I'd already been railroaded, I helped him. "I see you've been getting in a lot of reading time."

While I generally disliked lying, I saw no need to be upfront with the woman, who'd tried to give me my very own slave and clues about what I should be doing with him. "I have, thank you. I made use of my brand-new slave once to fetch me dinner so I wouldn't interrupt my book reading. I appreciate that, by the way. It's nice having a slave who is willing to fetch food without the ship's crew getting upset he's pilfering plates and cutlery."

"It helps he returns them in a reasonable time. I meant for you to be doing other things with him, though. I didn't give him to you to play fetch!"

Edward snorted. "I told you it wouldn't work, darling. She's too ethical."

Like hell I was too ethical to take advantage of Rick's offers of company in bed. I shrugged. "Anyway, this cruise is about your happy marriage. I'm sure I can handle finding adult companionship after the cruise."

"I was more hoping you'd take pity on Rick, as he is dense, is incapable of finding a good woman, and you're a good woman who comes with a good family, with a notable exception."

Oy. Amy again. "What did she do now?"

"She's whining as usual. She's friends with some of our family, but truth be told? We're all hoping Mat will be a steadying influence on her. She has issues, but it is what it is."

Right. "I did my part. They're married, and they're going to have a kid, so I really hope everything works out for them. As for Rick, does he really need anyone's pity?"

"When it comes to his lack of a love life, yes. Even Aunt Carolina is starting to want to meddle," Elizabeth replied. "For Rick's sake, save him. If Aunt Carolina starts meddling, he'll want to become a hermit for the rest of his life."

If he did, I hoped he would take me with him. I could think of a few small towns we could move to. "I am committing to nothing, but I will hear you out."

Edward and I carried the last of the presents into my cabin, leaving me with a walkway to get to my bed. He went about stacking everything in an orderly fashion, organizing by size, possibly weight, and some other metric only he understood.

"I have a plan."

And there it was, the moment I'd figure out just what the minx had been contemplating the entire cruise. "Those are four terrifying words, but as promised, I will hear you out."

"I may have called your boss and asked if you could have a few extra days to handle an unforeseen family matter. Once I explained the unforeseen family matter, he said he had no problems if you needed to call out for a few extra days. By a few extra days, I mean a week."

"Technically, I don't think I'm supposed to have that much extra time off for a few more months."

"You've put in so much overtime you've earned the time off, and he cleared it already. Also, I've been told to tell you that you work too much and that you need the vacation."

Damn, the woman was out for my blood. "Okay. I may need the vacation. What do you have in mind?"

"Before I tell you, I feel it is important to say I also called Rick's minions and explained I had a plan."

"Did they laugh at you? It's not usual for family members to do this sort of thing." I doubted his employees would actually laugh at her, as Rick seemed like the kind to want professionalism in the face of absurdity, but I could never be sure with him. He liked to surprise me.

"It's really not. Honestly, when I called your boss, I begged for my request to not harm you in any way because you had no idea I was doing it, and that I was really sorry I didn't just have you ask for two weeks off."

"Edward, I don't suppose you can tame your wife, can you?"

"I like her just as she is," he replied with a smile. "It's a good deal for you, but it does require some cooperation on your part."

"What sort of cooperation?"

"I want you to wear the skimpiest bikini Juliette gave you and lure Rick off so you can make use of your permission slip and a special package we gave him at the reception," Elizabeth announced. "He will know what package I mean."

Yep, Rick's cousin was trying to sell him into sexual servitude, and he was enjoying every minute of it.

"Does this special package happen to be themed around the one gift card I received along with the permission slip?"

"As a matter of fact, yes. It's a win-win! You both get laid, you have a great week, and if something comes of it, that's great. You handle Aunt Carolina like a champion, and honestly, that's the only accolade the rest of the family needs. And if you two don't work out like that, well, you get to spend a week at a nice place where you can read books."

"Oh! That reminds me. I wanted to thank you for so many gift cards, especially to the dog-friendly bookstores in the area. Edgar Allan Paw loves going into them, and they don't mind if Lenore comes in, too. Her being leashed helps with that. I tell them she's his seeing-eye cat despite his unimpaired vision."

"Yeah, I figured you were the type who liked taking your dog to as many places as possible. I'd asked your brother. I think he's a little jealous over how much you love your dog."

"My brother can be an idiot sometimes. Ignore him. How many perverted gifts are in this?" I asked, gesturing to the new gifts and my unopened presents.

Edward snickered. "Thanks to me, very few. I limited her to the gift card and your permission slip, as I thought you'd be overwhelmed with perverted purchases otherwise. Juliette refused to be contained, but having stepped into women's boutiques before, I figured you would not complain if you received such things. Mr. Carter is having an interesting time keeping her under some form of control on the cruise, though. If she has more than half a shot, she goes from fine to drunk, and while she's the happiest drunk I've ever seen in my life, she's a danger to herself. Mr. Carter has had to fish her out of the various pools more times than I can count. Honestly, I think she's falling in on purpose so he'll rescue her, but I've been advised I should not ruin her fun by sharing that with her husband."

I laughed at the thought of Juliette falling into pools so her doting husband would have to fetch her. "She really would, too. I'm very grateful for the clothing. My wallet cries every time I need to go shopping. I am sorry I haven't opened everything yet, though. I found the books, chocolate, and checked some of the baskets for edibles, and at that point, did I need any of the other gifts right away?"

Edward grinned. "The only edibles are the hard sausages, the stuff in your fridge, and the chocolates."

"The stuff in my fridge was not long for this world," I admitted. "I'm guessing Mat confessed about my love of cheese."

"Your brother made an excellent informant, yes. Open the presents with Rick tomorrow. Honestly, he has a lot more presents, too, but they're at your destination tomorrow. I wanted him to feel like he was in the doghouse for moving to the United States. I'll confess now he has a permission slip, too. I even made your parents sign it."

Oh no. "You made my parents sign *what*?"

"A permission slip for Rick to have his wicked way with you. Okay, it was more along the lines of properly court and treat you well, but that's what I meant. Your mother figured out what I meant. Your father is convinced you're an eternal innocent."

The bride and groom were going to be the death of me, and I'd never be able to show my face in public again—or at least look my mother in the eyes. "Can tomorrow's adventures include an escape to a different country? Once my brother finds out about this, it'll be World War Family, and I'll be the main target."

"I'm sure he'll get over Rick's wise acquisition of your person," Elizabeth replied with a grin. "And he better not have a problem with Rick being interested in you. I'll set him straight myself if I must. You supported his choices, so he damned well better support yours!"

"I'm sure Mat can handle however I decide to proceed with my personal relationships in the future. It's bad enough his wife hates me, so I'll just pretend he can be an adult should I decide to involve a man in my life. I let him make his mistakes, so he damned well better let me make mine."

"Rick won't be a mistake, that much I can promise you."

"Mat will most certainly think so."

"Mat can kiss my ass." Elizabeth snorted. "I'll handle your brother around the same time everyone notices that you and Rick missed the ship in a tragic oversight. The crew will be emptying your cabin as soon as we disembark for the snorkeling adventure, and I have a boat that'll take you to your new home for the next week and a half. That's when you'll have to lure Rick off alone, and thus need a most excellent bikini for your job."

"How about we just bring our e-readers and read on one of these boats, and then we don't have to worry about any luring?"

"But snorkeling!"

"Reading."

"Snorkeling."

"Reading. Nonnegotiable."

Edward snickered. "You're dealing with the book-crazed, Elizabeth. Rick's been this way since the day he learned how to read. Just give them their books and let them pretend they're snorkeling. Nobody is going to notice, and if their new e-readers get wet, well, they'll just have to amuse each other."

"Throw the e-readers into the ocean!"

"Absolutely not." I pointed at her. "That's blasphemy. No. Edward, tell her no."

"You want a happy couple, not a murderous one, darling. Don't endanger their e-readers. You're more likely to get what you want if they're happy rather than murderous."

"Listen to him."

"Fine. Your e-readers are safe. For now."

"What sort of place are you sending us to?"

"It's a private villa. I had the kitchen stocked, and someone will come pick you up for your trip back to New York City at the appropriate time. I shall, of course, appear properly saddened you are unable to attend the gala. Such a pity."

"A true tragedy."

"You're just like Rick, and it disgusts me. You two really would prefer to read books than go to a party!"

"Yes."

Edward snickered. "Let's leave her be for a while, darling. I'm sure she'll be able to handle her cruel imprisonment at a villa for the next while. Rick will like it, too. Anyway, the ship you'll want to read and relax on is a small sailing ship named *Harmony*. Her captain will take you to the villa as soon as you two are the only ones left on board. I've already made arrangements for all of your gifts to make it back to New York for delivery to your place, as I was unable to acquire Rick's address, much to my disgust."

"Rick can pick everything up from my place, sure."

"Good. Don't try to escape my plans, Hope. If you are not in your skimpiest bikini, I will make Juliette help you find the right one, and when hungover, Juliette is a bit of a bear."

"Her? A bear? Never. She's so nice."

"Hungover Juliette is a force of nature."

I frowned. "But she's a force of nature sober, too."

"Fine. Don't make me send Juliette in here, you!"

I laughed. "I will cooperate with your plan, but I am only doing so because I could use another week of vacation."

"Good woman. I'll see you bright and early in the morning."

TWENTY-FIVE

They were discussing destroying my e-reader if I didn't dress appropriately.

WHILE I HAD no idea there were snorkeling locations in North Carolina, the cruise ship docked in Charleston, where we left on a collection of tour and sailing vessels from a nearby marina. The weather cooperated, which made wearing the ridiculously skimpy bikini somewhat comfortable. To be safe rather than sorry, I brought a wrap, which would keep me warm if the wind picked up over the water.

Rick had opted for jeans and a button-up shirt, which he'd left unbuttoned in a half-hearted attempt to pretend he might actually swim.

"This is ridiculous," he muttered, and he clutched his e-reader while casting suspicious glances around. "Where are those two menaces?"

"You mean Elizabeth and Edward?"

"Yes, them."

I pointed at where they waited by the small sailing vessel that would kidnap us. "Over there. You best get your scolding in now, else they may escape your wrath, and that wouldn't do."

"You better come with me, or you might be taken by your jerk of a brother."

"What did Mat do now?"

"He complained at me for stealing all your attention. All I said was that it was no wonder you liked staying in your cabin. You like peace and quiet to read. I did slip and say you had invited me to read on your balcony once as long as I could stay quiet."

My brother would drive me crazy if I stayed on the cruise. I would miss my brother if he goaded me into killing him. "Okay. I can witness your attempt to scold the bride and groom. I don't think you'll get far in your scolding attempts, but I respect that you're going to try."

"I see you've sided with them."

"No, I just got told last night what would happen to me if I disobeyed. It was not a good situation. I decided cooperation would work out better for me." I gestured to my bikini. "They were discussing destroying my e-reader if I didn't dress appropriately and show up on time."

"That's a potent threat."

"It really is."

Rick heaved a sigh and marched towards Elizabeth and Edward. "Really, you two?"

Elizabeth pointed at the small sailing ship. "Board or walk the plank. And I might make Hope be the one to walk the plank while you watch. Oh, actually, sign this first." Elizabeth held out two slips of paper and a pen, which declared they were tourist fishing licenses filled out with our names and my address. She pointed at the fishing shop nearby. "I picked these up for you just in case, because I've heard readers often pretend to fish while enjoying their book."

Rick's eyes lit up, and he scribbled his signature, checked over the copies, and took the page that declared itself to be a fishing license. I followed his example. While I didn't go fishing often, I did sometimes, and I usually liked it.

"I can't tell if you're encouraging or discouraging me, Elizabeth. Well, you're encouraging me to go fishing, but I'm not sure I want to walk the plank knowing I might be able to go fishing."

"Board!"

I got behind Rick and pushed him in the direction of the ship, which was tied close enough to the pier we could just step on. "Do what she wants, otherwise our e-readers will get thrown overboard."

He boarded the boat, and I followed him.

While the ship could easily fit six or seven people, Elizabeth made shooing gestures with her hands. "Take these two away, far away! Don't bother returning them. They're extras."

I laughed, as I was aware of what she had in mind. "You're something else, Elizabeth."

"Enjoy your sailing, have a good time, and don't drown. There's suntan lotion there somewhere, and aloe in case you get burned. Rick, defend her pale countenance! Don't miss any spots."

I rolled my eyes, as I was hardly pale, tended to dodge burning, and likely wouldn't need any aloe. However, I'd accept Rick's attention, especially once we had some form of privacy. "Really, Elizabeth?"

"I've been hearing that question a lot today for some reason."

"It's because you keep saying ridiculous things," Rick muttered.

Elizabeth huffed. "Make him walk the plank for me, Hope."

I rolled my eyes, as I had far better ideas of what I could be doing with Rick. "Sure, Elizabeth. I'll make him walk the plank."

After she left, the captain, a younger man with a friendly grin and windswept hair, started the engine of his sailing boat. "The wind isn't ideal, I'm lazy, and I figured you'd rather have a pleasant cruise rather than listen to me curse at the rigging. Some of the purists make fun of my motor, but when they're stuck on dead waters, I'm cruising along. I'm John, and I've been tasked with giving you two some peace and quiet."

Rick sat, twisted around and hollered at

his cousin, "I changed my mind about you for now."

Elizabeth waved and laughed. "Have fun."

"Rick really likes his peace and quiet." I held up my e-reader. "If you dump us somewhere peaceful and quiet, you won't even hear us complain as long as there's food and water nearby."

"Since there's only the two of you, we can get out ahead of the rest of the group. The marina will be chaos while everyone comes in and out. The spot they picked to snorkel is about thirty minutes away, and they'll have their hands full, as there are instructors coming in to teach those who've never done it before. It's really an impressive venture. There are a lot of islands near here, so everyone should have a good time. The spot I'm taking you to is on the coast, but you'll find it a pleasant getaway."

"See, Rick? Elizabeth cares. She's not actually making us deal with your aunt all day—or my brother. You'll have to give her a card later."

"Can I give her a hard time instead?"

"Sure, just don't forget the card when you do it."

JOHN TOOK us on a cruise around the islands nearby Charleston before showing us the coast, telling us the history of the area, what lurked beneath the waters, and about the local wildlife we might spot if we were patient and had a good eye. Every time a new bird flew overhead, he took the time to tell us the species, where they usually lived, and how often we might see them.

Several hours after leaving the marina, John killed the engine and coasted his ship alongside a long pier leading up to a villa perched on a rocky outcropping overlooking the ocean. I whistled, wondering how the hell Elizabeth had pulled off acquiring such a place for us on short notice—or if the tricky woman had been planning the getaway for longer than I thought.

"If you would like to walk the plank, I recommend you use the end of the pier and just walk off," John announced with a grin. "I have been told to kick you off my ship, and that everything you need is inside. Enjoy your stay. Someone will be by to tell you how long you'll be tragically stranded here."

"Wait, what?" Rick blurted.

I laughed. "We've been kidnapped and marooned, Rick."

"I didn't think she'd actually do it," he spluttered.

"Ah, but you were hoping she would." I grabbed my e-reader and stepped onto the pier. "Thank you very much for the tour, John. It was lovely."

"You're welcome. Enjoy your stay. If you

want to go on another tour, my card should be inside."

"I'll keep that in mind," I lied, as I had zero intention of going anywhere with a week and a half of peace, quiet, and Rick to enjoy. Rick followed me, and he went through the motions of thanking John although his attention remained fixed on the villa above.

I waited for John to leave before saying, "How terrible. We've been marooned. Whatever shall we do?"

"Read books, keep each other company, and go fishing."

According to his tone, I would be battling the fish for Rick's attention, but I could handle that—for the most part. "You'll just have to hope there's fishing rods and bait here somewhere."

"I can improvise if needed."

"How does one improvise fishing rods and bait?"

"I can dig for worms a little inland, and I'm sure I can think of something."

Part of me wanted to have Rick show me how a desperate man made himself fishing gear, but the rest of me selfishly wanted as much of his time as possible. "I'm sure she wouldn't have gotten us fishing licenses without providing fishing gear, and I am willing to negotiate for fishing time, assuming I'm properly cared for prior."

"So, if I want to fish, I have to tire you out

so much you're okay with fishing while you recover?"

That sounded nice. "Yes, please."

"I'm sure an arrangement can be made. I guess I do need to get her a card, don't I?"

"I've been told you have presents inside, and one of them is a permission slip from my parents to court me."

Rick slapped his forehead. "Are you serious?"

"I'm serious. It seems your family believes you need a great deal of help with your eviction from the pool of eligible bachelors. My father seems oblivious to what all the permission slip entails, and my mother is a pervert and has made certain assumptions."

"Your mother isn't blind, and my mother tells me I'm handsome. It just means she's smart and your father is blind."

I nodded my agreement with his assessment of the situation. "I'm obviously pure and innocent."

Rick snorted at that. "Sure."

"I am!"

"Obviously, I have not despoiled you sufficiently, then, if you believe there's anything pure and innocent left about you. Shall we go inside and rectify that?"

"I want to see this permission slip and your presents. I want to open some presents, too. Elizabeth said she'd have everything sent here. I'm still not clear on how we're getting home, but I guess we'll figure it out."

Rick took my hand and led me up the staircase leading up to the top of the cliff and the villa at its top. A wraparound porch offered an excellent view of the ocean, and on the other side of a wall-to-wall window, two familiar furry noses pressed to the glass, and their tails wagged a mile a minute. "Our puppies!"

I bolted for the door, discovered it was unlocked, and knelt so I could greet my old man of a dog. He washed my face with his tongue, and Lenore strolled over with her tail bannered high, joining in for her fair share of attention. Annabel Lee plowed over her owner and bounced on him in her excitement to see him.

It took a while to calm our animals enough we could escape them, and Rick made sure the door was firmly closed to prevent any escapees. I picked up Lenore and snuggled with her, making happy sounds in my throat while burying my face in her fur. "Elizabeth is sneaky! How did she get our animals?"

"Well, truth be told, I asked Jacob to watch Annabelle Lee since I knew he'd also have Edgar Allan Paw and Lenore. And you told Elizabeth who was watching your pets. And I, fool that I am, didn't insist my dog stay out of my cousin's fiendish hands—and I bet Jacob knew we'd both appreciate seeing our pets."

"We've been played, Rick."

"We really have been, but I can't say I mind."

I didn't mind, either. "We have our dogs, we have a week and a half, and I think we should make the most of it before we pretend we have absolutely no interest in each other just to see how long we can give those jerks the run around for setting us up."

"In my defense, I was working up to trying to do something about this situation myself. I was starting to lose sleep worrying another man might step up."

"Please. Are other men going to try to charm me with hilarious news headlines?"

"Probably not. I will admit, I had no idea such an odd hobby would have won me so much."

"I feel the same about a baseball to the head," I admitted. "Without that baseball, I'd probably still be at the same old job doing the same old thing stuck in the same old routine. Who knew something so bad could be so good?"

Rick leered at me. "I can show you all about how something so bad can be so good."

He really could. "I will take you up on that after we open presents and convince our dogs and my cat that we're not abandoning them in the next ten minutes. We're going to have to negotiate about living arrangements in the future, however. I need heated floors, a fireplace, and a nice tub. I've become spoiled, Rick."

"Conveniently, my deep, dark, and dirty secret involves the penthouse floor of your building, where I happen to live. I, too, have heated floors, a most excellent tub, and a fireplace. When I realized you had moved into the same building, I had to take precautions so you wouldn't spot me or my car."

"Why were you hiding it?"

"I didn't want to come across like some weird stalker. I'd even purchased first, since the penthouse was in a good location. It was more than I wanted to spend, but the view is great, the condo is even better, and I had enough to pay it off in full. I'm doing some upgrades, though."

"Upgrades? How can you upgrade perfection?"

"My perfection didn't have fully heated floors; only the bathroom and the bedroom had them, so I had everything else done upon learning how much you and your dog enjoy them. I also upgraded the fireplace, as mine was too small for two people, two dogs, and a cat to comfortably enjoy. Honestly, I might join you in your apartment for a few weeks, if you're all right with that, while the renovations are finished. There's nothing quite like getting up in the morning and dodging construction workers. I made the mistake of telling them they could start as early as Jacob would allow. The person below me leaves at six and didn't mind the workers starting that early."

My bed would become quite cozy with two dogs, two people, and a cat, but I could deal with it for a few weeks. "I think I could be convinced with little work on your part. You'll have to take me on dates to the bookstore, where we bring our pets and shop. Your aunt already said I should have you hold leashes while I browse, but honestly, I think we'll be taking turns being the leash holders."

"I like this plan. It involves buying books. The condo is pretty large, and I had a library installed in one of the larger rooms. I'm not sure what the designers were thinking, but I underestimated how much room I have. I have two offices, a library, a study, the living room, which is where the fireplace is, a ridiculously large kitchen, three full bathrooms, and some rooms that might actually be closets? I'm not sure. It's weird."

"But is it as weird as a bathroom in a kitchen?"

"Nothing is as weird as a bathroom in a kitchen, Hope."

"True."

We explored the villa to discover the entire living room overwhelmed with wrapped gifts, all in red. I shook my head at the insanity. "Elizabeth had warned me she'd gotten you extra presents, but this is ridiculous. What could possibly be in all of these boxes?"

"Well, one of these boxes has a permission slip from your parents, so I refuse to quit unwrapping presents until I find it. Do you know how often men want the approval of potential in-laws? That thing is priceless, and I need to secure it. That way, I can use it when your brother tries to kill me for making off with you."

"You're not making off with me. I'm stealing you. I will defend my newly acquired territory viciously."

Rick furrowed his brows. "I'm not sure what I'm supposed to do here."

"Smile smugly at my brother, knowing you're the victor."

"You're going to hold a grudge against him for life, aren't you?"

"No, I'm just going to make him think I will for a while. I shall also indulge in some smug smiles over having stolen one of his friends. It's his fault for tossing you my way."

"It's Annabel Lee's fault for chewing up my wedding invitation."

I knelt in front of Rick's dog and rewarded her with the petting she deserved. "And you're just the sweetest little girl, doing your best to make sure your wayward master couldn't leave you. Don't worry. I'll help you keep him close to home most of the time, and if he does have to wander off, we can sulk in front of the fireplace."

"Already decided you're going to sulk in front of the fireplace should I have to leave for a trip?"

"Yep. I'll indulge in a good sulk with a good book and our pets."

"Is it really sulking if you're enjoying yourself?"

"Absolutely."

"I will do my best to limit the number of times per month you must sulk, although traveling will happen."

"I can accept that, but I will expect a trip to the bookstore to refuel after I've indulged in my sulk. Sulking is tiring business, you know."

"I'm sure an arrangement can be made. I'll even offer some pampering in the tub should I be forced away on business trips. You'll be so tired and worn out after sulking, after all."

I liked the sound of that, so I nodded. "I'll require intensive therapy every time you return, but I'm sure Annabelle Lee will forgive you the instant you walk in the door."

"Obviously, the solution to this is to properly wear you out before every business trip."

I could work with that. "And what if I have to go on a business trip?"

"It seems only fair you'll have to offer me pampering and intensive therapy sessions before and after your trips."

"That does seem fair." I laughed at the absurdity of it all. "Your cousin wants me to charm you, then she wants me to seduce you. I believe she wants this to be a permanent arrangement, considering you have been gifted with a permission slip signed by my parents. I thought you should know."

Rick looked over the pile of presents and

shook his head, gesturing at the hoard awaiting our attention. "She could have the entire world packed away in those boxes, and that would easily be the best gift I've ever received in my life. I mean, having their approval is worth a lot, but you're beyond compare."

It would take me a long time to get used to the idea of someone holding me in such high regard. "You're not so bad yourself for a British lord. I think I'm winning this deal."

"No, I'm winning. I get you. Titles are cheap."

"Says the lordling!"

"This is going to be one of those fights we have for the rest of our lives, isn't it?"

I sure as hell hoped so. "Very probably."

"Good. I don't know about you, but I intend to enjoy every minute of it."

About Bernadette Franklin

Bernadette Franklin is a figment of imagination owned and operated by two cats, some plants, and a human.

The human also writes as R.J. Blain and Susan Copperfield.

Want to hear from the author when a new book releases? You can sign up at her website (thesneakykittycritic.com). Please note this newsletter is operated by the Furred & Frond Management. Expect to be sassed by a cat. (With guest features of other animals, including dogs.)

A complete list of books written by RJ and her various pen names is available at https://www.thesneakykittycritic.com/complete-list-of-books-by-year-of-publication/

RJ Blain suffers from a Moleskine journal obsession, a pen fixation, and a terrible tendency to pun without warning.

When she isn't playing pretend, she likes to

think she's a cartographer and a sumi-e painter.

In her spare time, she daydreams about being a spy. Should that fail, her contingency plan involves tying her best of enemies to spinning wheels and quoting James Bond villains until she is satisfied.

RJ also writes as Susan Copperfield and Bernadette Franklin. Visit RJ and her pets (the Management) at thesneakykittycritic.com.

FOLLOW RJ & HER ALTER EGOS ON BOOKBUB:
RJ BLAIN
SUSAN COPPERFIELD
BERNADETTE FRANKLIN

CPSIA information can be obtained
at www.ICGtesting.com
Printed in the USA
LVHW112019260422
717291LV00004B/165

9 781649 640628